195

I, Sherlock Holmes

I, Sherlock Holmes

Memoirs of Mr Sherlock Holmes, OM, late Consulting
Private Detective-in-Ordinary to Their Majesties Queen Victoria,
King Edward VII and King George V

Edited and Annotated by

MICHAEL HARRISON

E. P. DUTTON / NEW YORK

Library of Congress Cataloging in Publication Data
Harrison, Michael.
    I, Sherlock Holmes.
    Bibliography: p.
    Includes index.
    I. Title.
PZ3.H2472Iad3   [PR6058.A694]   823'.9'12   76-11874
ISBN: 0-525-13085-3

Published simultaneously in
Canada by Clarke, Irwin & Company
Limited, Toronto and Vancouver

Designed by Ann Gold

10 9 8 7 6 5 4 3 2 1

First Edition

Canon to right of her,
Canon to left of her,
Canon in front of her,
  Lest galleys blundered;
Calmly she checked and well,
Checking each fault that fell,
On guard 'gainst the gremlins' spell,
Saving the author hell,
When critics thundered . . .

Contents

List of Illustrations

All illustrations, except as indicated, obtained through Contrad Research Library

The Holmes memoirs

. . . an introductory and explanatory note

Mr Sherlock Holmes, though an inordinately busy (as well as unusually successful) solver of problems—usually, but not by any means exclusively, of a criminal nature—was not a prolific writer, and what he did write was invariably of a technical nature, and then mostly relevant to his profession as a detective. Of the eleven monographs listed under his name in the British Museum, only three—*Upon the Polyphonic Motets of Lassus, A Study of the Chaldean Roots in the Ancient Cornish Language* and *Practical Bee-keeping, with Some Observations upon the Segregation of the Queen*—have no apparent relevance to the philosophy of his profession. Only three articles in professional journals have been attributed to him—at least, under his own name; and two of his cases (both published in 1927) have been attributed to his pen; in the opinion of this Editor, on quite insufficient internal and external evidence.

In addition to the above testimony to Mr Holmes's liking and capacity for writing, we have his half-promise to Dr Watson that, on Mr Holmes's retirement, he would set about the production of *The Art of Detection*, the MS. of which is now being prepared for publication by the present editor.

That Mr Holmes intended to give the world the full record of his remarkable life cannot be doubted, for, to him, Dr Watson's incomplete (and, as we see from the Memoirs, not always completely veridical), and—as Mr Holmes complained—'romanticized' accounts of selected cases could hardly have replaced, in Mr Holmes's opinion, his own account of his professional career. He has, as we see, both enlarged and supplemented the synoptic Watson account—at times differing from it—and the edited memoirs of the first ten years of his association with Dr Watson are here offered to the reader for the first time.

The reader will not meet, in these pages, a new Sherlock Holmes, for all that he, rather than Dr Watson, presents his own *persona* for our inspection and—the autobiographer must have hoped—our approval. Few, if any, men see themselves as they truly *are;* only as they would wish themselves to be—and if Sherlock Holmes seems at times to have a blind eye for the deficiencies and faults of Sherlock Holmes, Dr Watson was no less prejudiced in favour of the man who ('warts and all') came to be Dr Watson's hero.

So, as I said above, these memoirs supplement those of Dr Watson—both of which are as tender (though not less truthful) as obsessed hero-worship can make history. The difference, as I see it, between the memoirs of Dr Watson and those of Mr Holmes is that the latter is not frightened occasionally to record the unflattering truth.

THE MANUSCRIPT OF THE MEMOIRS

The Memoirs, as printed here, cover the ten years from 1881, when Mr Holmes first met Dr Watson in the Pathological Laboratory of St Bartholomew's Hospital, until 1891, when Mr Holmes 'disappeared' for nearly three years, in that personal effacement that Sherlockian scholars call 'the Great Hiatus'.

From a note on the cover of the packet in which the sheets of the Memoirs are wrapped, as well as from a more formal copy of a receipt in the archives of the British Museum Library, the Memoirs were handed over to Sir Frederick Kenyon * for safe-keeping until after a period of sixty years should have elapsed. The transfer of the Memoirs—recorded, I may mention, in passing, by Sir Frederick in his diary—took place on Monday, 12th July, 1915. By the arrangement that Mr Holmes had made with Sir Frederick and the Trustees of the British Museum, the Memoirs were released from the Museum's care on Monday, 14th July, 1975—exactly (allowing for the week-end in 1975) sixty years after Mr Holmes had deposited the first part of his Memoirs with Sir Frederick Kenyon.

The Holmes Memoirs were placed in my hands, according to my diary, on Tuesday, 21st October (Nelson's Day), 1975; the edited and annotated text being delivered to the American publishers, Messrs E. P. Dutton and Company, on Wednesday, 5th May, 1976.

TEXTUAL REVISIONS

That the text of Mr Holmes's memoirs has been greatly—and, at times, radically—revised is indicated by the changes of writing-paper, of pens, of

* Sir Frederick G. Kenyon, GBE, KCB, was Director of the British Museum from 1909 to 1931.—*Editor*

ink, and—to the extent of forty-two pages in the first instance, seventy-six pages in the second—a re-writing of an original draft in typescript.

I am indebted to Mr Philip Poole, the well-known stationer and calligraphic archivist-antiquary of Drury-lane, for having identified the two makes of typewriter used: the earlier, a Remington, the later, a Yost. A brief note, which was reproduced on page xix, was written in ink on the torn-out page of a Letts' diary.

All the text of the Memoirs, including the typewritten one hundred and eighteen pages, is on paper of foolscap size or the near equivalent (*e.g.*, Regina or Albert). The colour of the paper used varies between cream and azure, unruled and ruled feint. Twenty-four pages are on what was then called "Sermon paper"—cream laid foolscap 4to fly,* ruled feint on four sides.

Altogether, by watermarks and other evidence, eight papers have been identified as the products of existing or extinct stationers:-

STATIONER	ADDRESS	PAPER	SIZE	COLOUR
J. & J. Cowan	London	Laid	4to fcp	cream
Grosvenor Chater	"	Abbey Mill	" "	azure
Henningham & Hollis	"	Laid	" "	azure
H. & M. Massey	"	Cartridge	" "	azure
Houghton & Gunn	"	Bond	Albert	cream
Geo. New	Eton	Laid	4to fcp	azure
Henry Roberts	London	Bond	" "	azure
Thorburn Bain	"	Charterhouse Parchment	Regina	azure
" "	"	Sermon (fly)	4to fcp	cream

N.B.: The paper from George New, of Eton, a firm which held a Royal Warrant, appears to have been obtained by Mr Holmes from Windsor Castle, doubtless when he was staying there as a guest of (in all probability) King Edward VII.

The variations in the types of pens used, as well as in the styles of handwriting, indicate—when added to the evidence of the many types of paper and the fact that two fairly large sections of the text have been re-written on typewriters—that the revisions were, as I have said, on a large scale, and (it is obvious) carried out over a considerable length of time.

The text, in its final form—that is to say, in the state in which it was handed over to Sir Frederick Kenyon, bears the clearest indication that Mr Holmes continued to revise it right up to the latter half of 1915, though he

* "Fly" = each pair of sheets joined at the left-hand side.—*Editor*

does not refer to events between 1891 (at which point the 'narrative' ends) and the date at which he finished revising the text.

SELECTIVITY OF EDITING

Those who are familiar with 'the Canon'—that is, the sixty-one stories, long and short, in which Dr Watson (with some editorial collaboration by Dr Conan Doyle) has presented the character and described the adventures of Mr Sherlock Holmes—may be astonished at some 'gaps' in what, after all, is a fairly continuous narrative of Mr Holmes's progress from 1881 to 1891—the most formative years of his adult life.

I should have been puzzled, too, by these gaps—where is the Hound of the Baskervilles, for instance, in all this?—had not that other of Mr Holmes's writings, *The Art of Detection*, come into my hands, discovered recently by me in quite exceptional circumstances: no less, in fact, than the happy accident of my having 'ratiocinated' (as Poe might have said) their certain existence and *almost* certain location hardly a moment before the demolition-men had begun to tear down the old building in which it had lain for many years.

The Art of Detection is complete—at least, in the sense that it says all that Mr Holmes wished to say in this particular book; but that leaves us with the question posed by the incompleteness of the autobiography. Are these pages here, covering only the first ten years of the Watson-Holmes professional-friendly relationship, all that exist—that ever existed? Did Mr Holmes write no more than an account of his life up to that still-undescribed three-year period that Sherlockians call 'the Great Hiatus'? It is not only unlikely; it is impossible. There are references in *The Art of Detection* to what obviously fascinated Mr Holmes: the *reasons* behind Dr Watson's or Dr Conan Doyle's choice of some particular name, rather than of another—and in these references, Mr Holmes often makes use of the phrase "As I explained when writing [of the Ferrers Documents]" or "As I pointed out when describing [the significance of the name, 'Saltire']." As he mentions neither the Ferrers Documents nor the Duke of Holdernesse's odious little heir in this first part of his autobiography, we may, I think, feel justified in assuming that Mr Holmes completed the tale of his own life—at least up to, and perhaps beyond, 1915. That the missing parts of the autobiography are irretrievably lost, I for one, do not believe. I have an extraordinary reliance—not at all unbased on experience—on paper's ability to survive where even hardy Man may succumb. After all, I found *The Art of Detection;* saved it, as the ram in the thicket saved Isaac: at the very moment of its threatened destruction. I am certain that we shall have—I trust that I shall be still here to welcome it—the missing portions of *I, Sherlock Holmes*.

In the meanwhile, here, with my notes, is the first part of an autobiography for which, I feel, the world has been too long waiting. It is no very different Mr Holmes which greets the reader from the pages that he wrote himself; but, in ways often too subtle to be analyzed, it is a Sherlock Holmes that Dr Watson could never have given us.

Acknowledgements

The books and journals that I, as Editor of Mr Holmes's memoirs, have had to consult are listed in the Bibliography. In addition to my indebtedness to these books and journals—as well as the several Librarians who enabled me to read them—I confess myself under a grateful obligation to the following, whose suggestions have been of great help to me in elucidating Mr Holmes's not always easily decipherable text.

MR FRANK ALLEN, FPS, for a professional pharmaceutical chemist's opinion of, and check on, Mr Holmes's method of synthesizing indigotin disulphonic acid.

HEER HARALD ALTHIN, of the Stockholm *Stadsmuseum*, for the photograph of, and much valuable information on, the prototype submarine of Torsten Nordenfelt.

MR P. W. AYLING, B SC, C ENG, FRINA, Secretary of The Royal Institution of Naval Architects, for a splendid photograph of the late Sir George Holmes and a copy of his Obituary, as it appeared in the *I.N.A. Volume of Transactions for 1926*.

HEER TED BERGMAN, BSI, of *The Solitary Cyclists of Stockholm*, for valuable information regarding Thorsten Nordenfelt's work on the Submarine, and for important suggestions in respect of the attempted intrigues of Kaiser Wilhelm II to the intended disadvantage of the Swedish Royal Family.

MR ALAN BRADLEY, BSI, of Saskatoon, a dedicated Holmesian, for having given me two valuable clues to the interpretation of Mr Holmes's somewhat, and Dr Watson's *very*, guarded references to two most sensational crimes. To Mr Bradley I am also indebted for a rare item of Victorian ephemeral publishing from Canada, as well as some quite exceptional "candid camera" snapshots of Mr Holmes at work.

HEER JAN BROBERG, MA, the noted Swedish historian of Crime, for filling-in the background of Crown Prince Oscar, Duke of Vermland, and for clarifying Mr Holmes's references to the Duke's friendship with August Strindberg.

MONSIEUR CHARLES GLAUSER, Consul at the Swiss Embassy, London, for information regarding the career of Henry Vernet, Swiss Consul-general in London from 1876 to 1891.

MR GEORGE W. LOCKE, the antiquarian and specialized bookseller of London, for having brought to my notice certain aspects of the Pseudo-History of Mr Sherlock Holmes; and, in particular, for having given me the opportunity of evaluating the implications of the non-Canonical "Case of the Missing Compression", and similar works.

MR DAVID PEARSON, BSI, for those invaluable pictures of Old New York which enabled me to follow the topographical references far better than any map could have done, and let me trace the footsteps of Mr Sherlock Holmes, visually rather than on plan, as he trod the pavements of still pre-skyscraper Manhattan, on his way to serve a Stewart or a Vanderbilt, or to call at the Russian Legation.

MR PHILIP POOLE, collector, historian and archivist of pens, inks, paper and "office sundries", now of Drury-lane, for technical information which enabled me to identify the various papers, inks and pens used by Mr Holmes in the writing of his memoirs.

FRØKEN SIGYN REIMERS, of the Royal Library, Stockholm, for giving me permission to use the photograph of the Duke of Vermland (King Gustav V) from her private collection, and for giving me additional information on the title bestowed on Torsten Nordenfelt.

MR JOHN THORNTON, Librarian of St Bartholomew's Hospital—'Barts'—in whose Pathological Laboratory Mr Holmes met Dr Watson in 1881; for a map of 'Bart's' in the 'Eighties, and much valuable information on the conditions in which members of the great teaching Hospital were admitted and in which they studied around 1881.

HEER F. A. C. VAN OORSCHOT, a Sherlockophile, of The Hague, for valuable information which enabled me to check Mr Holmes's references to both the Dutch Royal Family over the period, 1880–1890, and the founding of what is now Royal Dutch Shell in the last year of the decade.

LIEUTENANT-COLONEL R. F. WALTER, Commandant, The Corps of Commissionaires, for having kindly searched his records to identify Commissionaire No. 278 as Serjeant James Eldon, ex-5th Lancers, and give me the greatly appreciated details of the serjeant's length of service with the Corps that Colonel Walter now commands.

NOTE BY THE EDITOR

The following fragment of a note, in Mr Holmes's (pen-written) hand, was found amongst his papers. It is jotted down—apparently in the careless script of haste or preoccupation—on a torn-out page of a diary (Saturday, 11th March, 1882). The fragment seems to be part of a much fuller autobiographical note; but both the beginning and the end of the fragment are missing and, in all probability, now irrecoverable. The 'Captain MDB' referred to is that "Captain Marmaduke Dacre-Buttsworth' who was one of Mr Holmes's 'substitute personalities'. It is to be regretted, in the light of the comments on this 'altera persona', that the rest of the fragment is gone.

1882   31 Days   *11*   Saturday [70—295]   *March*

since I am something of a silent man, in the company of my fellows, as Dr Watson has remarked more than once. But I am no silent *thinker*—I seem to recall that I once told W[atson] that my mind was like a racing engine—tearing itself to pieces because it wasn't connected up with the machine for which it was intended.*

I look back over these jottings of a professional lifetime, and feel that I ought to be amazed (considering my perhaps not undeserved reputation for a relative taciturnity!) at my lack of reserve—even my garrulity—

But, I ask myself, *who* is this writing here? The official egomet,† William Escott Sherlock Holmes—'William the Silent, the Second'—or that far too real character, conceived in a moment of whimsicality, but now—'an image in the round'—living his own and robust and not-so-silent life: Captain MDB?

Hyde is—especially by the modern psychologists of the Vienna school—considered the 'release' of Dr Jekyll; the 'repressed' Jekyll finding the 'release' for his 'inhibitions' in Hyde—in the contrary, contradictory and mirror-image of 'Hyde'—I put his name in apostrophes. Has it never occurred to anyone—did it never occur to Stevenson?—that Hyde was the *persona*, and Jekyll the *altera persona;* that the *real* Hyde might have been seeking release and respite from the too frantic pattern of his *normal* life in the make-believe quiet of being Dr Jekyll? Did it never occur to anyone—perhaps least of all to myself—that I might wish to 'cool my overheated racing engine' by stepping, as it were, into the silent pools of non-intellectuality (almost of non-being) represented by my several 'other selves'—notably that splendid and satisfying fiction, Captain MDB?

If I might

[Here the fragment ends.—*Editor*]

* Dr Watson quotes this, with slight variations, in *Wisteria Lodge.*—*Editor*
† Latin for 'I myself'.—*Editor*

I, Sherlock Holmes

ONE

The author introduces himself

I have felt at a loss to know in which manner I ought to introduce the following memoirs of my professional life to the reader. I should have been inclined to launch them without a word of preface, but that it might be thought that I had formed an exaggerated estimate of their intrinsic merit, which is certainly not the case.

What I have striven to do, and trust that I have succeeded in doing, has been to adhere strictly to facts in the incidents recorded; and the conclusions expressed are the honest results of such experience as a long professional life, not unmixed with other associations, has enabled me to form.

Like many another man, I have been often disagreeably impressed by the failure of clear-minded military officers or lawyers of established practice or physicians of deserved reputation—experienced men, who have been able succinctly and unambiguously to set out their hypotheses and conclusions in writing—to set out the facts of their own successful lives with the same clarity. They may describe a victorious battle, a brilliant pleading, a masterly diagnosis followed by a surgical operation that it is now the fashion to describe as 'classic'; but they fail dismally to write, in any convincing (or even entertaining) manner, of their own lives—the lives of men responsible for heroic achievements in military, forensic or medical art. I think that this must be because the setting-down of the facts of a *life* is—though few seem to appreciate this truth—fundamentally different from the setting-down of the facts of a battle lost or won, of a law-case handled badly or well, of a surgical operation which did, or did not, prove successful.

And the reason for this fundamental difference, in my opinion, is that a life—any man's life—may be described by others, but never by the subject himself. The general-officer—be he Caesar or Gustavus Adolphus, Napoleon or Lord Wolseley, Robert E. Lee or Colonel Roosevelt—may well recall in perfectly understood detail the initiation and conclusion of a single involvement or a complete campaign; but which of us has any vivid memory of his birth or (despite the fables of the pietistic and moralistic romancers) any better perception of his death? Our lives begin and end in facts unperceived by us—and it is in *this* essential character that they differ from the clear accounts of battles and law-cases and experimental surgical techniques. Those who fought the battles and law-cases and the invidious malice of disease—*these* were conscious of, and commanded every step in, the progress from imagined beginning to factual * end. In other—and far simpler—words: the General who writes a clear, detailed despatch and fails to write an equally clear autobiography is writing, in the first instance, about the matters of which he is informed; in the second, of matters which, when he is not completely ignorant of them, he has received only at second hand. How much of the so-called 'memories' of our childhood have we not received from parents and relatives and—more generally—from servants? I have been told that I 'recollected', on my second visit to Pau in September, 1868, my first visit to the beautiful capital of Béarn—the city of Jeanne III d'Albret, of Henry IV and of Bernadotte—though that first visit took place in the July of 1855, when I was barely eighteen months old. Let me confess that, through this persuasion that I 'remembered', I have truly 'remembered'—thus, perhaps, justifying the faith of others as well as flattering my own childish desire to be different from others who remember less. But do I, in truth, recall that warm Southern summer of 1855—when the new Napoleon had been but three years on his inherently shaky throne?—or do I merely fill the gaps of memory with an imagined picture limned with the pencils and colours of the memories received from others? I confess that I do not know. But I also confess that this uncertainty makes me reluctant to include in my memoirs any recollected material save from a time at which I had complete control of my faculties. I think that old men may justly recall what they, as young men, did; I think that old men—and, perhaps, even young men—waste their time in recording the memories, true or false, of childhood.

I have, then, selected a date at which I propose to begin this story of (not so much my life, as) my *professional* life; but before I begin my narrative on that cold day in January, 1881, in the then newly-built Pharmaceutical Laboratory, I must recall a meeting that I had at around that same time—a meeting that I had quite forgotten until I set out to make the notes for these

---

* This modern word—an import from American English—had been received into accepted English usage by 1915, when Mr Holmes used it.—*Editor*

memoirs. The meeting to which I now refer was with that most brilliant of
all forensic pleaders, the late Mr Serjeant Ballantine, one of the few lawyers, let me say, with whom I could place myself on friendly terms, and
certainly one of the scant half-dozen for whom I have entertained any respect at all.

Only a few weeks after my return from America at the beginning of
August, 1880, I had, to what I admit was my intense gratification, a letter
from the secretary of the Union Club, informing me that, on the recommendation of Mr Serjeant Ballantine, supported by Lord Wicklow, I had
been elected a member of that well-known London club. This was, the
reader may imagine, a source of considerable gratification to me. In the first
place, I was only a few months over twenty-six—and though Dickens had
become a member of the Royal Society at the 'tender' age of twenty-seven,
I did not then—and still, thank Heavens!, do not—rank myself with that
greatest of all English novelists. I had been fortunate in an ability to be of
some small assistance to Mr Ballantine in the matter of an infringement of
patent in connection with the steam-driven submersible vessel of the Reverend Mr William George Garrett, then Curate of Holy Cross, Manchester.
Mr Garrett and his partner, Mr Nordenfelt, the Swedish engineer, have
progressed to higher—or lower, as you may like to think—achievements; of
which both Germany and the United States of America have taken due cognizance. But of that, more anon: here I am speaking of the pride that I felt
that, at twenty-six, I should have been elected a member of the Union
Club, then some seventy-five years old, having been founded in the year of
Trafalgar. From its inception, the Club had been patronized by men of
rank, and among the nearly sixty members who had belonged to the House
of Peers were the Dukes of York and Sussex, Richmond and Devonshire,
the Marquess of Wellesley, Lord Granville and—most eminent of all—Lord
Byron. At the time when my self-esteem was delightfully soothed by admission to the Union, it had changed somewhat from its original aristocratic
character, and the membership was now more strongly represented by the
banking interests—though members of the firm of Baring's and of Hoare's
had belonged from the Club's foundation—and by the Law. The peer who
supported Mr Serjeant Ballantine's motion to elect me to this august assem-
bly of legal luminaries, bankers, physicians and divines—I trust that I have
mentioned the classes in the strictest order of precedence!—was Lord
Wicklow, who had succeeded to his title in 1869 only after his right to inherit had been demonstrated by a long and costly law-suit, in which both
fraud and effrontery were employed against him in almost equal measures
to deprive him of his lawful rank. Unlike the Claimant in the Tichborne
Baronetcy case, whom a prison sentence effectively subdued—at least as

regards the rightful holder of the title—the impudent claimants to the Wicklow title still persecuted the rightful peer even after their case had been contemptuously thrown out of Court. Appealed to in his distress by Lord Wicklow, I was able to suggest how the criminally insolent pests might be silenced; and though they returned to attack a *future* holder of the title, they never again troubled my client, who had, as all who have read the proceedings know, suffered enough in establishing his just rights.

For this small service, his Lordship professed himself under the heaviest obligations, and he willingly complied with Mr Ballantine's request that my application to join the Union should be supported. And so I became a member of the Union Club at the age of twenty-six—the first professional consulting detective ever to be enrolled on the Club's membership list.

Of course, as Mr Ballantine (and indeed, Lord Wicklow) pointed out to me, in disclaiming my thanks for their having obtained me my membership, no relative of the famous 'Tom' Holmes—then the unchallenged 'Father' of the Club—would be likely to be excluded. Certainly nothing like the grotesque experience which attended Tom Holmes's own election in 1828 could have befallen me: an Irish member, deciding to play an elaborate Hibernian joke, saved up his black balls and—Tom Holmes being the last in the ballot—placed *seven* black balls in the box.

Fortunately, some suspicion had attached to the Irish member in consequence, Mr Ballantine explained to me, of 'former proceedings'. The unhappy prank was detected; the Irish member was asked to resign forthwith; and Tom Holmes was elected there-and-then. When I met him at the Union Club, my venerable relative, son of the Tory Whip of George IV's day, and one of the earliest promoters—with Lord Lowther—of the Union Club, had been a member for fifty-two years.

In the changes which have overtaken Society and, indeed, the world generally, in the decades which have passed since 1880, it is still a fact that advancement in this world, especially at the commencement of any career, is greatly facilitated by the interest of highly-placed and influential persons. 'Tom'—as even I, young as I was, soon came to call him—was highly respected by the survivors of a world of which I knew only a little by hearsay, and nothing at all by experience. Tom's father had been an intimate friend of an earlier Lord Rivers (not the Lord Rivers who died in 1880), noted, even in those days of high play, for the recklessness of his gambling. On one occasion, Tom's father told his son, Lord Rivers had shewn the elder Holmes no less a sum than £100,000 in bank-notes.

I was, at that time, faintly scandalized—and afterwards, as I became more accommodated to my impressive surroundings, somewhat amused—

to see what respect old Tom commanded through his having known the men of a more licensed Age.

There was a further connection with, if not precisely the Union Club, then at least one of its principal ornaments, which was to serve me well in getting myself established in my chosen and unusual profession. I refer again to Mr Serjeant Ballantine, who had made his name familiar throughout the English-speaking world (and, I dare say, other parts, too) through his having led for the Claimant in the notorious Tichborne Baronetcy Trial.

At this time—a few months before that date on which I propose 'officially' to begin my memoirs—I was living, if not meanly, then at any rate in decidedly straitened circumstances, in Montague-street, Russell-square, just around the corner from the British Museum, whose grass-grown forecourt and blank side walls behind its massive iron railings I saw every day from the windows of my third-floor apartment. I was comfortable enough at No. 24; for food was cheap in those days, and coals—equally cheap—were never missing from the scuttles which flanked the cast-iron grate-cum-hot-water-boiler in the Georgian fireplace. I had the great Reading Room of the Museum around the corner, as I have said; St Bartholomew's was only a penny bus-ride away—and well within walking distance on those days when even that penny was better kept for a bread-roll and piece of cheese. I *should* have returned from New York in August, 1880, with money—even a lot of money—for the Stewart family had offered the immense sum of $50,000 for the recovery of the body robbed from its grave. At the proper time, I shall give the details of this interesting case, and, in the course of my doing so, explain how it was that I decided not to accept the reward that Mrs Stewart offered. I came back, indeed, not with money, but in debt. My elder brother, Mycroft, had advanced me the money to cover my three years' fees at Bart's, and because one gained a discount of seven guineas by paying the fee for the three years' tuition in one sum—125 guineas—instead of over three years (in payments of one of 40 guineas and two of 46 guineas), Mycroft generously insisted on my accepting of the whole 125 guineas. "Now that's paid!" he said. It was true . . . unfortunately. And now it had to be paid back.

I had had considerable difficulty in paying the terms of subscription at the Union Club, even though these had been set as long ago as 3rd February, 1807: ten guineas a-year and one guinea for the servants. There was, I was happy to know, an absence of that entrance-fee which has now become a permanent item in Club dues.

I must make it clear that I was far from insolvency at this critical time of my life; indeed, I was not even aware of the bitter grind of poverty; not as poverty was known in the London of the 'Eighties. In the few months before that date in January, 1881, on which I have fixed as my 'official' beginning—I talk now of these proposed memoirs, and not, of course, of my life, or even of my professional career—I had become involved in, and had 'wound up', as the modern phrase has it, no fewer than nine cases, not all of the same importance. In listing these cases here, I shall give them, for the moment, the identity-concealing titles given to them in Dr Watson's record of my activities. Later, I shall give the details of some of these titled but unrecorded cases, with, of course what must be their correct appellations. Here, then, are the nine cases which occupied my attention and brought me in a few professional guineas between my return from New York in August, 1880, and my first meeting with Dr Watson, late of the Army Medical Service, in January, 1881—a matter of a little less than five months. Against each entry I have made a note of the fee asked. An asterisk denotes non-payment of the fee.

	GUINEAS
The Tarleton Murders	10
The Case of Vamberry, the Wine Merchant	50
The Adventure of the Old Russian Woman	5*
The Singular Affair of the Aluminium Crutch	25
Riccoletti of the Club Foot and His Abominable Wife	30*
The Trifling Affair of Mortimer Maberley	30
The Taking of Brooks and Woodhouse	15
The *Matilda Briggs* and the Giant Rat of Sumatra	75
The Case of Mrs Farintosh (concerned with an Opal Tiara)	25

TOTAL (actual) 230 guineas

"Two hundred and thirty guineas—£241 10s.—nearly two hundred and fifty pounds for little more than four months' work! Why, that's—let me see—about fifty pounds a-month—why, good gracious!, that's about six hundred a year . . . between four and three times what a bank-manager receives in salary! Why . . ."

But let me not continue with what was said—and, for all that I know, is said still—about what so many unthinking people have condemned as my 'discontent with my lot' of those apprentice days.

It is true, as the list printed above shews, that I earned, between mid-August, 1880, and early January, 1881, nearly two hundred and fifty pounds, and—had defaulting clients paid up—a further £37. But my expenses were heavy; I had begun my professional practice in a day when long credit was demanded and given without question on either side, and in which, to compound the difficulties caused by a situation in which one might wait for years before seeing the money that one had earned, it was, to recall a monitory phrase of the time, 'professional suicide' to press for the payment of one's outstanding fees.

As I look back over a practice of now some forty years long, I see that this social obligation to *keep up appearances*, no matter what resolution, what sacrifices, what so-called 'hypocrisy', were entailed, imposed on all of that generation some cardinal virtues, as well as some trivial vices. Our domestic and professional difficulties we were forced, by that Draconian code of Society that no-one dared to defy, to keep to ourselves. We were *forced*—we had no choice—to invent and adopt a 'public face', a public deportment of (how shall I express it?) unruffled self-assurance, at once responsibly grave and unobtrusively light-hearted. We were not, I think, justly to be condemned—as it seems now that it is the fashion to condemn us Late Victorians—for our 'hypocrisy', in that we all went to what now are called 'extraordinary lengths', to keep our troubles to ourselves or to our immediate relatives; to conceal our difficulties and—even more important—to conceal the means that we were adopting to cope with those difficulties. I was reminded of our social attitude by two books that I read recently: the first, a novelette by a popular present-day writer, Mr William Le Queux; the other, a short-story by an equally popular but far better writer, Sir Arthur Conan Doyle. In Mr Le Queux's novel * we are shewn a man who for years has been 'off the Social List'—after having fallen into disgrace—in the act of preparing to attend a grand reception in Rome. He is about to accept an invitation of the sort to which he is socially accustomed, but which has not come his way for a long time. Mr Le Queux now shews us this man as he examines—and with never a touch of self-pity—his meagre and mean wardrobe. He still has his Orders and Decorations, preserved, God knows how, from the pawnshop; but his dress-coat, though by Poole or Davies, is green with age and shiny with wear. In no sense of reducing his hero in our estimation, Mr Le Queux now shews him removing both green and shine with black marking-ink.

In the short story by Sir Arthur Conan Doyle, we have a situation not dissimilar. Two men who have achieved worldly success are travelling in great style in Egypt, when one of them encounters an old friend, or, rather, a friend from the old days. Disgraced in England, this man went into exile, where his social descent has been deep indeed. The wealthy traveller invites the outcast to join him and his companion for dinner; the outcast accepts—with gratitude. At dinner that night, the traveller who tells the story re-

* Presumably *The Unknown.*—Editor

marks on the fact that, though the outcast's dress-coat looks as crumpled as though it had been kept for years in an Army kit-bag, he has managed to dress himself correctly for dinner, even to the extent of fashioning a white tie out of a handkerchief.

Now, I recall these Hiders-of-Poverty, not so much because I find *them* typical Late Victorians, as because the literary inventiveness which created these fictitious adventures is typically Late Victorian. These 'outcasts' who are held up for our admiration, though 'heroes' of the adventures, are in no sense intended to be accepted as heroic. They may be bounders, even criminals; in any event, Society has exacted from them terrible penalties. But if there be a moral in such stories—and many hundreds have been written—it is that, *no matter what the temptations, the gravest offence against Society is the failure to conform.* In the case of Sir Arthur Conan Doyle's tale, we are asked to accept the truth of his argument that the Outcast, for all the shocking behaviour which has exiled him from his native land and from all decent company, has partly—perhaps, even wholly—redeemed himself in the eyes of honest men by turning up in a tent in the desert, in a shabby old dress-coat and a white tie fashioned from a torn handkerchief.

Born when I was, and *how* I was, I could no more reject the emotion and the reasoning behind such presentations of behaviour than I could fly. I mention this 'polite' secretiveness—to me, I confess, the mark of a really civilized society—because, for all that Dr Watson has recorded what may appear to be much confidential unburdening of my soul, I did not, in truth, confide in Dr Watson more than in any other person of my acquaintance—certainly not in those earlier days of our sharing lodgings together.

I see that Dr Watson records that I mentioned bitterly 'my all too abundant time', when living in Montague-street. This, I think, conveys a false impression of unprofitable and resented idleness. In fact, the time was 'too abundant' because my too abundant *energy* needed more opportunities to discharge itself than were provided by the nine cases listed above, by legal and medical studies, and by the many other activities in which I sought to satisfy the demands of my restless energy. I think that other men might not have found the time 'too abundant'—but I have always had, it seems, ten times the energy of the average man; and so I have felt the need for ten times the occupation.

This brings me back to an evening in the late November of 1880, only a few weeks after I had been elected to membership of the Union Club. I had been invited by my excellent friend, Mr Serjeant Ballantine, to join a party by the big fireplace; a party which, as I recall, included not only old Tom Holmes, but also Sir George Honyman, Q.C., who had been 'on the op-

posite side' to Mr Ballantine in the Tichborne Trial, and Colonel R.
Phayre, the Viceroy's Resident at Baroda: the man (an officious nincom-
poop, in my opinion, then and now) who ignorantly and dangerously
stirred up the trouble which culminated in the trial and dethronement of
the Gaekwar of Baroda. However, at this small gathering of members of the
Union Club, the affairs in India of six years earlier were not being discussed: the subject was the manner in which Mr Serjeant Ballantine proposed
to set forth those memoirs which had been requested of him by Mr Richard
Bentley, son and successor to that Richard Bentley who had been one of
Dickens's earlier publishers. Like his father, the younger Mr Bentley was
also Publisher-in-Ordinary to Her Majesty the Queen.

A book, its binding of gilt-stamped purple cloth now somewhat faded
with the years, meets my eye as I glance at the bookcases which flank my
fireplace; it records, for ever, the decisions taken in discussion at that party
in the Union Club. I take the book from its place, and open it at the title-
page: *Some Experiences of a Barrister's Life, by Mr Serjeant Ballantine.** On the
facing page, the kindly, intelligent, humorous face of my old friend regards
the reader with shrewd yet sympathetic gaze. I then turn to the *Contents*—
and I find this:—

CHAPTER I.
Autobiography

CHAPTER II.
London during My Pupilage

CHAPTER III.
Commencement of My Professional Life

—and so forth, just as the learned pleader of my earlier days would have set
forth, under their progressive heads, the several stages of his argument.

I do not propose to treat of my own biography in this manner; a descrip-

* Mr Holmes's mention of this book, as well as of the name of its author, raises some interesting—and, at present, quite unanswerable—questions. It will not escape the notice of students of late Victorian autobiographical literature that the first two paragraphs of Mr Holmes's
memoirs are almost word-for-word reproductions of the first two in the 'Prefatory Notice' to
Mr Serjeant Ballantine's book. Was this copying—for such it must be—voluntary or involun-
tary on Mr Holmes's part? Was the copying the subconsciously dictated reproduction of writing that Mr Holmes admired? Or was the copying part of a complimentary tribute to Mr Serjeant Ballantine of what is to-day called an ' "in" joke' nature? Or did Mr Holmes copy out the
first two paragraphs from the Serjeant's 'Prefatory Note' as an excellent example of how a biography should be begun; find the copy years later, forget that it was a copy, rather than original work; and thinking that it was his own, 'continued from there'? Literature—especially
modern literature—is full of such not very important problems; perhaps the still missing second part of Mr Holmes's memoirs may give us the solution.—*Editor*

tion of my childhood and youth and adolescence hardly merits space in the account of myself that I propose to give.

I turn up the account of my family that I gave to Dr Watson these many years gone; and I have little here to add to it. My family were yeomen, settled for generations—centuries, even—on their freeholding in the North Riding. My father, Siger Holmes, a captain in the Honourable East India Company's service, was invalided home, his career, in all practical meaning of that word, finished, in April, 1844. My grandmother, as I told Dr Watson, was a sister of Horace Vernet, the noted French painter. I may add here that I was the third of three sons, my elder brothers, Sherrinford and Mycroft (the latter named after my family's estate in the North Riding), being born in, respectively, 1845 and 1847. I myself was born on 6th January, 1854, at Mycroft.

My father, Captain Siger Holmes, died in 1877. I deeply regret that my persistent—what, unhappily, he chose to see as merely 'obstinate and wilful'—attempts to obtain his blessing on my choice of career met with no success, and that he died, I am grieved to record, estranged, if not from me, his son, then from his son's decision. I trust that, if we go, as they say, to a higher, more comprehending life after this, he will long ago have understood me—and, having understood, forgiven my seeming defiance of his own ambitions for his youngest son.

His death, I also grieve to record, left my mother in circumstances in which she had never expected to find herself at any time, let alone at an age approaching sixty; for my father's pension of some £1,200 a-year was not the only source of income which had died with him. During the thirty years and more which had elapsed between his retirement (for that is what his being invalided home turned out to be) and his death, several depressions of trade and commerce had affected this country, with an adverse effect on the value of the pound sterling, and a consequent rise in the price of staple commodities. With three sons to educate in the traditional manner—my father's restless nature took us all over the Continent during my younger years, so that I enjoyed the benefits of none but the most haphazard schooling; but we three boys all went up to the University—my father, it is now clear, was often at his wits' end to know how to meet his bills. I think now, with the charity, not so much of hindsight, as of the understanding which comes with age, that what he did was rather forced upon him than chosen by him out of weakness. But the fact of the matter is that he mortgaged Mycroft up, as they say, to the hilt; and when he died—never having the courage to confide his desperate situation to my poor mother—she found herself, within a matter of weeks, dispossessed by creditors who foreclosed on the property.

Like my brothers at the time, I was indignant with what I *then* called my father's 'cowardice'. But many decades have now passed; and I may, I am happy to say, see his actions in a different—and more kindly (as, indeed, a more tolerant)—light. We are, as Cervantes said, as we are made—and my father *did* no better because he *knew* no better. It at once shames and gladdens me that my mother, for all the shock that she experienced in finding herself a virtual pauper at fifty-six, never joined in our triple condemnation of my father; always rebuked us in her gentle manner; telling us—which, indeed, as we all afterwards learned, was the truth—that whatever Captain Holmes had done or not done, he had acted out of—at the worst, thoughtlessness; never out of selfishness. Far less, said my dear mother, out of malice.

This was a time on which I prefer not to look back, though, in all conscience, I can say that it is not now the *suffering* which repels the memories of that time; rather is it the *bitterness*, of which I am now so deeply ashamed, that self-pity generated in me.

I was forced to leave the University without a degree; I accepted employment as badly-paid as it was demeaning. For a time—and this honesty now compels me to admit—I hated the memory of my father, who had left my mother (and me, too, I know now that I was complaining) in such straits.

The fact of the matter is that I was still young—and I did not realize, even as I bitterly condemned his 'bad management', his 'irresponsibility', his 'self-centeredness' (for so, in my youthful ignorance, I named them), how much I owed, and was to owe, to the good character that he enjoyed among his relatives and friends; a good character that he had never enjoyed had he been even the fool, let alone the knave, of my childish reproaches.

My mother was not left to starve, even though none of her sons was at that time in a position to help her. Ours has always been a fairly large family, and members of it were to be found in almost every profession. (I shall afterwards mention two members of St Bartholomew's Hospital, whose family feeling helped me immeasurably in the bitter days following my father's death.) These, as they say, rallied around—and my dear mother was provided with a competency sufficient for her modest needs; a slender but adequate allowance to which, I am glad to say, I was able soon to contribute, and which, through the success which came soon to both Sherrinford and myself, was greatly augmented before her regretted death in the year of the Diamond Jubilee.

And now, let me anticipate the question that both friend and stranger must reasonably ask: why do you wish to give us your memoirs?

I do not, as I hope that I have explained, wish to give the reader a detailed account of those trivial domestic progresses or setbacks common to us all. But I do feel an obligation enforced on me to explain what I think, without immodesty, I have given to the world.

Let me make myself clear. When I decided to embark on the profession of private consulting detective, *there was no such profession*. True, there were private inquiry-agents—you may find their names in the reference-books of the day, and sometimes they acquired some newspaper eminence. One of their unprofessional company, a Mr Wendel Scherer, gained himself some momentary fame when he was rebuked by Mr Bushby, one of the two magistrates at Worship-street Police-court, for claiming the right of 'professional privilege', in refusing to divulge information imparted in confidence by a client. Mr Bushby was exceedingly angry at this assumption of 'professional status', and Mr Wendel Scherer, standing firm, would have been committed to prison for contempt of Court, had he not been rescued by the client on whose behalf he was being silent. I felt much admiration for Mr Scherer, who came of a family of shorthand writers greatly respected in legal circles, and afterwards I called on him; a call which developed into a mild friendship.

But when I say that Mr Scherer's dressing-down by Mr Bushby came late in 1881, some years after I had embarked on my profession of private consulting detective, the reader may well imagine against what apparently insurmountable obstacles of prejudice I have had to battle to get my profession noticed, let alone 'recognized'.

I look back with, I think, a satisfaction which is wholly pardonable. I *did* succeed in establishing the art—the science—of deduction on a professional basis. I became the first (and so far, the only) Private Consulting Detective-in-Ordinary to a reigning Sovereign. I have served three British monarchs; to two of whom I was able to give respectful affection as well as that service that it behoves every loyal subject to give to his Sovereign. In the third case, though I was not able to give this affection, I gave of my best service, and this King was not unmindful of my help.

There is another reason why I should, I feel, write and publish my memoirs. I was the first, not to apply scientific methods to the business of preventing or solving crime, but to apply the scientific method generally in all matters criminal. I was, I think that I may now say, one who sought in every scientific advance some help in strengthening the armoury of the weapons with which crime was to be fought. There is something paradoxical—and not a little amusing—in the reflection that, in making Science the handmaiden of Justice, I not only 'professionalized' my own chosen career, but, after a fashion, 'professionalized' Crime itself. How all this happened, I now propose to tell.

TWO

I meet
Dr John Watson

One often hears it said that "the Terms at our great teaching hospitals are the same as those kept in our Universities." This may be so to-day; certainly it was not the case in the late 'Seventies and early 'Eighties, when I first became acquainted with the more practical side of the Aesculapian Art. For one thing, our terms—we called them 'Sessions'—were longer, with the inevitable consequence that our vacations were shorter. Thus, to refer precisely to that period at which my story opens, the Winter Sessions of 1880–1881 began on 1st October, dividing at 23rd December (a Thursday, in that Leap Year, I recall), and resuming on Sunday, 9th January, 1881. Compare this with the Hilary, Trinity and Michaelmas Terms of Oxford, or the Lent, Easter and Michaelmas Terms of Cambridge, and you will comprehend how the less dedicated of our fellow-students at Bart's groaned under the 'tyranny' of the Hospital's time-table.

Although I was not resident at the Hospital—for reasons that I shall explain later—I attended, with the others, on that bleak Sunday afternoon, to 'report in', and receive (a mere formality, this, since the time-table never varied from one decade to the next) my printed *Days and Hours of Attendance on Lectures and Demonstrations.*

On the following morning, which was as cold as on the previous day, but which was even less sympathetic because of the normal 'Monday-morning blues' adding themselves to the equally normal 'first-day-back depression', I took the *Atlas* 'bus along Holborn, over the new cast-iron viaduct, to the corner of Giltspur-street, from which I walked briskly, through a thin, drizzling rain, to the King Henry the Eighth Gate, now the entrance to the almost totally renovated and rearranged south-west part of the ancient foundation.

I had timed my arrival to give myself full opportunity to arrange my notes for the Chemistry Lecture which was given at ten o'clock on Monday mornings during the Winter Session. The Lecturer on that particular day was, I remember, the learned but immensely 'wide-awake' (if I may use this vividly expressive colloquial term with all respect for one who had well deserved his Fellowship of the Royal Society) Dr William Russell, Treasurer of the Chemical Society and Lecturer on Chemistry at Christ's Hospital—from over the wall of which old school I could hear the mist-muted voices of "the little bareheaded men in blue petticoats and yellow stockings" * as they took their school-break in the Western Quadrangle.

I was soon—though of course, I had no premonition of the fact—to find a friend who would be my almost constant companion over the next quarter-century; but, in the loneliness of my life during those first weeks at Bart's, I sought and found solace for the unhappiness of my condition in the sight and sound of 'the Blue Coat boys'—the scholars of Christ's Hospital. For this had been my Father's school, and since, though the old mediaeval buildings had been replaced by the modern structure in 1825, the dress that my Father wore, and that the schoolboys of 1880 were wearing, was that in which the boys had been apparelled when, ten days before his death, the boy-king Edward VI had founded, on 26th June, 1553, a 'hospital' for poor fatherless children and foundlings—the pious origin of so many of our most 'select' English public schools. Nothing in the school's architecture linked the modern Blue Coat foundation with the Greyfriars monastery in which it had had its origin—even the attached mediaeval Christ Church, which had escaped the Great Fire of 1666, had been rebuilt by Wren in 1704—but the Tudor dress of the boys not only linked the nineteenth-century present with the school's sixteenth-century past, it linked the boys that I was seeing and hearing each day with that Father of mine who, fifty years before, had played and shouted, in this same archaic dress of blue gown and long yellow stockings, in this very Western Quadrangle, separated from us at Bart's by no more than an old stone wall.

There is a sadness in all recollection—people talk incorrectly of 'happy memories'; they should talk of 'the memories of happy things'. But in this sadness of recollection there is a power to cure the pain of loneliness; and seeing the boys at play, I could imagine that almost any one of these 'little victims' was my Father; and that I had been drawn back, as it were,

---

* Mr Sherlock Holmes would be gratified to know that, for all the fundamental changes of an age which finds a profit in any change, the boys of Christ's Hospital ('The Bluecoat School'), removed from Smithfield to Horsham in 1902, still wear their Tudor dress of long blue coat and long yellow stockings.—*Editor*

through time, to be spared the loneliness of the empty present in finding the warm, heedless companionship of time past.

I was eager that morning, not only to hear Dr Russell, but to get back to some experiments which had been inspired, if not altogether suggested, by the Lecturer in Forensic Medicine, Dr Ernst Klein—another Fellow of the Royal Society. Dr Klein used also to lecture in General Histology or Microscopical Analysis; and in one or the other of his allied lectures—I forget now which—he had deplored the necessity of relying on the guaiacum test for ascertaining whether or not certain appearances are those of blood. He instanced several—indeed, many—cases in which the accused had had to go free because of the impossibility of demonstrating *beyond all reasonable doubt* that the stains on an apparently blood-stained garment were, in fact, what they seemed to be. "We need," said Dr Klein, in that thick German accent which so irritated the more John-Bullish of our students, "some test far more precise, far more reliable, than any that guaiacum may provide. As you know, the test by microscopical analysis is grossly defective by reason of the fact that the microscopical detection of blood corpuscles is impossible after the blood is but a few hours old. We require a reagent which will detect the presence of blood even centuries—even millennia—old. We require a reagent so positive, so sensitive, so *consistently* reliable, that it will verify the presence of blood in the mummy of an Egyptian Pharaoh or in the frozen desiccation of a Siberian mammoth. Gentlemen," he added, "if you wish a problem whose solution will bring you not only honour but also the no less acceptable material rewards—the baronetcy and other emoluments of Sir James Simpson will serve as examples—then find such a reagent as I have described! Gentlemen, if you—one of you (I dare hope for no more!)—should find this reagent, future ages will not only heap blessings on your memory, Her Majesty, in the present, will indubitably offer you at least a knighthood. Think on it!"

It would be idle to affirm that Dr Klein was in any way popular either with us students or with the staff of Bart's. Since the revolutions of 1848, Germans had been arriving in this country in ever greater numbers, and from all levels of that society that they had left. Not all were Jewish, but many were; and with that easy adaptability which is one of the most remarkable characteristics of that industrious and ingenious race, not a few had contrived to enter the professions—including that of politics—and to reap what one may hardly deny were the just rewards of their efforts.

But the spectacle of German Jews in the House of Commons; in the Justiciary; in Medicine, Education, Law, Engineering, and so on—to say nothing of Banking and Commerce—was one which brought to the surface the never very deeply submerged xenophobia of the native British. I dare say that Germans—Jewish or Christian—were even more disliked in the British Isles of 1881 than they are to-day.* This general dislike did not spare Dr Klein.

Yet his classes and lectures were always fully—and even enthusiastically—attended, not least by those who affected to hold him in contempt. There is, fortunately, a practical side to us English which permits us, at times, to recognize that even our enemies may teach us for our good.

The *seeming* paradox of the popularity of an unpopular Lecturer was not, of course, lost upon the somewhat cynical Dr Klein, who was by no means backward in alluding to his unpopularity in those sarcastic remarks—mostly of a very personal flavour—with which he would interpolate his lectures.

"Gentlemen," he said to us one day, "make no mistake: there is nothing small about me but my name.† If I were not disliked, I should begin to wonder what was wrong with me. I should be disliked if I were English; as I am German, with a German accent, it is inevitable that I be disliked. But, what some of you gentlemen don't seem to realize is this: *the dislike is not reserved to one side.* Ah! you did not realize that? But, *ach!*, you should! As, gentlemen, you should also realize that *my* dislike for *you* is that much more intelligent than *your* dislike for me, as I am, indeed, more intelligent than you.

"You challenge my argument? But reflect, gentlemen! *You* dislike me because I am not English; because I do not pronounce English as you pronounce it. These are trivialities, gentlemen; but my dislike of you—of *some* of you, I ought to say—is not based on similar trivialities: it is based on the fact that you are ignorant, lazy and seemingly contemptuous of the brains that the good God has given you. Tchah!"

I did not dislike Dr Klein, and he did not dislike me. My plainly irregular upbringing, which had taken me to France and Germany, Holland and Belgium, and which had deprived me (in my opinion, no great loss) of a normal English education, made me, at Bart's, almost more of an outsider than was Dr Klein. A fellow-feeling, the poet says, makes us wondrous kind; and such 'sheep without the fold' as Dr. Klein and I were, must have tended to establish some sort of intimacy, though it were merely to emphasize the fact of our individual and common separateness.

Besides, I spoke German; not perfectly, for I had had little practice since, as a boy, I had spoken it fluently in Cologne—then the most Roman, the

---

* Mr Holmes is, of course, writing in 1915, when the military fortunes of Great Britain seemed at their lowest ebb.—*Editor*

† German *klein* means 'small'.—*Editor*

most German, the most Jewish, and, above all, the most independent of all the Rhine cities. The opportunity of polishing up my German that conversation with Dr Klein offered was one that I seized eagerly, and this again, whilst drawing us ever closer, sensibly widened the gap which separated me from the majority of my fellow-students.

Dr Klein spoke English well, but there were times when the English equivalent of a German word did not come instantly to his mind. The 'purification' of the 'Imperial' German tongue, with which the name of Von Stephan will always be associated, had not spared Dr Klein, and he was mostly at a loss when trying to find an English word of Latin or Greek origin, but which, in modern, 'purified' German, has been replaced by a word of 'pure Teutonic' type.

Such a word—or phrase, rather—in English was the translation of the German *Stickstoff*, that Dr Klein, at one lecture, tried vainly to find. I ventured a diffident: "Nitrogen, sir."

"*Ach! danke!*" said the Professor, and passed on to other matters in which his command of the English tongue was not to be impugned.

But he had not forgotten, and, soon, he 'came back to me', as they say. I noticed that, after he had translated for us a passage from one of the many German journals that he received from his home-land, his firm grip on the idiom of the British Isles was apt to falter. Let Dr Klein read out—translating as he went—some interesting piece from the *Berichte der deutschen chemischen Gesellschaft* or *Hoppe-Seylers Zeitschrift für physiologische Chemie* (both of which he regularly 'took'), and, for some small time after, he would lose his firm grip on the tongue that Shakespeare spake. The German journals would have returned him, in spirit, to his home-land, and that return would have returned him to his mother-tongue.

At such times, I would translate for the class—at first, with an open or implied request for his permission; but, after a short while, with no apology. It was understood by us all that when Dr Klein was at a loss for the English version of a word or sentence, then Sherlock Holmes was at liberty to supply it. Insensibly, then, Dr Klein began to use me as his interpreter— a development which was of great benefit to me, and which did his students no disservice. This was more notable when the subject under discussion was one for which, to use a phrase not then invented, Dr Klein 'felt deeply'.

And for no subject did Dr Klein 'feel more deeply' than for blood . . . or, rather, haemoglobin. So bound up in his subject did he become, that all his English deserted him—but quite, as we saw, without his noticing the fact. And at such moments, instead of saying that, for instance, the red blood corpuscles in man are circular, biconcave, elastic disks, or that the white corpuscles are larger than the red corpuscles, Dr Klein would declaim that *die roten Blutkörperchen des Menschen sind runde, bikonkave, elastische Scheiben* or that *die farblosen Blutkörperchen des Menschen sind grosser als die roten.*

All such unconscious lapses into his native language, I translated, *sotto voce*, for the Professor, to the benefit of his students ignorant of German. In this manner, I not only acquired valuable practice in translation; I soon realized that my voluntary interpretership was forging a strong bond of friendship between Dr Klein and myself.

Not all the Lecturer's use of German was unconscious: there was a phrase that it always amused me to hear; a phrase with which the good Doctor sarcastically expressed his impatience with the more obtuse of his students. This phrase—reiterated several times; the number of reiterations depending on his degree of impatience—was *"Zweimal zwei ist vier"*— "Twice two are four"—and implied that Dr. Klein had at last consented to state a fact within the comprehension of his dull-witted class.

But there was another German phrase—almost never translated into English by the Doctor—from which I think I derived more mental and spiritual benefit than I should have got from a hundred of the learned books or a thousand of the academic journals that Dr Klein was wont to lend me. But I must have heard this phrase many times before its deeper significance struck me; and an even longer time had to pass before I realized its significance for *me*.

The phrase was this. Dr Klein, positive though he was in speech and manner, never expressed his conclusion otherwise than in saying "The convincing proof . . . as *I* see it"—"Der nach meiner Ansicht starke Beweis". The significance of this choice of expression may—and I trust that it will— be more readily apparent to the reader than it was to a young and somewhat conceited Chemistry student of nearly forty years ago. For those readers who may still be as uncomprehending—or 'slow on the uptake', as Dr Watson rather more colloquially used to express it—I may point out that Dr Klein deplored the setting up of Axiomatic and Absolute so-called 'facts'. A fact, he explained, was what reason saw as a fact; but a fact could not exist outside of the reasoning mind of the observer. "Think for yourselves," he used to tell us; "accept no conclusions but those to which you shall have come by your trained but unaided *reason*." He had little time for the Objective—that is, the fact divorced from its environment; for him only the Subjective had reality and functional purpose; and it is more than merely interesting to reflect that a younger German professor, of brilliant intellect—Dr Albert Einstein—has evolved his Theory of Relativity by rejecting as unproven the 'facts' of cosmogony accepted by generations of post-Newtonian astronomers as axiomatic.

In a word, it was Dr Klein who first taught me really to think. . . .

Let me state here quite frankly that, at first unconsciously, and, later, consciously, I resisted the influence that Dr Klein was obtaining over me. At Cambridge, I had met and read under the man who, for many years, was to remain for me the *beau idéal* of English scholarship: Lord Rayleigh, then Professor of Experimental Physics, and one of the foremost scientists of our age.

Like most young men of my age and time, I was not insensible of the glamour of Rank, and this Lord Rayleigh, a peer and the great-grandson of a Duke of Leinster, had in a marked degree. But, besides his undisputed claim to Rank, Lord Rayleigh might well assert his equally undisputed claim to the aristocracy of Intellect. He was a skilled teacher—patient and imaginative; he was an inventor of a severely *practical* type, whose work had earned him the honours of governments and universities throughout the world. He had a lively interest in the improvement of everything, and his scientific interests ranged, as is well known, from the production of pure milk to the discovery of the gas, argon. In accepting the influence of Dr Klein, I felt, in an irrational but (I think that I may say) a normally youthful way, that I was being in some fashion disloyal to my ungrudged admiration for my old Cambridge professor, who had taught me so much—and, let me put the fact on record, so very pleasantly.

For, except that both these excellent men shared learning and the ability to impart their knowledge to others, no two could have been more dissimilar: on one hand, the descendant of an Irish ducal house, of both assured social position and *indigenous* academic standing, as well as of that physical type that it is the convention to call 'Anglo-Saxon'—an English gentleman, in short; on the other hand, a man of perhaps even more ancient descent— but that descent remotely Oriental and more recently Teutonic; a man whose every gesture, every word (whether in German or in English) betrayed his exotic origins. One would have to be decidedly unfamiliar with the mental attitudes of the English not to understand how it was that I was more attracted towards Lord Rayleigh than I was to Dr Klein. However, as it turned out, both these academic luminaries became my close friends, but that, as Mr Kipling says, is another story, and one which will be held over until its proper time for telling.

Women, as Dr Watson has seen fit to remark, have always troubled me; but Dr Watson, for all his interest in me which often bordered on the inquisitive, never asked me why. I am sure that a misconceived 'delicacy' forbade him to raise subjects which, to use the modern jargon, are—or might be held to be—'taboo'. I know that he has interpreted my *noli me tangere* attitude towards women as some proof of my innate ideal of celibacy. In fact, women—Woman, rather—has always troubled me because I feel at a disadvantage in her presence; at a disadvantage, to be more precise, in my dealings with her. For she has a quality that I have tried unsuccessfully to cultivate; a quality—a trick of reasoning—which gives her the decided advantage of securing a short cut to the truth, without the tedious necessity of reasoning out conclusions from observed evidence, or deducing causes from observed results. This quality is called 'intuition'—and so long as Woman retains the use of this tremendous mental weapon, she will always be superior to what the lady novelists call (and it seems rightly!) 'mere Man'.

But this does not mean to say that 'mere Man' does not have his occasional flashes of intuition. There are problems for which I have been seeking a solution this half-century and more; there have been problems whose solution came to me, as the common phrase has it, in a flash—a flash of intuition. I shall not deny that I had been inspired to effort by Dr Klein's urging us to go forth to our laboratory benches and there find the substance which could react as positively to the desiccated blood corpuscles of a five-thousand-year-old mummy as to the 'claret' flowing from the freshly tapped nose. But the fact is that the discovery of what I sought *did* come in a flash of inspiration—and it was at that very moment of discovery and triumph that I was interrupted by the approach of two visitors: the young doctor whom Watson calls 'Stamford', and an older man who, I had learnt within a few seconds, was Dr John Watson, M.D.—the fully qualified 'old boy' of a hospital in which I was a recently admitted student. This difference in our respective academic standings is one that Dr Watson has never mentioned in his well-known account of our first meeting—it may be that Dr Watson was unaware of it; or, aware of it, attached no importance to it—but it was one which certainly influenced my attitude towards Dr Watson, not merely at this moment of our first meeting, but subsequently; indeed, throughout our long friendship.

The world has been able to read, since the year of the first Jubilee, what Dr Watson thought of me when we met, on that bleak January day of 1881, in the then new 'Path. Lab.' of Bart's. It is, if I may point this out, a record remarkable for its reticence. Dr Watson tells us that I startled him by remarking, after 'Stamford' had introduced us, and we had shaken hands: "You have been in Afghanistan, I perceive?"

But, as 'Stamford' had introduced my other visitor as 'Dr Watson'—adding "late of the Army Medical Service"—it had taken far less detective skill than I possessed to make a fair guess that, having seen active service and been invalided out (that he had suffered some injury to his shoulder was evident), he had seen action in a recent war—and what else would that war be but the trouble in Afghanistan? (Watson still thinks my guess 'inspired'; I think of it merely as the expression of plain common sense.)

Did Watson forget that 'Stamford' had told me that his friend had served with the Army Medical Service, and that Dr Watson's visiting-card, proclaiming him an 'M.D.', made it pretty clear that the Doctor was no regular Army man? For 'Stamford' had not introduced his friend as 'Surgeon-captain' or a higher rank; this Watson, then, though a fully-qualified doctor of medicine, was of a military rank below that of captain—and that fact could argue only that Dr Watson had joined the Army Medical Service late . . . and left (it would seem) early. That whatever it was which was paining him in the region of the shoulder was connected in some fashion with his army service, I could not doubt. He had not, say, fallen downstairs or been knocked down by an omnibus or hansom. He bore his affliction, if not with overt pride, then at least without apology; and that the injury was of fairly recent happening, his intermittent wincing made apparent. It would have been hard for me not to have come to the conclusion that he had been in Afghanistan.

Shakespeare talks somewhere, I believe, of "the confederate circumstance"—the right happening at the right time. There is no doubt that the entry of 'Stamford', with Dr Watson in tow, could have happened—*rightly*—at no other time. A few seconds *before* I had obtained what, for me, was the decisive proof that I had succeeded, and I should angrily have sent the two intruders about their business; a few seconds *later*, and I should have recovered that equilibrium momentarily disturbed by my triumph—and greeted 'Stamford' and his friend with what was then my usual reserve. I know that, in either case, I should not have found myself, some days later, sharing the expenses of a modest but spacious and comfortable set of chambers in Baker-street, Marylebone.*

But, as it happened, my two visitors *did* intrude upon me at the right—the one right time. I understand that I greeted them effusively: I am not astonished that I did—I would have greeted one of the porters or the charwomen with the same effusiveness! I understand, too, that I shouted (shades of—or, rather, echoes of—'Eureka' † as Archimedes leapt naked from the bath!), "I've found it; I've found it! A reagent which is precipitated by haemoglobin—*and nothing else!*"

Well . . . why not? I *had* found it. Was I not (like Archimedes) entitled to take a pride—nay, even more, a *joy*—in my achievement? I understand that I shouted aloud for joy—for which, with all respect, I may plead Biblical precedence—before even 'Stamford' had had the opportunity to introduce me to Dr Watson. Well, again . . . why not? It was a splendid moment, and only good came out of it.

* Mr Holmes specifies that his chambers were in Baker-street, Marylebone, because, at that time (1881), there were other Baker-streets in the London postal area.—*Editor*
† The MS. spells the word (properly 'heureka') in Greek characters.—*Editor*

For, a few seconds earlier, or a few seconds later, I might have resented what I saw (but, in my happiness, charitably refrained from remarking): that both 'Stamford' and Dr Watson had been, in a phrase current at that time, 'doing themselves very well'. In other words, though not *quite* drunk, the pair were not far off 'half seas over', and it was clear that Dr Watson had had to make a strong effort to dredge up from his abandoned sense of reality a hesitating: "Chemically it is interesting, but practically . . .", when I had observed: "Of course, you see the significance of this discovery . . . ?"

The fact was—as I readily perceived—that neither Dr Watson nor 'Stamford' could, at that moment, see very much very clearly: certainly not the significance of a reagent which might precipitate haemoglobin, however old. To give the Doctor a chance to recover somewhat, I pulled forward a hard windsor chair, invited him to be seated, and then—to give myself an excuse to ignore his deranged condition—repeated the experiment.

"It seems a very delicate test," he said, mopping his forehead with a large handkerchief of that *khaki* colour only recently introduced into Army use. "Very delicate indeed. . . ."

Let us grant that, from the bar of *The Criterion*, in which he had met 'Stamford', to a late—and large—luncheon at *The Holborn*, Dr Watson had covered a distance of about one mile and some five hours; and that, on that journey through time and distance, he had managed to lose, even though momentarily, a perfect sobriety, one may well ask how it was that I accepted him as my fellow-lodger? Did I wish to share the apartment on which I had settled—but whose rent I could, at that time, ill afford—with one who was at best a toper and at worse an inebriate? Even to-day, after the lapse of nearly forty years, I cannot *exactly* explain what it was about Dr Watson's appearance and personality which inclined me to overlook his tipsy condition, and to try to see, in the swaying body, the glazed eyes, the man who he ought to have been. I thank God that I did see that man. . . .

Dr Watson, through the romanticized versions of my adventures, has described me often enough—and, generally speaking, I have no fault to find with his delineation of my physical and mental characteristics. Living with me over many years at 221B, Baker-street, John Watson got to know me pretty well; though people are inclined to forget that his pen-pictures of me are the truer as we both got older. The written portrait of me which appears in the first of the Watsonian chronicles—the long account of the Jefferson Hope case that the Editor of *Beeton's Christmas Annual for 1887* (and *not* Dr Watson) called "A Study in Scarlet"—is not, I think, an accurate portrait of me, even as I was at the age of twenty-seven. But I shall not quarrel with that presentation seriously: I am there, it would seem, as Watson saw me—and, for all that I know, it may be as other people saw me, too.

But what of Watson? Who has described him—in writing? Certainly not John H. Watson, self-authorized biographer (and sometime critic) of Sherlock Holmes. So that, to fill a long-empty gap in the chronicles—and, incidentally, to explain how it was that, despite his 'heavy' luncheon at *The Holborn*, Dr Watson and I did arrange to share the chambers at Baker-street—let me recall what I saw, as, in answer to a hail from the door, I looked up to see 'Stamford', with a stranger.

The stranger—Dr Watson—had been drinking: that much was evident: his broad, high-cheekboned face was flushed, his gait was controlled to the point of unsteadiness, his gaze was indirect, and his speech had lost the fine edge of precision.

On the other hand, as I saw, he had none of those unmistakable signs by which the habitual toper may easily and unambiguously be recognized. His clothes, of formal and subtly military cut—I thought that I recognized, in the cut of black frock-coat and sponge-bag trousers, the skill of Davies or of Hacker & Rowell—were pressed and brushed; his linen, from high military collar to tight military shirt-cuffs, spotless, for all that it was now the gas-lit tea-time of a winter's day. Yet, as I saw by the lining of his silk hat, as he held it somewhat nervously in a slightly trembling hand, he was no half-pay West End dandy: the lining was the red satin of some Oxford-street or Cornhill hatter, and not the white satin of St James's-street or Jermyn street.

I was to learn shortly that this well-set-up man of broad chest and open 'East Anglian' face—honest and none-too-bright under its short fair hair—was, as they say, 'quite somebody' at Bart's, being the nephew of one of that ancient Hospital's most distinguished Governors, Sir Thomas Watson, Bart., M.D., D.C.L., LL.D., President of the Royal College of Physicians, the first representative of the Royal College of Physicians on the Medical Council, and a Physician-in-Ordinary to Her Majesty the Queen. I knew nothing of Dr Watson's distinguished patronage when I first met him in the 'Path. Lab.' of Bart's, and he has never mentioned his eminent relative in his writings.

Sometimes, some of the few people who have known the truth of that first meeting, have wondered that I should have taken on 'the companion of a lifetime' in the snap judgement of a few minutes' duration. But this is entirely to misunderstand my relationship with Dr Watson: when I accepted him as the sharer of the lodgings on which I had set my heart, I had no intention of choosing a companion for life. I had no thought that, in taking up lodgings in Baker-street, I was to make No. 221B my home for nearly a quarter-of-a-century. In asking 'Stamford' to look around for a room-mate to share my rent, I had no permanent tenancy in view. I simply hoped that, for the few months that I should need to wait for my clients to pay their bills, half of my domestic expenses would be defrayed by a tolerable companion.

As everyone knows, I did accept Dr Watson as my fellow-tenant. In that snap judgement of which I have just spoken, I put down his having taken rather too much to drink to his having too little to do, and too much time to do it in. I had seen before what havoc could be played in a professional man's life by some accidental interruption of daily routine—I suspected that the wound which had terminated (even if but temporarily) Dr Watson's military career had caused other and perhaps more serious suffering than a post-operative twinge in the scapular region.

I look back, with a gentle, half-wondering pity, not only for Dr Watson but for my immature self as well—and I see in my refusal to accept the *evident* signs of Dr Watson's intemperance, in my determination to see that intemperance as only a temporary lapse, caused by an enforced idleness, a sentimental *naïveté* of whose existence in me I was quite unaware, and whose possession I should indignantly have denied.

For, of course, I could have been wrong—entirely so. Dr Watson could have been a case-hardened tosspot, of valid but wasted talent, whose neat and soldierly appearance he owed more to a valet than to his strict military training. I knew—or thought then that I knew—that the unprepossessing appearance with which he first presented himself to my sight was an irregular, and so unimportant, matter. I could have been wrong—young men of determined prejudices and a disinclination to admit even the possibility that they might be at fault, very often *are* wrong.

But, as all now know, I was not wrong. Yet it was not my reason—or, rather, my reasoning—which guided me aright; it was that quality of unreasoning perception which, encountered in women, I had always viewed with such mistrust.

Yes—pure reason would have betrayed me: would have counselled me to send this idle toper (for all his medical doctorate) to the Deuce. It was intuition which saved me. . . .

THREE

No. 221B, Baker-street

Once we had shaken hands on our compact, Dr Watson, for all his abstracted manner, seemed unusually eager to close the deal.

I had intended to be present, on the following day, at the first of the two demonstrations of Morbid Anatomy, which began at twelve o'clock, noon (this was the Medical; the Surgical began at 2.30 p.m.). But so insistent was Dr Watson that we 'look over' the diggings at Baker-street that I agreed to forego the earlier Morbid Anatomy, and meet him, in this same Pathological Laboratory, on the following day at noon, upon which we should proceed to Baker-street.

He presented himself on the following day, with not only military punctuality, but with military smartness, too. Of the earlier day's indulgence there were few physical traces—and those only minor: a slight yellowing of the eye, a slight ruddiness of the nose . . . nothing important. I was delighted that I had (as I told myself) judged him so well. And, since 'Stamford' had, by this time, told me something of the history of this nephew of our famous 'Nestor of English Physicians', I was proud as well as satisfied as a hansom took us to Pentonville-road by way of St John-street, and so, past the three great northern railway termini, along Euston-road and the New Road to York-buildings and Baker-street.

As we talked in the cab, the cold wind entering above the apron causing us to huddle into our frieze greatcoats, I learned for certain what I had half-suspected: that Dr Watson's short and disastrous Afghan campaign had not been his first experience of the horrors of modern warfare. Nor did his somewhat halting account of his adventures—begun in the hansom and continued at intervals in the days which followed our taking rooms together—make it clear that warfare was any more 'civilized' in Europe than Dr Watson had found it when fighting the murderous Ghazis north of Quetta and west of Peshawar—places that I was to know well in the years to come.

In this first 'serious' talk that I had with the Doctor, certain of his idio-syncrasies made themselves unmistakably apparent; and of these, that which made most impression on my mind was Dr Watson's reluctance to talk of himself—especially of those aspects of his life which might be thought to throw some credit on himself. He was the most modest—as well (I am happy and grateful to say) as the most honest—man whom I have ever met. It is true that, under the thawing influences of our domestic hearth—the first true 'home' that this man of a restless life-pattern had known—he became more confidential. But he never lost his habit of reti-cence; and this led him to a practice of *concealment for its own sake;* a practice that I propose to describe shortly, as its indulgence tells us much of the psychology of this seemingly ordinary but, in reality, distinctly unusual man.

What I learned as we bowled along the slushy, dirty streets towards Marylebone, was that Dr Watson had gone out to Turkey, to offer his ser-vices, either as a medically-trained civilian or as a member of the Ottoman Medical Service, in the war with Russia. Through one of his numerous 'connections'—Watson was always inclined to be both bashful and reticent when he had to admit to his having used Influence; and he rarely named the 'connection'—he had joined Colonel William Coope (a member of the wealthy family of brewers), who was going out to Constantinople, to take up a post under Colonel Valentine Baker, who had received a *firman* from the Sultan to organize and command an Imperial Ottoman Gendarmerie. Colonel Coope and Watson travelled overland to Trieste, where they em-barked on the Austrain Lloyd's steamer 'Danubio', arriving at the Turkish capital on 22nd May, 1877. The voyage down the Adriatic and through the Aegean into the Dardanelles had been enlivened, Dr Watson told me with a reminiscent smile, by the presence aboard the 'Danubio' of the eccentric and famed Baron Zubowitz, the Hungarian nobleman who had ridden horseback from Vienna to Paris in six days, in the course of which ride he had crossed the Danube mounted—horse and rider being carried by a spe-cial inflatable saddle, invented by the Baron, over the water.

The Baron was on his way to the Sublime Porte with two ambitions: to get a *firman* from the Caliph to raise an Hungarian Legion for the Turkish Army, and to get a substantial order from that same Army for the Zubo-witz Inflatable Saddle—to demonstrate the virtues of which the Baron pro-posed to swim his horse, supported by the gutta-percha saddle, across the Bosphorus.

I recall that Dr Watson's description of the Baron and his freaks was so amusing that I often laughed during the telling; but there was nothing amusing in Dr Watson's account of the terrible sights which were his after he had—through Baker Pasha's influence—joined the Stafford House Committee, under Mr Barrington Kennett, its Commissioner, who provided the only effective expression of those sentiments implicit in the organization of the Turkish Government's 'Red Crescent' (the Mussulman counterpart of the Christian nations' 'Red Cross').

The shocking introduction to the Turkish wounded and dying—and their total neglect by their still healthy superiors—Watson had on his first visit to the base-hospital at Scutari: that same hospital in which our own men, a quarter-of-a-century earlier, had lain neglected and dying—until Miss Florence Nightingale, 'The Lady of the Lamp', had brought them hope and comfort and—in many cases—recovery.

But now there was no Miss Nightingale to mitigate the horrible sufferings of the Turks, than whom, Dr Watson assured me, no braver soldiers, whether fighting or dying, existed.

Had Dr Watson had his way, he informed me, he would have stayed on at Scutari, attempting to introduce into the Turkish military hospitals something of those reforms with which Miss Nightingale had saved so many from suffering and death during the Crimean War.

However, Turkish officialdom being then what it was, Dr Watson was forced to accompany the main medical body leaving to collect the wounded—estimated at upwards of six thousand—from the battlefield of Plevna. The wounded were being brought from Plevna, through Sophia, to Orhanye, and to this village in a plain surrounded by mountains, Dr Watson went with Drs MacKellar, Vachell, Manooric, Douglas and Sarell, with Colonel Coope as both guide and guard.

What Dr Watson saw there sickened him; but what sickened him was not the blood, the untended wounds, the nightmare of pain and putrefaction. Like me, he had seen too much of these in our own hospitals, where, less than forty years ago, the operating table was still a blood-stained butcher's block, and where the Big Man performed his surgical operations in his 'operating coat'—a garment stiff and stinking with ancient blood and pus. In no other sphere of human activity have there been more—and more fundamental—changes than in the internal management of our great hospitals, and in the surgeon's approach to his necessary tasks.

What did sicken Dr Watson was the appalling inefficiency of Turkish officialdom; an inefficiency allied with, and supported by, an inhuman tolerance of *others'* suffering and a smug self-satisfaction to be described only as insane. Aware of his inability to effect the least change in a barbarous system, for all that his conscience troubled him in thus abandoning (as he told it) his helpless charges to mutilation and death, Dr Watson returned to England, took the final degree that he had postponed for his fruitless Turkish adventure; qualified at Netley for an Army commission, and got himself gazetted to the Medical Service as a subaltern—rather an elderly subaltern, to be sure!—and so, after posting to the Berkshires, to the heat and horror of the North-West Frontier—and beyond. As he admitted somewhat rue-fully to me, he had been able to do little more for his fellow-men within the discipline of the British Army than he had resigned himself to doing—which was precisely nothing—within the complacent inanity of the Sultan's military command.

Dr Watson, as I soon perceived, spoke always from a sense, not so much of loss, as of failure to realize some deep-rooted but quite undefined ambi-tion; which, of course, never having been defined, could not therefore ever be realized.

Had he been a bad man, or even a mildly dishonest one—and he was neither—one might have thought him the victim of some tremendous bur-den of guilt; a man enduring, rather than living, a life terrible with the con-sciousness of a wrong never to be amended, for all that it had long ago been repented.

The truth about Dr Watson took a long time—many years, in fact—to become known to me, and the sum of all this knowledge became mine only after I had lived with him and broken down his reserve through the com-mon events of a shared experience. But I shall anticipate my long-sought discovery here, and tell at the beginning of my memoirs what I knew about Dr Watson only after I was more than half-way on to the age at which I now am.

John Hamish Watson, as his name makes clear, was of Scotch descent, but the family had migrated to England at the beginning of the last century, when the novels of Scott and Galt and Miss Porter, the poetry of Ramsay and Burns, Moir and Hogg, *Blackwood's* and *The Edinburgh Quarterly*—to say nothing of the extravagant but sincere patronage of George IV—had made Scotland, the Scotch and Scotch institutions fashionable (in which we should include the many excellent Scotch assurance companies).

Even to this present time, Dr Watson has preserved an inviolable reti-cence about the troubles which overtook his family; troubles which left him an orphan in fact if not in the strict legal sense of that word. That there was—or, rather, *there had been*—'money in the family', he gave me to under-stand not long after we had first met, but he also made it clear beyond argument that nothing short of a miracle could bring him within reach of that money. He confessed frankly that, at present, he had no other income than the eleven-and-sixpence * a day that Government allowed him.

---

* Then equivalent to $2.76.—*Editor*

The Watson family—or that part of it to which Dr Watson belonged—had come south from Edinburgh, to settle in Devon, where, after the death or disappearance of his natural parents, he was brought up by an elderly aunt on his mother's side: an acidulated spinster (by Watson's account) whose narrow religious beliefs imposed on both her and her charge an existence which, for joylessness, could hardly have been matched within the walls of the neighbouring Dartmoor Penitentiary.

His aunt, Watson admitted, had denied him little on the *material* side: there was always plenty to eat, he had clothing adequate for his needs; he was sent to a good school—the ancient * establishment of Blundell's School, at Tiverton, of which I had then never heard, although the novel which had made it famous, Mr R. D. Blackmore's *Lorna Doone*, had been published over ten years before. Afterwards, on Watson's urging, I borrowed this fine novel from Mudie's, and *thought* that I saw, in the splendidly romantic character of Jan Ridd, much of the origin of John Watson's discontent.

For all Dr Watson's trouble might, I saw, be reduced to its simplest terms in a statement that he needed a hero to admire and to serve—*whether or not that hero were himself or another*. I saw that, in his going out to Turkey and war-ravaged Bulgaria; in his changing a fairly near theatre of war for a fairly remote one—Afghanistan—he had been a-hero-hunting. He had hoped—poor, good old Watson!—that, in this atmosphere of the heroic, he might become a hero himself, or, at least, meet one who was.

As it happened, the real heroes of that inconclusive campaign were the locals who were killing—or doing their best to kill—our own men; and on our side, the only hero that Watson met was his humble orderly, Murray, who saved a Watson incapable of saving himself. And now, here he was, in a hansom smelling of stale leather and mouldy stuffing, on his way to share diggings with a stranger whom young 'Stamford' must already have represented as someone so deuced odd as almost to verge on the Heroic.

Watson, for all his apparent lack of emotional and mental complexity, is not at all easily defined. One might say of him that he was simple, but in no way a simpleton; that he was very observant in that he *noticed* things, but that he saw little, since he drew few conclusions from what he so minutely saw; that he was scrupulously honest, but both reticent and devious, seeming almost to love concealment for its own sake, as I have already observed.

Not all of this, naturally, I gathered or deduced as we moved slowly westwards through the dismal London streets; and, again, I write now from the wisdom of a man who has passed his sixtieth year. I neither saw nor

* Founded 1604, and still flourishing.— *Editor*

knew so much at twenty-seven. But I could not guess that I should have the opportunity, over more than twenty-four years, of discovering all that there was to be known about the man who sat by my side in that musty hansom.

In taking a prospective fellow-tenant to the apartments at 221B, Baker-street, I was, I may now confess, taking him to apartments that I was determined to rent. I nearly said, "that I was determined at all costs to rent"— but what sense would the addition make? Obviously, I could not hope to force a reluctant Dr Watson to share the rent of apartments that he did not like. Yet I think that I was determined to use every permissible argument— should every permissible argument be called for—to overcome his possible reluctance, and gain his agreement. For I dearly wished to become the sub-tenant-in-chief of the most desirable diggings that I had found in several months of more or less dedicated room-hunting.

So much has been written by Dr Watson of our rooms at Baker-street, and so few details have been given, that I should explain here exactly what it was that we rented in the January of 1881, and acquired in the years to follow: exactly what it was which made those rooms so desirable in *my* estimation.

What Mrs Hudson, the head-tenant of 221B, had to offer was not merely the drawing-room floor of what had once been a spacious West End private house, built, as I afterwards learned, some ninety years earlier by Sir Edward Baker of Ranston, who assisted Mr Portman to build his suburb north of Oxford-street.

Mrs Hudson's lease did not include the whole of the property: the tailor's shop, which had been constructed out of the house's original ground-floor—parlour, morning-room and some smaller rooms at the back, looking on to the small garden—was the subject of a separate lease. Mrs Hudson's territory comprised the three floors and attic above the shop, as well as part of the basement, including the kitchen, scullery, servants' hall and butler's pantry. Access to both the upper and the lower portions of the house was by way of a side-door opening on the street. One reached the first floor by a pair of stairs, with a break-landing between; there were seventeen treads to the first floor.

The accommodation which was offered to us consisted, first, in the double-drawing room, the front and back rooms being divided by folding doors. The front part, with two round-headed windows * looking on to Baker-street, was 20 ft x 18 ft; the back room, looking on to what was left of the garden, was a trifle smaller. With the folding doors thrown back, the original drawing-room must have been a noble apartment, nearly forty feet

* Watson calls them 'bow' windows—the term is correct but obsolete.—*Editor*

in length by eighteen feet wide at its larger breadth. This back room, however, had been converted into a bedroom, whilst a second bedroom had
been constructed on the site of a conservatory which had projected, supported by pillars of wrought iron, over the rear area. All three rooms had
communicating doors, but all three were accessible by doors opening into
the corridor.

To this modest but still fairly spacious accommodation, we were able, a
year or two later, to add a small dining-room, converted to that necessary
use from a front bedroom on the floor above.

At the end of the corridor, a small but adequate bathroom, equipped
with the most modern fittings, had been added to the conveniences of the
house, and, as Mrs Hudson pointed out, with some understandable pride,
not only the bathroom but fixed wash-hand-stands in the bedrooms ran
both cold and hot water, the latter provided by the system of the well-
known sanitary engineers, Messrs Dent & Hellyer. We were also offered the
use of part of the attic, for the storage of such property as we might not
require to hand.

I had answered an advertisement of Mrs Hudson's in *The Times*, and I
had, before I rang the bell, 'scouted', as the military say, the surroundings,
front and back. I was notably impressed—and attracted—by a fact which,
to most people, would have set the accommodation at a disadvantage: I
mean the fact that the garden at the rear of the house had been almost entirely covered over, in the course of a century, with a haphazard collection
of small buildings—a pastry-room, a drying-room, and so on—so as to
unite the coach-house in the mews with the house itself. A casual enquiry
assured me of the truth of what I had suspected from a survey of the property's rear: that, through this collection of rooms, it was possible to reach
the house from the mews, *entirely unobserved*. When at last I called at the
house, and was shewn over by Mrs Hudson, I enquired if, perhaps, there
might be a small room to let in the mews house, above the coach-room and
stables, since it was obvious that Mrs Hudson did not keep her carriage?

The coach-room and stables, she told me, were let to a jobmaster, but to
my delight I learned that the rooms above, once occupied by the coachman,
were empty. I resolved, should I find a suitable fellow-tenant, that I would
make a bargain to rent these rooms in the mews.

Well, Watson came, saw—and was conquered. By the standards of those
days, the accommodation was not cheap: for our three rooms, baths, coals
and full board (four meals a day, if one include afternoon tea), Mrs Hudson
asked four-and-a-half * guineas a week; we settled for four.* It was more
than I had intended to pay, and considerably more than Dr Watson was

* Respectively: $22.68 and $21.16—*Editor*

paying at his seedy Strand hotel; but, on the other hand, he had been taking all his meals in chop-houses and coffee-rooms—with the Bunsen-burner
and gas cooking-ring that I intended to instal, some economies in Dr Watson's dietary could surely be effected?

The fact that the furniture provided by the landlady was no more than
adequate was something that we both saw as an advantage: Dr Watson's
aunt had bequeathed him some few pieces in a modest legacy of which only
the furniture—now in store at Hampton's—remained. At Montague-street,
Mrs Holmes * was looking after a few pieces of my own: some framed original drawings and a dozen lithographs of *Cries of London* and *Cries of Paris* by
my great-uncle, Carle Vernet; a handsome break-front bookcase which had
belonged to my Sherrinford grandfather; some curiosities that my father
had brought back from India and Persia—nothing much, and nothing of
value, but dear to me nonetheless, who now saw, for the first time since
leaving home, the prospect of a 'home of my own'. There was room and to
spare at Baker-street to accommodate both Watson's and my own few domestic treasures.

We struck our bargain there and then, with no formal lease, but with that
handshake which is still the seal of our English compacts. I brushed aside
that slight hesitation that I noticed in my fellow-lodger-to-be—I felt that he
needed someone like me to make up his mind for him. And when we had
given Mrs Hudson a cheque on Watson's account at Cox's for one month's
rent in advance: £18 4s. od., I made a separate bargain with our landlady—
a bargain, that is to say, on my own account, and not involving Dr Watson.
I handed her a sovereign and twenty pence: one month's rent in advance, at
five shillings a week, of the empty rooms above the coach-house.

Dr Watson took possession of our new apartment that same evening—
Monday, 10th January, 1881. I heard the noise of wheels, and, looking out,
saw that a London growler of typically dilapidated state had drawn up outside the house, its top loaded with that traditional military luggage of
tinned iron cases—cases for uniforms, hats, swords, papers—all daubed
with black and red blobs, in a crude imitation of tortoiseshell. All were
carefully marked, *John H. Watson, M.D., A.M.S.*

---

* Despite some interesting surmises concerning her identity and her relationship to Holmes,
Mrs Holmes—mentioned here by Holmes for the first and last time—remains a character as
enigmatical as undefined. All that we know of her, up to the present, is that she held a lease
from the Bedford Estate, in respect of 24, Montague-street, Russell-square, from 1877 to 1884,
and that it was of this address that Holmes was talking when he informed Dr Watson that
"When I first came up to London, I had rooms in Montague-street, just round the corner from
the British Museum." Further research may yet identify the Mrs Holmes of 24, Montague-
street as a member of Sherlock Holmes's family—it has even been suggested that Mrs Holmes
was . . . *Mrs* Holmes—but the fact is that, so far, no-one has found out who she really was.—
Editor

We dined well that night off game soup, lemon sole, roast beef, cabinet pudding and welsh rarebit. Why this gastronomically detailed recollection should be among the most vivid memories of my earliest Baker-street existence is explained by Watson's enthusiastically exclaiming, as he wiped his moustache and flung down his napkin: "Well, by Jove, Holmes, I congratulate you!"

"How so?" I asked, though I knew well what he meant.

"Why, on account of this excellent dinner. It's been a long while since I ate anything half so good."

"But it was Mrs Hudson—or, rather, her cook—who gave us this dinner. . . ."

"Ah, but, Holmes," he said, wagging a forefinger at me in facetious mock-reproof, "it was *you* who found, out of the hundreds, perhaps thousands, of London landladies, one whose table was as commendable—and as lavish—as this! It is you, my dear Holmes, and not Mrs Hudson, who deserves *my* praise!"

"Hm!" I muttered, affecting a judicial frown; "this fine first dinner may be in the nature of what the Germans call a *Heimgeschenk* . . . do you know the word? No . . . ? It is the gift that neighbours and other friends make to those who enter on a new home. *Heimgeschenk* . . . 'Home-gift'. This may well be the good Mrs Hudson's version of an acceptable *Heimgeschenk*. Tomorrow we may be back to the traditional English boarding-house menu of minced scrag-end in the lumpy mashed potato of shepherd's pie! Or," I added, smiling at his open consternation, "perhaps rissoles from what's left of this sirloin . . . and bread-and-butter pudding from those crusts on your plate!"

Dr Watson shook his head as seriously as vigorously.

"No, no," he said indignantly. "I won't believe it. I am convinced, my dear fellow, that here at least you are mistaken."

And in this one respect, at least, it was Dr Watson who was right, and I who was wrong. Mrs Hudson's services—which included her excellent fare—continued at the same high level at which they had begun. We had—both Dr Watson and myself—some occasional small *contretemps* with our good landlady; none, I am happy to say, having to do with money; but, by and by, as Watson and I grew, by constant association, to understand and tolerate each other, so did Mrs Hudson, our landlady for many years, come to understand and tolerate her sometimes irritating and almost always irregular lodgers.

And that phrase, "for many years", reminds me that, at the proper place, I must tell the story of Mrs Hudson's strange and—as the newspapers would say—'dramatic' change of condition. She became, though entirely by her own efforts, the successful subject of what I should fully agree that the newspapers should call 'a romance'. In our quiet, efficient, handsome and strong-willed landlady there hid a character that only time was to reveal, and that Watson and I never suspected, until it so astonishingly manifested itself.

Mention has been made of Mrs Hudson's status of 'respectable widow'. She was nothing of the sort; respectable, yes—but widow, no. Her husband was alive and serving in the Viceroy's army when we first knew her, and not until many years afterwards did she find herself a widow, with results which are certainly not the least imaginable happenings in that life of mine which has had its full measure of surprises, pleasant and otherwise.

FOUR

London in the 'Eighties

Dr Watson and I soon settled down into an orderly routine at 221B, Baker-street, where much of our free time—he had a lot of free time; I little enough—was spent, not so much in my trying to analyze his psychology, as in trying to find out enough about him so as to fit him usefully into a pattern that I had still only half worked out.

In one important respect, I was at fault in my relations with Dr Watson—and that from almost the first day of our meeting. His apparent *naïveté* was such that I simply could not resist the unhappy impulse to tease him: the slang expression 'to pull his leg' perfectly expresses what Dr Watson's perpetual simplicity?—innocence? (I could not, at the beginning of our long association, decide whether it was natural or cleverly assumed)— tempted me to do.

Yes, I began that 'leg-pulling', now that I look back, even in the Pathological Laboratory at Bart's, and an old man's memory for the distant past brings back our conversation word for word—though I believe that Watson has written it down in one of his stories.

I asked the chance-met stranger if he didn't mind the smell of strong tobacco.

"I always smoke 'ship's' myself," he replied.

"That's good enough. I generally have chemicals about, and occasionally do experiments. Would that annoy you?"

"Not at all."

"Let me see—what are my other shortcomings? I get in the dumps at times, and don't open my mouth for days. Don't think me sulky when I do that—just let me alone, and I'll soon be all right. Now, what do you have to confess?"

35

"Well, I object to rows because my nerves are shaken, and I get up at all sorts of ungodly hours, and I am extremely lazy. I have another set of vices when I'm well, but those are the principal ones at present."

After we had got to Baker-street, I multiplied my eccentricities—'piled them on', as they say—simply to see what Watson would say. One day, when he was out, I wrote a patriotic *V.R.* in bullet-pocks on the wall of our sitting-room (having got, and paid for, Mrs Hudson's permission before-hand); I put my shag into the toe of a Persian slipper, and put that into the brass-mounted oak *perdonium*—as they affected to call a coal-box in those days. I gathered together a few unpaid bills (it was an age of bills—most of them long 'a-maturing'), and pinned them to the mantelshelf with a murderous Eastern dagger.

All these follies, Dr Watson has solemnly recorded in writing, though there were others that he has not seen fit to mention. Did he recognize my little jokes for what they were? Or did he really take as acceptable the 'eccentricities of a man of genius'? Even to this day, I cannot be *sure*. . . .

Of course, looking back, I see that we both had the Bump of Reticence developed in the highest degree. He never, after he had come to live at Baker-street, defined those vices that he had "when I'm well," and it was long before I told him that the *tic douloureux* induced by an unskilful dental operation had led me, first to Mariani's Coca Wine, and then (let me pass quickly over the cocoa lozenges, tea, pastilles and other products of that thriving coca industry which arose, it seemed overnight, at the end of the 'Seventies) to the deadly cocaine, which had been available for medical use for longer than had Mariani's Coca Wine—relatively harmless, save that it provided an almost inevitable introduction to cocaine.

I was never a slave to cocaine, as were Coleridge, Poe and De Quincey to opium—though, even with his terrible addiction, the last-named managed to cast off 'the accursed chains'. However, I was never in any doubt of the dangers, and grave dangers, too, inherent in the use of the coca plant in any of its derivatives. I had been recommended to take Mariani's Coca Wine by an advertisement calling attention to the fact that it had given relief, not only to Pope Leo XIII—who shewed his gratitude to Mariani by presenting a medal to the young Italian-French chemist—but to many of my favourite and most respected musicians: Gounod, Fauré, Massenet and Thomas among them. Many members of the Royal Families of Europe were known patrons of Coca Wine. I cannot feel a sense of guilt—though I do feel a sense of regret—that I should ever have been led to indulge in cocaine through my introduction to the 'harmless' Coca Wine. What happened to me must have happened to thousands of others—with far more disastrous results.

In my case, the taking of, first an infusion of coca, and then the seven per cent. solution of the alkaloid, was not without a beneficial effect—was it *this* that I endeavoured to conceal?

Both the Coca Wine and the cocaine greatly relieved the distressing symptoms of the *tic*, an appalling infliction whose terrors only the sufferer may understand. And, of course, cocaine's remarkable effects upon the human organism were not absent in my own case: I enjoyed its marked stimulating effect on the higher levels of the brain, and the increase in physical and mental power that such stimulation invariably brings. But there came a time—inevitably so—when I found that I had turned to cocaine, not as an anodyne, but as a stimulant; and at this stage, on the very verge of addiction (or had I, in truth, overstepped that dangerous limiting line?), I began seriously to question, not only my use of the drug, but my reasons for having come to it in the first place.

It must be borne in mind that the *moral*—or, perhaps, *moralizing* is the more precise word—attitude towards the recourse to drugs, whether as an opium-eater or what has come of recent years to be called a 'morphinomaniac', was not, in the late 'Seventies and early 'Eighties, one of the common social prejudices. Our greatest writer on the subject of opium-eating—himself a victim of the addiction—sought to "break the accursed chains" (and advise his readers to avoid opium-eating), not on any 'moral' grounds, but simply to rid himself of the terrible "pains of opium", as he calls them. There is no more 'moral guilt' in De Quincey than in an indifferent horseman, who has rejected the advice of the knowledgeable, and has bought himself a fractious mount which has given him a dislocated shoulder.

The attitude towards drugs, at the time that I left Mariani's Coca Wine for a seven per cent. solution of cocaine, was rather more than merely tolerant—it was, to put the matter plainly, quite indifferent. The average person, in those days, unless it happened that he was a medical man, was no more concerned with the fact of another's drug-taking than with another's choice of neck-tie or boots. And even medical opinion was not at all unanimous on the question of drugs' dangers. My favourite author—he is also my favourite and most-to-be-trusted philosopher—was a respected medical man of wide practice and long experience: yet neither alcohol nor any narcotic drug earned his condemnation. Listen, then, to one of the greatest of all doctors, Oliver Wendell Holmes:

> Throw out opium, which the Creator himself seems to prescribe, for we often see the scarlet poppy growing in the cornfields, as if it were foreseen that wherever there is hunger to be fed there must also be pain to be soothed; throw out a few specifics which our art did not discover; . . . throw out wine, which is a food, and the vapors of which produce the miracle of anaesthesia—and I firmly

believe that if the whole *materia medica*, as now used, could be sunk to the bottom of the sea, it would be all the better for mankind—and all the worse for the fishes.

Nor was this tolerance of stimulants confined to an American doctor of mid-Victorian times: two generations later, a well-known British doctor, associated with Watson in the romantic presentation of some cases from my career, expressed his opinion on both drink and drugs in even more tolerant terms.

Let me try to explain the nature of my dilemma. I had had recourse to cocaine, in the first place, as I might have had recourse to any other pain-killing medicament. Then, after the (first Coca Wine, followed by) cocaine had sensibly relieved the frightful agony of the *tic douloureux*, I began to notice—and, I admit, to value—some, as it were, 'extra' benefits to be had from the taking of cocaine.

One often hears of cocaine's 'powers to stimulate the higher centres', an empty phrase when mouthed by any who have never taken cocaine, for who but one who has experienced the results of cocaine may describe exactly *how*—and *what*—cocaine stimulates?

The first miraculous revelation that the first dose of cocaine makes to its 'victim' is that he has the ability to concentrate—and this in a manner which makes all previous and accepted meanings of the word 'concentrate' without significance. Before magnifying-glasses were invented, there must have been invented a means of concentrating upon material objects that schoolboys still use: a pin-hole in a piece of dark paper.

Look at the object to be scrutinized—through this pin-hole. There is a clarity of vision, a depth of perception, which is quite incredible. Why is this? Because the pin-hole permits one to see the object without the disturbing, blinding light which habitually falls on both object and eye from all around: this disturbing (and, indeed, distracting) light is completely cut out. Through the pin-hole, one sees what one needs to see—only that and nothing more.

So with the concentration that cocaine permits, save that the concentration of cocaine may be applied to *happenings* as well as to things. Let me give an instance that I recall well. (I even remember the date, without consulting my somewhat haphazardly kept diary.)

It was Saturday, 5th March, 1881, that Watson and I went to St James's Hall to hear Madame Norman-Neruda—now better known under the name of Lady Hallé—execute, as only she might, Handel's Sonata in D Major. I know well that it was a Saturday, for I had something 'important'—forgotten now!—that I had reluctantly to abandon, so that we might hear our favourite *lady* violinist (the favourite *gentleman* violinist was Señor Sarasate) in her last appearance of that particular season.

On the previous day, Watson, for the first time, had acted as my assistant—amanuensis—coadjutor—for the life of me I don't know which title to give him!—had, shall we say?, accompanied me on a detective errand in more or less the capacity of one involved, and not merely as an interested onlooker. This was the case which, first taking us down to an empty house in a block of five in the Brixton-road that Watson calls 'Lauriston-gardens',* involved matters which had happened five or six thousand miles away, and provided us—Watson, Lestrade and myself—with a fresh proof (had we ever needed one) that 'old sins cast long shadows'.

Between the finding of the dead body of the Mormon, 'Drebber' (as Watson calls him), in the empty house, and the tracking-down of the culprit—I hesitate to call him 'murderer'—I had drawn heavily upon my reserves of both mental and physical strength, and before leaving for St James's Hall for the afternoon concert, I had given myself a cocaine pick-me-up. Thus it was that when we got to the Hall, the drug was exerting its greatest influence on me.

Now I forget in which piece of virtuoso playing it was—it was not in Madame Norman-Neruda's, that I *can* affirm—I noticed, or thought that I noticed, a slight—a *very* slight—defect in execution. Yes—I do remember now, so very clearly: it was in an orchestral composition, in which the performance of the second violin seemed to be in slight—oh, very slight!—error.

And here only cocaine—or that heroin by which, later, Dr Watson tried to wean me from the earlier drug—could have enabled me to do what I then did: *listen* to the second violin, *to the exclusion of all other sound.*

There is something more in this power of cocaine to isolate the object (person, thing or happening) of one's minutest scrutiny: a power—I hardly know how to express this—which affects *time* as well as place. Before the invention of motion-pictures, this power would have been quite impossible to describe, but, even though description is still difficult, an analogy with the motion-picture may help us here.

In running a strip of celluloid † through the motion-picture projector, one may, *theoretically* (since it is dangerous to expose a single frame of the motion-picture to the intense heat of the projecting-lamp), 'hold up the ac-

* The five houses comprising the block are of late Georgian date, and have recently been restored by the local Council; they are numbered 152–160 (inclusive, even numbers only).—*Editor.*

† In 1915, when these words were written, this dangerously inflammable mixture of nitrocellulose and camphor had not been replaced by less explosive substances.—*Editor*

tion'—by stopping the run of the continuous progress of the pictures. One may, then, in a manner of speaking, halt time in its passage—and what one may *theoretically* do with a motion-picture projection, one may do *actually* under the influence of cocaine. I cannot explain this, though the theories of the fashionable German mathematician Herr Einstein seem to hint at some understanding of the differing *natures* of Time. All that I can say is that, under the influence of cocaine, one may not only pick out something for one's intense yet calm scrutiny—and study it to the exclusion of all other things—*but one may spend as much time on that study as one wishes*. Through the quite inexplicable paradox of a power that, to my knowledge, only cocaine and heroin may bestow, one may stretch out the instantaneous-ephemeral to eternity; I seemed to halt time as I listened to that wrong note of the second violin—isolating, not merely the man and his playing, but the one false note which was the object of my study.

To a man of my peculiar temperament, that power of concentration accessible through—and (then) only through—cocaine was not one lightly to be abandoned, either on shaky 'moral' grounds or because of the strong possibility that physical degeneration might, at some time, succeed to the exhilaration and exaltation of the drug. Besides, the French blood that I had inherited through my Vernet grandmother had given me the legacy of a solidly practical streak in my composition: I was quite prepared to weigh the advantages and disadvantages of cocaine, with as nice a sense of values as any shewn by a French *bonne-à-tout-faire* shopping in the local market. If the taking of cocaine offered me unusual—almost, one might say, super-human—powers of concentration and a complete elimination of that spirit of aggression which seems, ordinarily, to go hand-in-hand with that driving ambition which had always possessed me . . . why, then, could I not face with equanimity the price that I might have to pay for this boon?

I was not at all sure of my new friend's attitude towards the taking of drugs. I had noticed that, as Samuel Butler * remarked long ago, the self-indulgent were most prejudiced against self-indulgences of a different sort in others—and with a doctor who, as the servants say, obviously liked his drop, it was risky to assume that he would not come down hard on my own idiosyncratic indulgence, and comb my hair with a vengeance whenever I should reach for the hypodermic syringe. Common prudence, then, dictated that I did not include an admission of cocaine-taking in the parcel of those intimacies with which two fairly young men decide to set up a shared establishment. (I realized, of course, that none but the most obtuse

* The author of *Hudibras*, not the late-Victorian novelist.—*Editor*

medical man—and Watson, with his excellent London M.D., could hardly have been that—would fail to observe at least the more obvious symptoms of cocaine-addiction: first, and far and away the most noticeable, the characteristic 'pin-point' pupil, that all art or contrivance may never hide in the patient. But I was ready then to let the future take care of itself.)

Besides, I was possessed of an unreasoning confidence that the text-book warnings in the matter of cocaine had no application to *me*. Degeneration as ghastly as any promised to the cocaine-taker threatened, according to the 'authoritative opinion,' not merely the habitual dram-drinker, but anyone who raised a glass of ardent waters to his lips. Yet, regarding this matter of so-called self-indulgence with an unprejudiced eye, how many of the millions who touched alcohol in the forms of cyder, beer, wine or distilled spirits, came to the shocking ends depicted with lurid exaggeration in the Blue Ribbon tracts? And—if one might get the truth here—how many of the thousands who took cocaine came to the arachnation, that dreadful itching, as though the skin is covered with spiders and their webs, which was the prelude to the complete mental and physical collapse of the text-books' awful warnings?

One who had read as widely and as deeply as I knew that there has been hardly one substance introduced into the *materia medica* which has not had its defenders and its detractors—both equally vociferous and dogmatic. Who remembers now the great Antimony Dispute of the Seventeenth Century, begun with the publication of 'Basil Valentine's' book in 1604 and carried through into the beginning of the last century—when Napoleon preferred to die slowly of cancer than quickly (though no less painfully) of the Irish doctor's tartar emetic?

In short, I believed even then—and my belief has been happily vindicated—that I was one of those persons who may use and not abuse every stimulant, however potentially dangerous.

And, on the less practical and more metaphysical side, I would recall the saying of an old Spaniard who worked in the garden when we lived at Pau: "Take what you want from God . . . and pay for it."

All the same, I decided to say nothing of my cocaine-taking to Dr Watson; always remembering to don blue spectacles ("to shield my sensitive eyes from the glare") whenever I felt the need for my seven per cent. solution.

FIVE ❧

John H. Watson,
M.D. (Lond.)

I have said that I felt a spontaneous attraction towards Dr Watson when 'Stamford' brought him—both rather unsteadily!—into the new Pathological Laboratory at Bart's. But, though my affection for this temporarily aimless man did not lessen as we took up our new corporate life in Baker-street, I soon found that my interest in him was rapidly outpacing my affection. I found his character, with its many contradictions, of such engrossing interest that I often found myself forgetting, in my experimental attempts to reveal new quirks and crotchets in his personality, that I held this new-found acquaintance in the warmest regard. I look back now over nearly forty years to realize—often with some astonishment—how skilfully he evaded my most direct questioning!

As I came, not so much to know him better, as to know better his habits, I was struck by his insistence on concealing what, for the life of me, I could not find worth the concealing. That he was at some pains to suppress the main facts of his earlier life, I understood; and with this I sympathized. But that he would, for instance, change the name of the man who introduced us from Templeton (his real name) to 'Stamford', I could not understand. It was—and still is—true that there were excellent legal reasons for concealing the identity of those persons who appeared in the accounts of my cases by which Watson, eventually, 'found his niche', as they say; there was every reason why Watson should have concealed the identity of Prince Alexander of Battenberg (brother of that Court favourite who has only recently re-signed as First Lord of the Admiralty) under the novelettish style of "Wilhelm Gottsreich Sigismond von Ormstein, Grand Duke of Cassel-Falstein, and hereditary King of Bohemia". (I often thought that Watson had more than a mere tendency to lay it on thick!)

But if it be conceded that a case involving the indiscretions of a Prince—and a Prince who was a darling of the Queen—ought to be wrapped up in pseudonyms, why had Templeton's name to be altered, when there was nothing wrong in his having visited the bar of *The Criterion*, eaten at *The Holborn*, and introduced Dr Watson to me? The answer is that concealment became a habit with Watson; inspired and justified in the first place by the dangerous libel laws of the time, the giving of false names by Watson soon developed into an unthinking response to imagined need; what, in a jargon grown fashionable recently, is now called 'an automatic reflex'.

Yet, having decided, once and for all, to conceal true identities under imaginary names, Watson, whether on his own initiative or at the suggestion of his very wide-awake literary agent (to whom I shall come in due course), never selected a name capriciously, 'out of the blue', as they say. The choice was always dictated by the strange necessities of what must be called only an elaborate code, in which every chosen name will refer either to some event in Watson's life or to some prejudice that he has developed in the course of it.

For instance, I noticed that, in telling me of his experiences on his way to Turkey with Colonel Coope's party and the Doctor's later seeing active service with Mr Barrington Kennett's Stafford House Committee, Dr Watson managed to avoid all mention of Colonel Valentine Baker—'Baker Pasha'—who had accepted a commission from the Sultan to found, organize and command a force of Turkish Gendarmerie, and through whose personal intervention the Stafford House Committee was permitted to offer its charitable services to the Turkish wounded. I wondered at the time whether or not this failure to mention the name of Colonel Baker was intentional; whether or not—supposing that the failure *were* intentional—the failure indicated an implicit condemnation of the Colonel, and a reluctance, on Watson's part, to speak of him at all. I had already gathered that Dr Watson was something of a prude—I have no objection to prudishness, myself—and from what I knew of Colonel Baker (which was something more, I may add, than was revealed even in the most lurid of the daily and weekly sheets), I could well understand the reluctance of a man of prudish mind to discuss him.

The case is forgotten now, though not, I should add, by me, since there were the gravest inconsistencies in the story told by the young person involved—inconsistencies which have never permitted me to forget this strangest of all cases by which a senior military officer was condemned to complete and final disgrace.

Colonel Valentine Baker was the brother of Sir Samuel Baker, the famous explorer; and in his own right, the younger Baker—Valentine—had made a considerable reputation for himself as a soldier who had seen much active service both as a servant of the Crown and (as was not uncommon in those days) a free-lance: he had been awarded many medals for gallantry by both his Sovereign and by other monarchs. The regiment of which he was Colonel—H.R.H. the Prince of Wales being the Colonel-in-Chief—was the famous (and, I regret to say, to many the notorious) Tenth (Prince of Wales's) Hussars, into which crack cavalry regiment went all which was aristocratic, wealthy, irresponsible and—for what my opinion is worth— useless in the younger male Society of the last century's final quarter. There was, as a matter of plain fact, hardly a scandal of late Victorian times, from a relatively simple matter of a fight between two gentlemen in Hyde Park to a libel action arising out of some 'funny business' at the Jockey Club, from a noticeably unsavoury divorce action to the murderous business of 'Jack the Ripper', in which the name of the crack Tenth Hussars was not (I had almost added 'inevitably') mentioned. In many of these cases, I was later to find myself professionally involved; I never closed the file on one without a feeling of profound relief, and a hope that the 'nasty taste in my mouth' would soon go.

The facts in the case of Colonel Valentine Baker—such facts, that is to say, which were given in evidence at Croydon Assizes, before Mr Justice Brett; I have admitted that I have reservations—are quickly told.

The charge against Colonel Baker was that he had committed an indecent assault upon the person of one Miss Rebecca Kate Dickenson, a young lady chance-met in a railway carriage.

On 17th June, 1875, Miss Dickenson, having bought a first-class ticket, got into the London train at Midhurst. It was a sunny afternoon, and the window by which Miss Dickenson seated herself had been lowered, so that she might enjoy the breeze.

When the train arrived at Liphook, Colonel Baker entered the compart-ment in which Miss Dickenson was sitting by an open window. He had never seen the young lady before; nor had she ever seen the Colonel.

They entered into conversation: Miss Dickenson was not questioned later on any doubts that she may have felt as to the propriety of permitting a stranger to speak to her. They talked pleasantly, so she said, as the train sped on towards Woking, the train's last stop before reaching the terminus of Waterloo.

Then, according to the story that Miss Dickenson was later to tell, the Colonel's manner changed abruptly—and frighteningly. Bluntly (so she said) Baker suggested that, after they should have reached London, the young lady should correspond with him—his tone making it quite clear on what terms they should correspond. A little belatedly, Miss Dickenson recalled the generally sound principle that one should not encourage strangers to talk to young ladies in railway-compartments.

She rejected the Colonel's invitation—only to discover, she said, that she was face-to-face with a 'maniac'.

The Colonel 'leapt at her'; planted himself down beside her; caught her around the waist, and kissed her again and again.

She could not help but scream—yet there was no hope of aid: there was no corridor; both doors opened only on to the tracks. The communication-cord, even had she been able to reach it, appeared to be broken.

Terror gave her strength—so she said—and, struggling to her feet, Miss Dickenson broke free of the Colonel's grasp. Her hand, panic-guided, shot through the open window, grasped the door-handle, and turned it. The door swung open, with the lady hanging on it.

Her screams had already brought heads poking out of the windows of ad-joining carriages; now the horrified watchers saw a young woman, with dishevelled hair and disordered clothing, hanging from the opened door of a train rushing through Surrey at forty miles an hour.

Somebody, with almost as much presence of mind as Miss Dickenson said that she had shewn, pulled the communication-cord. With a roar of es-caping steam and a shudder of brakes, the train came to a halt, as the young lady tumbled down on to the permanent way.

The evidence of the guard, who hurried up to where a crowd of people had already gathered about the young woman, put the darkest construction upon the Colonel's behaviour. According to this servant of the railway-company, the "gentleman who was standing beside the young lady" said: "Don't say anything. If you do, you don't know what trouble you'll get me into. Just tell him you were frightened."

This, unfortunately for Baker, was just what the young lady was to tell the police—and to tell them, too, *why* she had been frightened.

The guard was of that type of public functionary not to be intimidated by Rank. He asked a clergyman, who was standing by, to look after the young lady; Colonel Baker, the guard sternly ordered into a carriage oc-cupied by two gentlemen, the carriage doors then being locked.

The train resumed its interrupted journey; when it reached Waterloo, the guard asked Colonel Baker to accompany him to the superintendent's office, where the Colonel was asked his name and address. These he gave cor-rectly.

Asked to explain how the young lady had come to be hanging, in a dis-traught state, from the open door of a moving train, the Colonel replied curtly that the young lady had 'reported the case incorrectly'. On the following day, the Deputy-Chief Constable of Surrey served Colonel Baker with a warrant of arrest.

This was one of those unfortunate cases, only too common still in our society, in which the guilt or innocence of the party charged will be 'obvious', not from the facts, but according to the social position or social sympathies (they are not invariably the same) of the observer.

To his brother-officers, active or retired, as to most of the male members of his social class, the Colonel's 'harmless' gallantry—apparently he had done no more than to steal a kiss—was rather a compliment than an insult to the young lady. It is needless to say what others—including Mr Justice Brett (afterwards the first Lord Esher) thought of such behaviour! On the face of it, Baker had, in legal language, 'assaulted' Miss Dickenson; whether or not his offensive conduct merited its being described as 'criminal assault' is another matter; for myself, I am inclined to think that these old-fashioned phrases, relics of a darker world than ours, do, by their having become meaningless to the world outside the law-courts, pre-judge the issue, and cause the return of verdicts hardly justified by either the gravity of the charge or the evidence adduced to support it.

In the dock, the Colonel gained much admiration, and not a little sympathy, by his refusal to permit his counsel, the very able Mr Henry Hawkins (afterwards Lord Brampton), to cross-examine the principal Crown witness—the young person herself. By his gentlemanlike refusal to expose his accuser to the rigours of a cross-examination by the deadly Mr Hawkins—most will remember him, not altogether justly, as 'The Hanging Judge'—Colonel Baker 'gave the case away', and entered in effect a plea of Guilty. That the Judge was unduly harsh in condemning the Colonel to a fine of £500, in addition to the payment of all costs and a year's *rigorous* imprisonment (which, in those days, implied the picking of oakum, sewing of canvas mailbags and walking the treadmill) is, I think, generally admitted. Nor was the Colonel permitted to resign his commission: at the insistence of Her Majesty, the Colonel of the 10th Hussars was cashiered—and only the most earnest representations by the Secretary at War and other highly-placed persons, including Her Majesty's cousin, the Duke of Cambridge (then Commander-in-Chief) spared the Colonel the frightful ignominy of a full military degradation within a square of his own troops, to the awful sound of the muffled drums.

I was never happy about this case; it seemed to me to be so rich with improbabilities—if I may so express it—that it must have been with the gravest sense of frustration that Mr Hawkins obeyed his client's instructions not to proceed to the cross-examination of the principal witness.

No-one challenged the evidence of the clergyman that he had looked out of his carriage-window to see an open carriage-door, from the inner window-frame of which a young person was hanging; and the guard, summoned by the pulling-down of the alarm-chain, supported the clergyman's evidence. But, I used to ask myself, *how*—not *why*, but *how*—came the young person to be hanging by her finger-tips to the inner side of the carriage-door, *when the hinges of that door were on the side nearer to the engine?*

At the speed at which the train was moving—some thirty-five to forty miles an hour—the forward motion would have been more than sufficient to fling an open door shut—in this case, catching the legs of the young person between door and running-board. To have seen—as the clergyman said that he had seen—an open door with the young person hanging from its inner side, he would have had to lower his window and look out and back *at the very moment that the door of the distressed girl's carriage flew open;* a moment more, and the velocity of the train would have flung the open door shut. I do not say that this coincidence in time is impossible; but my long experience of happening has taught me to beware of coincidences, especially in criminal evidence. And there remains another question, which was never raised, by either prosecution or defence, at the trial: how—and why—was the door open at all? Why had not the guard locked it, as was customary in those days, and is still a custom on our longer runs?

But, as I once said to Watson, circumstantial evidence is a very tricky thing. It may well seem to point very straight to one thing, but if one shifts one's own point of view a little, one may find it pointing in an equally uncompromising manner to something entirely different. There is, in fact, in studying evidence, a way of its being looked at which bears the most striking analogy to that parallactic displacement by which the apparent relative position of observed objects changes as the position of the observer changes. In this case, in any event, we shall now never, in all probability, know the real truth of the matter.

Colonel Baker, his sentence completed (with remission for good behaviour) and his fine and heavy costs paid, left for Turkey, where the common view of incivilities offered to young persons in railway-carriages is different from our own.

As a Turkish officer, he routed a Russian army; then, promoted general, he organized that International Gendarmerie for the Sultan by which the autocrat of the Sublime Porte hoped to evade the provisions of the Berlin Congress whilst seeming to conform to them. And when Arabi Pasha's revolt against the Khedive made British and Egyptian soldiers companions in arms, General Baker found himself sharing a mess with those who had formerly been his brother-officers.

Watson never mentioned the Colonel; so that only indirectly did my friend make plain his opinion of Baker Pasha. In the first place, he changed the real name of Hucknall, owner of the lost goose (in the case that Watson calls "The Blue Carbuncle"), to 'Baker'—and if one turn up that amusing little tale, one may find why the change was made: "A touch of red in nose and cheeks, with a slight tremor of his extended hand, recalled Holmes's surmise as to his habits". And in the second place, his setting the action of "The Cardboard Box" in Croydon and nearby Wallington—when, in fact, the real places were Chatham and Strood—as well as his use of the name Beddington (a mile or two from Croydon) as a surname (in the case of "The Stockbroker's Clerk") shew well how vivid in Watson's memory was the tragedy of the *Croydon Assizes* at which Colonel Baker was sentenced to gaol.

But, as I ponder now on these half-forgotten things, I recall an even more significant—and even plainer—indication of Watson's opinion of Baker. In the case of "The Bruce-Partington Plans", which concerned the theft of naval secrets, a man of distinction is arrested: the younger brother of the Head of the Submarine Department at Woolwich Arsenal. Now, Watson has given to this brother both the military title and the Christian name of what *must* be the despised Baker: *Colonel Valentine* Walter—and even the altered surname, *Walter*, has not been chosen haphazardly, or so it would seem to me.

Watson was—and has put it upon record that he was—irritated by my identifying a caller in mufti as an ex-sergeant of the Royal Marines, now with the Corps of Commissionaires. We had both been looking through one of the tall windows on Baker-street when we saw this man look up, scan the houses on our side of the road, and cross over; a moment or two later, we heard his tread upon the stairs. I had already deduced the man's occupation—even, at Watson's insistence, made a guess at the man's former regiment. Watson has written that this display of my simple deductive skill left him as annoyed as incredulous.

In any case, it was plain enough to see what he was thinking. ("Brag and bounce!" he tells us that he thought.)

"Very well," I said. "If you think that I am mistaken, pray ask the man himself. If I am not mistaken, here he is."

The tall, well-set-up, soberly dressed man came into our room after a sharp but in no way insolent knock.

Watson, with a triumphant glance at me, addressed our caller.

"May I ask what your trade may be?" he asked, after the man had handed over the letter to me that he was carrying.

"Commissionaire, sir," the man said gruffly. "Uniform away for repairs."

"And you were?" Watson continued, though a little less confidently.

"A sergeant, sir. Royal Marine Light Infantry . . ."

Now, I had no idea that this small exchange had had the power to rankle Watson so much. I did not crow over him; merely opened the letter, and read there the summons from Gregson, of Scotland Yard, which began the case that Watson calls "A Study in Scarlet". As far as I remember, the commissionaire in mufti was never mentioned again.

But Watson had not forgotten him. Seven or eight years ago,* Watson's account of the theft of the Bruce-Partington plans (actually the submarine was properly to be called the 'Garrett-Nordenfelt', joint achievement of the Reverend Mr William George Garrett, formerly curate of Holy Cross, Manchester, and Hr Nordenfelt, the Swedish inventor of the machine-gun which bears his name) appeared, and I saw—I confess to my amusement— that, in his selection of the name 'Walter', was the proof that even after *twenty-seven* years, the episode of the sergeant of Marines retained all its power of annoying Watson. But perhaps I had better explain the connection between the name 'Walter' and the episode of the commissionaire.

I know that Watson is aware of this connection, for we once discussed it—though not in connection with the sergeant's call.

In 1859, an unemployed regular Army officer, who had fought in the Crimean War, was distressed to observe the condition of many fit ex-soldiers, who, with no work, were turning—or had already turned—into street-corner loafers.

The officer conceived a plan for putting these men—or, at least, some of them—to useful employment; and to this end, he organized them (after having taken up their references) into an uniformed body, subject to military discipline. Borrowing a title from France, where the licensed free-lance street-messenger has long been a recognized figure in French social life, the officer called his uniformed band of messengers the Corps of Commissionaires. The officer—who was afterwards knighted for his work in helping unemployed ex-soldiers of good character to find employment and regain their self-respect—was . . . Captain *Walter*. Since the term 'commissionaire' had been sticking in Watson's throat since 1881, the name 'Walter' was still not one, in 1908, to hold any attraction for him—it was typically, in Watson's opinion, the name to give a man accused of High Treason!

As for Watson's having given Templeton, who brought us together, the name 'Stamford', here, too, we have the now-familiar Watsonian device of choosing a pseudonym which will, in some fashion, link his own history, his own prejudices, with the history of our partnership. Wondering why he had chosen 'Stamford', I one day reached for our *Debrett*, and turned up the

* In fact, seven years: the story was published in both *The Strand Magazine* and *Collier's Weekly*, in December, 1908.—*Editor*

Earl of Stamford, whose family name is 'Grey'. Running my finger along the list of collaterals, I found that once again, Watson had been true to his obscure principles: Lady Mary Grey, daughter of the 8th Earl of Stamford and Warrington, had married, in 1884, none other than *John Watson, M.D.*

My John Watson, M.D.? Oh no! But his existence in that part of *Debrett* dedicated to the Earls of Stamford sufficiently explains the use of the name 'Stamford' in a write-up of the Brixton-road case that *my* Watson prepared in either 1886 or 1887. Years later, I did touch cautiously on this other John Watson, M.D. (he died in the year of the Diamond Jubilee, 1897): it was as I had suspected—this other Watson was a fairly near relative of my Watson. By the anything-but-capricious change of the real name, 'Templeton', to the imaginary name, 'Stamford', Watson had made a secret but permanent record of that distinguished relationship.

John Watson was older than I—by how much he was never precisely to define. He used to talk as though there were no more than the difference of some two or three years in our ages, and though, of course, I could have found out his true age by a few minutes' search at Somerset House, this I had no inclination to do. If his true age was among the many facts that Dr Watson's curious reticence caused him to conceal, well—so be it! I had no wish to know what he had rather kept hidden from me. What my observation and deductive powers might tell me about my friend—well, that was a different matter; constituted as I am—and was even then—I could no more resist deducing the facts about a man or woman whom I encountered than I might resist opening my eyes—and what I deduced about Dr John Watson left little of importance to be gathered from official records.

I knew that he was older than I, for all that he had a youthful air that I had never, even as a youth, commanded. I often recalled a remark that I had overheard in the comfortable members' bar of the Royal Society of Medicine, to which Watson had taken me for what he would, in those days, persist in calling a *chota peg*. Two other members, unaware that they could be overheard by me, were discussing Watson's age. The comment of one pleased me by its simple wit.

"Well," he said, "whatever it is, *he certainly doesn't look it!*"

I reckoned that Watson might be even as much as ten years my senior: there were far too many—and too long—undescribed passages in his history for him to have been, in 1881, very much the sunny side of forty. I was, in 1881, when we met, just twenty-seven; I put Watson down as about thirty-five or thirty-six. Frankly, I wondered what had gone wrong with him.

I have mentioned his extreme credulity; the literal manner in which he accepted and recorded statements as wild and as (one would have thought) obviously ludicrous as my irresistible desire to pull his leg forced me to make. The ease with which my verbal follies shocked him tempted me, I am afraid, to even wilder excesses—as, for instance, when I affected a complete ignorance of Thomas Carlyle—"Carlyle . . . ? Who the dickens is *he?*"—and then quoted from the Sage of Cheyne-row; and also (you will find the record in *The Sign of the Four*) when I discussed with Watson Carlyle's connection with Jean-Paul Richter. Extraordinary! But there was something more: genuinely—or merely affecting to be (I never knew which)—shocked by my 'ignorance', he would even forget what exactly had been the outrageous statement which had shocked him. Thus, I see that he does quote me correctly in "A Study in Scarlet", when I exclaim impatiently: "You say that we go round the sun. If we went round the moon, it wouldn't make a penn'orth of difference to me or to my work." (Indeed, how should it?) But, in *The Hound of the Baskervilles*—a real surname for once, for a change!—Watson makes me say that it didn't matter to me whether the earth went round the sun or the sun round the earth. In fact, *that* difference would be of no consequence to me, either—but, in his almost pathological instinct for hiding facts, he does, unfortunately—and far too often—hide the truth under an incorrect or downright nonsensical statement, as when, in "A Case of Identity", he fathers me with the meaningless expression 'bisulphate of baryta'; invents a jewel unknown to geologists or gemmologists, a 'blue carbuncle'; and even puts himself on record as having prescribed large doses of strychnine as a *sedative!*

But, leaving this mock or true credulity, this disarming literal-mindedness, aside, it did not take me long to understand the basic differences between Watson's character and my own—and to attribute much of the quality of those differences to a difference in upbringing; specifically, to a difference in *education.*

It is not in school-curricula that types of education differ; it is in the different types of character that each type of education has the aim of producing. Despite his unhappy childhood (for uncles and aunts are the indulgent relatives only of children who have parents—with whom, of course, the aunts and uncles are in conscious or unconscious competition), Watson's education had been of the sort designed to produce the conventional middle-class citizen of the mid-Nineteenth Century. After his dame-school, he had been sent—by the afore-mentioned strict aunt—to a good preparatory-school at Sampford Peverell, about five miles from Tiverton, to whose famous public school Watson proceeded at the age of thirteen, remaining there for five years. As his aunt's villa was at Norton Fitzwarren, half-way between Milverton and Taunton, on the road from Tiverton—the aunt's

house was some twenty-five miles distant from Tiverton by road—it was
not possible for young Watson to attend Blundell's as a day-scholar. He was
entered at Blundell's as a boarder, and here, as I said, he passed the next
five years, going 'home' only for the holidays: two months of the Long
Vacation, and a day or two at Easter, Whitsun and Christmas. He told me
that he never spent half-holidays with his aunt; but would use his exeat to
explore the beautiful Devon countryside, or visit the silk and lace manufac-
tories on which the commercial prosperity of the small town mainly de-
pended, or, if he were sufficiently well in funds, take train for Exeter, fourteen miles to the south, and there wander about the ancient Celtic-Roman
city of Isca Dumnoniorum. There is no doubt that school, with all its
boredom and bullying, was to him far preferable to the cold justice of his
aunt's grudged hospitality.*

Watson grew up, then, under the dominant influence of his academic,
rather than his domestic, education. He played the traditional and enforced
games of his school: cricket, fives, Rugby football: group activities from
which, thank Heaven!, I was early released. He rowed, on the River Exe,
in both House and School eights; his sculling brought him a trumpery but
valued silver pot or two (polished by Mrs Hudson's maid-of-all-work, they
shone resplendent on our study mantelshelf at Baker-street). He absorbed
all that his public-school had to teach him—which was to uphold the system by which a world-empire is managed and controlled; and to uphold
that system in becoming, actively or potentially, its willing and efficient
servant. The radical change in the public-school system, which will always
be associated with the name of Dr Arnold of Rugby (though he developed,
rather than initiated it) came when the school-system changed from a general system of education to a system designed to educate for a special purpose: to provide administrators, at every level, for our Empire. It had no
other purpose; and, indeed, that purpose absorbed all its energies, as it
directed all its will.

The public-school system did not set out to train its scholars for banking,
even though many of those in that occupation have attended public-schools;
it certainly did not set out to teach its scholars how to make money—*that*
useful art it left to less admired types of academy to impart! What it did set
out to do was to produce administrators—and call him what you will; call
him by whatever magniloquent title of honour seem proper to enhance the
glory of full-bottomed wig, of silk robe, of gold-lace, of scarlet coat, of stars
and garters; an administrator, however exalted in rank, is still a servant, and

* Dr Watson's memories of childhood cannot have been otherwise than unpleasant, seeing
that he gave the name of his birth-place, Milverton, to 'the Worst Man in London'—'Charles
Augustus Milverton'.—*Editor*

no more than a servant, with (if he be a honest man) all a servant's excellent qualities, but never (since he *is* a servant) completely without a servant's faults—perhaps even a servant's vices.

One must grant that, if a nation have the care of an extensive and—even at this day—expanding empire, that nation must ensure a steady output of men (and, to a growing degree, women) trained to administer and support that empire.

But that training must ask, on the part of those whom it trains, the sacrifice of what, to me, is the least dispensable part of my personality—my *will*.

Administrators, of whatever rank, from the silk-hatted and frock-coated station-master to the ermine-cloaked and knee-breeched Viceroy; from the time-keeper of a factory to the adjutant of a regiment; all have *authority*— but it is an authority derived from, and supported by, the authority of that system of government that they are helping, each in his appointed place, to maintain. Not one, *as an administrator*, works—advises, determines, orders, commands—by the authority of his own will, but only as the servant of that anonymous, completely impersonal will that we call Government. Watson—like so many hundreds of thousands of others who had been reared, with no more care for the development of his essential character than a gardener gives for the espaliered peach-tree—had been denied the development of his individual will, that he might the more willingly, the more loyally, and the more unthinkingly serve the purpose of that system which had moulded him to effect its blind purposes.

Not indeed in every way—but in so many important ways—Dr Watson and I were the complete antithesis one of the other. Even in the games and other forms of physical exercise that we had mastered, we were different. He played—and enjoyed playing—all those games which call for the corporate effort of a team, and in which individual effort is neither asked nor welcomed; I, on the other hand, excelled—where I excelled at all—in those sports which either demanded no partner or which demanded, at the most, a single opponent. Watson liked cricket, football, rowing in an eight, following harriers or beagles—preferably in the company of many others; I preferred—and excelled at—single-stick, boxing and fencing. The essential differences in our characters will be, I think, apparent from the differences in our sporting tastes.

And then it was, after having considered well the character of my new fellow-lodger, I realized clearly what was wrong with him. At some time, in fairly recent years, he had been deprived of his vocation. I don't mean that he had been deprived of his qualifications as a medical man—though I did doubt his ability, at this particular time, to practise medicine or surgery (he was both an M.R.C.S and an L.R.C.P. before taking his final M.D.). Why, I did not know—it could have been the effect of the *jezail* bullet in his shoulder, or that less easily defined injury to his leg (or both?)—but it was patent to me, as it must have been to Templeton and to any other who had known him well, that Dr Watson had, for the moment at least, 'lost his nerve', as we say of a soldier or a boxer who will not fight or of a horse who refuses the easiest of jumps.

It seems to me that, in these idle jottings, I have come a long way from a description of life at Baker-street and of the second phase of a career which had begun well in the United States, during my brief spell as an actor; and it did occur to me to wonder if, perhaps, I had not given too much space to an analysis, not only of Dr Watson's character, but also of my relationship with him.

But on consideration, I think not. I had no prevision, when Dr Watson accepted my proposition that he go shares in an apartment that I could not afford on my own, that we would be together for more than a few weeks—for a few months, at most: until, say, I had either gathered in what was then owing to me, or had secured consultations which would be paid for as is done in Harley-street: in cash. It had never occurred to me that the man with whom I was agreeing to share a temporary furnished accommodation was a companion who would share my life for a quarter-of-a-century—that I was entering upon a bachelor *ménage à deux* in which the ever-closer relationship of us both would have the profoundest effect upon the character of each.

However, all this lay in the future, as, over many a pipeful of Brumfit's Latakia, I considered the problem of Dr Watson—both from his point-of-view and from my own. I could see that his present unsatisfactory condition might well be summed up in the statement that, as Grant Allen (a friend of Watson's Agent of later years, by the way) used to write, Watson 'had been denied fulfilment'—though it was never of middle-aged medical men, but of flighty, 'misunderstood' females that Mr Allen was writing.

Still, that phrase of Grant Allen's does express what I felt to be the fact. Here was my companion, at a loose end, driven by the boredom of idleness to spend too much time in too many bars and smoking-rooms and coffee-houses, and spending far too much of his meagre income in doing so. His profession he was unable—even had he been competent—to resume; in those days, there were few openings for employment to qualified medical men without a private practice—and I knew that Dr Watson had no capital to buy one (even though he did have a little more money to spend, I was happy in suspecting, than his declared Army pension of eleven-and-six-pence per diem).

But here he was, without a clearly defined ambition—perhaps without a real ambition: only (as Dr Spooner *should* have said!) a half-formed wish that someone—somewhere—would realize a need of his services; would seek him out; and offer him what he felt, even though instinctively rather than consciously, as his 'fulfilment'—for he too, I knew, had read Grant Allen. His 'fulfilment': the ability to 'be of some use'—the administrator's somewhat embarrassing euphemism for the declaration that, without the authority of Authority, he might hardly earn a sixpenny piece.

Well, well!—and here was I, not only literally feverish with ambition, but with an ambition clearly realized and plainly set out. I emptied my pipe, put it with some others in the pipe-rack of the five-barred-gate pattern which was one grateful client's total payment; I took up the fairly new calabash from Weingott's and charged it with a full load of Navy Cut Plug: my favourite stimulus for constructive introspection. But this, I knew, would be no three-pipe problem. I could see, even after one pipeful of Latakia, how I could help Dr Watson—how I could solve his painful problem. And yes—why not, now, after thirty-four years, admit it?—and help myself, too. . . .

SIX ❦

More lives than one...

Watson has recorded that, on the occasion of our first meeting, I had warned him that "I generally have chemicals about, and occasionally do experiments. Would that annoy you?" His "Not at all", I took in the perfunctory spirit in which it had been uttered—a mere conventional complaisance with no comprehension of the facts behind it.

Now, at the end of my first month as Dr Watson's companion, he was about to learn exactly what that carelessly given permission was to mean to him in the way of discomfort.

I have mentioned that it was through the good offices of Mr Serjeant Ballantine that I became a member of the Union Club, not only at an extraordinarily early age, but also—apart from my having the recommendation of old Tom Holmes—quite wthout those qualifications of wealth or worldly position of which admission to membership of the Union is considered to be the full and respectful acknowledgment.

Mr Ballantine, it will be remembered, had been one of the defenders of the so-called Tichborne Claimant—that gross, ignorant Wapping butcher who cheated a great and ancient English family * by forcing it to defend its patrimony against the criminal insolence of Arthur Orton.

I have already said that I could never understand why the Serjeant † had consented to assist in the defence of this patent humbug; but, after having mentioned this once to him, it is obvious that the special facts of my rela-

* One of the few of the old English families which had been in settled possession of its landed estates since before the Norman Conquest.—*Editor*

† The legal rank of 'Serjeant-at-Law'—the title surviving now only in that of the City of London's 'Common Serjeant'—was the most ancient of all, its members belonging to the Order of the Coif, and wearing a distinctive type of legal wig. The Order itself was abolished in the 'reforms' of 1873, and the headquarters of the Order—Serjeants' Inn—sold.—*Editor*

tionship with Serjeant Ballantine forbade my ever mentioning his decision again.

But there was one curious aspect of the case which, I felt, might be discussed without my risking an offence against clubbability in particular and good manners in general. I mean the curious affair of the *unmentioned* tattoo-marks, known to literally dozens of competent and respectable witnesses to have been on the arms of the missing nobleman, Sir Roger Doughty-Tichborne, 11th baronet of Tichborne, Hampshire, who disappeared—presumed lost at sea—at some date before 1869, the year in which the Wapping butcher, Arthur Orton, presented himself to the world as the missing Heir.

The facts of this scandalous case, which all but ruined an ancient English family, settled on its estates since Saxon times, are so well known that I need touch only briefly upon them here. It says much for the weakness of our English legal system that such a case should have been permitted to come before the courts; had there been a Grand Jury for civil cases, as there is in criminal,* Orton's impudent attempt to claim the baronetcy would have been dismissed with the contempt that it deserved.

The missing Heir, Roger Doughty-Tichborne, had been educated at the well-known Jesuit school at Stoneyhurst (for the Tichbornes were of the Romish persuasion); he had held a commission in the crack Sixth Dragoon Guards (the Carabineers); and he spoke excellent French, his mother being French, and he having passed a great part of his life in France. He had visited South America; had taken ship for England; and had not been heard of again.

That this English aristocrat—a man-of-the-world; speaking excellent French; slim of build, and with the upright carriage of an English military officer—should so have changed as to turn up in the guise of a hugely fat, ill-spoken, almost illiterate butcher should have seemed a proposition outside all serious consideration. How anyone could have supported this man's claim to be the missing Sir Roger passes my comprehension. When he presented himself in England, claiming to be the missing Sir Roger, Colonel Lushington, chairman of the trustees of the Tichborne Estates, promptly shewed the impudent blackguard the door. And, as promptly, Orton, *alias* 'Sir Roger Doughty-Tichborne, baronet', brought suit against Colonel Lushington for the handing over to 'Sir Roger' of 'his rightful patrimony'!

The case, known officially as *Tichborne versus Lushington*, opened before the Lord Chief Justice, Sir Alexander Cockburn, Mr Justice Mellor, and Mr Justice Lush. For the Plaintiff, Orton, my friend, for so I may now call

---

* The inexplicable abolition of the Grand Jury had not taken place when Mr Holmes wrote these words.—*Editor*

him, led; and with Mr Serjeant Ballantine were associated some of the brightest ornaments of the English Bar. For the defendants—the trustees of the Tichborne Estates—that greatest of English advocates, Sir John (afterwards Lord) Coleridge, led an equally brilliant array of forensic talent.

It was an array too brilliant for Orton, who, seeing the hopelessness of his case, accepted the advice of his counsel, and elected (as the lawyers say) to be non-suited—that is, given leave to withdraw his claim. His trial for perjury followed as a matter of course, and he eventually went down for seven years at hard labour—his brilliant but misguided counsel, Dr Kenealy, joining the Wapping butcher 'in durance vile'.

Now, one night at the Union Club, as I was sharing a bottle of the Club's Château Margaux, 1864 * with Mr Serjeant Ballantine, we were joined by that eminent judge, Sir Henry Hawkins, afterwards Lord Brampton. The conversation then turned upon one of the most curious of all the curious aspects of this extraordinary case: the suppression, *by the Trustees of the Tichborne Estates*, of an argument—indeed, one might well say *the* clinching argument—in *their* favour.

"Sir Roger's tattoo-marks," I ventured: "I have often wondered why they were never brought forward as evidence against the Claimant—who patently bore none on *his* arms?"

Now, in bringing up this subject, I was, I knew well, venturing upon most delicate ground. For whilst Mr Serjeant Ballantine had led for the plaintiff—that is, the odious Orton—Mr Henry Hawkins (as he was then, before being raised to the Bench) had been one of the four counsel led by the Solicitor-General, Sir John Coleridge. And whilst the brilliant pleading of Mr Serjeant Ballantine on behalf of his client came to nothing—indeed, in an almost unprecedented exercise of judicial authority, the Lord Chief Justice of the Common Pleas ordered Orton into immediate custody on the withdrawal of his claim—Mr Hawkins, as we all knew, had been bitterly disappointed in Sir John Coleridge's assessment of the evidence available against Orton.

"Well, well," said Sir Henry, with a slight smile for my daring to raise what might have seemed a dangerous subject, "that's all so much water under the bridge now. I dare say that I should have been pleased to use as powerful an argument as the absence of witnessed tattoo-marks upon the Claimant's arms or arms; but Coleridge did well enough with what he had—brilliantly, indeed. I don't think that the Claimant had a chance after my brother Coleridge had finished with him: exhibiting his utter ignorance of French, that the real Sir Roger, with a French mother, had spoken

---

* In 1971, for a magnum of Château Lafite of this same year, a 'Swiss syndicate' paid £3,600 at a Geneva sale. In 1881, the Château Margaux cost 98s. (then $23.52) a dozen.—*Editor*

fluently. Besides, Coleridge's perfect familiarity, not only with French but with the classics also, let him expose the witness upon these subjects in both startling and ridiculous lights. No, Ballantine, I would have *liked* the evidence of the tattoo-marks—but I did not need them. All the same," he added, "it really is curious that this evidence regarding the tattooing was never placed in our hands. I wonder why . . . ?"

"Which evidence, sir?"

Sir Henry looked puzzled by my question.

"Why Holmes, the evidence that the missing Sir Roger carried the marks of tattooing. . . ."

"No, sir. The only evidence which could have been given on the subject of tattooing, in respect of Sir Roger, was that he *had been* tattooed. You say that the two gentlemen who, as boys, had done the tattooing, were ready to give evidence. They could have testified only to one fact: that they had tattooed Sir Roger. They could not have testified that the marks were still upon him—for they had no knowledge of that."

Mr Serjeant Ballantine looked positively startled.

"Why, goodness gracious me!" he exclaimed; "do you imply that tattoo-marks are *not* indelible?—that they may be, as one would say, 'bleached out'?"

"I cannot say for certain. All my enquiries, so far, of the many tattooing artists who serve the military and marine customers of London tell me that the marks are quite indelible—that they are often asked to erase them. . . ."

"To change 'Eternal Love, Rosa' to 'Eternal Love, Mary'?" Sir Henry observed, smiling.

"Precisely so. But, in this instance—an important instance, indeed—they are unable to oblige. The most that they can do to erase the mark is to superimpose some design sufficiently complicated that the original is hidden beneath it."

"Then a tattoo-mark *is* indelible . . . ?"

"No, Sir Henry: *only as far as we know.* And I confess that I have often wondered if the possibility—even the probability—of a successful erasure of tattooing were known to Colonel Lushington; and that the Colonel entertained the possibility that such erasure was known to the Claimant."

"But . . . Holmes, I confess that you do indeed puzzle me. Why should the Claimant have any knowledge of this erasing method—supposing that such a method should exist?"

"For two reasons. In the first place, a method of erasure would be of benefit to criminals, who are often tattooed by foreign prison officials; and this would tend to keep the method secret. And Arthur Orton, from the docks of Wapping, could well be familiar with the secrets of a world infested with foreign seamen and others—many of them fugitives from justice. In the second place, the art of tattooing is practised brilliantly by the aboriginal inhabitants of our Australian and New Zealand colonies. It is not, I think, beyond the bounds of possibility that these natives have discovered a means of erasing the marks of tattooing. Had Orton known that erasure was even a possibility, and had Colonel Lushington instructed his legal representatives to raise the matter of Sir Roger's tattoo-marks, Orton could have claimed that the marks had been erased—and I am afraid that Sir John Coleridge would have suffered a forensic reverse."

"Orton shewing that marks *may* be erased . . . ?"

"No, sir: shewing that—or merely suggesting that—tattoo-marks are not necessarily indelible. Suggesting to the jury, of course . . ."

"Of course. But, you say that you have not come across any evidence that the marks may be erased?"

"If it were of use to criminals, I should not expect to find that evidence—at least, on first enquiry."

"Just so. And what is your own interest in this matter? Have you marks"—and here Sir Henry smiled—"that you would wish erased . . . or *altered?*"

"A purely scientific interest, Sir Henry. If I could find a means by which the marks might be erased, I should be able to answer at least one question which has been troubling me."

"And that is . . . ?" asked Mr Serjeant Ballantine.

"Why the matter of Sir Roger's tattoo-marks was never raised in Court. I know that it has puzzled you, Sir Henry, and you, Mr Serjeant"—both nodded—"but at least I can try not to let it further puzzle me."

"And how shall you set about this?" Sir Henry asked.

"I shall continue to make enquiries, and I shall also see whether or not I may find a chemical means of effecting the erasure. If I can discover such a means, it must be assumed than another experimenter may—or has already done so."

"You are a chemical experimenter? I did not know this."

"Yes, sir: I am studying Chemistry under both Dr Armstrong and Dr Russell at Bart's, as well as Forensic Medicine under Dr Southey."

"Excellent! You are reading for . . . what? . . . your first M.B.?"

"If I can. But my primary interest is to fit myself—to qualify myself professionally. . . ."

"Oh," said Sir Henry: "you mean, qualify professionally as a doctor of medicine?"

"Not primarily, sir, though I should like, of course, to do that. But primarily, I wish to qualify myself for a profession of my own devising." It was, I must say now, after nearly forty years, not easy to continue. The warm friendliness had left Sir Henry's lean face; and his features were beginning to assume that harsh and relentless cast better known when he was passing judgment in the Central Criminal Court. Yet I knew that I must test the validity of my claim to professional status; I had already survived the essay with both Templeton and Dr Watson; the American millionaire Mr William H. Vanderbilt had accepted my claimed profession without question, as had all the lesser clients whom I had served. I must not falter or withdraw *now*. So that, braving Sir Henry's most intimidating frown, I ploughed on, only too unhappily aware that my face was red, but hoping that my two fellow-members would charitably attribute my heightened colour to the heat of the blazing fire. I said, "I perceive that you think that I am joking, Sir Henry. Let me assure you that I have too much respect for you to do that. I have invented the profession of private consulting detective—so far an unique profession, in that I believe that I am its only member. But I do assure you, sir, that this is what I intend to be—for what I am qualifying myself."

I could see that Sir Henry's expression had softened; but only because he could see that I was in earnest. I could not flatter myself that he thought any more highly of me in hearing what to him must have sounded my most impudent claim to professional status. However, he said, cordially enough:

"And have you made an actual start in this—er—*profession* of yours? Permit me to ask, in no offensive way, I assure you: but in which respect does your work differ from that of the private enquiry agents whom one sees about the courts, and often in the witness-box?"

I told Sir Henry; I am afraid that it was not on that occasion that I succeeded in explaining the difference!

"And your clients, Holmes? Of what standing are they?"

Here I was on more solid ground—and my confidence, sadly shaken by Sir Henry's patent lack of sympathy (perhaps, even, a momentary contempt), returned.

"Well, sir, I have not many at the moment; but my ledgers do contain the names of a well-known English baronet of very ancient family; the Russian Ambassador in this country, and the Russian Consul-general in New York; half-a-dozen members of some of our best London clubs; a lady well-known in Society who had some trouble with her opal tiara; and—oh yes—the richest man (or I am told that he is the richest man) in the world."

"Are you joking, Holmes?"

"No, sir, indeed I am not."

"But the richest man in the world . . .?"

"Mr William Vanderbilt, of New York."

"*The* Mr Vanderbilt . . .?"

I saw, with a pleasure that (I think) I contrived to hide, that Sir Henry was impressed despite himself. However, that shrewd judge of human nature was not one to abandon an opinion—far less a suspicion—on the persuasion of an acceptable phrase.

"And is it permitted by your—hm!—*professional* etiquette, Holmes, to tell us how Mr Vanderbilt came to use your services? How, for that matter, he came to hear of them?"

I smiled.

"Oh, he heard of me by his coming to see *Hamlet,* in which I played the part of Horatio. Apparently my performance pleased him; and that of Horatio is, so I understood, Mr Vanderbilt's favourite Shakespearean *rôle*—as we say on the stage."

"Holmes! you more and more astonish me! An actor—*you!*"

"Why not, sir? I toured the United States for eight months with the well-known Sasanoff Shakespearean Company—we were most successful; and the long and short of it was that Mr Vanderbilt invited a few of us to have dinner with him at his town-house, and to see the splendid objects of art with which his father's legacy and his own acquisitions had filled it. You know, I suppose, gentlemen, that the founder of the family fortune had died only a year or two before I arrived in New York in November, '79? And you may well have heard that there was a deal of litigation in connection with the settlement of the immense estate—valued, so I believe, at more than two hundred millions of dollars; about forty millions, sterling. The late Cornelius Vanderbilt had been a rapacious if never very discriminating collector; and all his treasures had necessarily to be valued and inventoried by expert appraisers.

"Now you may recall that, about twenty years ago, Commodore Vanderbilt, as he liked to be called, came with his lady to England; was here received with doubtful warmth by Society, and moved, first to Paris, and then to St Petersburg, where His Imperial Majesty—possibly to be different from his Cousin of England—received the Vanderbilts with truly regal hospitality, and even placed one of the finest carriages from the Imperial manège at the service of the two American visitors.

"The Russian Court has always been famous for its lavish generosity. Besides the customary orders and decorations always bestowed on distinguished foreigners, Commodore Vanderbilt was given the great urn of malachite, over eight feet in height, which still stands in the New York mansion, and some . . . eggs."

"*Eggs,* sir! Holmes, I fear that you trifle with us—you do, sir!"

"The eggs, sir, are Easter eggs—what the Russians call *yaitsa paschaia;* the Imperial Family and the nobility give them to each other, and they are masterpieces of the jeweller's skill; both artistically and intrinsically, of very great value. The Czar presented a dozen of these to Mr—Commodore, rather—Vanderbilt; the Czarina, an equal number (though not of inferior quality) to Mrs Vanderbilt. Enchanted with the beauty and the costliness of these trinkets, the Commodore sent out his professional collectors to acquire more. When he died a couple of years ago, the cabinets in his house in Fifth-avenue held as many as three hundred—exactly how many it was now the duty of the executors to ascertain by taking careful inventory. The Commodore's acquisitiveness had many of the characteristics of that of the magpie.

"Well, as so often happens, the inventory held some surprises. In the first place, there were a good deal more of these richly jewelled eggs than there should have been. It was often said of the Commodore, especially in his last days, that he did not know what he possessed—but I take leave to doubt that; and, in any case, a note was made of all acquisitions by his very competent secretaries, and the inventory taken at regular and short intervals. It was in comparing the inventory of 1879 with that of only a few years earlier that the discrepancy had come to light."

"And the discrepancy?" Mr Serjeant Ballantine asked.

"Not fewer than eighty-three."

"And where had they come from?"

"Ah!—that was the question that Mr Vanderbilt, the Commodore's heir, suggested that I try to answer."

"And did you suceed, Holmes?"

"By good fortune, sir—yes."

"You say 'good fortune'. Not, then, by deductive skill?"

"The 'good fortune', sir, was in recalling that I *might* be able to put my hand on some information having a bearing on the case. I sought out this possible information—and applied it to the solution of the excess of Easter eggs. The whole art of deduction, gentlemen, is not more than the whole art of using one's common sense."

"Indeed!"

"Yes—so I conceive; so I conduct my affairs."

"And this information . . . ?" Sir Henry prompted; his manner now sensibly warmer than it had been only a short while earlier.

"I recalled that Mr Sasanoff, the proprietor and manager of our Shakespearean Company, had once mentioned that an uncle was or had been a jeweller of repute in St Petersburg. I wondered if perhaps Mr Sasanoff had himself ever been in the same trade. It was a happy thought: he had. And it was by his expert advice that I found out where the additional eggs had come from—and what they were doing in Mr Vanderbilt Junior's cabinets."

"And what were they doing?"

"If you wished to hide some needles, Sir Henry, where, in your opinion, would be the best place in which to hide them?"

"A haystack, Holmes?"

"No, sir: for even a random plunging of the hand into the hay might get a luckily pricked finger. No, sir, the best place in which to hide needles would be in a quantity of other needles—as the best place to hide stolen Easter eggs was in a rarely-inspected and never questioned collection of Easter eggs. Has either of you gentlemen ever seen the mansion that Mr Vanderbilt inhabits in New York City . . . ? No . . . ? Well, it is magnificent, and it is crowded with the furniture and works of art, with the trinkets and curiosities that both his father and he bought—either personally or through agents all over the world. Only an inventory could tell what is in the house—and only an inventory did.

"And what information—properly estimated, of course—that inventory had to give us! A well-organized traffic in Russian works of art—not merely the priceless Easter eggs, but all those other works for which the Russian jeweller and artist is famous—had been organized to provide funds for the Nihilists and other revolutionary bodies. Yes, indeed!

"Revolutionists, working as servants in the Vanderbilt household, simply took in the treasures imported by other Revolutionists working as sailors and stewards on Russian ships, that other revolutionists employed as stevedores had unloaded at the docks. It was a well-organized trade in stolen goods—and the crowded art-collection of a New York millionaire provided an ideal place in which the goods might be stored whilst arrangements for their sale were being made with a 'fence'—if you know that word, Sir Henry?"

The eminent judge smiled—perhaps a little bleakly.

"Forty years in the service of the Law,* Holmes, have made me fairly well acquainted with criminals' cant. Yes, I do know what 'fence' means—and so, I imagine, does my learned friend on your right."

"Well, sir, that trade was stopped. Having detected *what* was happening, it was no difficult task to detect *who* were involved. The Russian Consul-general was privately given the proofs that two of his staff—senior members, too—were involved, and by those methods that the Russian Government understands so well, were transported back to their native land with-

---

* Born 1817, Hawkins was called to the Bar of the Middle Temple, 1843; Q.C. and Bencher, 1858; Judge of High Court of Justice, 1876; knighted, 1876; Privy Councillor and raised to peerage as Baron Brampton, 1899.—*Editor*

out the knowledge of anyone save a few close colleagues that they had gone. The same discreet return to Russia was arranged for the servants and stevedores and crew-members.

"On my return, I was called to the Russian Embassy, to receive the thanks of His Imperial Majesty, and the award of an order, that I have the Queen's permission to wear—should I ever wish to do so. His Imperial Majesty also asked my acceptance of a splendid cigar-case, with the double-headed eagle, in diamonds, on the cover, and a most flattering inscription within. It is, however, a little too flamboyant for a consulting private detective just embarking on his career. I never make a practice of carrying it—it is rich; too rich; with a richness which, amongst us, sir, would be looked upon as akin to bad taste."

This, by the way, is the true account of that adventure which appears in Watson's record as "The Case of Vanderbilt and the Yeggman". That a 'yeggman' does exist in America—he is a safe-breaker who uses the simplest tools —is well known; but in the matter of the revolutionists' using the Vanderbilt art-collection as a 'transit depot', no yeggman was needed. For any smuggled stolen object of art to be lost to sight amongst a profusion of the world's costliest treasures was a better hiding-place than any safe might have provided. I think that I must have referred to the head revolutionist in the Russian consulate as 'the egg-man', and that Watson either mis-heard me or assumed, from his less than perfect knowledge of American criminality, that I *must* have said 'Vanderbilt and the yeggman', rather than 'Vanderbilt and the egg-man'.

Our discussion of the mystery of the tattoo-marks which were never mentioned (I was reminded of them, years later, by a dog which did not bark in the night) filled me with a desire to 'prove my point' which soon grew to be a positive obsession. I could hardly give my full attention to my regular duties—not least of them, Dr Russell's lectures at 10 a.m. on Mondays, Wednesdays and Fridays—for my impatience to set about finding out whether or not tattoo-marks were indelible.

But at last I found my opportunity to set about my long-desired experiment. I came out of the St James's Hall late one afternoon, walked a short way along Piccadilly, and turned into Swallow-street, where I selected a fine fore-quarter of pork at Bisney & Jones's shop, and told the butcher to send it immediately to Baker-street. I chose pork as being the flesh nearest to that of the human being; I should have preferred to experiment upon living human flesh, but that, I realized, was—at any rate, for the present—out of the question. I must make do with fresh-killed pork—and the assistant assured me that the porker had been taken to the shambles only on the previous evening. I walked in a leisurely manner through Vigo-street, Cork-street, New Bond-street, Cavendish-square and the several small stretches which then made up the length of modern Wigmore-street, and so home. When I put my key into the lock, Mrs Hudson came upstairs to tell me that the meat had just been delivered by the boy.

"How will you want this done, Mr Holmes?—roast, baked, boiled or pickled? Or perhaps you and the Doctor would like half of it roasted, the other half pickled? Pickled's nice and handy for sandwiches, especially if you're going out at night." (This was an allusion, hardly veiled, to Mrs Hudson's disapproval of my nocturnal 'business'.)

"Give it to me, and I'll take it upstairs as it is."

Mrs Hudson looked her horror of this suggestion.

"Why, my goodness gracious *me*, Mr Holmes: surely you don't mean to eat it *raw!*"

"I need it for an experiment, Mrs Hudson. I shalln't eat it at all. Pray be good enough to fetch it up from the larder, and I'll take it up with me."

She hurried off, disapproval in every line of her starched cap and black bombazine dress. I caught the muttered words: "Best English pork at sixpence a pound . . . and ten pounds there, if there's an ounce. A sin and a shame. . . ."

Watson was out; and, speedily divesting myself of hat and ulster, I laid out the tools of tattooing with which I had provided myself on a visit to Burdett-road, and set about the pricking of a design on the remarkably human-looking skin of the *porcus domesticus*. As I wished to leave the attempted eradication of the marks until at least the following day, it followed that I should have to ask Mrs Hudson to put the tattooed pork into her larder. The design, then, called for some thought: on the one hand, anything facetious or disloyal (and she would certainly consider a Union Flag and the letters 'V.R.' both) would not only scandalize Mrs Hudson; but would probably mean an abrupt termination of our tenancy; on the other, I felt that her openly expressed disapproval of my pork-buying merited *some* rebuke.

I lit a pipe of Carlin's *Golden Bar*, that I had bought in Piccadilly that afternoon, on my way to the St James's Hall, and considered the problem of the tattoo. The inspiration came to me with the end of my second pipe—it was evidently no more than a two-pipe problem. I took a sheet of paper, and sketched this design, which will be familiar to all who have seen the well-known advertisements of the furniture-moving company which advertises its service with a Greek word, 'Ecoscevephoron' *—Hudson's.

* In his MS., Mr Holmes also writes the word in Greek characters.—*Editor*

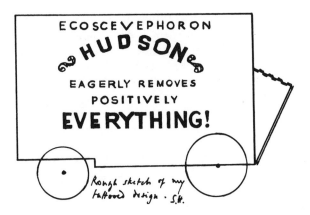

ECOSCEVEPHORON
HUDSON
EAGERLY REMOVES
POSITIVELY
EVERYTHING!

Rough sketch of my tattooed design . S.H.

I transferred the design, with opaque water-colour and Indian-ink, to the skin of the porker; and then, with my needles, made what I still consider to be a most creditable job of tattooing—perhaps not *quite* up to the professional standards of York-road or Great Alie-street; but better than I had expected that I should be able to do. I finished the tattooing, and took the joint down to Mrs Hudson, with a request that she had better put it away in the larder with a note attached, so that the kitchen-maid should not cook it.

She cast a dubious glance at the tattooing, but said nothing; and I had cleared away needles and ink by the time that Dr Watson arrived back from playing a hundred up at Thurston's.

On the following day, I once again had the apartment to myself—at least, for a sufficient length of time that I might work at my experiment untroubled by Dr Watson's always somewhat inquisitive (*he* called it 'interested') presence.

I had discussed the proposed experiment with Dr Russell, and for reasons that I shall not go into here, but which will be acceptable, at least hypothetically, to an experienced analytical chemist, I had decided to try what effect indigotin disulphonic acid would have upon the supposedly indelible stains of the tattooist's needle.

I had already, in the Pathological Laboratory at Bart's, put in a good many hours of useless experimentation; I was attracted by the prospects offered in my synthesizing indigotin disulphonic acid, and this I resolved to do at home.

There was considerable history behind this acid: it had been synthesized from indigo in about 1750, and made synthetically about a century later. It is a simple chemical operation, this synthesis, which is effected by the action of pyrosulphuric (or fuming sulphuric) acid on indigo—otherwise in-digotin. I thought it best to prepare my indigotin disulphonic acid both from the pure indigo and from the artificial, which was synthesized first by Baeyer from o-nitrobenzene. I had performed both these operations when Dr Watson returned, to complain (I thought with excessive warmth) about the smell.

I left the attempt at eradication of the tattoo-marks until the evening of the day next-but-one, since I had several calls on the following day. Dr Watson was again out when I asked Mrs Hudson to bring up the tattooed fore-quarter of pork, and I did not need to notice the wrinkling of her nose to observe that, despite the cold weather, the meat smelt distinctly gamey. Perhaps the butchers had deceived me, and the meat had not been as fresh as they had claimed. However, she put it, on its dish, on the side-table by the fireplace, and I immediately got to work on the pig's tattoo.

I confess that the combination of disulphonic acid and gamey pork be-came, within a short time, almost insufferable even to me, who had been hardened to offensive odours in a long experience of dissecting-rooms and mortuaries. I tied a silk handkerchief about my nose, after having first sprinkled it with some eau-de-Cologne from Watson's cut-glass scent decan-ter, and though the poisonous nidor penetrated even the scent-laden silk, my interest in my experiment enabled me to pursue my research with un-diminished ardour.

Alas!—all that the indigotin disulphonic acid—both 'natural' and syn-thetic—did was to add a bit more darkness to the already dark pigment. I wondered if I might have more success with the leuco form of indigo, which exists as 'indigo white', and which is usually made by using an alkaline reducing agent, rather than an acid one—when, at that moment, remembering that Watson was due to arrive, I hastily gathered up the joint of pork, as hastily clapped on its wire-mesh fly-cover, and put it as hastily out of my bedroom window, on to the sill, which is unusually wide in the Baker-street houses of this date. I cleaned up the chemicals and apparatus, and put them neatly away in the cupboard. And then, as 'camouflage', to use the phrase which has been introduced with the present war, I lit a pipe filled with the coarsest shag in my possession. I picked up *The Martyrdom of Man*, and sat down in our wicker-work arm-chair to await the arrival of Dr. Watson and my belated dinner.

But not even the shag could disguise the odour that my experiment had left behind, and though the gamey pork was now inoffensively outside the window of the next room, one could still, I admit, detect the ghost of its disturbing presence.

It was then that Dr. Watson and I had our first disagreement. . . .

One important aspect of my professional career to which Dr Watson was never privy was the creation and maintenance of some six or eight (the number varied with my professional needs) carefully planned *personae:* alternative identities, as it were, into whose very distinct characters I could slip at will. Of course, Dr Watson knew that I had occasionally to 'don disguise', as he called it; but what he never knew were the 'disguises' that I 'donned'—nor did he know that I did not merely 'make up' (as they say on the Stage) to spend an hour or two in the character of a loafer, a navvy, a groom out of livery or a clerk out of collar, but really gave these assumed personalities an established existence—with friends, acquaintances, an occupation (of sorts) and a settled, regularly paid-up address which would bear up under all but the most penetrating police enquiries.

I have pulled half-a-pint of Allsopp's sixty-shilling bitter at Wetjen's *Redan Hotel* in Notting-hill-gate, at what time Dr Watson has slipped out of the Coronet Theatre; and I have served him 'the Best Shilling Dinner' at the adjoining *Devonshire Arms*—soup, joint or entrée, two vegetables, bread and cheese—and thanked him for the tuppenny tip . . . and all this without his having the least idea that the barman so skilled with the beer-engine, the waiter so deft with the service of the shilling dinner . . . was yours truly! I have steadied his shaking hand and jumping stomach with a pick-me-up passed over the counter at Barritt's, the Perfumer and Foreign Chemist at the Oxford-street end of Charing-cross-road; I even tried to sell him one of Pococks' twenty-five-guinea 'Continental' overstrung pianos, when I saw him, one day, peering into the window of their shop in West-bourne-grove. I even, on several occasions, asked him directions in the street, and on one of them was so grossly insolent that the outraged Doctor bade me take myself off, or he would summon a constable!

But it was—and is still—my theory that these *ad hoc* impersonations are useful only for gathering in one piece of information, and that quickly. For the establishment of what I may call a focus of observation, from which one may seek information for days, perhaps weeks, on end; and to which, by the very fact of that focus's relative stability, information shall trickle through to the watcher; only what the stockbrokers call the 'long-term investment' will yield a profit. One must *establish* the character; round it off; give it depth; make it known to the neighbours, to the shopkeepers—so that, as I have said, if the police start to make enquiries, they will find that there is such a person. A momentary apparition of any person, with no discernible past and no discernible future, is always mysterious to the police; and what is mysterious to them is *always* suspect.

So that, with considerable application, and the laying out of money that I could ill afford, I had set up the following *permanent* characters with whom

I could exchange my own. I flatter myself that my careful attention to the *minutiae* of those idiosyncrasies which distinguish—at least outwardly—one person from another: intonations of speech, tricks of manner, gestures of face and hands, modes of walking and of holding the body: each of these I had, through the closest observation of others, mastered, until I had created—there is no other word—six persons of highly individual mould, all as different from all of the others as chalk is from cheese.

Over the years, the six altered: some dropped out, to be replaced by others. In 1888, an exceptionally busy year for me, I had no fewer than eight 'alternate' identities ready "to post o'er land and ocean without rest", to do my bidding. But at the time that I first met Dr Watson, I had but six, and they were these:—

1. Henry Beatson, aged thirty-four; a clerk out of collar. Had begun work at fourteen with the Titanic & General Fire & Life Insurance Company (ceased trading as a result of a creditors' petition in 1879; a collapse which had thrown Beatson out of work). As assiduous as unsuccessful in his efforts to get regular employment, he eked out a living by such irregular jobs as the addressing of envelopes, delivery of circular-letters, etc. Not above cadging a few coppers by singing at the doors of public-houses and gin-palaces. Unmarried. Lived in a neat room in Barham-street, Camden Town.

2. Albert Edward de Fratteville, aged twenty-eight; a groom out of livery, supporting himself modestly but comfortably as a part-time barman at *The Running Horse*, Shepherd-market; *The Running Footman, The Guinea* and *The Coach and Horses*, all off Berkeley-square. Language laced with racing terms; gave most people the impression that he knew much of horses, and that he was on friendly terms with one or two of the better-known jockeys and trainers. Unmarried. Lived in a room owned by a jobbing-master in a small way of business, owning two stables in Lambeth-mews, Berkeley-square. One conviction—a fine of One Pound—for acting as 'bookie's runner'.

3. Friedrich ('Fritz') Kassel, aged forty-two; German free-lance waiter, employed regularly (mostly at night) at *The Gambrinus Bar*, Glasshouse-street; *Apenrodt's German Restaurant*, Piccadilly-circus, and *Das Muenchener Haus*, Charlotte-street; less frequently at *The Criterion Restaurant* and *The Continental Hotel*. Kept 'out of trouble' by associating mostly with his fellow German nationals. Known to the police after he had volunteered to translate in the case of an arrest in Denman-street, after which he had been regularly called upon to give his services—free—as an interpreter at Vine-street Police Station and Marlborough-street Metropolitan Magistrate's court. Unmarried. Lived in two rooms (with many books and newspapers of the 'respectable' sort, in both German and English) in a shabby house kept by a German widow in Litchfield-street, Charing-cross-road. Popular with his customers, who all called him 'Fritz'.

4. Augustus Walker, aged fifty-six; an ex-schoolmaster, and now 'Travelling Inspector' (*vide* visiting-card) for The British & Imperial Heraldic & Genealogical College of Research, an establishment with (very small) offices, from which this perfectly genuine but not very well known 'College' communicated with the outer world on writing-paper of an extraordinarily impressive nature. By the time that I took up my share of the diggings in Baker-street, the Heraldic College had already acquired not a little of that respectability which comes with age—and it was already some six years old. I had foreseen the need for such a 'cover' (as the Americans now happily call it) as far back as the Long Vacation of 1874, when, at the invitation of my fellow-undergraduate, Victor Trevor, I solved the case of 'The *Gloria Scott*'. As Watson has recorded, I had already—even by that early date—formed habits of observation and inference into a system, although I had not yet fully appreciated the part that they were to play in my life. All the same, I did foresee the need for such an 'imaginary' (perhaps 'factitious' is the more precise word?) headquarters as the Heraldic College, to and from which I might come and go as I pleased, and to which my other *personae* might come without comment from neighbours or the police. Accordingly, in my second year at Caius College, Cambridge, I founded the Heraldic College in two rooms over a Welsh dairy and an antiquarian bookseller's in the Gray's-inn-road, a few yards only from the Royal Free Hospital. This, for me, was a 'cover' of quite unusual value: not only could I visit myself as 'Henry Beatson' and other literate but 'invisible' callers—I employed 'Beatson' on many occasions, as a clerical assistant, mostly to give him money for which he might account; money which was punctiliously entered into the 'College's' day-book. Few doors were kept permanently closed to the Travelling Inspector, Mr Walker, since his peregrinations, which could and often did—take him very far from London, were all concerned, not so much with tracing family-trees, but with tracing 'missing heirs'—a subject on which most people are willing to be respectfully examined. Augustus Walker was a widower. He looked like a widower. No-one ever doubted his claim to be such, and so no-one ever asked about his dead wife. He did not smoke, but took snuff: a mixture of *Rose Rapee*, *Cardinal* and *Paris* that he bought at Smith's, in the Charing-cross-road. He played chess, and spent many hours at *Simpson's*, in the Strand, where, for a shilling, he had a cup of coffee, a cigar (that he took home, since he did not smoke) and watched the Grand Masters play their classic games. Sometimes, at *Simpson's*, he enquired after Mr Sherlock Holmes, and finding that Holmes had not been in recently but 'was expected', Mr Walker left a note, so carelessly closed that all the staff might read it. All such notes concerned the proof of some genealogical link or the hoped-for tracing of a missing heir.

5. Captain Marmaduke Dacre-Buttsworth, aged thirty-five; a somewhat flashy gentleman of vaguely military and positively Turfite background, who dressed well in the silk hat, frock-coat and varnished boots of West End convention, but whose two-pair-back in the Haymarket end of Jermyn-street was furnished for use rather than comfort. Unlike so many others of his type—the

living nexus between the world of the established aristocracy 'on a night out' and the world of seedy tipsters, prize-fighters and (at its lowest) fob-divers and out-and-out panders—the 'Captain' had flown no kites in the several dubious clubs of which he was a member; had drawn no bills or signed promissory notes. The Cork-street 'financiers' knew him not—save by name (and then only to wonder which of their rivals he was patronizing). But, as Captain Dacre-Buttsworth, I could not afford—in both senses of the word—to risk even a judgement-summons as a means of bringing me to the notice of Authority. Of course, I pretended, in my loud boasting to the Duke of Teck at Sandown or to the Duke of Hamilton at the Alsatian Club, that I was heavily in debt to the money-lenders, and that I had to employ a dozen subterfuges to get in and out of lodgings ambushed by the sheriff's officers. But all this was untrue: I did not owe a penny. I know that I was an object of both suspicion and contempt in that I did settle my bills—even at Romano's—but I dared not do otherwise, and that I called down upon me the disdain of the smarter men by settling my bills was the price that I had to pay to be allowed to keep out of the Courts.

Captain Dacre-Buttsworth had been educated at St Cyprian's Academy for Young Gentlemen at Balham (closed, on the death of the proprietor, in 1872); his commission, it was understood, had been gained during the Franco-Prussian War, where he had commanded a company of the French National Guard during the siege of Paris. He played whist well. He was a friend, if not exactly an intimate, of Fred Archer ('The Tinman'), England's greatest jockey. He occasionally, through his knowledge of English genealogy, earned a guinea or two at the Heraldic College in Gray's-inn-road. He was not married, but he was rarely unaccompanied when seen at the Oxford Music Hall or the St James's Restaurant.

6. Mrs Salubria Hempseed, forty-four; a widow. Her husband had been an assistant-manager in a bank at Rainham, Essex, and had died in a railway accident, which made him "too painful to discuss, if you will excuse me!" Mrs Hempseed's afflictions included an inflamed and very red nose, caused by what the medical men call *acne rosacea*, and which is less professionally known as 'grog-blossom' or 'gin-flush'. This affliction Mrs Hempseed, who was of a religious—evangelically religious—turn of mind, attributed to 'God's punishment' for her having once pointed the finger of scorn at a drunkard, as he came reeling out of *The Horseshoe*, in the Tottenham-court-road. Mrs Hempseed lived in one room above an ironmonger's in Marchmont-street, Bloomsbury, which was principally decorated with no fewer than nine photographs of her dead husband and an illuminated testimonial from the Rainham branch of the City & Suburban Bank. She confined her cooking to making tea and boiling an egg on the single gas-ring supplied by a landlady as high-principled as herself. Her days and nights—I am talking of Mrs Hempseed, and not of the landlady—were spent in distributing religious tracts and exhorting women of the streets to change their habit of life. Of all my 'alternative selves', none

was so literally unrecognizable as Mrs Hempseed, since her disturbing nasal
irregularity made it difficult for even the most ill-bred to look her in the face,
lest he might be accused of 'staring'.

Well, there were my six 'characters' as they lined up on the day that I
met Dr Watson. Of course, no serious detective investigation could have
failed to expose the fraudulent—or, at least, the insubstantial—nature of
their greatly differing identities. But no serious investigation was ever un-
dertaken, for the good reason that I took care never to call official attention
to any, from Captain Dacre-Buttsworth to Mrs Salubria Hempseed. The illuminated address in her room in Marchmont-street I bought for five shillings in a second-hand shop in the Hampstead-road. Originally it had borne
the name of a publican and that of his 'house', but for a guinea the illumi-
nating artist in Lincoln's-inn-fields erased the publican's name and address,
and substituted that of the late, 'highly respected', Mr Cuthbert Hempseed.

Looking back over forty years, I think that I may account for my complete identification with these impossible and in many ways grotesque cre-
ations of my fanciful younger self by the fact that *real*—even though sometimes comic or embarrassing—adventures came their way. Imaginary,
fanciful, insubstantial, factitious as they might have been, these creatures of
my imagination were, indeed, given reality by the undeniable fact that they
were swept up into the undeniable reality of living.

For instance, there was the embarrassing encounter between Mrs Hempseed and the Prime Minister of England.

Whatever advantages may be urged for the broad new street connecting
High Holborn and the Strand, there is no doubt that the Clare Market
which was swept away some ten years ago was a much livelier place than
modern Kingsway and Aldwych will ever be.

On one balmy evening in the late autumn of 1880 (I had returned from
the United States in the previous August), Mrs Hempseed, having left her
lodgings in Marchmont-street, and walked to the Strand through Brunswick-
square, Red Lion-street and Chancery-lane, found herself outside charming
old Dane's Inn—now, alas, as so much of our older London, gone beyond
recall! Ahead of her was all the bustle of Holywell-street and Wych-street.
As the clock of St Clement's struck eight, Mrs Hempseed pressed on
through Holywell-street, ignoring, not only the indecent displays of even
more indecent wares in the shop-windows, but no less the invitations to
partake of "half-a-dozen native oysters, with roll and butter, for sixpence";
deaf to the chant of the tout at the door of the snide picture-sale, with his
monotonous "Now on, gentlemen; now on . . .", and caring nothing for
the egg-hawker's cry of "Ten-a-penny, all cracked!" On she went, a sheaf of

tracts clasped in her cotton-mittened hand; past the alley with the outlet in Drury-lane which was the favourite bolt-hole of so many watch-snatchers; on past the doorway of the once red-hot Newmarket Club; past *Short's Wine Bar* and *The Gaiety Bar;* until she found herself outside *The Wellington*, at the corner of Wellington-street and the Strand. And here, as usual, a half-dozen Strandite Cyprians were standing, looking for custom. Mrs Hemp-seed's experienced eye fixed on the least abandoned of the six, and march-ing up to the lady of the night, asked in ringing tones some direct questions pertinent to her occupation *here* and her likely occupation *hereafter.*

Taken aback more by the sight of Mrs Hempseed's crimson 'hooter' than by the personal character of the attack, the young lady paused before an-swering in *her* characteristic way—when, from the direction of the Lyceum Theatre, came another soul-saver: an old gentelman with long grey hair, dark eagle eyes and a nose which, if not so highly coloured as Mrs Hemp-seed's, was quite as commanding. Only Mrs Hempseed recognized, in the proselytizing stranger, the 'Grand Old Man' of British politics—the Right Honourable William Ewart Gladstone, Prime Minister of Great Britain.

Ignoring Mrs Hempseed in his arrogant way, the 'G.O.M.' button-holed the same lady as she on whom Mrs Hempseed had already fired an opening salvo for Redemption. Now doubly angered by this interference with her rightful trade, the Cyprian proclaimed her indignation so loudly and so of-fensively that the point-man on the island in the Strand came over to see what the commotion was all about. The Cyprians he, of course, recog-nized—but, to his astonishment and indignation, he also recognized the old gentleman who had, as it were, usurped Mrs Hempseed's prerogative.

" 'Ere!" said the peeler, fumbling for his billy: "I knows *you!* You're the ole bloke as got hisself pinched in 'Yde Park or Piccadilly for a-doin' exactly of what you're a-doin' of now—*molestin' females!*" *

"Be off with you, my man!" The Prime Minister ordered, with a pe-remptory (and not very courteous) shake of his walking-cane.

"Ho! it's like *that*, is it, then?" said the pride of 'E' Division: "Well, it's Bow-street *you* gets, me ole cockalorum!" And with that the constable ad-vanced to make what seemed now the inevitable arrest.

I doubted that my disguise would stand up against the scrutiny of the

* This is true: Mr Gladstone was actually arrested in Hyde Park and charged with having 'molested females'—and, despite his loud protestations of innocence and a lot of indignant Vic-torian "Do you know who I am, my man?", was carted off to the local police-office. After this painful episode, the Grand Old Man judged it more prudent to take his Wife with him on his tour of the Haymarket and Piccadilly Cyprians—not all of whom shewed him the respect that his 'devoted service to the Nation' ought to have earned him. But—sometimes (even after the episode of the arrest)—Mrs Gladstone could not accompany him; and, rather than let the great work of Redemption suffer, the Grand Old Man went out alone, as we have seen.—*Editor*

Chief Metropolitan Magistrate and the sharp-eyed ushers and young barristers of the court—in any case, I had no wish to appear as a witness in *any* court; in *any* case. And what quickened my decision to rescue Mr Gladstone—I should have said, what quickened *Mrs Hempseed's* decision to rescue Mr Gladstone—was the sight of Arthur William Hill, contributor of 'Vigilant's Note Book' to *The Sportsman*, the leading article to *The Newcastle Daily Chronicle*, and a regular article to *The Manchester Sporting Telegraph* (of which esteemed journal he was for a time the Editor) headed obviously in our direction.

Hill—facetiously called 'Kangaroo' in playful allusion to his trouserial rotundity and a temporary sojourn in New South Wales—was as obviously far from sober. It was clear that he had left his frowsty lodgings in Cecil-street to open a keg of nails at the old Adelphi Club—I use his terminology—and followed that with a few *steins* of *Muenchener Loewenbräu* at Darmstatter's German restaurant and bar. It was imperative that Hill be diverted before he came up to what the penny-journalists call a *fracas;* for if Mr Gladstone did not know Mr Hill, the same could not be said of the reverse. I beckoned the constable to one side; and, rather reluctantly, he stepped aside a pace or two.

"Young man," I said, with all the authority at my command: "I have no wish to see you ruin your career for a paltry business like this—but ruin it you surely will if you persist in arresting this elderly person. So I warn you: leave the matter alone!"

"What's it to you, ma'am?" he asked, rudely. "Why should I let him go? Is he a relation of yourn?"

"He is nothing to me, constable. Carry on: arrest him if you like. But remember who he is!"

"And who is he, then?"

"Sir Charles Warren, constable—and don't say that I didn't give you fair warning!"

As the constable beat a hasty retreat from the supposed Commissioner of Metropolitan Police, I drew Mr Gladstone aside.

"Mr Prime Minister," I said: "do you see a very fat man, just passing Gow's—and headed straight for us? Well, that is Mr Hill, Editor of *The Manchester Sporting Telegraph*. He is a hopeless inebriate—I know, because I have failed to turn him from drink—and he is no supporter, either of you, sir, or of your Party. I should advise you to follow the constable up Wellington-street or take this hansom."

Hill came up just as Gladstone was closing the apron of the hanson. The fat man stared, frowning.

"Gladstone, for a pound!" I heard him mutter. He turned to me. "Was it

Mr Gladstone, ma'am?"—wincing as he saw Mrs Hempseed's strawberry nose.

"I am sure that I could not tell you," I answered, coldly. "I have not the honour of the Prime Minister's acquaintance. However, I should say that it was unlikely that Mr Gladstone could spare time from his pressing political duties. Young man, let us be practical: ARE YOU TO BE A BRAND SAVED FROM THE BURNING? I—"

"Excuse *me* ma'am, but I find that I have a very pressing engagement."

He raised his hat, and hurried off, as fast as his immense weight would permit him, in the direction of *The Gaiety Bar*.

Years later, as I sat in the Cabinet Room, talking to Mr Gladstone of the second "Adventure of the Second Stain",* and observing sadly how political defeat, no less than extreme age, had blunted the force of "that white-hot face, stern as a Covenanter's yet mobile as a comedian's, those restless, flashing eyes", of which an admiring opponent has written, I wondered if even those "flashing eyes" could have recognized in me the preposterous female tract-walloper who had saved him from disgrace and—yes, I am sure—political extinction, over a decade earlier?

To Captain Dacre-Buttsworth, too, came unsought adventure—unsought involvement in matters which might have endangered the carefully contrived but essentially insubstantial *persona* of that gentleman of shadowy antecedents and dubious connections.

The Captain had just enjoyed a modest supper at the Cavendish Hotel in Jermyn-street, and 'looked in' (as they say) for a b. & s. at the *Criterion American Bar*, and had just stepped out into Regent-circus,† when he observed a considerable commotion on his left—a crowd of blackguards from the Haymarket, all armed with broken bottles and tumblers, were attacking a tall man, who, with his back to the wall at the side of the Criterion Theatre's entrance, was defending himself with amazing courage and—as I saw when two of the foremost ruffians went staggering back into the road—with not a little fistic skill. That the victim of this brutal and cowardly assault was a gentleman, I did not deduce from his now-torn frock-coat or the silk hat which lay crushed at his feet; I could see from the man's *bearing* and a something unmistakable of what the French call *race*. It was almost impossible to see the lone combatant's face, so cut and streaked with blood was it; and it was apparent that the broken glass—the 'shivs'—had already inflicted fearful injury. It was no time now to consider the preservation of 'Captain Dacre-Buttsworth's' delicate identity: without hesitation, I seized two of the

---

* This is the only occasion on which Mr Holmes refers to this business of the *second* "Second Stain", but *see* the late W. Baring-Gould's *Sherlock Holmes of Baker Street.—Editor*

† Now called 'Piccadilly-circus'.—*Editor*

ruffians by their collars, and, hurling them out of the way, jumped over the two prone bodies to stand by the gentleman's side.

"You're not alone, sir, now!" I said, now, for the first time, seeing that the blood-dabbled hair was white.

"Thank God for that!" said the old man, still hitting out as (I learned afterwards) he had hit out at both Pekin and Lucknow. "Where on earth are the peelers!"

But now the ruffians had another victim, and half the band—there must have been a round dozen of these larrikins—began to close on me. I raised my cane to my lips, and blew two long trills on the police-whistle hidden in the knob—and, that done, I drew nearly a yard of shining Solingen steel from the sword-stick, warding off two attacks with *savate* kicks as I did so.

To one who had studied fencing under such a tutor as Bencin, it was child's play to keep the blackguards at bay, even as the trills of answering police-whistles began to sound from all the side-streets. I pinked two or three of the ruffians and the ring began to fall back. I caught sight of the dark blue Roman helmets with the silver badges of the always-missing-when-they're-needed constabulary. But at that moment, I was in no mood to carp at their habitual tardiness—I was so glad to see them that I shouted: "Officers! Over here!" even as the cry, "Nark it! It's the pigs!" * sent the attackers scurrying; though not before three had been caught by the advancing police. And now the crowd which, with its customary apathy, had been willing to see an old gentleman half-murdered by a gang of cowardly brutes, acquired some courage from the presence of the police—or acquired some shame: perhaps both. At any rate, as the rest of the ruffians, throwing their glasses and bottles away, tried to force their way through the dense crowd, three or four were tripped up, and these, truncheoned into insensibility and handcuffed to each other, made up no fewer than nine due to appear at Bow-street on the following morning.

But first we carried the victim, fearfully gashed and bleeding from a dozen savage cuts, into the hall of the Criterion, whilst one of the waiters ran off to Jozeau, the Haymarket chemist, for assistance, and another hurried off to fetch a doctor. I called for warm water and sponge to begin to clean up the blood-stained face—imagine my horror and indignation when I discovered that, at some time in the past, the subject of my ministrations had been involved in some accident so grave that it appeared to have lifted the top of his head off. A terrible scar ran completely around his head—and that anyone should have ventured to attack (and that so brutally) a man already gravely mutilated, filled me with such indignation that my hand trembled as I gently washed the blood away.

* There is nothing new about this term of opprobrium for the police; it dates from at least as far back as the eighteenth century.—*Editor*

Jozeau's man arrived, with iodine and gauze and all other necessary things; and I first accompanied the victim to Charing Cross Hospital—where I discovered that I had rescued none other than the redoubtable (and eccentric) Major 'Bob' Hope-Johnstone, favourite aide-de-camp of the Commander-in-Chief, and unsuccessful claimant to the abeyant marquessate of Annandale—and then went back with the police-inspector and his serjeant to Vine-street, to make a statement.

It is not my usual practice to dictate such statements, but here prudence counselled a departure from my customary behaviour. I had no desire to play the hero; to give the police a version of the incident out of which some police-court reporter, hunting for 'copy', would concoct a wildly romantic story which would bring me the last thing that I wished: the notice of the public.

As it was, it was touch-and-go, for Major Hope-Johnstone had permanently closed the right eye of one of his assailants; but, as my luck would have it, it was the Major on whom the attention of the Court reporters became fixed; *he* was the hero—and rightly so. It was about *him* that the reporters, to my relief, wrote columns for their newspapers. And, to calm my fears even more, the reporters had faulted both the rank and the name of Captain Marmaduke Dacre-Buttsworth. He appeared briefly and unimportantly as "a witness to this cowardly assault, who summoned the police by a blast on his whistle". Not a word, thank goodness!, of the Captain's having defied the gang, sword-stick in hand, and wounded, as well as repelled, not a few. Such small credit as the newspapers decided to award went to 'Colonel Archibald Akers-Douglas', an entry in the historical record that the family of the present Viscount Chilston may find puzzling.

Only one small happening came to ruffle the surface of my contentment as I walked down the few steps to the pavement outside Bow-street Magistrate's Court. A voice—a voice that I knew only too well!—murmured:

"I am about to have a bottle of Boy—Moët & Chandon, I think, since both Her Majesty and the Heir drink it; and they can afford the best—at *Romano's*. Will you join me? It occurred to me that they might not have got your name right—I heard some of the reporters giving quite an incorrect name to the others—and it then occurred to me that you might need some fortifying against the shock of seeing your name misspelt in *The Star* or, worse still, *The St James's Gazette*. Shall we take this hansom?"

It was 'Kangaroo' Hill, the cleverest as well as the most impudent of all those well-educated, fundamentally lazy, effortlessly brilliant men who, living a life of the most unregulated Bohemianism, brought English journalism to a splendour which has been equalled neither before or since.

Wittily described by a brother-scribe as "unconventional to a fault and having as little veneration for ancient lineage as a chicken born in an incuba-

tor", Hill, besides being "a skilled and gentlemanly exponent of turf literature", was, in my opinion at least, one of the shrewdest men whom I ever
knew—but with a shrewdness, like that of Lucius Brutus, hidden beneath a
well-carried affectation of seemingly stupid irresponsibility.

There were innumerable stories told about Hill. One of the most representative—they were all true, by the way—was of his returning to England
from Australia, to see most of his school-fellows grown up, and usually
unrecognizable.

One day, Hill saw one whom he did recognize: a portly gentleman
pounding across Newmarket Heath on a coal-black cob.

"Hi, Bentinck!" Hill shouted. "Pull up, dash you! Pull up!"

The horseman, unhearing or unheeding, swept by, whilst some brother
scribblers, suitably shocked—or affecting to be—told Hill who the horseman was.

"What?" Hill cried. "Is *he* the Duke of Portland? Why, the last time we
were out together, I lent the beggar five bob!"—which was as true as any
recollection of a man's schooldays may be.

This, then, was the man with whom I was now seated behind the closed
apron of a hansom, whose mare, in fine early-morning fettle, was stepping
it out briskly as we went down Wellington-street, making for the Strand.

But it was not until 'the Roman'—*Romano's* still is with us, though somewhat dimmed as to glory; but Romano himself is gone to that Land where
is credit but no more giving of credit—until 'the Roman', I say, had
snapped his ringed Italian fingers at a crop-poll German waiter to fetch us
the champagne that Hill had already ordered, that 'Kangaroo' returned to
the subject that he had delicately hinted at in the entrance to the Magistrate's Court. He waited until Fritz had poured out two glasses of Moët &
Chandon; and then, after a silent raising of his glass, he said bluntly:

"No-one has a name like 'Dacre-Buttsworth' outside of the novels that
they print in *The Pink 'Un*. It's just too pat to be true. *Ergo*, it isn't true.
And, by the same token, one might enquire the why and the wherefore of a
nom de guerre which is a reproach to every man who can't see through a
simple pun. And, equally by the same token, one might enquire what is the
real name that so humorous a concoction as 'Dacre-Buttsworth' hides? "

Now I truly was puzzled. For the first time that I might remember since
I had left the ignorance of childhood behind me, *I did not know what the other
man was talking about!*

"Pun . . . ?" I murmured, not having anything else to say.

"Well," said Hill, "the slang term has gone out of fashion; but both my
grandfather and my father used it a lot. 'Lady Dacre's wine'—you know the
expression, of course?"

But I shook my head.

"You don't? You honestly don't?"

"No, I've never heard the expression. I imagine that all of us must have missed knowing what is common knowledge to many others. What does it mean?"

"Extraordinary! I'd never have credited it—I mean to say: that I'd ever find anyone who honestly didn't know what 'Lady Dacre's wine' was. I suppose you don't know who Lady Dacre was?"

"Indeed I do. She was the very rich lady of the last century—or, perhaps, of the century before—who founded almshouses and schools and on whose land most of Victoria-street and the tributary streets have been built."

"You know this, I take it, because the lady is a collateral of your family?"

"Precisely."

"And you don't know, then, what 'Lady Dacre's wine' is?"

"No; I have told you that I don't. What is it?"

"Well . . . if you say that you *don't* know: it's gin."

"It's a slang phrase for gin? No, I didn't know that."

"So, as you see, the name 'Buttsworth' after that of 'gin' . . . a butt's worth of gin . . . Do you wonder that I thought your name a little suspect?"

"No. Except that there are hundreds of such names—names which appear to be significant phrases. Obviously, mine is such a name. Equally obviously, if its significance had struck any one of my family, he—or she—would have changed it."

Hill stared at me, then nodded, and then, winking his right eye, laid his finger along his nose in a gesture as expressive as vulgar.

"All right, then," he said; "I shalln't peach. But are you a 'D'? * You may even be Captain Dacre-Buttsworth, for all that I know—or care. But you're not 'one of the Boys', for all that you wear a suit brighter than any that even the well-known Billy Savernake, 'Ducks' Ailesbury, would dare to wear.† (I'm talking, of course, of when you go to Sandown or Newmarket; not of your perhaps rather too sober garb of the present moment.)"

"I have never pretended to be, as you put it, 'one of the Boys'. I like racing—I wear the customary clothes for a meeting. I bet; I—"

"Ah, but that's just *it!* You *bet*. Of course. But you *pay*. Why, you've got more credit with Charlie Head or any of the other bookies than Lord Durham or Prince Soltykoff or the Duchess of Montrose—for though they

* A detective.—*Editor*

† George William Thomas, 4th Marquess of Ailesbury and Viscount Savernake; *b.* 1863, *d.* 1894, reputed to be the most insolent and foul-mouthed Turfite of his day. Nicknamed 'Ducks' after the town of Aylesbury (note the spelling), famous for its ducklings.—*Editor*

do pay up when they lose, they don't always pay up slap-bang, as I know that you invariably do."

"Short reckonings make long friendships, as the French say."

Hill snorted.

"To h-ll with the French—and, in any case, what friendships have you with Charlie Head and his like that you should wish to preserve them? Be sensible, Captain: *what's the dodge?*"

"I'm sure that I can't say," I answered, with well-affected unconcern. "But this must surely be the first time in the world's history that a man came under suspicion because he paid his debts—or, rather, paid them promptly." I signed to Fritz to replenish the wine-cooler. "And now, perhaps you will permit *me* to ask a question? Of what, exactly, am I suspected?"

"Oh, that's easily answered," said Hill, cheerfully. "I suspect you of being something different from what you have taken such trouble to appear. That's all. I thought that you might be a 'D'—you say that you're not; and I don't much care for the notion myself, seeing what the usual 'D' sounds like. So we'll agree that you're not a 'D'. But, then, that leaves us with the question: what precisely *are* you?"

"Captain Marmaduke Dacre-Buttsworth—at your service."

"Yes . . . I suppose so. Shall we drop the subject?"

"With pleasure," I said. "Have you another subject to discuss?"

"Yes. Bob Hope-Johnstone. I wonder why they attacked him? You know, and I know—and, presumably, the mob knows—that poor old Bob hasn't a ha' penny to rattle on a tombstone."

"But he is a gentleman—and dressed as a gentleman—"

"My dear good man, a Haymarket mob of cads will not bestir itself save in what it considers, not merely a good, but a profitable, cause. They must have thought that our Crimean and Mutiny hero had a sufficiency of the spondulicks, to have lured them out of their kennels to spiflicate him. *You* know—at least, I assume that you do?—and *I* know that the poor old chap is stoney, but why did that mob think differently? Pity you're *not* a 'D'—otherwise you might have made a stab at the answer!"

I was anxious, as one may well imagine, to change the subject. I said negligently, "At least, I was able to do the Major a good turn. A few minutes more, and those brutes would have killed him."

"Yes, indeed. Well, Buttsworth, I don't know why they should have attacked him; but you certainly did yourself no disservice in coming to his rescue. The Hope-Johnstones always remember their obligations."

There were, as I afterwards found out, good reasons for a gang's having attacked Major Hope-Johnstone—though those reasons did not concern me.

But, in one respect, 'Kangaroo' Hill was right: I had done myself no disservice by my coming to the aid of the Major, for all that it was rather 'Captain' Dacre-Buttsworth than Mr Sherlock Holmes who proved to be the beneficiary of an impulsive action to protect another.

Yet, despite the benefits that Hill confidently promised me as a result of my having helped the Major, it was not any possible advantage to come from the Hope-Johnstone 'connexion' which occupied my thoughts for that and for several succeeding days. To tell the truth, I had been not a little alarmed by Hill's openly doubting my identity—and not a little disgusted with myself that I should have given him cause to doubt it. I look back upon that doubting, though, as one of the most important happenings of my life.

Hill was a shrewd man, to be sure—but there were (whether or not I had met them) many far more shrewd. If there were, to arouse Hill's suspicion, that certain, albeit trivial, element of the *not quite right* in the counterfeit personality of 'Captain Marmaduke Dacre-Buttsworth', it would be not the less present—and dangerous to me—in the acute observation of those shrewder than was Hill.

One lesson that near-revelation of my imposture had taught me: that 'nearly right' is never 'quite right'—and that I had relied upon mere *disguise* to serve me as only *a complete assumption of identity* could do. I realized that my assumed *persona* of 'Dacre-Buttsworth' was only superficial (though I had thought otherwise), and that I should have, as Henry Irving or another of my more famous theatrical friends might have said, 'to go more deeply into character'.

This I did. Dacre-Buttsworth was not abandoned—that would have been fatal; nor did he become more 'one of the Boys' by some financial irregularity more in keeping with a cashiered-or-never-commissioned Captain: that would have been even more dangerous. I 'retained' the *persona* of the Captain, but, to borrow a phrase from the painters, I 'filled in the background'.

On the following day, I caught the Gunter's Arms 'bus from Coventry-street to the bottom of Fleet-street, and after a sherry-and-bitters and a free Welsh rarebit at the *King Lud*—not, of course, in my *persona* of Captain Dacre-Buttsworth, but in that of Augustus Walker, of the Imperial Heraldic College—I visited the bookstalls in Farringdon-road, and bought three 16mo. Bibles for threepence each. For a further three guineas—paid in gold and silver—a 'reformed' forger of my acquaintance annotated the Bibles to provide evidence of the existence of the Dacres and the Buttsworths (and their collaterals) over the past two centuries. One of these annotated Bibles I 'forgot' in *The Adelphi Club*—the old 'Spooferies', to which

Kangaroo was a frequent visitor—; another I also 'forgot' to collect, after having asked the porter of *The Star Club*, in Denman-street, to 'be sure and don't lose it'; the third I left in the *Criterion Bar*, and recovered it by advertising for it in *The Times* and *The Daily Telegraph*. By the time that a week had gone by, I felt reasonably certain that all the London which mattered to Captain Dacre-Buttsworth knew that his name, at least, was genuine. And now let us return to the leg of pork, somewhat rapidly corrupting (in those days before electric refrigerators) in Mrs Hudson's larder.

There is not a great deal left to tell. The man-of-all-work brought up the meat with a red handkerchief held to his nose.

I had, I saw, failed to remove the tattoo-marks by the indigotin disulphonic acid that I had synthesized by the action of fuming sulphuric acid on indigo; now I resolved to essay the powers of the leuco-form of indigo, which differs from the other in that it is made, as I said, by using an alkaline reducing agent, rather than an acid.

The leuco-form was equally useless to remove the marks. So far as I could tell, tatooing *was* indelible—a fact that I was sure would be of interest to both Serjeant Ballantine and Sir Henry. Now all that was left was to rid myself—and our apartments—of the appalling stench of the pork.

I lit a couple of those joss-sticks that Barritt, the perfumer, of Charing-cross-road, used to sell—but that only made the noxious aroma even more noxious. I moved the bell-handle by the fireplace, and, after a few minutes, the old handyman appeared.

"Get rid of this!" I told him, adding a shilling to the order. Clapping a different handkerchief—blue, this time—to his nose, he carried off the offending meat.

I mention these seeming trivialities, for they were to have important results.

Watson, I recall, came in about ten o'clock: he had been at the Victoria Club, playing billiards with Tom Tuffey, five hundred up, fifty shillings a-side. (It was as well for both of us that he won!)

No sooner had he opened the door of our sitting-room than he clapped his fingers to his nose, and cried out:

"Gracious goodness! what is that appalling smell? Holmes, this really is too bad of you! Chemical experiments . . . yes: you warned me of them. But this smells like a dissecting-room . . . in an Indian temple!"

I laughed, and told him what I had been doing. It was indiscreet of me—how indiscreet, I was not to know until the following day—but Watson's indignation was so comical that my judgement, for the moment, was at fault.

"Tattoo-marks . . . ?" he echoed; his indignation vanishing in his always-easily-aroused interest. "By Jove! you think that they may be removed?"

"As to that, I could not say. Let us settle the matter for the moment by saying that I have embarked upon some tests."

"And made an infernal stench in doing so? Are you sure that you have opened *all* the windows?"

"Is the fire as hot as all that?"

"I don't know how I shall be able to sleep in this stink. Hasn't Mrs Hudson complained?"

"Not yet. But I shall be astonished if she don't. Light another joss-stick, and I'll fill up with Navy. . . ."

The sequel was quicker in coming than sequels usually are.

As I came into our sitting-room on the following night, I found Watson awaiting me, my copy of Reade's *Martyrdom of Man* open on the red plush tablecloth at his elbow. He did not look so much worried as irritated, and I guessed—rightly, as it turned out—that one of my visitors had annoyed him.

"Which of my callers," I asked lightly, taking off my ulster and shaking the night-dew from my hat, "has managed to put you in the dumps?"

"How did you . . ." he began; and then, smiling a little at his own irritation, he continued: "It was that Scotland Yard man. . . ."

"Which one?" I asked, moving to the fire, so as to warm my hand. "Gregson?"

"No, the other. The one with the foreign name."

"Lestrade. Not exactly foreign; it's a Channel Islands name. And what's Lestrade done to annoy you?"

"Oh, he came in, making a great to-do about the smell of—well, of whatever it was that you were experimenting on or with last night . . . yesterday. He really is an odious man, Holmes; *must* you admit him to terms of such intimacy?"

"I'm afraid that I must," I said, moving from the fire to the sideboard, to pour myself a whisky. "I can hardly take a retaining fee from Scotland Yard and refuse to know their officers. But—yes, let us admit his vulgarity— what *precisely* did he say or do to irritate you?"

"Oh, I don't know. After having gone through a perfect pantomime of his pretending to have been asphyxiated by the deadly fumes—Holmes, I really cannot describe this clown's ludicrous behaviour! He kept on shouting 'My canary-bird's done me down; my canary-bird's done me down! I'm *dying!*' Holmes: what on earth did he mean? What has a—why should he be talking of a canary-bird? To be honest with you, I think that the most charitable explanation of his behaviour would be to assume that he was drunk."

I laughed.

"Perhaps he was. But his reference to a canary-bird is no proof of that. Coal-miners take a canary-bird down with them so that the creature may detect the presence of fire-damp. No, Doctor, I am afraid that vulgarity is the most which may be charged against our friend Lestrade. Was it that which annoyed you?"

"Indeed not. There was much more. I certainly cannot recall most of the rubbish that the man talked, but one remark was so extraordinary that— but, well, Holmes: he suddenly shouted, through a handkerchief that he held up to his nose: 'Want a pen-and-ink!' I thought that he wished to leave a note for you; so I said: 'There's pen and ink on that desk, if you need them.' Upon which, he gave a great bellow of a laugh, and said, 'Tell Holmes to get the place fumigated before I come again!' Why, if he needed a pen and ink, did he not avail himself of my offer?"

I laid my hand on the Doctor's shoulder.

"I am afraid, my dear Watson," I said, "that you will have to adjust your sentiments to a very different way of life, if you continue to share these apartments. Lestrade is, indeed, what you find him; but, knowing that, bear in mind that his speech is that of the Cockney. He was not asking you for writing materials—he did not say, as you thought that he said—'*Want* a pen and ink!', but '*What* a pen-and-ink!' 'Pen-and-ink', my dear Doctor, is Cockney for 'stink'. Did you not know this? Well, well: Lestrade shall, I have no doubt, teach you much more of this quaint dialect. And what did you answer him when he complained of the—I admit, most offensive— smell?"

"I . . . ? I merely told him that the odour was the result of one of your chemical experiments."

"I know Lestrade well. I shall be astonished if you tell me that he did not ask you on what I was experimenting."

"Well, as a matter of fact, he did."

"And did you tell him?"

"Not really. I was not in a position to do so. I merely said that you were trying to eradicate the marks of tattooing. Did I do wrong?"

"Let us say that I had rather you had not been so specific. But, pray, don't look so dejected. I expect that no harm has been done. But remember this: Lestrade *always* asks questions; he will think you contemptibly green if you do him the favour of answering them."

But in reassuring myself that no harm had been done by Dr Watson's in- discreet candour, I was mistaken—as I was to discover before long.

SEVEN

At The Pelican *Club*

I have said that my bold interference to save Major Hope-Johnstone from the mob in Regent-circus was to serve me well; and so it proved. I was thereafter received—as Captain Dacre-Buttsworth, of course—by the decidedly dubious company of *The Adelphi*, *The Star* (re-named *The Pelican*), *The Flamingo*, *The Victoria* and similar clubs, not merely as 'one of the Boys', but as one of themselves. As a class, the membership of such clubs, which included the regular custom of such bars as *Romano's*, *The Cri'*, *Jimmy's* and *Jubber's*,* as well as *Evans's*, *The Coal Hole*, *The Continental* and *The Gaiety*, were not given overmuch to that sentimental-intellectual exercise known to Carlyle as 'hero-worship'; and so I never became a hero in these places.

But—these subtle shades of *standing* are not at all easily defined—I had, by my impulsive and vigorous defence of a man whom they all admired, put myself into a new position *vis-à-vis* my company. A casual visitor to those places at which, in their gratitude for my having saved the Major, I was treated 'differently', might not have noticed even the slightest difference in the 'regulars'' attitude towards me. My fellow-guests of the fourth-rate hotels and restaurants, my fellow-members of the sixth-rate clubs, still touched me for 'the odd jimmy o' goblin,† dear old chap?'; still invited me to sit in on games of skill and chance in which their own mastery was undoubted; mine, scarcely more than that of a tyro. They still practised, at my expense, the same small frauds—never greater in yield than what was needed to settle a pressing bar-bill or stand a round of popularity-supporting drinks.

The men—for it was an exclusively masculine society—who comprised

---

* '*Jimmy's*' was the bar of the old St James's Restaurant, in Piccadilly, demolished in 1905; '*Jubber's*' was the 'in' name of Long's Hotel (favoured by Byron), at the corner of Bond-street and Clifford-street.—*Editor*

† 'Jimmy o' goblin'=a sovereign, the gold £1.—*Editor*

the constantly changing membership of this socially unclassifiable association of the (for the most part) impecunious idle, were of all sorts, both as regards nominal occupations and as regards their defined social ranks. These ranks they kept, whilst entering the no-rank companionship of what I may call, for purposes of generalization, 'the *Pelican* Class'. The common bond uniting such originally different persons as Hugh Drummond,* "best and brightest of the sons of the morning", as his fellow-Pelicans, Arthur Binstead and Ernest Wells, have called him in print,† and, say, 'Repartee' Robbins, 'the man who was never nonplussed'; the 'Mate' (Sir John Astley, I add, for readers of the far future) and Fatty Coleman; Lord Queensberry (the one who put Mr Wilde in gaol) and Teddy Solomon, organizer of the club's smoking concerts; 'Billy' Fitzwilliam ** and Ike Lyons, the *schlemiel;* 'Kim' Mandeville †† and 'Chops' Trussell;—the common bond was, like the Caesar's Gaul of our schooldays, or the head of Cerberus, three-fold: a common addiction to the Turf; a temporary or chronic lack of money; and a resolution, not merely to avoid paying, but to court indebtedness—whether to a Cork-street moneylender for fifty thousand; to Charlie Head, the bookie, for a monkey; or the somnolent cabby from the Glasshouse-street rank for the fare to Old Barrack-yard.

No-one paid, unless forced to do so. Clubs were opened on 'capital' which was completely credit—with the landlord owed for the rent, the builders for the alterations, the upholsterers for the furniture, the electricians for the wiring and fittings, the local tradesmen for the food and as much of the cellar as might be stocked 'on tick'. If these never-paid tradesmen failed to close the premises down, the members, by refusing to pay either subscriptions or dining-room bills, got there first. *The Pelican* was a most popular club: when Hugh Drummond led a party of its members to invade and attack, with no inconsiderable display of force, the officers' quarters at St James's Palace, and Colonel Brabazon, collecting a party of his toughest young bloods, got into hansoms to avenge the assault-at-arms—the Colonel leading the attacking party because the Pelicans' assault had been witnessed by H.R.H. the Prince of Wales—the Guardsmen, with their Colonel, stayed after the furniture-breaking and eye-blacking battle, to enjoy the hospitality of the club, and, in many instances, to join it.

I came in that night as Colonel Brabazon, with blood over his shirt-front

---

* Of the family of Viscount Strathallen—the Drummonds who had founded the aristocratic Drummonds' Bank.—*Editor*

† Presumably Mr Holmes alludes here to their joint book, *A Pink 'Un and a Pelican;* London: Sands & Company, (first edition) March, 1898. It was a popular work, several times reprinted.—*Editor*

** The Honourable William Reginald Wentworth-Fitzwilliam, 4th son (they were all named 'William') of William, 6th Earl Fitzwilliam, K.G.—*Editor*

†† Later 8th Duke of Manchester; married Consuelo Yznaga, of U.S.A.—*Editor*

and waistcoat, was being 'introduced' to 'Chops' Thrussell (so called because, irritated, he had once thrown a friend through the plate-glass window of a Regent-circus chop-house on to the red-hot grill), whilst Phil May,
only slightly drunk, was making a rapid sketch of the two strangely-con-
trasted chance-mets for that week's *Black and White*. As 'Chops' once observed to the club in general: "Say wot yer like, yer do meet the *toffs*
'ere!"—and the original membership committee bears him out: the Marquess of Queensberry; Lord Mandeville (afterwards Duke of Manchester);
Lord de Clifford; Lord Churston; the Honourable Daniel Finch, the Honourable Clement Finch; * Sir John Astley, Bart ('The Mate'); Captain Archibald Drummond, Scots Guards; John Corlett, 'Master' of the *Pink
'Un*—and all his talented staff of artists and writers, two of whom had
founded the club—; Walter Dickson ('Dicky the Driver'), the greatest whip
of the last century; George Edwardes, who has since become (at Daly's
Theatre) our greatest impresario—and several others, though of rank somewhat inferior to that of the Duke and the Marquess. I give these names to
explain how it was that when, for unpaid rent, 'the man in possession' took
up his quarters in *The Pelican*, and was, though far less sober than he had
been on arrival, got rid of with the leisurely-collected arrears of rent, he
should have taken his temporary farewell of us Pelicans in the following af-
fectionate terms:

"Me lords an' gentlemen, it's sorry indeed I am to leave yer—but I still
'ave 'opes; and tonight I shall pray on me biscuits † as I shall be put in 'ere
every quarter-day 's long 's I live! Wiv all respeck—*good*-day!"

As I said, no club was more popular than *The Pelican*—but the members,
and not their creditors, brought about its certain ruin. Banded together in
an emotional defiance of Debt—by whomever or whatever represented—
they forgot to exclude their own well-loved and most useful club from the
ranks of the Enemy. I recall going to have a wash-and-brush-up, and finding this notice wafered on to the chimney-glass of the cloak-room:—

N O T I C E
Members who have reason to believe
that Writs, Judgments, or any other
Legal Blisters are out against them,
are warned against Washing, etc.,
downstairs, as

THE CLUB LAVATORY IS FULL OF BAILIFFS.

* Sons of the 6th Earl of Aylesford.—*Editor*

† 'Biscuits', in Cockney rhyming slang, is 'knees'. ('Biscuits' is the colloquially contracted
form of 'biscuits-and-cheese', which rhymes with, and therefore means, 'knees'.)—*Editor*

But not even that could make the members 'brass up', and the club eventually foundered, leaving the outraged members to complain, to the barmen of *The Cri'*, *Jimmy's*, *Jubber's*, *The Alsatian*, end the rest, that they didn't know what things were coming to!

The Pelican, as I see by my diary, opened on a wet, cold night of January, 1887; it was like a famous brand of whisky, 'still going strong' when I 'disappeared' on Monday, 4th May, 1891, at Meiringen, in Switzerland.

When I returned on Thursday, 5th April, 1894, it was to find that *The Pelican* had closed down; that Watson had begun to publish my over-romanticized adventures in the new *Strand Magazine;* that he had lost his wife through valvular disease of the heart, in the early part of 1892; and that, only a few weeks before Mrs Watson had died, Prince 'Eddy' had, by a terrible but just decision, left his place vacant for a brother more fitted to be a King.

I once asked Dr Watson to meet me at *The Pelican*.

"It's a new place," I explained; "and I hear that it's not too bad. Queensberry and Mandeville and Churston are on the committee—"

"That's no great recommendation."

"Possibly not. But from what I hear, it might be a useful place to join. One could have a sherry, read the papers. At any rate, a man I know has invited me to look in. I'm going. Would you care to join me there later?"

Mr Sherlock Holmes had left his apologies for Dr Watson; but the member, Captain Dacre-Buttsworth, was 'happy to look after Mr Holmes's friend'.

Dr Watson and the Captain had a drink or two; played two games of a hundred up on the rather worn baize—Dr Watson won the first game; the Captain, his revenge—and then, sitting in the Library, the Captain tried to discuss Mr Holmes. In a huff of—as it happened—quite misplaced loyalty, Dr Watson excused himself. He told me that he did not like *The Pelican;* he didn't like what he had seen of its membership; he particularly disliked Captain Dacre-Buttsworth, and took leave to cast doubts on the quality of his commission ("I can't imagine any officer, outside of the pages of Ouida, calling his servant a 'batman'—but, then, you never know what *anything's* coming to, these days—even the Army!") and expressed himself firmly on the subject of his never returning to "that perfectly *dreadful* place"—"Holmes, you missed *nothing*—nothing at all! I assure you that, had you seen it, you have felt about it as I felt—*quite* outside consideration!"

This suited me excellently. Even though Mr Holmes had not yet visited, *in propria persona*, *The Pelican*, I did not wish that Dr Watson should become a member, least of all an habitué. That he disliked the club suited me very well.

As for me, or, rather, my professional needs, the club suited excellently—no other place that I can imagine was so generous in its yield of information or of hints as to where information might be got.

The Pelican had not been founded as a resort of criminals, nor were they criminals who resorted to it; but they were all racing-men, supporters of the Turf. That is to say that, though several of the members—indeed, many— were members of some of our most exclusive hunts, their main interest in horses derived from the money that they hoped to win from them. And Racing is an activity which attracts rogues as sugar attracts wasps. What Mr Baron Alderson had to say at the close of the *Running Rein* case, forty years earlier, applied no less in the days when *The Pelican* opened its doors in Denman-street on 19th January, 1887:

> . . . If gentlemen would make it a rule to associate only with gentlemen, such practices [*as the 'Running Rein' swindle*] would be impossible. But if gentlemen will condescend to race with blackguards, they must expect to be cheated.

When bookmakers are considered fair game to be cheated even by gentlemen, then it is idle to pretend that one is not in a society where at least a strong element of criminality is present, even if the society do not deserve altogether the condemnation as criminal.

It was a tolerant society, that of *The Pelican*, and one may half-sympathize with those persons of rigid morality who see rather in tolerance than in the love of money the root of all evil; for, from a free-and-easy attitude towards owing money, these Pelicans had long come to an equally free-and-easy attitude towards cheating—at first in its pettier forms of bilking cabbies and diddling tradesmen; then to the more serious forms involving stumer cheques and irregular promissory-notes—and from *that* tolerance, it was not difficult to regard the graver forms of crime with a lenient eye. It was not long before our membership included, not only genuine criminals, but criminals who made no secret of their 'profession'.

In respect of only one grave moral irregularity were the Pelicans, to a man, completely intolerant: that unnatural vice whose permeation of so much of our society was revealed, not so much in the Cleveland-street Case of 1889, as in the Wilde Case of five years later. After the oddity of Wiggins's appearance had alerted me to what might be happening to corrupt our youth, it was to *The Pelican* that I first repaired; it was from the members of *The Pelican* that I heard the rumours that I afterwards proved to be facts.

In that adventure of mine that Dr Watson has told under the title "The Abbey Grange", he records a chance remark of mine that I have no reason to wish forgotten. I observed that "once or twice in my career I feel that I have done more real harm by my discovery of the criminal than ever he had done by his crime. I have learned caution now; and I had rather play tricks with the law of England than with my own conscience". Similar sentiments were never far from my mind whenever I found myself at *The Pelican* and similar places; and recalling them remind me, too, of another remark of mine, recorded by my Boswell: "It is always awkward doing business with an *alias*." *

I think that there must be an element of criminality in us all: certainly, I had more enjoyable times at *The Pelican* than ever at *The Athenaeum*, *The Beefsteak* or *The Garrick;* the carefree, light-hearted, completely irresponsible *Pelican* cheered one up; made one forget one's prejudices, one's worries and, perhaps, even one's lighter principles. We even acquired a forger as member; introduced by a *fairly* respectable 'Pelican'; and the forger entertained us through one winter's evening with his boastful tales of how he, the finest maker of 'smash tosheroons' † in the world, had even got the Yarders baffled to prove them snide. It seems strange to me, as I look back at the pleasure that this good, if not honest, workman gave us that night, that it never then occurred to any of us (certainly it did not to me) that each of us was guilty, in our not reporting this man to the police, of the serious crime of misprision of felony. But no 'Pelican'—least of all Captain Dacre-Buttsworth—could have denounced the forger, and dared look himself in the face afterwards.

I find it difficult to 'explain' *The Pelican*. I have asserted that it had in it an element of petty criminality—but I could affirm the same thing of fifty other London clubs of the day. Yet, though that statement may not be going too far, it is a statement which deserves, in all justice, to be modified: there *was* an element of petty criminality, *but it was a product of something not in itself criminal.* It was the product of a guileless irresponsibility; of something no more evil than the unthinking impulse of the child to satisfy its unconsidered wants. Give the child the desired sugarplum; all is well. Deny the child its sweetmeat; and—if it can—it will take it. ('Take', be it noted; not 'steal'. The action justifies itself by the pressure of the imperative need; there is no criminality here.)

I did not cultivate the world of the shabby, ephemeral club; of the longer-lasting, but quite as shabby, bar; in order to apprehend criminals; not even to study them. It was this submerged *milieu* that I wished to

* 'The Blue Carbuncle'.—*Editor*
† Counterfeit half-crowns.—*Editor*

study; and if I never gave a thought to catching a self-declared forger, it was still in these dubious surroundings that, as I shall tell later, I caught the first faint whispers of something far above and beyond even the biggest coups of 'The Boys' ' most daring plots. As I told Dr Watson, though without ever hinting at the identity of my *alterae personae*, there was no one who knew the higher criminal world of London as well as I did. And for years, as I told him, I had been continually conscious of some power behind the malefactor; some deep organizing power which for ever stood in the way of the law, and threw its shield over the wrong-doer.

I did not find this organizing power in *The Pelican;* but it was there, and in similar institutions, that I first caught the faint, elusive scent of my quarry. For that, my days and nights in seedier London were richly rewarded.

EIGHT

My friend
Charlie Peace... and others

In recording that I once referred to the late Charles Peace, musician, burglar and murderer, as my friend, Watson has, I am afraid, caused much
head-wagging amongst those in whose throats that phrase, 'my friend', may
hardly be expected *not* to stick. Of these, those who would be 'just' to me
excuse the reference in the 'admission' that my detective work must cause
me to be acquainted—as indeed, they point out, priests and doctors and
judges and alienists must necessarily be acquainted—with persons of a class
not likely to be encountered in a Berkeley-square drawing-room; whilst
those who do not conceive it to be their duty to find excuses for me maintain, loudly or *sotto voce,* that evil communications *must* corrupt good manners—and that professional tolerance *must* eventually degenerate into a careless acceptance of evil.

Perhaps I should have explained to Watson how it was that I came to
know Charles Peace; and perhaps—for the comfort of those who have been
troubled by my kindly reference to one who was undoubtedly a vicious
criminal—I should have explained further that Peace consulted me in matters which, so far from being even mildly illegal, were, as I shall now
explain, of the most practical benefit to mankind. If it seem hard to put
aside the image of Charles Peace the daring and ruthless criminal, that it be
replaced by that of Charles Peace the ingenious inventor, the substitution
must, nevertheless, be made—for it was in the latter capacity, and in no
other, that I had my sole acquaintance with this extraordinary man.

Had I never been a reader of the daily sheets, I should have been in no
ignorance of the career and dreadful end of Peace, since the learned Judge
Mr Justice Lopes, Q.C. (afterwards Lord Ludlow), and counsel for both
prosecution and defence—Mr Campbell Foster, Q.C., and Mr Frank Lock-

wood, Q.C. (later Solicitor-general), respectively—were all afterwards known to me. But it was in no criminal connection that Peace came to see me, on the introduction of Mr Samuel Plimsoll, M.P., a few weeks before the Christmas of 1877, in which year I had come down from Cambridge and, from an address in Montague-street, Russell-square, had embarked upon my private consultative detective practice.

My acquaintance with Peace had come about in this way. In about July or August, 1877, I had written to Mr Plimsoll, then busy with his now famous campaign to abolish the 'coffin ship' by enforcing the markings justly called 'Plimsoll marks'. Some account of these marks and the reasoning behind them had appeared in *The Times*, and, thinking that they might be improved in point of clarity, I ventured to write to Mr Plimsoll, with my suggestions.

In reply, I received a letter inviting me to take tea with this bold fighter for seamen's rights, and, on the Terrace of the House of Commons, in a day of high summer, I was not only invited to make my suggestions for improving the Plimsoll markings, but also to tell this eminent (and, as it proved, eminently successful) reformer, something of myself. That I did not make myself sufficiently clear, or that Mr Plimsoll had misunderstood me, is evident from the sequel.

It was, as I say, an evening in the late summer of 1877 that the house-boy at No. 24, Montague-street, brought up a card, with the request that the owner might 'have a word or two' with me. The visiting-card was not engraved, though it had been printed in a style a little better than those which are run off 'while you wait', at two shillings a hundred. It was a trade-card, and bore the following legend:

JOHN THOMPSON
Dealer in Musical Instruments

5, East-terrace,
Evelina-road, Peckham Rye,
London, S.E.

"Ask him to come up," I told the house-boy.

A minute or so passed, and the door again opened to admit a short man whose appearance, at any rate, might hardly have inspired me with confidence. He was neatly dressed in a long grey ulster, above which shewed a well-starched collar and a silk four-in-hand neck-tie. In his hand he carried a neatly brushed and ironed silk hat. So far as his clothes went, Mr Thompson looked what his card proclaimed him to be: a dealer in a modest way of business who had risen to be his own master from long employment in the artisan class. It occured to me that his calling on me might have some connection with a violin that I had bought recently at a pawnbroker's in the Tottenham-court-road, and as, in those days, I was less in command of my discretion than I was later to become, I asked:

"Have you come about the violin . . . ?"

He looked puzzled, working his mouth in a peculiar manner impossible to describe. When he answered me, it was as though his tongue was too big for his mouth. He shook his head.

"No . . . not about a violin. Why, have you a violin to sell?"

"I am not sure, yet. But if you haven't come to see me about a violin—"

"You are Mr Sherlock Holmes, sir?"

"Yes."

"Ah, that's all right, then!" he answered, rubbing his hands, from one of which, I saw, he had lost an index finger. "The fact is that it was Mr Samuel Plimsoll who give me your name, sir, and suggested that you might be able to help me, like; professionally, in course."

"Indeed, I know Mr Plimsoll; and shall be happy to help you, if I can. Pray be seated, and tell me in which way I may be of service."

Mr Thompson had not been speaking long before I saw that Mr Plimsoll had recommended me, and my visitor had come, because of a complete misunderstanding of my profession. To this day I am not sure what Thompson wanted me to do; but it was nothing which might fairly be called under the heading of 'private consulting detective work'. Yet the story that he had to tell was of such fascination that I could not bring myself to dismiss Mr Thompson until I had heard it all.

In brief, he had, in partnership with a certain Henry Fersey Brion, a near neighbour, invented a system for raising sunken vessels; a system which, so far as I might judge, had both ingenuity and practicality to recommend it. He shewed me an appropriate entry in *The Patent Gazette,* and there, to be sure, was the grant of a patent to the two inventors.*

I had, of course, no means of assessing the strictly practical value of this invention. Were divers to seal the funnel, hatches, holes and other inlets into the hull, and then pump air into the sealed hull by means of the most powerful compressors, would the sunken ship rise to the surface? It seemed

---

* The patent, No. 2635, was granted to Henry Fersey Brion, 22, Philip-road, Peckham Rye, London, S.E., and John Thompson, 5, East-terrace, Evelina-road, Peckham Rye, London, S.E., for an invention for raising sunken vessels by the displacement of water within the vessels by air and gases. It is a system which, since Peace's death by hanging, has recovered millions of tons of sunken shipping.—*Editor*

probable that it would, but I was—and am—no hydraulic engineer, and was in no position to make final judgment on the scheme's practicality. I was, however, impressed, not only by the *seeming* practicality of the invention, but also by the energy with which my visitor expounded the merits of his scheme.

"What do you think of it, sir?" my visitor asked, his small, bright eyes alight with the eagerness—if not, perhaps, the fanaticism—of the inventor. "Mr Plimsoll thought highly of it, sir—said it might be the means of recovering I-don't-know-how-many tons of shipping. So that's why he give me your name, sir, and suggested you might be helpful with a little advice."

"Certainly. But advice in which respect—?"

"On Brion."

"On your partner! But I know nothing of him, beyond his name. How may I advise you?"

"He's planning to cheat me, sir; diddle me out of my share—and, in any case, it's me what thought up the wheeze in the first place."

"Then why is he in the project at all? Has Mr Brion put money into the venture?"

"He's an engineer—and them drawings cost a bit; and, then, what with the fees for the Patent Office, like, and—"

"Yes, I see. But goodness gracious, Mr Thompson, what can I say? You claim that your partner is planning to cheat you. How may he do that? Have you no watertight deed of partnership? If you have, then—heavens! you mean to tell me that you have not?"

"Should it be drawn up, then?"

"At once. The sooner the better—and without a moment's delay. Gracious heavens! what were you doing, not to have had a deed of partnership engrossed!"

"You couldn't do it for me, I suppose? I'd expect to pay, of course."

"I regret, no. I am not a solicitor; but any competent solicitor—there must be many in Peckham Rye—could do it for you."

He sat silently for a moment or two, nodding his head in confirmation of some private decision—I did not doubt that it was to confirm his decision to effect a deed of partnership. Then he looked up—a quick, bird-like gesture—and said, quietly:

"You mentioned something about a violin? Considering selling it, perhaps?"

"No, I merely mentioned it because I thought, mistakenly, that you had called about it. I picked it up recently in the Tottenham-court-road."

"And you're not thinking of selling it?"

"I hadn't given it a thought. It cost me only a few shillings."

"Do you play, sir?"

"I do. And you. . .?"

He laughed.

"In me own fashion. Self-taught—in that as in most other things. But, yes, sir, I do play—to please myself, at any rate, if not others. Sir . . . ?"

"Yes, Mr Thompson?"

"Without no question of buying and selling, I'm interested in all musical instruments—especially violins. Would you think me too bold if I was to ask you to shew me yourn?"

"Not a bit." I walked over to the sideboard, and picked up the rather shabby old case. Unlocking it, I took out the violin, which had cost me only a few shillings, and passed the piece of velvet over the smooth surface of the wood. Mr Thompson took it from me with a gentleness that one had never guessed could reside in those rough hands.

Still seated, he bent over the instrument, smoothing the wood with his finger-tips, and peering within. He took a folding magnifying-glass from his pocket, the better to aid his vision, and then, rising and carrying the violin with him, moved over to the lamp. At last, he laid the violin gently in its case.

"You've been very patient with me, sir, and so I'm going to tell you what I shouldn't care to tell *many* people. . . ."

"And that, Mr Thompson—?"

He gave that strange grin of his, and passed his too-large tongue over his protruding lips: he was certainly no very inviting figure at the moment, and I felt the strongest inclination then to cut short our interview. But, though of a personality at times almost repellent, there was that about my strange visitor which compelled attention—sometimes, almost a sympathetic hearing. I found myself reflecting that this Mr Thompson was, despite his rough, uncultured speech; his labourer's mannerisms; his air at once boasting and sly; no cypher. He was a man to be taken *au sérieux*—and I gave him, as they say, the floor.

"Well, Mr Holmes, sir, in the first place, let me tell you, sir, that I'd be much obliged if you was to tell me what I owe you, sir, for advice and that—and, of course, taking up your time?"

"Owe me, Mr Thompson—?" I shook my head. "You owe me nothing. I have done nothing for you. Why, then, should I charge you anything?"

"A lawyer would've," he muttered.

"Doubtless. But, as I told you, I am not a lawyer. I am a private consulting detective. You came to me in the belief that I was something different; I could not help you. *Ergo*, I have no claim on your cheque-book, Mr Thompson."

But, as all the world was to know not much later, my visitor was a dogged man.

"But you do charge professional fees?" he persisted.

"Indeed yes—for professional work."

"Like the lawyers' six-and-eightpence, like?" *

"Not quite," I answered, smiling. "I work to a somewhat different monetary standard. But," I added, more seriously, "it is true that I do have a fixed scale of professional charges, and that I never vary them, save when I remit them altogether."

"Then, Mr Holmes, sir, kindly allow me—"

"No, Mr Thompson: let us have done with this. You owe me nothing; that is to say, in the way of a professional fee. No . . . no more, pray! If anything, *I* am in *your* debt; since your description of the ship-raising invention interested me greatly: I wish you and your partner much joy of it!"

His strange twinkling little eyes lit up at this modest praise of his ingenuity. It was impossible to ignore the fact that Mr Thompson was not only a born boaster—one might even say, facetiously (but accurately) that he was always 'bursting to boast'—but that he was, in truth, what the modern psychologists call an 'extrovert'. Praise, then, of his invention, could not but be interpreted, by this exceedingly odd person, as praise of himself—and all such 'tribute' to his worth pleased him mightily.

"Then, Mr Holmes, sir, may I ask you to do me the kindness to let me put you, as you say, further in my debt?"

"How so, sir?"

"With a bit of information, Mr Holmes, that I see you don't have. You appreciate useful information, Mr Holmes? Of course you do. Then," as he saw that I was endeavouring to discover his meaning, "pray be so good as to take this here magnifying-glass and have a screw—I beg your pardon!: a *look*—into the innards of your fiddle." I took the glass, and did as I was bid—though not without, I confess, a wary look at my side and rear. "What do you see, Mr Holmes? A dirty old paper label?"

"Yes."

"Can you read what's writ on that there label? You shake your head, Mr Holmes. Quite right, too: for you ain't the only one not to pay no mind to that there label. If someone *had* read and understood what's writ on it, you wouldn't have had it, not for no few shillings, even in the Tom Corroa' † you wouldn't have." He looked at me with so cunning a look, yet one

* Six shillings and eightpence (6s. 8d.), half-a-mark or one-third of a pound sterling, was the standard minimum fee of an English solicitor until after the first World War.—*Editor*

† Standard colloquial pronunciation of 'Tottenham-court-road' to this day.—*Editor*

so friendly withal, that I confess to a leap of my heart, as the implications of his remark forced themselves to be taken as the literal truth. He saw then that I had grasped his meaning, and nodded, screwing up his face in an extraordinary gesture of boasted superiority and unabashed self-satisfaction. "That's right, Mr Holmes, sir: I dare say you heard of Cremona, eh? It's a town in Italy, I believe? Eh? And I dare say you heard of the man who lived there not so *very* long ago—?"

Gently he repossessed himself of his magnifying-glass, whilst I gasped:

"But, good heavens!—it can't be—I mean to say: surely you—"

"That's right, sir: that there fiddle o' yourn was made by the very hands of Antonio Charivari, of Cremona."

I was too amazed—yes, even startled—by his confident opinion even to smile at his strange pronunciation of 'Stradivari'. I gazed down at the violin in my hands, as my visitor continued. "The secret, sir, is in the varnish. Oh, they've tried, all right!—oh, haven't they just, my eye! But there wasn't never no varnish like Charivari's before; nor hasn't never been one like it since. Look after that there fiddle, sir. And, if you should ever want to sell it, there's a tidy few *hundreds* you can always lay your hands on in need."

I remember only one more remark of one of the oddest of all my odd callers. I saw him downstairs and out into Montague-street. We shook hands, and he was about to walk off in the direction of Russell-square, when he turned, came back, and in a tone of the utmost seriousness, asked me:

"Don't you think it's sinful, sir, Mr Disraeli taking the side of them murdering Turks? What's Christianity and civilisation doing to let this awful war go on?" The Russo-Turkish War was in everyone's minds and on everyone's lips; I was in no doubt to what he was alluding. "I can't understand it, sir: us supporting them heathen Turks, and turning on the Christian Rooshians. It's downright scandalous, sir!"

I was spared the necessity of a comment; for he raised his hat, turned abruptly on his heel, and walked up Montague-street into a blazing red sunset. It was the last time that I saw Mr John Thompson, inventor, musician, lover of animals, amateur politician, skilled burglar and twice-times murderer—better known to the annals of criminality as Charlie Peace.

It was not, however, the last that I heard of him.

A fortnight or so after our meeting, I received a letter, in which was wrapped a small something about the size of a vesta-box. I opened the wrapping before reading the letter: the object was a well-used block of rosin. The letter ran as follows:—

5 East Terrace
Evelina Road
Peckham Rye. S.E.
September the 25th

Sir

I would like to thank you with heartfelt thanks for your kind advice and the fact that I fully appreciate that you would not accept a Fee although your Advice could not have been better if I had got it from a trained Lawyer. But there it is, you know better, and I am not one to Argue with someone so much my superior in book Learning and Brains if you will excuse the expression.

What I wrote about was I did take your Advice, and Brion and me are now Partners in a legal way. I think he will still try to Swindle me, but as you said what can He do? So I take the liberty of thanking you once again.

I also take the liberty of sending you the enclosed it is a piece of rosin and knowing your opinion of the VIOLIN!!!!! I went to the Hall the other night and asked Mr Sarah Sarty * if I could have a bit of his rosin for a souvenir. He kindly let me take a bit and I ask you to accept It as I feel sure that your Bow done with a touch of this rosin might improve even your Cremoner. Please accept it is the sincere wish of

I remain
Yours respectfully
[signed]   John Thompson

Sherlock Holmes esquire

There was one more communication from the man whom I shall now call by his rightful name of Charles Peace. As Watson has correctly recorded, I have a 'horror' of throwing away or destroying any documents, whether or not connected with solved or unsolved problems. So that Peace's two letters are before me as I write. I give a copy here of the second:—

H. M. Prison,
Armley,
February the 18th 1879

Sir,
Please forgive the liberty of writing to you a letter from the Condemned Cell but there is one thing that I should like to inform you of before I go to meet my Maker which they tell me is to take Place on February the 25th which is exactly a week to-day, I.E. that is on next Tuesday. I have made my Peace with my

* Pablo Sarasate, the eminent violinist.—*Editor*

Maker and them as have wronged me and I have no Fear. As I say in a poem I made up myself—

> Lion-hearted I've lived
> And when my time comes,
> Lion-hearted I'll die.

I think you will Agree, sir, that nobody could say no fairer than that, and this is what I Truly believe.

But what I wanted you to know was that you were quite right about the steps I ought to take regarding Brion. I said that he would try to Cheat me, and I was quite right. You then told me that I ought to have a Deed drawn up and you were quite Right too and that was what I wanted you to know and that I was grateful. I want to tell you that in my Opinion you are the only honest gentleman I have met for I don't know how many years and that is why I played Fair with you on my Part. When I asked you what you Charged you could have said anything but you did not. That was honest and honesty is a Quality I think very highly of being so rare in this World. So as I said I decided to play as honest with you. I told you what your violin was worth and if you haven't proved that I was right yet take it to Messrs Hill & Sons, the Violin Makers their Address is 140 New Bond Street London, W. They are Honest they have been making Violins since the time of I think it was King Charles the Second.* I have had dealings with them and have found them always Honest like yourself. And then again I made no attempt to rob you of your valuable Violin, I think that shews I am Honest too, at least in regards to my dealings with Yourself.

As to Brion I wish I could say the same but that is a very different kettle of Fish as they say. From the moment I took your valued Advice and saw a Solicitor to get him to draw up a Deed, Brion has steadily worked against me. He not only accompanied me on several of my expeditions for burglary so as to nark on me to the Police on their instructions, he also betrayed me first and now I hear has gone to the Treasury with Mrs Thompson [*Peace's mistress*] to claim the £100 reward for nicking me. On top of that he has come to Armley here to ask me to Confess that it was Brion's own invention and that I had nothing to do with it, he wanted me to sign a paper. I said no but said I would for £50, that is sell him my share, but as he is a Miser as well as Dishonest, he wouldn't Agree. However as I had decided to Repent of my Wickedness before keeping my Appointment with my Maker and that means forgiving everyone especially Them as have wronged you, I asked the Governor to arrange things so I could Deed my half-share to Brion and this was done according. Frankly, sir, I don't see what Good it can do him, because a Judas never makes anything out of his being a Judas, but if it makes him happy for a hour or so, then Good Luck to him.

Not that Brion is very important. I have something more important than him to worry about. There is a man in Prison for shooting Constable Cock. This man

---

* This is correct; the Firm, which is still flourishing after more than three centuries, made a 'kit' for Samuel Pepys.—*Editor*

was sent down after Justice Lindley had sentenced him to Death at Manchester in November 1876, they give him a reprieve two days before he was due to be done. He is now in prison for a crime that he never done and I did, though I never intended to kill Constable Cock, it was all a mistake through me using ball cartridge instead of blank as I should have done.

I could not have confessed it was me who shot the Constable for they would simply have taken me up instead and I should have been hanged. People will say I was a hardened wretch for allowing an innocent man to suffer for my crime but what man would have given himself up under such circumstances knowing I should certainly be hanged? But now that I am going to meet my Maker, my own life is gone and I have nothing to gain by holding my tongue any more. I think it is right in the sight of God and Man to clear this innocent young man. I am going to write out a confession and give it to the Governor who will I am sure see Justice is done.

In conclusion may I take the liberty of wishing you all the success and prosperity that your great Talents deserve? I shall go to my Maker with thoughts of an Honest Man such as you are yourself, Sir.

Yours respectfully,

[*signed*]   Charles Peace (known as John Thompson)

P.S.   I never meant to kill Dyson, as Mrs Dyson well knows. It was All an Accident. Her evidence put the rope round my neck.*

Well, as all the world now knows, justice *was* done. The man, William Habron, who had already begun the third year of his (legally) undeserved imprisonment, received, on the representation of the Secretary for Home Affairs, then Mr Cross, a Free Pardon from Her Majesty, and some £800 as a partial compensation for his sufferings. I may explain my slight reservation—expressed here by that interjected word, 'legally', in parentheses—by noting that, in the rush to acclaim Habron's 'innocence', the public forgot, as it so often does, that he was innocent in the particular, and that he may well have been by no means so innocent in the general. In other words, he was proved—or *assumed*—on the evidence of Peace's death-bed statement, to have been innocent of the crime of killing Constable Cock. Very well: but was Habron innocent *in an absolute sense?* The case against Habron and his mother was very strong; indeed, the editorial judgement of *The Manchester Guardian*, that "Few persons will be found to dispute the justice of the conclusions reached [*that William Habron was Guilty*]", was a pretty general expression of public opinion.

Nor, reviewing the evidence from a distance of forty years, may I fault

* The spelling has been corrected—Peace's spelling was phonetic, and not always that.—
Editor

the evidence which seemed to shew that footprints found near the dead constable matched those of Habron's boots—evidence which was certainly not rebutted, either in Law or in the jury's minds, by Habron's clumsy attempt to establish an *alibi*. The question which was never answered was this: If Habron was at the scene of the crime, *and if he did not fire the fatal shot*, why was he there at all?

I shewed the letter from Peace to Mr Justice Lopes (whose most friendly gesture to me of thirty years later I shall relate in its proper place). To Peace's comment that he thought it "right . . . to clear this innocent young man", Sir Henry Lopes supplied the additional and sour comment that it would have been more right in the sight of God and Man had Peace done it before—sparing Habron not only his imprisonment but the fearful experience of a condemnation to death.

In fairness to Mr Justice Lopes, it must be said that he never entertained the least doubt that the Crown had fully made out its charge, and that Peace was guilty of the murder of Dyson. Peace had stated that there had been a struggle between Dyson and himself, in the course of which the pistol had been accidentally discharged; but the learned Judge held that it had been clearly proved that no such alleged struggle had taken place, and that there was one witness (the labourer Brassington) to testify to *intention*.

I, on the other hand, have never been fully convinced of either Peace's complete culpability or of Habron's complete innocence. The flaw in the case, as I several times pointed out to some legal members of the Union Club, was that none of the Judiciary involved had had an opportunity to know Peace's character. He was an arrogant man—all brag and bounce; and to shoot the man whose wife Peace had seduced into an improper familiarity was the last thing that Peace might have been expected to do. Peace would have preferred, in the expressive popular phrase, to have rubbed Dyson's nose in the humiliating fact of his wife's infidelity. Peace liked to boast of his irregular conquests—never more so than to the betrayed husband. I am convinced that Dyson, enraged by Peace's taunts, rushed—naturally enough—at Peace, *whose pistol was drawn rather to intimidate Dyson than to wound or kill him*, and that it was as Peace claimed: a struggle, in which the pistol went off, fatally injuring the husband of the treacherous Mrs Dyson.

As to Habron's guilt, let us first consider another claim by Peace: that, like Dyson, Constable Cock was also shot 'by accident'. We know that Peace was arrested after having shot, but not fatally wounded, Constable Robinson, who, during a night of October, 1878, saw Peace prowling within the residence of a Mr Burness, of Blackheath. No-one—least of all Robinson, the police-officer—challenged the evidence that Peace had given the constable 'fair warning'. Peace had called out, when Robinson approached him: "Keep back!—or, by G—, I'll shoot you!" Peace then fired four shots as Robinson, with a rare bravery, rushed towards the burglar, and all shots missed—*even though Peace was known to be a marksman of singular skill.* (I make the point here that it would be hard to miss with all four shots, unless the miss were not accidental, seeing that, with each shot fired, the rapidly approaching target—in this case, Constable Robinson—*made itself the harder to miss.* The deduction is inescapable: the shots *were* intended not to hit the target.) Only when Robinson was almost upon him, did Peace, in desperation; crying out, "I'll settle you this time!"; fire the first shot which hit Robinson—and then only in the upper arm.

Concerning Robinson's dedication to his duty and the courage which accompanied that duty, there may be no doubt; he had already struck Peace in the face before the last shot had been fired, and after it he closed with the burglar, flinging Peace to the ground, taking the pistol from Peace's hand, and hitting him on the head with the weapon.

The other two officers, hearing the commotion, had run towards the struggling men; with their help Peace was secured—his villainous career was over.

But, forty years afterwards, I can honestly affirm that I do not find unacceptable Peace's claim that he had no intention of shooting Constable Cock, since he had five opportunities to kill Constable Robinson—and took not one of those five chances.

So, we ask ourselves, did Peace kill Constable Cock—or, to frame the question more precisely, was it Peace who fired the shot which killed Constable Cock? Or was it—as Mr Justice Lindley and a jury were satisfied was the case—William Habron, in understandable revenge for his having been 'persecuted' by the constable? I think that it was Habron; Habron, who had been heard to threaten that he would 'do for' Cock—would shoot 'the little bobby'. If the evidence of his guilt condemned Habron in the eyes of Judge and jury—as it has condemned in mine—did it not also condemn him in the eyes of the man who sat in the public gallery through the trial?—Charles Peace? I think that it did.

Now consider how that 'absence of good character' which, brought to the notice of the Court, is so often the clinching argument which 'proves' a prisoner's alleged guilt, may, in other circumstances, give him privileges that no 'man of proven good character' could hope to enjoy. As thus—

Charles Peace, in the condemned cell at Armley Gaol, was a 'bad' man; a convicted murderer whose frightful record of wrong-doing was now common knowledge. Had one asked any man in the street if he would accept Peace's word for anything, that passer-by would hotly have denied it—"No, sir, not if he swore the truth of the statement on a stack of Bibles!"

And, indeed, Charles Peace knew this; knew that his 'officially bad' character would prevent anyone from believing any statement of his—*save one*. And, too, he knew (since he was a shrewd man) that this one statement which *would* be believed would be accepted without challenge; that, unlike the statements of men known to be honest, this statement of a convicted murderer would be accepted without his being asked for the least proof. That he would make the statement would be all which would be required to make it instantly and universally credible . . . not because he was an honest man, *but because he was not*. When he claimed that it was he, and not William Habron, who had murdered (albeit by accident) Constable Cock, no-one asked Peace to adduce a scintilla of proof that he had the means, the motive and the opportunity to commit the crime. No—because it seemed 'logical', 'reasonable', 'in character', the crime was accepted as not only possible but probable, when Peace claimed to be the perpetrator. None but a criminal would have had his word accepted without supporting proof; an honest man would have had to supply, as they say, 'chapter and verse'.

"So," Watson commented, "Habron was really the murderer, as the Court had found. And Peace perjured himself to save a rogue's life. . . ."

"Not quite, Doctor."

"Not quite *what*, Holmes?"

"Not quite perjury. Peace's statement was not made on oath—the Governor did not even hand him a Bible. Peace's 'word'," I added, with a laugh, "was quite good enough for the Governor of Armley Gaol. It is amusing, don't you think—the reckless carelessness of professionally careful people?"

"But are you going to let this rest?—let a murderer like Habron go loose?"

"Why should I do anything? Besides, what proof have I? No: even had I the power to change matters, I should leave them as they are. Habron committed his murder in a *specialized* context: Constable Cock had gone out of his way to irritate the Habron brothers—the killing was revenge, no more. In all other aspects of his character, Habron is no criminal. We shall hear no more of him. Besides, it was splendid that Peace, leaving us so abruptly because he had taken—albeit accidentally—a human life, should have found the means to restore a human being to liberty. I would not take that pleasure away from my old friend Charlie Peace."

"So," Watson mused, stuffing Navy Cut into his old briar, "we have the life-taker, Peace, restoring life to another murderer—regaining his liberty for the murderous Habron."

"Why, as to that," I replied, stuffing my calabash with the rank shag from Watson's pewter pot, "Peace cannot take *all* the credit. He had some help—some inspiration; some pressure. Setting Habron free was not what the burglars call 'a one-man job'."

"Holmes, you astonish me! Who on earth was this accomplice? Someone in the prison—?"

"No; but someone who visited the prison. The accomplice, as you call him (he was only unwittingly that, of course) was—*Brion.*"

"Brion! But I thought that Brion had betrayed Peace?"

"So he had. In every way. In the first place, he had—as Peace had told me that he would—tried to cheat Peace out of his half of the invention. Then, when Peace took my advice, and protected himself by a Deed of Partnership, Brion, the respectable engineer, tried to put Peace away, even to the extent of acting as *agent provocateur.* That he really did so is proved by his claiming the reward for Peace's apprehension. Then, having got Peace into a condemned cell, he asks again for 'his half' of the invention."

"That Peace gives him—"

"Yes. I believe that Peace's declared religious beliefs were sincere. Certainly he forgave his enemies."

"But Brion—?"

"We shall never know for certain, of course, but what I surmise is this. Acting under some strong emotional and religious compulsion, Peace found that he had done something good for the one person who, in Peace's view— and, Watson, in mine, too—deserved nothing: Brion. In the loneliness of the condemned cell—the loneliness not lessened by the soft-voiced Death Guard of two warders—Peace must have found himself reasoning thus: I've done something for Brion, who doesn't deserve it. Is there anyone else, who might deserve it, for whom I may do a favour? There was someone: a man who had very nearly met the same fate as had overtaken Peace—and for the same crime. Peace 'confessed'—Habron was set free. But Peace would never have thought of 'obliging' Habron had he not already 'obliged' Brion.

"That is what I meant when I said that it was Brion who was responsible for setting Habron free. But, of course, Brion is not legally or even morally responsible for what, in truth, was a grave miscarriage of *official* justice."

" 'Official' justice, Holmes—?"

"Yes—'official'. The Law would say that Habron, a murderer, did not deserve to be pardoned—especially by means of a doomed man's cynical lie. To the narrow minds of those who live by the Law—aye, and kill by the Law—there would be something intolerable in the suggestion that a condemned felon had been pardoned by another criminal's 'perjury', however charitable the impulse behind that 'perjury'. (And I am not sure, even, that Peace's impulse *was* strictly charitable, as we understand that word.) But

. . . I am not so sure that Habron did not deserve his freedom, however it was obtained for him. . . ."

"Deserved it, Holmes! My dear chap, you astonish me; you positively do!"

I said, with an obvious deliberation which, I saw, was not lost on Dr Watson:

"I may change my opinion as I grow older; but now, not far off thirty and past my first youth, I seem to accept that what little we know of deserts makes us poor judges of what a man deserves. I find it easier—and, I think, more reasonable—to take the view that, if something comes to us, either of good or of ill, we must have deserved it. Or, to put the matter a little more precisely, whatever happens to us, it is doubtless right that it should have done so."

"But this is pure fatalism, Holmes!"

"You say that, Doctor, as though there were something wrong with fatalism. Pray tell me why that should be?"

"Well, you seem to deny us the merit of getting—of deserving—what we have striven for?"

"I do not, Doctor—and I think that a moment's reflection will remind you that you do not, either."

"Do not what, Holmes?"

"Do not think that I deny that we merit our rewards—good or bad—through our own strivings. No, I do not say that. I merely say that what we like to call rewards or punishments are better called consequences."

" 'As a man soweth, that also shall he reap—' "

"Precisely. I have never denied that St Paul spoke as good sense as does Winwood Reade." It amused me to see that Dr Watson was faintly shocked by my comparing saint and free-thinker; but these were early days in our relationship, and we moved around each other's prejudices with, as Byron said in a different context, the delicacy of a cat in avoiding the mantelpiece ornaments. "We don't know, Doctor, what we have sown. We may think that we do. But we don't. And, by consequence, we haven't the least idea what the crop will be. Heaven knows what Habron really did sow—the Law (and, in this case, I, too) said that he feloniously took the life of another human being. Perhaps he did. Human justice would condemn him to death; a jury found mitigating circumstances—recommended him to the judge's mercy. The judge was merciful: he passed on to the Home Secretary the jury's recommendation, and, because there was a slight suspicion, not that Constable Cock was killed by a Habron; but that the right Habron—John or William—had not been convicted; William was reprieved.

"And then Fate, in the person of a capricious impulse on the part of a

man in the condemned cell, steps in with something that purely official justice would never have contemplated: a free pardon and £800 compensation
for William Habron. But who are we to say that Habron did not 'deserve'
his freedom? Who are we to know how Providence—Fate—call it what you
will, sees and orders these things? I say that if a free pardon came to
Habron, *how* it came is irrelevant. I say that, if a pardon came to Habron, it
was right and proper that it should have done so. There is something higher
than morality in these matters, Doctor, and we poor humans may find ourselves doing good as accidentally as we find ourselves doing wrong. I don't
know why Peace confessed to Habron's crime, whether out of charity or
from pure facetiousness; but I am prepared to believe that what happened
because of that impulse happened for the best."

"I think that it was from charity rather than facetiousness. For see how
he—well, perhaps not forgave him, but—gave that appalling Brion what he
asked."

There is what the lady and ladylike novelists now fashionably call 'a little
pendant' to this conversation of forty years ago. I do not know which
angered Dr Watson the more: the thought of Brion's treachery towards his
partner, Peace, or that that treachery should have been rewarded in a most
'unjust' way. Perhaps both angered him equally, for his indignation against
Brion never truly died away.

"That that dastard, that *serpent*, should have bamboozled poor Peace—!"

"Heigh-ho! It's 'poor' Peace, now, eh?"

"No-one likes to think of a man on the scaffold—and Peace, for all his infamous life, did die bravely. It infuriates me, Holmes, to think that that
serpent Brion was the inheritor of his *honest* work!"

So that when, ten years later, Watson came to write of a woman who has
meant everything to me, but whom Watson held in mistrust and contempt,
the address that he invented for her in St John's Wood was 'Briony Lodge,
Serpentine-avenue'. What he had remembered of the 'serpent' Brion had
counselled the choice of that imaginary address.

NINE

'The' Woman
...and her Prince

In recalling here my first meeting with (though not my first sight of) that lady who to me was, as Watson has rightly written, always 'The' Woman, I am departing somewhat from a strict chronological order. But the matter was of such importance, and has had so many repercussions over the years, that I think that it properly belongs to this part of my memoirs.

It was, I see by my diary, in the March of the year 1888 that I received a call at Baker-street from His Serene Highness Prince Alexander of Battenberg, who had reigned as the first Sovereign Prince of newly-independent Bulgaria until the Russian secret police had deposed him, at pistol-point, on 21st August, 1886.

This call, and all which immediately resulted from it, has been told in a style which, for floridity and inaccuracy, could hardly have been bettered by Mr Anthony Hope. I refer, of course, to Dr Watson's account of "A Scandal in Bohemia", in which my services are requested by a masked visitor—"You may address me as the Count Von Kramm, a Bohemian nobleman."

'Bohemian', Dr Watson may be forgiven for having called him—for 'Bohemian' the Prince certainly was, in the colloquial sense of the word. But 'Von Kramm' he was not. In selecting that pseudonym for a nobleman of morganatic origin, how *intentional* was Dr Watson's choice? It is clear from his narrative how much my friend disliked Prince Alexander; but is not 'Von Kramm'—literally, 'from the haberdashery trade'—carrying dislike a little too far?

The Prince had been driven to our apartments in one of the Marlborough House 'discreet' broughams, drawn by the prettiest little pair of matched greys that I had ever seen, inside or outside of Tattersall's, and he had come to us straight from dinner at Buckingham Palace. He had come, I should add, by counsel of the Queen, who had already advised me in writing that "a brother of one of my sons-in-law is in some difficulty which would yield, I think, to *your* attention. He will be calling upon you—I should be grateful for anything that you may find to do to assist him".

The 'trouble' was simple—though by no means easily dealt with: Prince Alexander was merely yet one more of the many male members of his family who had entered upon an irregular intimacy with Mrs Edward Langtry. He had written some compromising letters to her, and the lady, in her usual manner, wished to derive some profit from her possessions.

Unfortunately, it was not a matter of simple monetary bargaining—Mrs 'Lillie' Langtry was inspired by considerable malice, since, in her opinion, the Prince had slighted her. She had determined to seek revenge as well as money.

Briefly, the simple background to this simple affair was this:

The Russian Government, deciding that the Sovereign Prince of Bulgaria was not prepared to be a puppet of Russia, sent in its secret police, who kidnapped Prince Alexander from his palace in Sophia, and, at pistol-point, forced him to sign an instrument of abdication. He was then replaced, as monarch of Bulgaria, by a more pliant Russian nominee; all this happening, as I have said, in August, 1886, since which date Prince Alexander had been without a throne. He was, of course, *de jure* Sovereign Prince, if not exactly so *de facto*, and it is in recognition of this truth that Dr Watson calls 'our visitor' *hereditary* King of Bohemia, rather than former or ex-King.

But, though 'Sandro', as he was familiarly called by our Royal Family, had lost his Balkan throne, he had not lost the affection of Queen Victoria and of her children, all of whom were more than eager to do everything to compensate 'Cousin Sandro' for his brutal treatment at the hands of the Russians. The immediate aim of this group of energetic and determined well-wishers was to marry 'Sandro' off to Princess Victoria of Prussia, daughter of the Crown Prince and Princess of Prussia—the Crown Princess being Victoria, Princess Royal of Great Britain, and the eldest daughter of Queen Victoria.

This marriage was bitterly opposed by Prince William of Prussia, Princess Victoria's brother, and the future Kaiser William II, against whom we are now fighting. The ages and health of the principal parties involved made it essential that the marriage, if it were to take place at all, must be celebrated with the utmost possible despatch. For these reasons:

Kaiser William I was over ninety, and obviously was very near the end of his life; but his heir, the Crown Prince, was also dying—of cancer of the throat—and it seemed unlikely that he would live long enough to inherit the Imperial throne. Should Prince William succeed to the Empire, the marriage of his sister to the morganatic 'Sandro' would be forbidden. Speed, then, was now of the essence of the affair; but a death, on the part of the ninety-one-year-old Kaiser William I—with the elevation of the dying Crown Prince Frederick to the throne—made a speedy tying-up of the marriage plans even more urgent. A few dates will make the matter clear.

On 10th February, 1888, the Prince of Wales went to San Remo to see his stricken brother-in-law, the Crown Prince, who, now that the squabbling surgeons had all had their chance to maul his body and shorten his life in the interests of Theory, was on the point of excruciating death.

Exactly a month later, the old Kaiser died; and Prince Frederick became Emperor—for fourteen weeks (though, of course, no-one guessed that the new Emperor's reign would be so short). Now, the urgency of the matter lay in this consideration: if the marriage of 'Sandro' and the Princess Victoria—to which the Dying Emperor had already given his consent—were to be consummated, the marriage must be celebrated without further delay, whilst the new Emperor was still alive to authorize it.

No *open* scandal, then, must strengthen Prince William's ever-stronger protests against the marriage; it was for *this* reason that recovery of 'Sandro's' incriminating letters from Mrs Langtry was now a matter of the first importance.

I recovered the letters—though not in the complicated and improbable way that Watson invented in order to make his account more 'romantic'. Mrs Langtry's character was well known to me; and I answered her threat to send the letters to Princess Victoria with a paraphrase of the Iron Duke's reply to a similar threat, made by a similar type of lady: "Publish!—and be damned!"

But—and here I ventured a step beyond what, I think, the Duke did—I explained what, in this context, 'damned' could, and would, mean to Mrs Langtry.

"Send them, by all means, madam—but, before you do, consider well, I pray you, the consequences of your act."

"Why should I care what happens to *him*, Mr Holmes?"

"I was speaking of the consequences to *you*, madam."

"To me—?"

"To you. You seek, you say, revenge. Might not others, later, seek *their* revenge, too?"

"How should the Princess know that the letters came from me? I should send them anonymously."

"I should tell her, madam."

"*You!* How infamous! And why should you do such a vile thing?"

"Because I wish to have the letters back. So that I am being quite explicit in telling you what will happen to you if you use them in any way against

the Prince. I have only to tell His Royal Highness the Prince of Wales that
you have insulted his sister's daughter, and—"

"Do you think that he would care a jot? Do you think that *anything* could
turn him against *me?* Do your worst, Mr Holmes!—we shall see who comes
out top in this contest: the woman or the man."

"Mrs Langtry," I said, quietly, "I am sure that His Royal Highness
would care a jot—and a great deal more than a jot, as you put it. Just as I
am sure that there are still a great many things which, for all your self-assurance, could turn His Royal Highness against you. And as for your
proposed contest, all that I have to say is—try it!"

In the third or the fourth post on the following day, a thick envelope
came through the door: it contained a bundle of letters, all still within their
covers; the flaps of the envelopes bearing elaborately engraved and coloured
armorial bearings: some of Bulgaria, some of Grand-ducal Hesse, not a few
(these had been sent from Windsor or Sandringham or Balmoral) of Great
Britain. Two or three, I recall, bore the three-feathers badge of the Prince
of Wales; one bore the 'coat-of-arms' of Claridge's Hotel.

There was no accompanying note. I did not read the letters, but enclosed
them, as I had received them, in a packet of stout paper, and sent them,
without a note, by a trusted commissionaire, Sergeant Eldon,* to the
Prince.

By return—Eldon had been told to wait an answer—I had what was
probably the most guarded note that Prince 'Sandro' had written in his entire life, and with it came—here Watson's account may be trusted— a gold
signet-ring set with an emerald of the finest water. And—Watson's romantic inaccuracy may be ignored here—I accepted the token of Royal gratitude. (It was to provide a fitting companion for the ring—whose origin, of
course, the Queen instantly recognized—that Her Majesty commissioned
Streeter's to make for me a tie-pin *en suite*. It strikes me as curious that Watson did not associate the tie-pin with the ring.)

Often, in the course of my long life, I have been asked why I have not married; doubtless, the question will continue to be put to me until I am no
longer in a condition to answer . . . that 'I had been too busy', or that 'a
detective's is a life that no lady should be asked to share', or that 'perhaps

* Sergeant Eldon, Commissionaire No. 278, joined the Corps of Commissionaires, from the
5th Lancers, on 6th December, 1878, and died, still a member of the Corps, on 20th March,
1909. From jottings among Mr Holmes's papers, he seems to have used Sergeant Eldon
frequently, on errands demanding a completely trustworthy messenger. It seems most likely
that Mr Holmes met Eldon at Simpson's, where the Sergeant was often employed: he is shewn
in the picture of the great Chess Tournament now hanging in the basement-bar of that well-
known restaurant. I am indebted to Lieut-colonel R. F. Walter, Commandant of the Corps of
Commissionaires, for the information on Sergeant Eldon.—*Editor*

the right lady has still to turn up'. All these half-facetious stock-replies are merely euphemisms for 'Why don't you mind your own business?'—and are generally accepted, with more or less of resignation, as such. On only one occasion have I answered truthfully—and without reservation. Looking back, I can suppose only that the question was so unexpected, *from that particular questioner*, that I answered without thinking.

The Queen said, thoughtfully,

"You have never married, Mr Holmes?"—and, seeing my reply in my face, had added quickly: "Perhaps you are not an admirer of our poor Sex—?"

"Oh, Ma'am!"

"Well, then—perhaps of their intellectual qualities only, Mr Holmes?"

"No, Ma'am. I am as—how may I put it?—as appreciative of all the qualities which make women so attractive to me as, well, as—as anybody else who is," I ended, rather lamely.

"Then, Mr Holmes, *why have you not married?*"

The completely truthful answer came out before I could stop myself. I said,

"I have an unhappy predilection, Ma'am, *for quite the wrong sort of woman.*" And, seeing that Her Majesty expected something more, by way, not so much of self-defence, as of explanation, I added: "It would be quite out of the question that I should marry the type of woman to whom I feel attracted. So, Ma'am—I have never married; nor, I think, am I likely ever to marry."

Most men would have asked me to go into details since I had come, in confession, this far—and *all* other women, I feel, would eagerly have urged me on to more and more imprudences of self-revelation.

But Her Majesty shared few faults with the ordinary man and woman. All that she said was,

"And the type of lady, Mr Holmes—?"

"As Your Majesty surmises, I am afraid."

She nodded.

"A pity! But you are not the only man, Mr Holmes, to look for attractiveness in the wrong direction—"

"Indeed not, Ma'am. Your Majesty and I both learned that in our youth. I mean: about a man attracted to the wrong women."

"I am not sure, Mr Holmes—?"

"Ulysses, Ma'am."

The Queen laughed.

"But he had a stout mast, Mr Holmes—and companions to lash him well to it. Have you a stout mast, Mr Holmes?"

I bowed.

"I thank Heaven yes, Ma'am—though I have, alas!, to tie the knots myself."

As I asked her for the letters to be returned to the Prince, Mrs Langtry, in a manner not at all untypically feminine, attacked the near-to-hand victim— me—in the absence of the one who, in her own words, "ought to be here to face the music". Among the very many words and phrases that she uttered in her (from a woman's point of view) just anger, was this:

"You have me at a disadvantage, Mr Holmes—*and well you know it*, d— your eyes! But, one of these days; you mark my words, I'll be revenged upon you!"

Poor woman, so far less clever than she imagined herself to be! Had she but had a tenth of the intelligence with which she credited herself, she would have known that I was for ever beyond the most fearful revenge that baleful thought could ever have imagined for me—that she was already revenged, and would always be, by the very fact of her inaccessibility to me; to me, who had loved her passionately since that day when she had met and hardly noticed me in Sir John Millais's studio in Palace-gate.* Sir John had not finished with his beautiful sitter when I was introduced into the studio; and I was asked to be seated whilst the eminent artist put the few final touches to the portrait which was to be the 'sensation' of 1879. Thus it was that I had the opportunity, vouchsafed to few men, to sit for many minutes in the permitted (or, at least, not forbidden) and rapt contempla- tion of what was, to me, the most perfect face that God ever gave a woman for man's undoing.

I was a young actor in those days; tall, too thin of face and body; neatly (I trust) but not richly dressed; far indeed from radiating that possession of power or wealth—or, preferably, both—that Mrs Langtry looked for in every male, and, not finding, saw nothing else. The last stroke of the brush; Sir John's carefully courteous handing-down of the lady from her throne; her modest retiring to adjust her dress for the street; his walking over to me, all ashine in silk-lapelled frock-coat, glossy linen, diamond tie-pin in gleaming satin stock; his practised kindliness in reassuring an impecunious, unimportant young man (I had come but to carry a message from him to an American client): all these trivial details I remember with a photographic clarity.

* Mr Holmes, in referring here to Millais as 'Sir John', is guilty of slight prolepsis, since John Everett Millais, President of the Royal Academy, was not created a baronet until 1885, by which time 'Lillie' Langtry was well and successfully launched on her career as a top- ranking harlot, one of the earliest publicizings of her charms being through the pictures that Millais and Watts painted of her, and displayed to admiring crowds in the Royal Academy.— *Editor*

No artist of Millais's experience can fail to be both a physiognomist or psychologist—an artist spends his whole life in the intense study of the human face—and what spoke volumes on my stricken visage only a half-wit could have failed to notice and correctly interpret.

"Won't keep you long now," he said, patting reassurance into my shoulder. He glanced over *his* shoulder at the portrait, now glowing, as though through a film of transparent gold—the light of a Spring sunset. "A regular stunner, eh?" he said—and he was not, I knew, referring to his splendid painting. He shook his head, and smiled, not at all unsympathetically. "But not for you, my dear fellow; not for you. . . ."

And Sir John was right: the lady was not for me—not then, without money or a profession; and not later, when I had made something of myself in a world where dog not only eats dog, but where dog prefers a diet of dog. The lady, I knew, was never to be for me.

During our conversation relative to Prince 'Sandro's' letters, Mrs Langtry had exclaimed, "You know nothing *of* me! You don't know the least little thing *about* me." I forget now which particular remark of mine had prompted this typically feminine fatuity; but I remember its prompting *me* to reflect that I probably knew more about her history than any other man in the world—certainly more than did her wretched, shamed and ruined husband; more than any of those gentlemen 'friends' who had been so many stepping-stones to more financially successful things.

I had—the Ulysses tied to his home-made mast—watched her progress through the ranks of our Society; making use of each rank to secure her admission to the next higher.

She had begun with the artists and the writers, who had, with their portraits and their paragraphs, advertised her presence and her charms. She had arrived in London, the daughter of a Dean and the wife of a man of unchallenged respectability; it was not long before London realized what Mrs Edward Langtry had set her heart on becoming—and to become which she would let no obstacle hinder her. It was no laudable ambition; but the whole-heartedness with which she pursued it might have been thought to have something admirable in it.

From the journalists, the novelists, the poets—the late Mr Oscar Wilde (whose two sons, I understand, were among the first to volunteer for the present fighting) was most active on her behalf, and even lent his rooms in Cecil-street for her assignations—Mrs Langtry passed on to the *déclassés* noble and *déclassés* rich: the Churchills, horse-racing Americans, such as Moreton Frewen (Randolph Churchill's brother-in-law) and Todhunter Sloan, who was warned-off by the Jockey Club; drunken brutes like Baird, who manhandled her so badly in a Paris hotel that she was confined to a nursing-home for three days.* From these wastrels and worse, the indomitable Mrs Langtry progressed to self-indulgent and none-too-moral Royalty: to Prince Leopold, to his brother, the Prince of Wales, gathering in, on her way, the Prince's Battenberg brothers-in-law, Prince Louis (until recently our First Sea Lord), and Prince Alexander, former Sovereign Prince of Bulgaria—the richly clad, masked nobleman of Watson's romantic memory, who had written too indiscreetly to Mrs Langtry.

With others, I had watched in fascinated incredulity as 'Lillie' Langtry had forced the Prince of Wales to induce his wife to receive her; and, more, had somehow managed to get herself received at Court by—of all people!—the Queen herself.

Yes, indeed, I knew much of Mrs Langtry's history; for I had been in a position to learn it, not merely as Mr Sherlock Holmes, but as Albert, the part-time barman of the Mayfair public-houses; as Fritz Kassel, the free-lance German waiter in the second- and third-rate West End restaurants; as Henry Beatson, the clerk out of collar; as Mrs Salubria Hempseed, whose chaste ears were often assaulted by a chant in which the women of the street condemned Mrs Langtry as a more successful—and thus envied—practitioner in their most ancient of professions.†

I even learned something of her through Mr Augustus Walker, the genealogist, for Mrs Langtry's pretentious, work-shy barrister brother, Clement le Breton, engaged Mr Walker to delve into 'documents and things' in a search for a quite imaginary 'Duke Clement le Breton', 'one of the Conqueror's men', after whom Mr Clement le Breton, of the Middle Temple, had been named.

Of all my *personae*, none, of course, heard more of the adventures, real or invented, than Captain Dacre-Buttsworth, into whose ears, at the *Pelican* and similar places, the gossips and professional name-blackeners—I think of the *Pink 'Un* writers here: Wells, Goldberg, Binstead, Newnham-Davis ('The Dwarf of Blood', as Bessie Bellwood christened him), Victor Hughes-Hallett, and the rest—told, all-but-nightly, the tales of Mrs Langtry, whose falsity he was unable to demonstrate, and whose slanderous nature he was not placed to rebuke.

To ask the question, "Has any man suffered as I suffered then?", would

* One of my happier recollections is of the unconscious Baird, lying in a pool of blood on the floor of *The Pelican Club*'s downstairs bar, after I—as Captain Dacre-Buttsworth, of course—had thrashed the cad into a well-merited insensibility. Mrs Langtry (now Lady de Bathe), still with us as I write, will never know that Sherlock Holmes was the champion who avenged her injuries at the hands of 'Squire of Abington' Baird.—*S.H.*

† Mr Holmes must be here referring to the vulgarly obscene "I'm Charlotte, the Harlot,/Queen of all the Whores," etc. 'Lillie' Langtry's baptismal names were 'Charlotte Emilie'.—*Editor*

be to ask a question as foolish as unnecessary. Thousands have so suffered. Tennyson tells us that a sorrow's crown of sorrow is remembering happier things. A sorrow's crown of sorrow is also *imagining* happier things—and the same poet who tells us that "we needs must love the highest when we see it", was not, as my own unhappy experience tells me, speaking for *all* mankind.

I am now turned of sixty, and the 'Lillie Langtry' that I knew is as gone as is the Sherlock Holmes who sent the cad Baird spinning with that famous Holmes left hook so many years ago. She is still alive, and—apparently—well; living in great comfort on what the moralists will call the gains of wrong-doing. I saw her last at Hendon, some three years ago; we had both turned up to cross stiles and negotiate the water-meadows, to see Mr Claude Grahame-White try out his new flying-machine.

We stood, with our friends, near each other against a quickset hedge, out of the way both of the sharp wind and Mr Grahame-White's propellors. She had a man much younger than herself with her. She did not look in my direction. I am sure that she did not recognize me.

But I talk thus calmly, as a man turned of sixty—and *because* I am turned of sixty. Yet, for all "that calm serene, that men call Age"—as a young modern poet puts it—it is not so long that, as another young poet of a generation since put it, I was "desolate and sick of an old passion"; not so much the desire of the moth for the star as the unthinking hunger of the thinking human being for what it *knows* to be its doom.

Dr Watson has more than once commented upon my apparent lack of normal human feelings—which is no more than to say that I am 'inhuman' or (perhaps more kindly) 'unhuman' only in respect of the fact that I have never been given to talking much of myself, let alone of my emotional needs and disappointments. I have certainly never worn my heart on my sleeve; least of all among the pencilled notes on my shirt-cuff. But here, since I have come this far in self-revelation, I feel that I must now go further, and admit that it would be the rankest hypocrisy were I to deny that I shared, with most of fallible mankind, those baser impulses that it is our hardship no less than our moral duty to overcome. Except for my obsessive ambition—and even that I shared with many thousands of others—I was, I think that I may say, a completely normal young man, given rather to self-indulgence (except where it seemed to threaten my ambition) than otherwise. I may have had a 'forbiddingly grave face', as a friend once expressed it; but my nature was not at all that grave. I could laugh—and often did: I liked the more innocent pleasures of the Town; I liked good food and good drink; I liked tobacco—both good and bad—in pipe, cigarette or cigar. I look back, and have to admit that, for all that I kept myself Muller- or Sandow-fit, * I was not above some sybaritic pampering of that kept-fit body of mine, especially by sitting for hours in the well-upholstered *fauteuils* of theatre or concert-hall or, even more sybaritically, passing an even greater number of idle hours in the steaming heat of a Turkish bath. Indeed, of the more common, so-called 'harmless' vices which keep Man permanently below the level of the Gods, I was guiltless of only one—I did not gamble, either at the tables or on the race-course. From indulgence in the one frailty that even the broadest-minded decline to classify as 'harmless', I have been happily free—but, in all honesty, I hesitate to claim this for virtue, as I am now determined to explain.

Of the so-called 'harmful' vices, I have indulged, as I have said, in one—but one only; yet, in the days when I first began to take cocaine, not even the general medical opinion regarded this habit as dangerous, let alone immoral. To-day, as we know, 'drug-taking' is viewed, in the common public opinion, with horror; but I am not sure, even now, that this opinion is founded on anything more admirable than a tendency to accept one's views from Father Bernard Vaughan and *The Daily Mail.* I am free of the habit now; since, with the passing of my *tic douloureux*, I no longer have need of any narcotic anodyne; and that love of not unpleasant introspection to which the taking of any narcotic drug inevitably leads was forgotten in the inescapable activity that professional success imposed. I am still unconvinced that my taking of cocaine was a 'vice'—I am not even convinced that it was what Dr Watson has called it, a 'weakness'. I have more than a mere suspicion that I needed that slowing down of my headlong, unthinking course that cocaine forced upon me; I *needed* those hours of physical immobility in which nothing moved save the unceasing activity of the brain, at once meditative and constructive. My friend Mr Kipling has rightly warned us against the thinking which may make thoughts our master; the dreaming which may cause the dream to become our aim; but throughout those hours of cocaine-induced physical immobility, I both thought and dreamed—yet at no time was *I* not the master of both thoughts and dreams. Without the curious influences of cocaine, could I ever have thought and dreamed—imagined and *planned*—undisturbed by bodily activity; undistracted by even the gentle sounds of Dr Watson's aimless pottering between window and fireside; between tantalus and basket-chair? No: I have no doubt, as most would say, that I am 'better off' without my seven per cent. solution; but I cling obstinately to the persuasion—though I have by now acquired more tact than to admit it publicly—that I would certainly not

* Professional 'Strong Men' of the period; both commercial exploiters of 'Physical Culture'.—*Editor*

have been 'better off' without cocaine during those first years of my sharing my life with Dr Watson.

But if I may not say under which head we shall classify my addiction to cocaine—under the Black or under the White (or even, perhaps, under the Grey?)—how may I, in the honesty that I should like to characterize every sentiment and line of these memoirs; how may I classify that quality of mind and spirit which was at once the motor and the brake which controlled and impelled me: my *pride?* Again I look back—and I see what my pride did for me . . . and so often stopped my doing. It was my pride which enabled me to bear that solitary life at my universities—that solitary life that a sometimes relative and sometimes absolute poverty imposed upon me; it was my pride which, *in all things,* forbade me to settle for the second-rate when I might not have the best; it was my pride which strengthened (though it was also strengthened by) my ambition to found, as it were, a new profession—that of private consulting detective; and it was certainly my pride which found me the courage to endure, for years even, the sneers covert and overt with which my naming of my profession was too often greeted. And—we are coming back now to a subject on which I touched a page or two since—it was, I feel, rather pride than principle which made me reject the temptation to some irregularities that few would have condemned—especially in a young bachelor, no longer living with his family.

Dr Watson was spared, I know, the temptations that the bachelor life that we led would seem to have offered. No man ever joined more readily in the jollifications of that pleasure-loving period; and my friend was as happy to join in the sing-song at *Evans's* or *The Coal Hole* as he was to listen, with me, to the superb bowing of Señor Sarasate or Madame Norman-Neruda—happier, perhaps, for there was nothing of what the Americans call the 'high brow' in the mental and spiritual composition of the Doctor. He preferred the music-hall to a lecture at the Royal Institution—though often his sense of duty would cause him to choose the latter. He liked melodrama; Irving and Miss Terry had no more devoted a regular attendant at the Lyceum, for the 'first nights' of which he would always try to obtain tickets, whether or not I was able to accompany him. Dr Watson, I discovered soon after our first meeting, was what one may call a 'sharply defined' man—a man for whom that lukewarm, Laodicean sentiment called 'liking' had no attraction—almost, one might say, no meaning. He either warmly admired or coldly disliked; and for such a hero and heroine as Mr Irving and Miss Terry his admiration was warm indeed. I remember the sternly righteous indignation—the adjectives come unbidden and unchecked, since there was always something 'Biblically righteous' about Watson's anger—

when, on the Doctor's having remarked on that perfect accord with which, on the stage, Irving and Miss Terry 'played up to each other', a tactless acquaintance repeated what was common gossip: that the relationship between the two 'stars' went somewhat further than mere stage-association.*

I have called Dr Watson's indignation 'righteous'—and so it was. Afterwards, one might smile at the old-fashioned expression of what had come to be, alas!, somewhat outmoded standards of opinion. But, though Watson would vehemently have denied that he had anything of the tyrant in his 'quiet' nature, there is no doubt that, in imposing his prudish—and some even said 'priggish'—views so as to silence (at least for the time being) the gossips, the rumour-mongers, the slanderers and the calumniators, Watson's rather 'pi' insistence on banning all derogatory references to others had something of the tyrannical in it.

"Phew, Holmes," Tom Browne, the artist, once remarked to me in *Jubber's;* "your Doctor pal's a holy terror when he gets on that morality nag of his! I'd only mentioned that—well, no matter—but I'd said something quite harmless about one of the lads at the Roman's—and, 'strewth!, the Doctor was so fast down my throat that I feared he'd he'd snag his stethoscope on my colon!"

It was Tom Browne, honoured member of the Royal Institute of Painters in Water Colour, as well as the very well-paid creator of Weary Willie and Tired Tim,† who one day presented me with a neat little sketch of Dr Watson as he sat in a box in the Lyceum; entranced with—I think it was—the last scene of *Becket,* in which Miss Terry, as the Nun, finds the dead body of the slain; I dare say, since I saw the play several times, one of the most moving scenes that the English stage has ever presented.

"Landseer," said Browne, in handing me the sketch of my friend, "used to choose as symbols of undying fidelity—no offence, old chap!—hounds lying on their masters' graves; chargers standing over dead troopers; that sort of thing. Know what I mean? Just so. Well, for *my* symbol of fidelity, I have a fancy, not for grave-haunting hounds or trooper-guarding chargers, but for your medical fidus Achates, the ever-faithful—"

"Faithful to me, do you mean?" I asked, not altogether happy with Browne's flippancy, in which I seemed to detect something of the Bohe-

---

* I permit myself to mention this gossip since, for all that Miss Terry, though now retired from the stage, is living as a neighbour of mine in Sussex, these memoirs will not see publication—if they see it at all!—until after Miss Terry and I and all of our older contemporaries are beyond the reach of either blame or praise.—*S.H.*

† A comic-strip pair of work-shy but ingenious tramps or hoboes, whose adventures Browne drew weekly, in *Comic Cuts;* their names have entered into British folklore as the Katzenjammer Kids' have into American.—*Editor*

mian insolence for which his drawings, rather than his manners, were noted.

"No, no. To everything. Faithful to everything that he thinks he ought to be faithful to. Principle. Here—take the drawing. It shews him being faithful to the Lyceum; I'll do one of him being faithful to *you*, if you like."

Yet, however flippant Browne's manner, what he had said was true enough; fidelity—to his principles, to his habits, to his opinions, to his friends—this was the master-characteristic by which Society might recognize and classify Dr Watson. And though a little nettled by Tom Browne's breezy dismissal of (though even in the full recognition of) this quality of Dr Watson's, I realized the truth that this fidelity had been for him what my pride had been for me: that which had saved him from the many follies to which we both had been tempted.

I think, looking back, that it was no difficult matter for Watson to reject constant appeals to irregularity that the gayer London of forty years ago made. Fidelity, as Browne's keen artist's eye had seen, came easily to Dr Watson; and love, for him, was no more—though no less—than fidelity to an ideal. He had; perhaps through his own fault, perhaps not; failed in his marriage. To Watson, this failure would be but the summons to a further trial. He wanted no light o' loves; he wanted another wife; and one, this time, with whom he would not fail.

As for me, though I was surrounded by all the temptations that a pleasure-seeking age laid out so seductively for a young bachelor who, he admits, liked *la vie sociale*, I had to endure a far more persuasive temptation than ever would have troubled a far less moral Dr Watson.

The temptation was this; and I take no little comfort in the fact that I overcame it: I could permit myself conduct, *as Captain Dacre-Buttsworth* (or, indeed, as others of my factitious selves), that I might never permit to the ambitious, set-fair-for-higher-things Mr Holmes. I recall one night, when the Captain, 'doing the Town' with the raffish *Punch* artist Harry Furniss, had, from a light supper at Belasco's Supper Club in Percy-street, Tottenham-court-road, gone on to the Oxford Music-hall, around the corner. I have only to say here that, as Hugh Drummond once remarked in the old *Corinthian* in York-street, St James's-square: "My thumbs are pricking—*it's going to be a terrible night for temptations.* . . ."

All that I need say of that night with Harry Furniss is this: it *was* a terrible night for temptations.

What saved me was that pride that I hesitate to call either vice or virtue—

though I may call it both sword and armour. But, as I stood in the Oxford, whilst Furniss did a quick sketch of Captain Dacre-Buttsworth on the block that the artist always carried in his pocket, I found myself rejecting with contempt the proposal that the Captain should do what Mr Sherlock Holmes refused—yes, or even *feared*—to do. The poet sings of the man who did good by stealth and blushed to find it fame. I would—either as the Captain or as Mr Holmes—have done more than blush to find that evil famous that I had done by stealth.

TEN 🙰

The Grave-robbers

Watson refers to the case as that of "The Dreadful Business of the Abernetty Family [of Baltimore]",* when, in fact, it should properly be called
"The Stewart Case of New York"—and how I came to be involved in that
affair (rather more sinister than 'dreadful', I should have said) I now propose to tell. Not for the first time, I was indebted to my friendship with Mr
William H. Vanderbilt for his recommending me to a prospective client at
once rich and influential, and who, as it turned out, was to shew herself
willing to further my ambitions. How it came about was in this way.

Exactly a year before I arrived in New York with the Sasanoff Shakespearean Company—I landed in New York from the Guion liner *Arizona*,
Captain Samuel Brooks, on Sunday, 30th November, 1879—an appalling
scandal, involving the family of one of the United States' richest and most
respected merchants, had set the country by the ears. The millionaire was
the late Alexander Turney Stewart, the eminently successful hotel-proprie-
tor and 'dry goods merchant'; the scandal lay in the 'snatching' (as the

* I have put the words, 'of Baltimore', between brackets since, in the reference to the Stewart
case in the adventure of "The Six Napoleons", as eventually printed, Dr Watson attaches his
'Abernetty Family' to no named town—neither to Baltimore nor to anywhere else. However, I do
know that it was his intension to 'locate' his imaginarily-named 'Abernetty Family' in Baltimore,
for, in casual conversation very many years before "The Six Napoleons" appeared in print—by
which time we had given up our Baker-street apartments, and I had purchased my modest
freeholding in Fulmer—he had mentioned to me that "your friends, the Stewarts of New York,
will be making a casual appearance in the story. I'm calling them, to be on the safe side, 'the
Abernethys'—we know *that* name well, Holmes, don't we?—and, to make assurance double-sure,
I'm settling them in Baltimore, rather than in New York." Why the name of Baltimore was
omitted from the printed version of the tale, I never knew—I forgot to ask the author. But that the
'Abernetty Family' were originally assigned by Dr Watson to Baltimore I may state as a fact, and I
have accordingly recorded this fact here.—*S.H.*

American phrase has it) of his dead body from the burial-ground of St Mark's-in-the-Bowery, at the north-west corner of Second-avenue, at Tenth-street.

This sacrilegious and posthumous kidnapping was immediately followed by a demand of Mrs Stewart, the deceased's widow, for a 'ransom' of $20,000; and when this outrageous demand was not promptly met—Mrs Stewart having called in the police—the demand was raised to $50,000.

The New York police had been unsuccessful in tracing either the violator of the Stewart tomb or the remains which had been taken from it; and when I arrived in New York, in the late November of the following year, the Stewarts had more or less reconciled themselves to their unseemly loss.* (And here I must record my own satisfaction that my having been called in, by Mr Vanderbilt, to 'take over' from the American private-detective Mr Wilson Hargreave, in no way prevented my establishing a most friendly relationship with Mr Hargreave, who was later to attain high position in the Metropolitan Police of New York City.)

Of course, to me, as to everyone else who had come to New York, the name of Stewart was familiar. One could hardly walk up Broadway without noticing the splendid cast-iron building which housed Mr Stewart's retail establishment; and almost my first call was on Anderson's, the photographer's studio at 785, Broadway, opposite both Grace Church and the Stewart store. What, of course, I did not know until Mr Vanderbilt had suggested to the Stewart family that I might help them to 'locate' (as the Americans say) the missing body of husband and father, was the interesting history of the young Irish-born Scottish-Protestant immigrant, who had come to the United States at the age of seventeen to make a fortune and to die a multi-millionaire.

This history, by the way, was certainly not related to me in any detail when I called upon Mrs Stewart at her white marble mansion on Fifth-avenue, at the north-west corner of Thirty-fourth-street. Built less than twenty years before, this elegant and imposing house, whose architecture was so reminiscent of the mansions of Belgravia and St James's, assured me—had I needed any further assurance—that the centre of the world's wealth had already moved from the Old World to the New. Here was wealth literally beyond the dreams of avarice—though, in recollecting Dr Johnson's phrase, I reflected that it was wealth which had not outlawed avarice.

I had seen something of the splendour in which these American millionaires lived—Mr William Henry Vanderbilt's 'palace' at 640, Fifth-avenue,

---

* The official account of this extraordinary affair is presented in *The Posthumous Relations of the late Alex. T. Stewart: Proceedings before the Surrogate. Burial Certificate No. 234, 380, N.Y.*—Editor

with its fifty-eight sumptuously furnished rooms, was no bad introduction to *la vie princière américaine*—but the restrained yet magnificent elegance of the Stewart mansion was positively breath-taking. In my long career as first the confidant and then (I think I may say) the friend of so many of the royalty and aristocracy of our time, I have visited perhaps the majority of the world's most famous palaces and mansions; I may say that only in Russia, Austria and Poland have I seen anything to compare with the palaces—for they were certainly something more than mere mansions—of those American families which had risen to wealth after the close of the Civil War. And of these palaces, I have seen nothing to compare with that of the Stewart family.

Mrs Stewart told me little of her late husband's rise to wealth; indeed, I had the impression that she knew nothing beyond the 'facts' that "he worked hard all his life, Mr Holmes", and that (this despite the evidence of the body-snatching!) "he never made an enemy in his whole life".

Now it was obvious that the late Mr Stewart had made at least one enemy; and it was not long before I had all the available details of Mr Stewart's not unadventurous career carefully entrusted to my note-book. He had ended as the owner of the world's largest retail store, covering the entire block bounded by Ninth- and Tenth-streets, Broadway and Fourth-avenue: a building which had cost nearly three million dollars to erect, and which employed no fewer than *two thousand* people, men and women, under one gigantic roof.

So much was common knowledge: but what of the journey up to these immense riches; this immense power? What lay between young Stewart's arrival in New York, on an emigrant ship, and his ownership of a retail store which, in the three years preceding his death in 1876, had sold goods to the value of $203,000,000—over £40,000,000?

The New York Public Library began to fill in the gaps: I discovered that Stewart had been bitterly attacked in the New York and national press as a *sweater of labour*—a charge as odious the other side the Atlantic as it is with us; a charge that Stewart's sending a shipload of potatoes to Ireland at the time of the famine did nothing to suppress.

There was, I decided, something altogether too *calculated* about the late Mr Stewart's generosity—and something a little too public: gifts to the Northern Government during the Civil War—"For every cheque that Commodore Vanderbilt gives, I promise the same!"—a gift of $10,000 for the relief of cotton-operatives ruined by the war; a shipload of flour to France after the defeat of '71; a building in New York to give working women and girls a comfortable lodging, with full board, at cost. . . . No, thought I: Mr Stewart has been *buying* his popularity—and the year in which he set out to buy the most was the mid-war year of 1862. Was there, I wondered, some special reason why Mr Stewart should have felt the need to appear at his most charitable in this particular year?

At this point, the wording of the 'ransom note' (as the American press called it) seemed to acquire a significance for me, as the solver of the puzzle. The police held the original note; but Mrs Stewart had taken a copy, and I was impressed by both the brevity and the *assurance* of the message; an assurance which hinted at the writer's firm belief that he had a *right* to make his demand. This was how the note was worded; it had neither salutation nor signature:—

> The body will be sent back for $20,000. If willing to do business just put notice in Times. Will fix details accordingly. Debts must be paid.

The second 'ransom note' ran as follows?—

> Now it will cost you $50,000. Will expect notice in Times. Debts must be paid.

But before Mrs Stewart could put the required notice in the *Times*, I had been sent to her by Mr Vanderbilt; and I had my own methods, which did not necessarily exclude the payment demanded. First, though, I had to determine the nature of the debt—for I strongly suspected that a genuine grievance lay behind the high-handed debt-collecting activities of our grave-robbing friend.

Now . . . suppose, I asked myself, that there had been a debt, owed by the late Mr Stewart to some person unknown, and not paid? The question—or so it seemed to me—which might yield the most valuable answer would be: for how long had this unpaid debt been outstanding? And that question seemed to me to involve the question: does the creditor expect interest on the unpaid debt? For, if so, then the interest will be *compound*. Of course, one may not calculate the interest owing until one may know the principal—but, let us suppose, I said, that the debt was contracted in that year of 1862 when Mr Stewart seemed to be doing so much in the way of purchasing popularity. Now, the time elapsed between 1862 and 1876, in which latter year Mr Stewart died, was between fourteen and fifteen years—and in fifteen years at compound interest of five per cent., the principal is doubled. Might one, then, not look for an unpaid debt of $10,000 (exactly the sum which had been *promised* for the relief of the cotton operatives in 1862)—incurred fourteen or fifteen years before Mr Stewart's death?

It was no difficult matter to trace this debt; though my search for it—or, rather, for the hypothetical creditor—was encouraged by the fact that the existence of an enemy in Mr Stewart's history had already been proven. In 1869, President Grant, that consistently good friend of the American business-man of enterprise, appointed Mr Stewart United States Secretary of Trade; it was commonly said, as a reward for the merchant's financial support of the Union Government during the late war. Almost immediately afterwards, it was announced that Mr Stewart, who had given a grand entertainment and banquet at his Fifth Avenue mansion, to celebrate his appointment, would be unable to continue as Secretary of Trade; an obscure—indeed, forgotten—Act of 2nd September, 1789, forbade the appointment to this Secretaryship of any citizen *engaged in trade.* I asked Mr Vanderbilt to open the relative Government records to my inspection; it was as I had supposed: the barring Act had been brought to the notice of the President by an anonymous letter. It was plainly evident that Mr Stewart had an active enemy.

"So, Mr Holmes," Vanderbilt asked me: "you know the identity of the grave-robber?"

"No, sir—not yet. But I think that I know the nature of the debt—the unpaid debt. And I think that I may name the State in which the creditor dwells."

"Indeed! And which State is that?" I told him. "And why, pray, that particular State?"

"Our grave-robbing friend is a traditionalist, sir. In that State, as I have taken the trouble to find out, the creditor has the right to seize the *person* of the debtor."

"Mr Holmes, you astonish me! But you said that you knew the nature of the debt. Would you explain?"

"It is unrecorded in writing—and it is *political* in nature."

"And your reasoning, Mr Holmes—?"

"Had it been a commercial debt, Mr Vanderbilt, it would have been recoverable at law. Ergo: it was—is—a debt of which the law may take no cognizance. Yours, sir, is a very litigious nation: it is quite unthinkable that the creditor would have refrained from instituting proceedings in a civil action had there not been good reasons why such an action could not have been brought. Our creditor has been forced to collect by other means."

"And how," Mr Vanderbilt asked, smiling at my reflection on American litigiousness, "shall you go about finding the grave-robber?"

"I shall begin by asking the accountants at present winding-up Mr Stewart's estate to search for some memorandum of payment—probably under the heading of 'Charitable Disbursements'—which is not recorded in the ledgers. The payee should be a resident—or institution—of the State of——."

"A Secessionist State," Mr Vanderbilt murmured, reflectively.

"Precisely. A State which found itself on the losing side."

"Mr Stewart changed his mind."

"But was not let off his promise."

"Would it not have been easier for him to pay? After all, ten thousand dollars would have been nothing to him."

"Would he have *dared*? The more the North looked like winning, the more dangerous it would have been to have aided the South—even by so 'trivial' a sum as ten thousand dollars. No, sir, he dared not. He began to change his manner of life; he, the vilified sweater of labour, began to be lavishly charitable. But he dared not pay that one regretted debt. And, besides, what chance would he have had of retaining that Secretaryship of Trade had it become known that he had made a payment to the South?"

Professional etiquette prevents my naming the man whom we found; and the police were never called in. On my shewing that a debt had been incurred by her late husband, the $20,000 was paid by Mrs Stewart to the grave-robber, and stated in the newspapers to have been the 'reward' promised by Mr Stewart's trustees.

The reward of $50,000 offered for the recovery of the body Mrs Stewart insisted on my accepting; but I declined, contenting myself with a modest bill for my professional services.

The corpse of the missing millionaire was reburied, but not in St Mark's graveyard; the reburial took place, in the early part of 1880, in Garden City, Hampstead Plains, Long Island, an estate that Mr Stewart had purchased to build thereon a 'model town' for persons of moderate means.

My success in finding the missing body of Mr Stewart was to serve my professional ambitions in good stead, both in the United States and in Great Britain.

I had returned from my American tour some four months when a death occurred which was to involve me once again in the grisly business of grave-robbing.

At Florence, on 13th December, 1880, there died the most famous book-collector that the modern world has known: Alexander William Crawford Lindsay, 25th Earl of Crawford and 8th Earl of Balcarres. His lordship's death, at the age of sixty-eight, had terminated a long period of ill-health; and it had been in a vain search for the restoration of his physical well-being that Lord Crawford had removed himself to Florence in April, 1880.

The traditions of our ancient families, especially those of North Britain, are observed with a punctilious regard for the formalities. It was the tradition in the Lindsay family to inter their dead in the ancestral cemetery of Dunecht, Aberdeenshire; and accordingly, to his tomb in Scotland the dead body of Lord Crawford, Premier Earl on the Union Roll of his kingdom, was conveyed from Florence, and buried, with the honours due to his rank, on Christmas Eve, 1880.

Almost exactly a year later—that is, on 2nd December, 1881—it was found that Lord Crawford's tomb had been broken open, and his corpse removed. Either the American sheets did not carry the report of this further grave-robbing, or Mr Vanderbilt remained unaware of the theft until he read, in March '82, of the unseemly efforts of some spiritualists to discover the whereabouts of Lord Crawford's body by asking the disembodied entity that his dead lordship had become. At any rate, on Friday, 25th March, 1882, I received a cablegram from Mr Vanderbilt:—

Can you help present Lord Crawford find father's stolen body as you did in Stewart case? Late Lord Crawford was friendly business rival and I would willingly help his son. If you can manage, you would greatly oblige me. Have written to Lord Crawford at No. 2, Cavendish-square to tell him you may be able to help. If so, let me know by cable. Letter follows express. Please send your account to me.

Best wishes and many thanks

Vanderbilt

The letter, which arrived at Baker-street a week later, informed me of what the new Lord Crawford had already told me: that his father and Mr Vanderbilt had found themselves in what Lord Crawford called 'warm rivalry', especially in the struggle to possess the famous Mazarin Bible, the pride of the Crawford collection—since, even against an art-loving American millionaire, Lord Crawford had triumphed.*

I called on the new Lord Crawford—who later became as eminent a collector as his father had been; though the younger collected postage-stamps and not books—at his town-house in Cavendish-square. In conversation with his lordship, I soon came to the conclusion that, though the violation of Lord Crawford's tomb had been a crime of a completely imitative nature—that is, an imitation of the stealing of Mr Stewart's body—there were differences in the two felonies.

---

* Note that Watson used the name of the Cardinal in "The Mazarin Stone" (published, London, October, 1921; New York, November, 1921). The sale of the Crawford Collection at Sotheby's in 1887 extended over ten days from 13th June, the Mazarin Bible fetching the then 'fabulous' sum of £2,500.—*Editor*

As I have told Watson on more than one occasion, my method of getting to the truth of any matter lies in the observation of trifles—but the importance or otherwise of trifles is not to be evaluated until after one had thoroughly observed them. I mention this truism because there were several trifles in the Crawford affair which positively *clamoured* for attention: not the least, that both the missing Lord Crawford and the missing-but-recovered Mr Stewart both bore the Christian name of 'Alexander'. This triviality was, in fact . . . a triviality; of no bearing at all upon the subject of the grave-robbing. And there were other trivialities which had to be examined before I felt that I might discard them.

It was by no means an *easy* case, and it was not until nearly three months had passed since the receipt of Mr Vanderbilt's cablegram that the body of the late Lord Crawford was recovered, and reburied. On 18th July, 1882, the body—as I had arranged with the tomb-violators—was found, decently arranged, by the side of the empty grave, whence it was conveyed to Haigh Hall, Wigan, his lordship's Lancashire seat, and there reburied.

The essential difficulty in this case was not so much in discovering the identity of the tomb-robber as in bringing him to justice; and the difficulty lay in the fact that, as in the Stewart grave-robbery (that this robbery imitated), *personal* animosities within the family had provided the motive from which all the unhappy events proceeded. It was, in fact, a ne'er-do-well member of Lord Lindsay's very large family who had employed—perhaps 'persuaded' is the better word here—a man named Taylor (or Taylour) to remove the body from the grave at Dunecht. Taylour himself was of gentle birth, and when arrested, gave his name in the Latinized form of 'Sutor', which, as 'Soutar' is a fairly common Scottish name, was accepted without question by the police; and it was as Thomas Soutar and not as Thomas Taylor that the man was sentenced to five years at hard labour as *accessory* to the crime. Though a rogue and a wastrel, 'Soutar' had retained some of the better instincts of a gentleman; he accepted his sentence without complaint and did not betray the secret of his own well-connected identity.

As for the actual instigator of the grave-robbing, *his* connection with Lord Lindsay was too close that *he* should have been charged—or even mentioned—in connection with the mischief. As a Justice of the Peace for both Lancashire and Aberdeenshire, the new Lord Lindsay had no difficulty in arranging that a commission in lunacy should pronounce the real culprit unfit to plead. And, save for an unhappy misconstruction of my advice, the man 'Soutar' would not have been arrested, either.

I mention this second case of grave-robbing in which I was involved, not that it gave me any notable chance of demonstrating my detective talents, but because it had the happiest and most far-reaching influences on my career, both in Europe and in America.

On the conclusion of the case—with the Court of Sessions' convicting 'Soutar'—Lord Lindsay invited me to dinner at his town-house; to thank me for my efforts in recovering the body of his father and in avoiding the scandal not always separable even from success, and to introduce me to some fellow-guests anxious to know the details of the body-snatching affair.

It was a 'mixed' dinner-party, though most of the ladies present were there with their husbands. A note made at the time not only recalls vividly that dinner of nearly forty years ago, but saddens me in the reflection that so many of my fellow-guests have passed on. (One hopes, sometimes against apparent *reason*, but never against the promptings of human nature, that they have all gone to some compensation hereafter; for, if there be none, then the world is indeed a cruel jest.)

I noted the names in no particular order of precedence, though one may be sure that we went into dinner according to the very precise reckoning of our rank—that Mr Sherlock Holmes and Miss Katharine Stephen did not bring up the rear was due solely to the fact that my fair companion * was the daughter of, and had been brought to Cavendish-square by, Sir James Stephen.† Here are the guests—as I remarked, in no special order of precedence:—

> *Sir Henry and Lady Seaton-Steuart*
>> (Watson told me afterwards that Sir Henry was Hereditary Armour-Bearer and Squire of the Royal Body in Scotland; I remember that I shocked Watson's Scottish sense of propriety by remarking that I hoped that Sir Henry would guard the Royal Body more efficiently than our host had guarded that of his father!)
>
> *Sir James Stephen and Miss Stephen*
> *Sir Archibald and Lady Campbell*
> *Lord and Lady Sudeley*
>> (A barrister friend of Mr Justice Stephen, and Lord-in-Waiting to H.M. from 1880 to 1885)
>
> *Mr Vernon Lushington*
>> (His Honour Judge Lushington)
>
> *Lord Edmond Fitzmaurice*
>> (Under-secretary of State for Foreign Affairs)
>
> *Lady Chitty*
>> (Wife of Sir Joseph Chitty, Lord Justice of Appeal)

* Afterwards Vice-principal of Newnham College, Cambridge.—*Editor*

† Sir James Fitzjames Stephen, Bart, K.C.S.I., D.C.L., LL.D., Judge of the High Court of Justice, 1879–1891. Died insane, 1894.—*Editor*

Mr Sherlock Holmes
Lord and Lady Tenterden
   (His lordship was Permanent Under-secretary for Foreign Affairs; he died that
   same year)
Mr and Mrs H. Hobhouse
Lady and Miss Thring
   (Lord Thring was a Parliamentary Counsel; he owed his peerage to the fact
   that his wife was the sister of Viscount Cardwell, of Army Reform fame.
   Miss—the Hon'ble Katharine Annie—Thring was just turned of twenty-one,
   and was, I recall, remarkably pretty for a lawyer's daughter)
Mr Cookson
Mr Claud Lindsay

A typical small dinner-party of the early 1880's—a thousand engagement-books of the period will not only shew the same pattern of guest-selection (if I may coin a phrase) but, in most cases, the combinations and variations possible in what was really a most limited selection of 'invitable people'. We still invite our friends and acquaintances to luncheon or dinner; but the habit of dining 'out'—that is, at an hotel or restaurant—had not then come widely into fashion; most entertaining was done at home. To be a host or hostess was to have adopted something of a time-consuming profession; and the profession of Hostess (the profession was most ably demonstrated on the distaff side) had necessarily called into essential being the profession of the Approved Guest or Licensed Diner-out. I was never much of a diner-out, and when Watson and I entertained, until we acquired our dining room, it was not at Baker-street, but always (in the case of our men friends) at our clubs, or (in the case of a mixed party) one of the more select hotels or restaurants: *Claridge's*, say, or *The Grand, Inns of Court* or *Westminster Palace*. (The last-named had the added attraction for me that the fine Oriental Turkish baths—long since demolished—stood hard by.)

Well, this dinner-party of forty years since did me no little good, though, as is always the way, the least of my benefits came from those fellow-guests of mature age and established social position; the most from the shy, twenty-one-year-old youth Claud Lindsay, a somewhat distant cousin of our noble host. Mr Lindsay's place at the dinner-table was near enough to mine that I might successfully include him in our conversation, and I had the satisfaction of seeing that, as the superb dinner progressed, something of the lad's diffidence left him, and that he was able to contribute a remark or two to the table-talk.

I was not deceived into thinking that something unique in my character appeared to have made me the lion of the evening; I was the centre of attraction only because of my having solved the mystery of the late Lord

Crawford's posthumous disappearance. During dinner, Miss Stephen, whom I had taken in, asked me some questions on the affair with all the directness which would have better suited her father, the Judge; after the ladies had retired, I had to tell the whole story over the port and cigars; and then, having joined the ladies in the drawing-room, I had to tell it yet again.

At dinner, whilst giving apparent full attention to the somewhat blue-stocking Miss Stephen, I noticed that Miss Thring, that pretty girl of twenty-one, was tremulously aware of Mr Lindsay's proximity—and as Mr Lindsay was a prepossessing young man of her own age, it seemed to me that a mutual attraction was not only the most natural, but also (as far as I could tell) the most desirable, thing in the world. In affairs of the heart my own life, I admit, has not followed a normal pattern—something on which I have to comment elsewhere in these memoirs—but vicariously I have always been able to respond to the sight of young love with all the completely impractical sentimentality of a lady novelist.

However, I saw that, far from welcoming Miss Thring's innocent but flattering attentions, Mr Lindsay appeared to be troubled, confused and—so it seemed—decidedly embarrassed by them; and, noticing this, I contrived to catch and hold Miss's eager attention by describing, as far as I might, the more obvious characteristics of the American Young Woman—then beginning to be a subject of common gossip by reason of her 'conquests' among our native aristocracy.

"I suppose," said Lady Campbell, who had been listening to me with more than half an ear, as they say; "I suppose that the attraction that they have for our young men is the age-old attraction of the exotic. But are they so *very* different from our young women, Mr Holmes?"

"Yes, Lady Campbell, I should say so—perhaps more different than even they appear to be."

"That sounds like something very clever, Mr Holmes. Is it?"

"Is it what, madam? Clever? I don't know. It may be that it's better than merely clever, since it's true."

"My goodness gracious, Mr Holmes: we *are* in an epigrammatic mood to-night! But in which way are the American women—the young women, especially; the young women who carry off our eligible young men—in which way are they different? Come, Mr Holmes, a definition of the truth oughtn't to trouble you?"

"It doesn't, Lady Campbell. American girls are different because they are permitted more liberty than we think proper to concede to our well-brought-up daughters. And they have more liberty because they have more money. The concept of 'pin-money' doesn't exist over there. A young lady, if her father or guardian be rich, expects to receive—and does, indeed, get—an allowance commensurate with her Papa's wealth. If he have, say, a couple of hundred thousand pounds a-year, Miss would certainly raise hob if Papa didn't make her an allowance of five thousand—*at least.*"

"Five *thousand*, Mr Holmes? Surely you must be joking?"

"On my honour, I assure you. Many young American ladies receive more—far more. Many even have their own capital."

"But five thousand is all that the Prime Minister gets. . . ."

"True, madam; and the Postmaster-general gets but half. Even the Lord High Chancellor gets but double. But it is so, I assure you. There is no primogeniture in the United States: all the children share—as under Kentish law—equally, with the exception that the daughters, especially if they have a brilliant future planned for them, do rather better than equally. I have the honour of knowing Mr William H. Vanderbilt, who is commonly reputed to be worth some fourteen to twenty millions of pounds sterling. The provision that he has made for his family passes belief— provision, be it noted, in his family's lifetime; they do not have to wait until his death to enjoy *some* of the good things of this only-too-transient life."

The Scotch baronet's lady looked what, to her, were the practical aspects of the matter 'squarely in the eye'.

"But, my goodness me, Mr Holmes," she exclaimed, "what chance will our poor young girls have against this Juggernaut of uncontrolled wealth? 'Be good, sweet maid' is all very well, but a bride with a hundred a-week and much more to come must be held to possess a *decided* advantage over our girls, whatever their qualities! Why, none of our young men is going to look at one of our girls!"

"It is hardly as bad as that, Lady Campbell," I said, laughing. "Have you a Debrett at home? Of course you have. Then may I suggest that you turn the pages, and count the hundreds—perhaps there may even be thousands—of well-bred young men who will have to be married some day. They cannot all marry the daughters of American millionaires—there are hardly enough millionaires; or hardly enough daughters; to go around. I feel that our young men will still look for their brides a little nearer home." And I glanced in a friendly and encouraging manner at Miss Thring, who blushed a little at the implied compliment. Mr Lindsay, however, looked a trifle glum, and within a few minutes, I was to learn why.

"But," Lady Campbell continued, "does not this liberty—this ability to have control of money without the necessity of accounting to anyone for its disbursement—does this not lead to, well, improper conduct?"

"As it surely would here? No, it does not," I said, firmly; "and for the same reason that the Eskimo does not perish of pneumonia or the Hottentot of sun-stroke: both have adapted to the unusual conditions in which each has been born. Thus with the American young lady: she is born, not so much to money—sometimes it happens that her father's fortune is still to be made—as to the understanding of money; what it is, how one acquires it, how one manages it. And this all without her losing a jot of her balance, and certainly not of her essential womanliness. She may be remarkably free-and-easy in her manner—I can assure you, Lady Campbell, that she is free-and-easy in no other way."

When the ladies had retired, Lord Sudeley, a dry stick of a lawyer turned Lord-in-Waiting, remarked to me, in no very warm tone:

"You seemed very amiable with your table-companions, Mr Holmes"—by which, I imagine, he intended to observe that I had spoken too much, especially for one not customarily invited to Lord Crawford's house. "You seem very well up in your subject. One understands that you approve of the Americans?"

"I could hardly permit the generalization, my lord," I answered. "I cannot say that I approve of Americans, since I know so few; I have met only a few—and of them, yes, I did approve. But, as they were all millionaires, I may hardly think of them as representative of America as a whole."

Lord Sudeley looked somewhat taken aback at this; but I noticed that Mr Lushington smiled, as did both my host and Lord Edmond, between whom and Lord Sudeley I fancied that I detected a certain *froideur*.

But of all who sat with me at table that night, it was young Mr Lindsay, of the decidedly retiring manner, who most took my attention. I have said that he was shy, but he was not so with me; and it was not long before I understood how he should be timid with others and not with me.

This timidity might be accounted for, as I told Watson afterwards, in two ways: a recent scandal involving the family of his mother, Lady Frances Howard, daughter of the 4th earl of Wicklow, * and by a choice of vocation of which, fortunately, his family—or that part of it represented by his father, the Hon'ble Colin Lindsay—approved: young Mr Lindsay was studying for Holy Orders in the Roman Church.

"I wish you every success and happiness," I told him, and he acknowledged my good wishes with a grave nod of his head.

"You are not of our Communion, Mr Holmes?"

"No," I said. "But my own family has an interesting place in Papal his-

---

* Though Mr Holmes does not say so here, he was involved professionally in some results of an impudent attempt to 'provide' an heir for the Wicklow earldom by means of a child 'adopted' from a Liverpool orphanage, a case referred to by Dr Watson as "The Darlington Substitution Scandal". See pages 3–4.—*Editor*

tory: my great-great-grandfather on the maternal side was Commander John Parker, and he was Admiral Commanding the Papal Navy."

"When was this, Mr Holmes?"

"At some time between 1740 and 1760."

"It was Pope Benedict XIV. Cardinal Lambertini. But how very interesting. Perhaps, who knows, the Pope may yet have a navy once more."

Later, as is well known, Mr Lindsay became the Right Reverend Monsignor Lindsay, Private Chamberlain to Pope Leo XIII, the latter rank being also held by Monsignor Lindsay's elder brother, Leonard, though he was not in Holy Orders.

This chance meeting was to have the most important results for me, which began to be apparent after Mr Lindsay had been ordained but long before he had risen to the rank of Monsignor.

It appears that, on his going home that night, he had told his mother, Lady Frances, that he had met (so, laughingly, her ladyship told me afterwards) "a most extraordinary young man, who's descended from a Commander-in-Chief of the Pope's navy"; had "talked of you all night, Mr Holmes"; and had eventually made my existence known to the Roman Catholic side of the large Lindsay family. Not long after, the young man had taken the story of my naval Papal ancestor to Rome, and thus made the Vatican aware of my existence, if not then of my talents.

The several cases in which I was able to be of service to the Vatican, both in Italy and elsewhere, came to me through the interest that young Mr Lindsay had taken in an idle conversation at his uncle's dinner-table. Thus—as idly, one might say!—are our destinies worked out.

We joined the ladies; and in the drawing-room I was forced, much to my mortification, to hold the floor with a minute description of the marvels of Mr Vanderbilt's 'palace' in Fifth-avenue.

A sequel to my solution of the Stewart mystery came about many years after the dinner-party at Lord Lindsay's—nearly twenty years after, in fact. But I shall describe this strange sequel here because, originating directly in both the Stewart and the Lindsay grave-robbings, it is linked, both in time and in fact, rather with 1882—the year in which the late Lord Lindsay's body was recovered—than with 1904, the year in which I received a courteous but puzzling letter from a firm of American attorneys with their offices in New York.

I suppose that, by now, it will seem inevitable that I should mention that the attorneys' letter concerned an American millionaire. It did—and the American millionaire was one whose name, if not his person, was well-known to the British people: Levi Zeigler Leiter (né Leitersburg), father of the wife of the then-Viceroy of India, Lord Curzon of Kedleston.

Mr Leiter had made his fortune—on his death he was found to have left some $30,000,000—in the 'dry-goods' trade; that same business which had provided Mr A. T. Stewart with his white marble palace and *his* immense fortune. The two millionaires knew each other, and had had some close commercial dealings; when Mr Stewart's body was stolen, Mr Leiter was deeply shocked—though how deeply, I was not to learn until nearly a quarter-of-a-century after I had effected its restoration to Mrs Stewart.

In brief, the letter informed me that, in his will, Mr Leiter had left the most elaborate precautions to be taken to provide him with a 'robber-proof' tomb; and that, in a letter to his attorneys, to be opened on the reading of the Will, he had instructed his attorneys to request my advice and superintendence in the construction of the proposed 'robber-proof' tomb. The letter from the attorneys assured me that it had been a wish of their late client that I should accept the charge, and as I knew, by this time, both Lord and Lady Curzon, I agreed to come to Washington, on a site four miles north of which, at Rock Creek, the curious tomb was to be constructed. I had 'officially' retired in the previous year, but like those 'retired' singers at whom I had often laughed, it now suited my convenience to return to the stage. As it turned out, this opportunity to serve the charming Lady Curzon (within two years of her father's death at the Vanderbilt cottage at Bar Harbor, Maine, she had joined him) gave me not only the pleasure of obliging a lady for whom I had both respect and affection, but, as it turned out, helped me, at no very distant date, to render my country signal service, that I shall describe later.

I made my 'headquarters' at Washington whilst the work of building Mr Leiter's tomb went on. Heaven knows why the millionaire had asked me to 'superintend' the construction; I was no architect or engineer; I knew nothing of rolled-steel joists or concrete—both of which were used to guard Mr Leiter's embalmed corpse from desecration. My classical education had spared me knowledge of all such things. But at a 'consultancy fee' of twenty guineas a-day (for so the Trustees of Mr Leiter's Will assured me was the rate at which it had been laid down that I should be paid), I mastered my repugnance to accept unearned money, and stood by the immense tomb—a hole some 4,000 square feet in area—whilst the engineers-in-charge made as it were a huge 'sandwich' of steel-and-concrete, coffin, and more steel-and-concrete.

Reverting to that classical education of which I spoke a line or two back, I know that some of the tombs of antiquity were of vast proportions. Herodotus has told why the tomb of Mausolus was accounted one of the seven wonders of the world; the tomb of Cyrus, according to Xenophon, was hardly less impressive; and many of us have seen such surviving funerary monuments as the Taj Mahal and the mausoleum of Hadrian—buildings which have defied time to justify Browne's opinion that "man is a noble animal, splendid in ashes, and pompous in the grave". I lack comparative dimensions in judging the 'pomposity' of the late Mr Leiter's last resting-place: two hundred feet by two hundred feet surely brings it within matching distance of some of the most impressive tombs of the past. But the technicalities of its construction were of a type unmatched in antiquity.

The foreman told me that they were 'laying a raft' of steel and concrete two feet deep, over the immense area of the excavation. "Then," he added, "we place the casket on this, and fill her"—that is, the excavation—"up with another raft of steel and concrete;" to which the *New York Times*, on the completion of the tomb, stated, as its opinion, that "only an earthquake or heavy charges of explosive could move the mass. The precautions were taken, as Mr Leiter had been much disturbed by the robbery of the body of the New York dry goods merchant, A. T. Stewart, some years before". I can never recall this oddest of all my experiences without my being reminded of those strange lines from the story of Edgar Allan Poe:

> No answer still. I thrust a torch through the remaining aperture and let it fall within. There came forth in return only a jingling of the bells. My heart grew sick; it was the dampness of the catacombs which made it so. I hastened to make an end of my labour. I forced the last stone into its position; I plastered it up. Against the new masonry I re-erected the old rampart of bones. For the half of a century no mortal has disturbed them. *In pace requiescat!*

It is, in fact, little more than a decade since the body of Mr Leiter was laid to rest, but so much has happened in the intervening few years that it seems an age ago that I stood in the sweltering heat of a Washington summer, and thoroughly despised myself for my paid condonation of a rich man's posthumous childishness.

And now you may well be wondering how—or why—Dr Watson came to refer to the Stewart case as that of "the Abernetty Family of Baltimore", when, as I have explained, it was the two cases of Mr A. T. Stewart of New York and of Lord Crawford and Balcarres of Dunecht.

A glance at the coat-of-arms of the earls of Crawford in any nobiliary will instantly reveal the source of Watson's change of name. The shield quarters the arms of Lindsay and *Abernethy*—the slight alteration to 'Abernetty' I attribute to a type-writer's mishearing or a compositor's error.

Her Majesty Queen Victoria. "The Head of the British Empire governs through nothing but the respect that she exacts from the governed . . ." *One of the portraits specially taken for the Golden Jubilee by W. & D. Downey.*

'Bart's': The King Henry the Eighth Gatehouse, erected between 1702 and 1730 to the design of Edward Strong, son of Sir Christopher Wren's master-mason.

Christ's Hospital ('The Blue-coat School'): the West Quadrangle, as it was in 1880, "from over the wall of which old school I could hear the mist-muted voices . . ."

"Our little dining-room at Baker-street." Obviously, despite his unhappy memories of Maiwand, Dr Watson could still acquire and display a pair of *tulwars* once used by 'the murderous Ghazis'.

Mr Serjeant William Ballantine. "The kindly, intelligent, humourous face of my old friend . . . that most brilliant of all forensic pleaders."

Colonel Valentine Baker, when commanding-officer of the 10th (Prince of Wales's) Hussars. ". . . this strangest of all cases by which a senior military officer was condemned to complete and final disgrace."

"I have often pulled a half-pint." Mr Holmes, in the *persona* of 'Albert', a groom out of livery, "supporting himself modestly but comfortably as a part-time barman . . ."

William Henry Vanderbilt, eldest son and principal heir of 'The Commodore'. In the eight years that he controlled the Vanderbilt wealth, W.H. made himself the richest man in the world—and laid much of the foundations of Mr Holmes's professional success.

The 'Grand Old Man' of Victorian politics: William Ewart Gladstone, friend and 'redeemer' of harlots, who did not always appreciate his evangelizing interest at its true worth.

". . . the restrained yet magnificent elegance of the Stewart mansion was positively breath-taking." Faced with white marble, this palace of an American merchant-prince (". . . so reminiscent of the mansions of Belgravia and St James's . . .") stood at the north-west corner of Thirty-fourth-street and Fifth-avenue. *Photograph by courtesy of the New-York Historical Society.*

His Imperial Majesty Alexander II, Czar of All the Russias (1818–1881), who conferred on Mr Holmes his first foreign decoration: the Order of St Anne.

Belgrave-square and the Imperial Russian Embassy, at the time when Mr Holmes
and Dr Watson attended the reception at the Embassy to celebrate the coronation of
the new Czar, Alexander III.

H.M. King Oscar II of Sweden and Norway, as he was
when he summoned Mr
Holmes to investigate a Royal
scandal. It was this monarch
who gave Mr Holmes his second foreign decoration: the
Order of the Polar Star. *Photograph from the private collection
of Hr Edward Bergman.*

H.R.H. Prince Oscar Gustav, Duke of Vermland, and Crown Prince of Sweden and Norway, aged 25. It was around the person and private life of this prince (later King Gustav V) that the scandal revolved—the scandal that Mr Holmes scotched. *Photograph from the private collection of Frøken Sigyn Reimers.*

Inanimate epicentre of the scandal: the Nordenfelt steam-driven submarine, seen here as she was in 1883, outside Karlsvik, on Kungsholmen, an island off Stockholm. For his inventions—and, in some measure, as compensation for having been innocently involved in scandal—Torsten Nordenfelt was given, in 1885, the title of Court Chamberlain (*Kammarherre*) by King Oscar II. *Photograph by Johannes Jaeger, from the private collection of Hr Harald Althin.*

"My cousin and good friend." Sir George Holmes, K.C.B., K.C.V.O., the distinguished naval and civil architect, founding Secretary of the Royal Institution of Naval Architects, and the recipient of many marks of honour from foreign governments. *Photograph by courtesy of the Secretary, the Royal Institution of Naval Architects, London.*

Albert Edward ('Bertie'), Prince of Wales, "at about the time that the Prince was defending his good name in the regrettable Rosenberg case." One of the long series of famous 'Spy' cartoons from *Vanity Fair.*

". . . he produced . . . some of the most contemptible scrawls that it has ever taxed my charity to praise." Here is one of the 'scrawls': Charles Doyle's conception of the scene at Lauriston-gardens, in which Mr Holmes, Dr Watson and the Scotland Yarder find the dead body of E. J. Drebber. Few will disagree with Mr Holmes's artistic judgement.

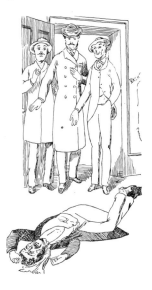

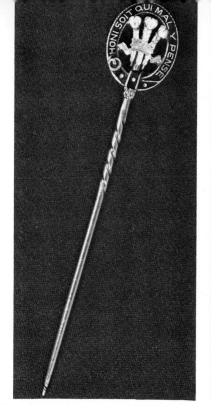

LEFT: Gold-and-enamel tie-pin of the very finest London craftsmanship (Streeter & Company), presented to Mr Holmes by the Prince of Wales, whose badge forms the head of the tie-pin. *Photograph specially taken by Anthony Mann, by kind permission of the present Owner.* RIGHT: ". . . I cannot lift my sword against my future Sovereign!" Lord Randolph Churchill, who felt that rivalry with the Prince of Wales should be confined to irregular conquests of the female; duels were such dangerous affairs.

Prince Otto von Bismarck, reviver of German Imperialism, creator of the Second Reich. "His Serene Highness esteems a professional consulting detective of the highest standing—yourself, my dear Herr Holmes!"

The Suppressed Lampoon. 'The Bridal Night', mocking the marriage of Queen Victoria and Prince Albert of Saxe-Coburg-Gotha, originally published by the 'underground press' in 1840. Re-publication was threatened as the Republicans' answer to the Golden Jubilee celebrations.

Buckingham Palace, as Mr Holmes first knew it. "Her Majesty received me in private audience in one of the smaller drawing-rooms . . ."

These are to Certify that on the *twenty eighth* day of *January* in the year One Thousand eight hundred and sixty *eight* Before us *Charles Kitson and Richard Elias Bishop* Two of the Perpetual Commissioners appointed — for the — County of *Devon* — for taking the acknowledgments of Deeds by Married Women pursuant to an Act passed in the third and fourth years of the reign of His late Majesty King William the Fourth, intituled "An Act for the Abolition of Fines and Recoveries, and for the substitution of more simple modes of Assurance." Appeared personally *Mary Ann* the wife of *John Watson* and produced a certain *indenture* marked **A** bearing date the *twenty eighth* day of *January* One thousand eight hundred and *sixty eight* — and made between the said *John Watson and Mary Ann his Wife of the one part and Frances Maria Holditch of the other part* — and acknowledged the same to be her act and deed. **And** we do hereby Certify that the said *Mary Ann* was at the time of her acknowledging the said Deed of full age and competent understanding, and that she was examined by us apart from her husband touching her knowledge of the contents of the said Deed, and that she freely and voluntarily consented to the same.

Chas. Kitson

Richard E. Bishop

Two complementary documents, dated 28th January, 1868, relating to John Watson and Mary Ann, his wife, and concerning the transfer of Mrs Watson's property to the purchaser, Mrs Frances Maria Holditch.

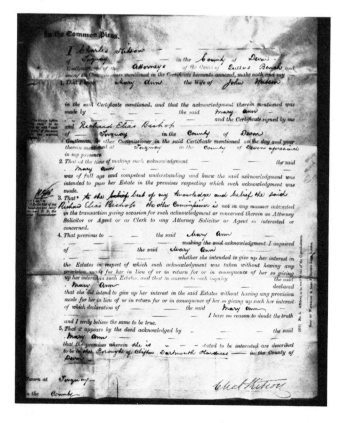

Prince Alexander ('Sandro') of Battenberg, first sovereign of independent Bulgaria, and the reality behind Dr Watson's fictionally presented 'Count von Kramm, Grand Duke of Cassel-Falstein, and hereditary King of Bohemia'. A *contemporary (1879) engraving by A. Weger, from a photograph taken especially for Alexander's coronation.*

Alexander's forced abdication: Russian 'military conspirators forcing open Prince Alexander's bed-room door', on the night of 21st August, 1886. Having shot or bayonetted the Prince's guards, the Russian secret police then forced him to sign a deed of abdication at pistol-point. *Photograph of contemporary engraving by courtesy of* The Illustrated London News.

To Mr Holmes, as Watson has somewhat sentimentally recorded, Lillie Langtry was always 'The Woman'. And so she was, in a somewhat different context, to far too many of the rich and powerful of Britain, Europe and America—one of the most rapacious harpies of all time.

"Watson, of course, was smitten beyond the reach of argument or warning." A pencilled note on the back of the original, in Mr Holmes's writing, records: "Stacey, the artist, sketched this of Dr Watson and Miss Morstan from memory, after we had all gone to hear Norman-Neruda at the St James's Hall. W wasn't too pleased with it, but he was waxy indeed when he found that Stacey had used it for an illustration in one of the *Strand* magazines."

". . . the gilt medal . . . which records that, in 1889, I made an ascent of the great iron tower erected by Monsieur Gustave Eiffel on the Champ-de-Mars." The reverse of the medal bears Mr Holmes's name. *Photograph specially taken by Anthony Mann, by kind permission of the Owner.*

On perpetual pleasure bent—but not the same type of pleasure. H.R.H. the Prince of Wales (*back view*) surveys the Park in the company of Lord Arthur Somerset, five years before scandal forced 'Podge's' exile on him. *Sketch from life by R. Caton Woodville, 1885.*

The selection, by Watson, of the name 'Baltimore' as that of the 'Abernetty's' place of residence is a little less obvious, but, as I said to Lord Kitchener recently, only to those who, unlike me, have not acquired the key to a deviousness more elaborate than subtle. However:—

1. Lord Crawford's body, after its abstraction from the grave at Dunecht, was hidden in a *culvert*. Lord Crawford's family name: *Lindsay*.
2. *Calvert* was the family name of the lords *Baltimore*.
3. *Lindsay*, a town of respectable size in the County of Victoria, Province of Ontario, Canada, is the important railway junction from which a branch line runs to, and ends at, Cobourg, Lake Ontario, the preceding station being . . . *Baltimore*. ('Lindsay' is thus linked with 'Baltimore'.)
4. The next town of any importance to the east of Baltimore, Co. Cork, is Castle*townsend*.
5. The full name of the then (6th) marquess Townshend was John James Dudley *Stuart*, a name which now links 'Stewart' with 'Townshend'—and thus with 'Baltimore'.

This is how the cases of Stewart of New York and Crawford (Lindsay) of Balcarres acquired the single designation of "The Dreadful Business of the Abernetty Family of Baltimore".

What I have never discovered—for I have never discussed my comprehension of his name-changing with Dr Watson—is how much of this name-changing (or, rather, of its *method*) we owe to Watson and how much to his friend and literary agent, Dr (now Sir) Arthur Conan Doyle. That Doyle was responsible for much of the changing, and for much of the more complicated changing, there is no doubt; but to ascribe *all* change to him would be wrong. Dr Watson was quite capable of using a pseudonym to work off an old grudge, as when he came to give a 'safe' name to the thief and traitor 'Joseph Harrison' in "The Naval Treaty", and make him the son of an *iron-master* (when, in fact, he was the son of a Horsham solicitor).

Only by chance, and after many years, did I learn whence this 'imaginary' name came. Dr Watson, believing that my identification of the commissionaire as a sergeant of Royal Marines had been a trick, decided to 'check up', as the Americans say, and, saying nothing to me of course, took the *Atlas* 'bus to Charing-cross. Alighting, he walked as fast as his mysteriously injured leg would let him to the Royal Marine Office of the Paymaster-general's Department, which, in those days, was at 40, Spring-gardens.

Dr Watson asked to see the Chief Clerk; was shewn in; and, why I do not know, received what my good old friend called (most indignantly) 'sauce'. In what this 'sauce' consisted, and why the Chief Clerk should have indulged in it, I cannot say; but Dr Watson did get his information—that the commissionaire had been a serjeant in the Royal Marines—but got, apparently, no apology from the touchy jack-in-office. When, ten years later, Watson was seeking a name for a thoroughly bad hat, the remembered insolence of the Chief Clerk still rankled sufficiently that Watson should have given his name to the villainous 'son of the *ironmaster*': *Quartermaster* Joseph Harrison.

ELEVEN ❧

I walk with Kings

I have often been asked, in that confidential manner in which one's friends ask one to betray one's most closely-guarded secrets, why, after so auspicious a beginning as an actor, I gave up the stage. The answer is simple: Mr Vanderbilt (who knew, of course, that I was 'playing' in New York under my *nom de théâtre* of 'William Escott') warned me that entry into New York Society would be impossible for me, were it to be known that 'William Escott' the stage-player and Mr Sherlock Holmes, the 'heuristician', were one and the same. The great ladies who ruled the salons of New York and Chicago—but more specially the former—had pronounced a total ban on actors and actresses; under the guidance of Mr Ward McAllister, 'creator of New York Society', the ladies of the Astor, Vanderbilt, Rockefeller and Wilson families (to name but the most ambitious and the most forceful), made the great mansions of New York decidedly harder to enter than Marlborough House or the town and country mansions of our nobility.

"Thank goodness," Mr Vanderbilt said to me, "I warned you in time. If my daughter, Alva, knew you were on the stage, she'd shew you the door. And if *she* didn't, the servants 'd go on strike until she did!"

It was in conversation with Mr Vanderbilt that the somewhat dishonest description of me as 'Consulting Heuristician' was invented.

"Got to call you something professional-sounding," he mused. "Something with a Greek or Latin twang. What's 'detective' in either? Or 'puzzle-solver', say. . . ?"

So it was that we arrived at 'heuristician'—and, to make assurance double-sure, 'Consulting Heuristician'.

"Best thing you can do," said Mr Vanderbilt, who liked to have his orders—he preferred to call them his 'suggestions'—carried out with the least delay, "is to take yourself off and get yourself some calling-cards engraved. George Rowell's Advertising Agency, in the *Times* Building, will do you a fast job—they're used to fixing up reporters with real and imaginary cards."

I have a packet of these cards still: I used them but infrequently, disliking the flavour of the, not so much fraudulent (for, after all, was I not a heuristician?), as catch-penny—something which smacked of the less reputable aspects of American commercialism: the 'Professors' of 'painless dentistry', chiropractics and even more dubious quasi-medical arts.

But, as I realized, Mr Vanderbilt had given me good advice: it would have been, in his vivid phrase, 'social felo-de-se' to have attempted to enter New York Society as an actor. I honoured my contract with Mr Sasanoff, and completed my tour with his Shakespearean Company; but, save in the course of adopting the various *personae* necessary to my business, I did no more acting—at least, none which was known to the world. On the night before they hanged him, old Baron Dowson—let Watson's invented name stay, since 'Dowson's' *family* was respectable, even if *he* was not—paid me the compliment of telling me: "In your case, what the Law has gained, the stage has lost." In fact, the stage had not lost any of my histrionic talent—it was simply that I acted on a stage before an audience unaware of my existence.

Mr Vanderbilt was exceedingly good to me, for, as he explained in his frank way, "I can afford to be helpful to those who aren't in competition with me—and you did me a good turn. I like to repay my debts—whatever they are."

Mr Vanderbilt's succession to the financial empire of his father, the Commodore, had surprised many, for it was succession by appointment, not by inheritance. William Henry Vanderbilt had always been 'the quiet one'; but the Commodore had made no mistake when he handed over to his son, to consolidate and extend, the financial power that the Commodore had created. As head of the Grand Central Railroad and many—perhaps most—of American 'basic' industries, Mr Vanderbilt proved himself entirely worthy of his father's trust: the son, when he died, had doubled his inherited fortune, and made himself the richest man in the world.

He liked to tell me stories of the Commodore, a self-made man, as the Americans say, of a ruthlessness to make Attila and Jenghis Khan seem like sucking-doves—but one of the stories planted a seed in my imagination which eventually flowered as the Baker Street Irregulars, that unofficial detective force that I was to recruit from among the street-arabs of the Marylebone slums.

In his middle years, the Commodore, exhausted by his energetic fight to destroy rivals and build his empire, suffered from a combination of more or less serious ailments, any one of which would have caused that insomnia which made his nights so painful. Insomnia was bad enough, but such short and broken sleep as he might have enjoyed was outwitted by legions of caterwauling felines—grimalkins that *did* mew in the night!

How the Commodore found Ikey Vesuvius, Mr Vanderbilt did not know—probably in no more mysterious a fashion (he was attempting some extremely amateur fob-diving at my expense) than that in which I first encountered Wiggins; but somewhere, at some time, in some fashion, the paths of the American multi-millionaire and the bare-footed guttersnipe met—and, reversing the usual *rôle* of the Commodore in these partnerships (a fight, said the Commodore, is no 'more'n mustard on my ham!'), Ikey Vesuvius, the street-gang leader, held the Commodore up to ransom.

Ikey, offered a dollar a-head for every dead cat that he could bring in, promptly ordered his gang out on a great cat-*battue*, and, before the next day, delivered a hundred dollars' worth of corpses to the Commodore. Realizing the almost illimitable possibilities of his rash offer to Ikey—possibilities already fully appreciated by Ikey—the Commodore withdrew his offer. That night, all the dead cats, with their tails tied together, went sailing over the walls of the Vanderbilts' garden. The Commodore, never one to ignore the rare defeat when it came, paid up. And, listening to how a street-arab bested a multi-millionaire, I saw the possibilities of recruiting my own band of urchins—though not to produce dead cats for me.

Mr Vanderbilt, I recall, was amused by my reluctance to 'jump in', as he expressed it, in the matter of my becoming a 'heuristician'. He accused me, though in the most friendly manner, of 'dragging my feet', of being 'too darned conservative', 'too much of the old John Bull'. He approved of my trying to professionalize my occupation, but could not understand how one false step in the beginning might jeopardize that professionalizing for ever— and this was the more curious, as he himself had warned me against the dangers of letting New York Society know that I was—or had been—an actor. When he asked me what I intended to call myself in England, and I answered that I had chosen, as the title of my profession, 'Private Consulting Detective', he shook his head.

"As bad as 'actor'! Worse, in my opinion. I think this die-hard attitude towards admitting actors and actresses will soften—after all, you can't have the Prince and Princess of Wales hobnobbing with the players—to say nothing of other royalties making a fuss over them—and our Society ladies standing aloof. But *detectives* . . . My, that's a different kettle of fish! There's only one type of detective they take seriously over here, and that's a

Pinkerton man—and whilst he's taken seriously and treated with respect, you see a Pink in your Wall-street office, and not in your drawing-room or home study. No, Mr Holmes, you take it from me: you're far better off with 'heuristician' than you are with 'private consulting detective'. I know. You say that you are the world's first private consulting detective—well, for land's sakes, has there ever been a professional *heuristician* before you had the title put on your calling-card?"

"Not to my knowledge," I admitted, smiling a little at Mr Vanderbilt's warmth.

"Well, then—" he said, with finality.

But I never became—officially, I mean—an heuristician; on my return to England, I put my somewhat absurd American visiting-cards away in a pigeon-hole of my desk, and reverted, as they say in the Army, to my former substantive rank: that of private consulting detective. The next few years were to prove me abundantly right.

To justify myself to Dr Watson in the matter of making our diggings free of the Scotland Yarders, whose unpolished and often impudent manner was a constant irritation to my friend, I told him what had been related to a few of us by Lord Coleridge,* one evening in the Athenaeum, shortly after his return from New York in 1883.

The eminent judge was amusing us with a vivid but appreciative description of the grand banquet in October, 1883, at which he had been entertained by the New York State Bar, when one of our company asked his lordship if there were any striking differences to be observed between English and New York law in either principle or practice.

"In principle, very little—hardly any, in fact. But, in practice—well, let me tell you of a conversation that I had with Mr Evarts, one of the most distinguished of New York barristers. I had asked Mr Evarts how American lawyers (they do not distinguish, as we do, between barristers and solicitors)—how American lawyers are remunerated for their work.

" 'Well, my lord,' said Mr Evarts, 'the clients pay them a retaining fee; it may be fifty dollars, or it may be five thousand dollars, or fifty thousand dollars.'

" 'Yes,' I said, 'and what does that cover?'

" 'Oh,' said Mr Evarts, 'that is simply the retainer. The rest is paid for as the work is done, and according to the work done.'

---

* Sir John Duke Coleridge, PC, *b.* 1820, *d.* 1894; Lord Chief Justice of England, 1880–1894; created Baron Coleridge (peerage of the United Kingdom), 1873. One of the greatest international jurists of the last century, honoured even more in the United States than in his home country.—*Editor*

" 'I see,' I said. 'But, Mr Evarts, do clients like that?'

" 'Not a bit, my lord,' he said; 'not a bit. They generally say: "I guess, Mr Evarts, I should like to know how deep down I shall have to go into my breeches pocket to see this business through." '

" 'And what do you say then?'

" 'Well, my lord, I have invented a formula, which I have found to answer very well. I say: "Sir (or Madam, as the case may be), I cannot undertake to say how many *judicial* errors I shall be called upon to correct before I obtain for you final justice!" ' "

"An amusing story, to be sure," said Dr Watson, "and a clever dig at the L.C.J. But, forgive me, Holmes, if I say that I fail to perceive the appositeness of the anecdote. Or is it not apposite of anything—?"

"Indeed it is. It is my justification for permitting Messrs Lestrade—especially Lestrade—Gregson, Peter Jones, Athelney Jones, and all the rest of the Yarders, to make free of both your half of this apartment as well as of my half; and for annoying you with their noisy and familiar vulgarity."

"But, Holmes," my poor friend said in patient bewilderment, "I cannot see—"

"The retainer, Watson—the retainer!—the one mark of a professional man's success which may never be gainsaid. I don't know how I managed it—Government Departments do almost never pay retainers, as I know from Mycroft—but manage it I did—"

"Manage *what*, for heavens sake!, Holmes?"

"To prise a retainer out of Scotland Yard. Ah, did you not know? I quite forgot to tell you. But that is my small—and, perhaps, not so small—triumph. Nor did I get it through the good offices of my cousin, Dr Timothy Holmes, who, as you know, is the Yard's Chief Surgeon.* I got it, Watson, by resolutely sticking to my ambition to professionalize myself; and my opportunity came when the Yarders began to consult me with ever-increasing frequency. Whenever Gregson, or Lestrade, or Athelney Jones were out of their depths—which, by the way, is their normal state—they laid their problems before me. At first I charged nothing; then I charged a fee for every consultation—have you ever tried to screw a debt out of a Government Department, Watson? Ah, yes: your pension is often in arrears, so you will understand. Then, bored with the constant and humiliating duty of presenting each small bill several times, I refused to continue to advise these impudent numskulls unless some satisfactory arrangement were made—satisfactory to me, that is to say—by which, in return for a regular yearly fee, I should hold myself at the disposal of Scotland Yard for

* Timothy Holmes, *b.* 1825, *d.* 1907, was a noted writer on Surgery, as well as the Metropolitan Police's Chief Surgeon for over twenty years.—*Editor*

a certain number of hours each month; hours in excess of these being paid for over and above the fee, which is paid, at my request, monthly rather than quarterly.

"There were difficulties, of course—there always are. I knew that I could not trust Lestrade or any of the others to present my case sympathetically; in any event, they were unsympathetic to the proposition. I took myself off to one of the Assistant-commissioners, Colonel Labalmondiere, who gave the scheme his approval, and sent me to the Director of Criminal Investigation, Mr Vincent, who also approved. The details of my remuneration were arranged between Mr Pennefather, the Receiver, and myself. So far, I have no reason to complain of the arrangement."

"Would it not have been better to have accepted an appointment to the staff of Scotland Yard, rather than continue as a free-lance?"

"And be junior to Gregson and the rest—? Come, come, Doctor, I see that you are in facetious mood! No, in all seriousness, this arrangement gives me most of the advantages of belonging to the Yard, with none—or very few—of the disadvantages. My time is my own; the Commissioner cannot command it; and I am certainly not at the beck-and-call of any of his subordinates. Yet I may use many—most—of the privileges which come to a Yarder: I may go where a private investigator may not; I speak, when I wish, with all the authority of the Yard—and, with my retainer (at which Mr Evarts would either laugh or curl his lip in no unjustified contempt) I have taken the first and most important step in professionalizing the occupation of a private detective. Doctor, shall you remember all this when Lestrade and Company's vulgarity weighs too heavily on your patience?"

I made steps—and often strides—towards the realization of my ambition in those first five years after returning from my tour with the Sasanoff Company. Even at the Union and other clubs most favoured of the professions, my pretensions—for, I may confess now that, at the beginning of my career, they were no more—were taken more and more seriously, though it seemed no hardship to the foreigner to concede professional rank to me. I think now, with vivid recollection of a grand reception at the Russian Embassy in 1883.

The Imperial Embassy, in those days, occupied, as it still does, Chesham House, Belgrave-square, a splendid mansion happily surviving, and the occasion was the coronation of the new Czar, Alexander III, on Sunday, 27th May, 1883, the reception at Chesham House being held on the day following.

I was young then, and no less easily impressed by the novel experience of imperial splendour than any other person of my age. As a Commander of the Order of St Anne—the first (and so still the most valued) of all my many decorations, I had my name entered in the Embassy's 'Book' as a matter of course, and my vanity was hardly offended by the fact that my invitation was brought to me at Baker-street by the Attaché (afterwards Ambassador), Baron de Stoeckl, himself. It was Watson, who, looking out of one of the windows which overlooked the street, drew my attention to the fact that Somebody Very Important Indeed was calling on us. It was a brougham, obviously from Hooper's, and I have never seen horseflesh to equal, let alone surpass, the pair of matched greys which drew the elegant equipage.

Hammercloth and panels bore vast coats-of-arms—I recognized at once the double-headed eagle of Imperial Russia; and both carriage and liveries were in the yellow of the Czars.

It was a happy chance which had brought Baron de Stoeckl in person; for though, in the Russian fashion, he was accompanied by his body-servant (an immense Cossack, in full uniform), he did not send my invitation up by a footman, but climbed the seventeen steps himself—though the door was open to await his entrance when he arrived on the first-floor landing.

I say that it was a happy chance, for having introduced Dr Watson to our distinguished visitor, and that visitor having accepted some slight refreshment from our tantalus and gasogene, my friend's experiences in Afghanistan almost inevitably came into the conversation. On learning that Dr Watson had served with the Berkshires at Maiwand, only some four years earlier, and had been wounded in that battle, the Baron most kindly extended the invitation to the Embassy to cover Dr Watson.

On the following Monday, we set off, in the best brougham that we could hire, for Belgrave-square. I flatter myself, even after this great lapse of years, that our joint and several appearances (as the lawyers say) were in no way inferior to those of anyone else at that magnificent reception.

I had chosen to wear the older type of Court-dress, of blue velvet, with knee-breeches, black silk stockings and with buttons and sword-hilt of cut-steel. It was the first time that I had worn such a dress, but some of its mildly embarrassing unfamiliarity I had rubbed off in my wearing it over several evenings in Baker-street. Against the blue velvet the cross of St Anne, on its light-red-and-yellow riband, looked well indeed; and Dr Watson positively blushed with pleasure to hear my compliments on his appearance in the full-dress uniform of the Army Medical Service, with three medals 'up' whose existence the modest Doctor had never mentioned to me.

The sumptuous mansion in Belgrave-square was illuminated by the recently-introduced electric-light; a fact which alone would have called out the immense crowd that police and embassy servants were politely but firmly keeping out of the carriages' way.

As our brougham pulled up before the marquee which extended the full width of the pavement before the *porte-cochère*, a footman in the distinctive Russian livery handed us out. Our cloaks we left in the cloak-room on the ground-floor, and, Watson's helmet under his left arm, and my cocked hat under mine, we ascended a grand staircase to where, on the broad landing, the Ambassador and his lady, Baron and Baroness Mohrenheim, waited to greet their guests.

Most of this diplomatic splendour is still with us—though three of the most splendid of the embassies are temporarily *en disponibilité*—and there is no need for me to relate in detail what may be found in any *Graphic, Queen, Times* or *Illustrated London News* of the date. What might well be recalled was a special 'British' quality in the occasion, for the new Czar was the brother-in-law of both H.R.H. the Princess of Wales and H.R.H. the Duke of Edinburgh. Whether it was this fact or some other which caused me to be sought out for special attention on that night, I cannot say; but singled out I seemed to be. His Excellency caused no little stir by keeping me in conversation for quite two minutes, whilst the people at my back waited, so that he could pass on to me a message of thanks from the Czar. My head spinning with this mark of condescension, I at first hardly noticed that Prince Ghika, whom I had met at one of Mrs Francis Spring-Rice's * political-legal dinner parties, was present. Prince Ghika, who was with the Princess, was then the Minister Plenipotentiary and Envoy Extraordinary from King Charles I of Roumania. I got permission from Princess Ghika to present Dr Watson to her; and hardly had the introductions been effected than a smart young Guards officer from the German Embassy came up, and asking politely if I were not Mr Sherlock Holmes—he had courteously greeted, of course, Prince and Princess Ghika—added that the German Ambassador, Count Muenster, would appreciate the honour of meeting and talking to Mr Holmes. Asking permission from Prince and Princess Ghika to meet the German Ambassador's request, I followed the young officer—Dr Watson bringing up the rear, at *my* especial request—to where the Count waited for me. With him were almost the entire senior staff of the Embassy: among them, the Councillor of Embassy, Count Herbert von Bismarck; the Secretary, Count von Vitzhum; the Attaché, Herr von Muller, and the Military Attaché, Commander Oldekop.

They all made much of us, greeting Dr Watson with the respect that the Germans always pay to a soldier honourably wounded in battle; and, indeed, that evening went, at first, as they say, like a dream. Of course, it is easy enough now—and was easy enough in the light of the following mor-

* Daughter of Sir Peter George FitzGerald, Knight of Kerry and first Baronet of Valentia (creation of 1880). In 1882, after her marriage, she entered the lists of 'Society hostesses'.—*Editor*

ning—to explain the Germans' interest in me: it was enough that I wore the cross of St Anne to set the Germans wondering why Imperial Russia should have found me important enough to honour with membership of an Order founded in 1735 and reorganized so as to reward, as the Statutes say, those *"étrangers qui ne sont pas au service de la Russie"*.

Nor, indeed, were the Germans the only ones to ask themselves this question, and to attempt an answer. Two gentlemen present that night shewed what, to me, seemed a quite extraordinary interest: Count Charles Piper, the Minister in London of Sweden and Norway, and Count Charles de Bylandt, the Minister of Holland—then a far more important country in its relations with ours than it is to-day.*

In a somewhat different manner, that night is also memorable for the clue that it provided towards an understanding of Dr Watson's (not so much character, as) 'attitude'.

We were in a group, at the buffet, which included the Siamese Military Attaché, Prince Sonabandity, when the talk, begun, as they say, by the sight of Dr Watson's medals and a polite enquiry as to their origins, turned inevitably towards the conduct of the campaign in which those medals had been won.

The professional military class among the Prussians hold the civilian, as is well known, in contempt, but this contempt is modified—often to an astonishing degree—in the case of those who hold the doctor's degree, so that, even had Watson never been a soldier, he would have been treated by the Prussians in our company with some degree of civility. I mention this to explain that what was then said by the German Military Attaché, Commander Oldekop, was said in no offensive spirit. That came later . . .

"Every nation, big or small," he said, "has both its defeats and its victories. The defeats should not shame it—provided that they be but the prelude to victories. But, *zut alors!"* (we were speaking French, for the benefit of Prince Sonabandity and some others) "—*what* a defeat that was! *What* Ayub Khan did to the British at Maiwand! Over fifty per cent. British casualties—and the rest sent hurrying back to safety at Kandahar." †

Watson bowed stiffly; I saw that, instead of the flush that anger or embarrassment usually brought to his very Saxon face, he was now extremely pale.

"I trust, sir," he said to the Commander, "that you will bear in mind that

---

* In 1882, Holland was the third largest exporter to Great Britain (£29,000,000).—*Editor*
† Going over this passage, I recall that Commander Oldekop's actual expression, in French, was far less polite. What he said was, *"Les anglais se sont barrés immédiatement"*—which, I suppose is best translated by the modern slang, 'They skedaddled toot-sweet'. Dr Watson's French was not sufficiently colloquial to appreciate the implications of the Commander's slang phrase.—*S.H.*

the odds were very great—very great indeed. Just over two thousand effective soldiers, against Ayub's twenty-five thousand—on their own ground. Would Germans have done better?"

"I doubt it," said the Commander, breezily, apparently unaware that Dr Watson was keeping his temper only with some difficulty. "But then," he added, putting fresh fuel on the flames of my friend's indignation, "look how badly led you were!"

"General Burrows was an excellent commander, sir! He did the best that he could, with what little he had."

"Oh," said Oldekop, "I wasn't thinking of the commander in the field; I was thinking of that Napoleon *manqué*, Sir Donald Stewart. But," as by now even the obtuse German could see that he had offended Dr Watson, "that was what I was saying about victory and defeat. Major Roberts's brilliant march from Kabul to Kandahar and his victory over Ayub—what could be more satisfying than that?—what more effective to wipe away the stain of defeat!"

"The stain of defeat . . ." The phrase turned over and over in my mind, as we sat in the brougham, in a silence broken only by the jingle of the harness, the clip-clop of the horses' feet, and an occasional snort or blow from the off-side mare. For, as soldiers—and especially German soldiers (at least, of that time)—were given to do, Oldekop grew eloquent upon the subject of military defeat, as well he might, who had watched Frenchmen savagely fighting Frenchmen for the capture of a Paris to be handed over to the Germans.

Commander Oldekop, whilst protesting that "the stain of defeat" could besmirch only the general or, in the case of subordinate officers or men, none but those who had behaved "in an unsoldierly manner", was still at great pains, I thought, to contradict himself, and to make it clear that he, at least, thought all defeat disgraceful—and all involved in defeat eternally disgraced. I have called the man obtuse, and so he was; but in his malicious attack upon the British in general and on Dr Watson in particular (for no-one could have supposed that his remarks were directed elsewhere), he shewed—in his obvious desire to insult and wound—a subtlety for which I, at least, would not have given him credit.

It was impossible to intervene, though I was not the only one present who would have wished to do so—I was well aware of what was causing embarrassment to others. Proverbial wisdom, crude though it often sounds, is rarely at fault, and we were all conscious of the old proverb about the cap's fitting—and of its inevitable appositeness should any of us seek to defend the defeated of Maiwand. In a phrase just as old, we had simply to grin and bear it.

And I must say, looking back, that the German certainly made his point: that the only way in which a man may wipe away the stain of defeat—"*si serait possible . . .*"—is to gain the effacing victory himself. No soldier, no general, no regiment, no army may wipe away the shame inflicted by defeat on *another* soldier, *another* general, *another* regiment, *another* army. "Do it yourself," said the German, contemptuously, "or don't do it at all. Another's success won't make up for your failure. Not," he added, with a sort of kack-handed 'fairness', "that the British Government thinks as we Germans do. For throwing away his soldiers' lives . . . well, had Sir Donald Stewart been a servant of His Imperial Majesty, he could have considered himself lucky to have ended up only in a fortress. As it was, his reward for this shameful mishandling of his plain military duty was the same as that given to the man who so brilliantly retrieved victory from defeat: a medal, the Grand Cross of the Order of the Bath, a baronetcy and—but this is the thing which so astonished us in Germany—*the thanks of Parliament!* Thank Sir Arthur Roberts, yes—thank him a million times for having restored the glory of British arms. But thank Sir Donald Stewart! What for, I should like to ask you, gentlemen—what for? Forgive my heat, but we are a nation of soldiers, we Germans; we reward richly—in both senses of the word. Indeed, *Herr Doktor*, is not true that Sir Donald got even more out of Parliament than did Sir Arthur?—that this incompetent general is now nothing less than the Commander-in-Chief of your vast Indian Empire? *Mein Gott!* what next!"

It was excessively painful to me to sit in our brougham and *feel* the anguish of spirit into which Commander Oldekop's deliberate insults had plunged my friend.

Yet I would not have had it otherwise. For the first time I understood my friend; understood into what torment of mind and soul that headlong flight from stricken Maiwand had plunged him, even though he had been unconscious when his orderly, Murray, had thrown the Doctor across a pack-mule and had led him out to safety.

For it was not in Dr Watson's nature to rejoice, as so many others—perhaps most of the others—would have rejoiced, in 'getting out with a whole skin'. My friend had no more objection to a sound skin than has anyone else; but he wished that whole skin, if I may so put it, to be free from stain—'*pas marquée de défaite*'. I understood now what Dr Watson had been asking himself since that terrible 27th July, 1880—and, far worse, what his unhappy imagination had been assuring him that all others were asking: did he leave that field of dishonour with his own honour intact? Who had witnessed his escape? Only Murray, who (in the Doctor's story) had taken on himself the responsibility of bearing his officer away from what must have seemed certain death. But who—and what—was Murray? A simple orderly—and a medical, non-combatant orderly at that. Which regular soldier would take the unsupported word of a 'poultice-walloper' that the time of *sauve qui peut* had truly come—and who would take the word of even an officer (albeit a medical one) supported only by the word of his 'poultice-walloping' orderly? One might imagine a dozen—a hundred—such derogatory questions, involving every prejudice to be encountered in a nation composed of so many races. Such questions as: "I wonder if he'd have got his orderly to carry him off so smartly had the orderly not been a Sandy, like his officer?"—and so on. Even I, as I sat by a dumb-struck Watson, could imagine many of them.

Then again, why, I asked myself, had this to happen on this night, of all nights? For the night had begun so well, with both of us in the highest spirits; pleased, in a childish sort of way, with our elegant dress and the opportunity to display our medals. Pride cometh before a fall, I suppose that the reader (if these memoirs ever find readers in the far distant future) will say—and that reader may well be right, though it was the pride of only one of us which took the fall.

This, then, was Watson's secret; the secret which had all but soured him; certainly had all but ruined him. The secret which had kept him away from old friends; had sent him, for company and comfort, to the dubious society of *The Criterion, The Continental, The Gaiety* and other even less reputable bars; which had caused him to forsake clubs, professional institutions, and any other places where he might be likely to meet those who had known him in the days before his 'disgrace'—such places as, for instance, the United Service Club (of which, I knew, he was a member), where he would almost certainly have met General Sir John Watson, V.C., not only the Doctor's cousin, but a soldier who had fought throughout the Afghan War.

I had never hesitated to 'keep in touch with' and to take assistance from, if necessary, those of my relatives who had achieved positions of respectability and influence. I won't say that my brother Mycroft had taught me to do this, but certainly his advice had not discouraged me from letting my relatives give yet another struggling Holmes a leg up.

I have already mentioned Dr Timothy Holmes, Chief Surgeon at Scotland Yard; I have not yet mentioned George Holmes, Secretary of the Institution of Naval Architects, nor Robert Holmes, the Treasury Remembrancer and Deputy Paymaster for Ireland; at different times the latter two were as ready to help me as was Dr Holmes. Then, again, there was my cousin on my mother's side: Henry Vernet, Agent and Consul-general for the Swiss Republic in London, whose help in effecting my 'disappearance' from his own country after the Moriarty affair of 1891 I may never sufficiently acknowledge.

Yet Watson had avoided even a relative influential in his own profession—a man of great fame and greater influence, who would, I know (since I afterwards asked him so, in confidence) have taken my friend's affairs in hand, and have put him in the way of taking up his medical practice once more. This was Sir Thomas Watson, Bart, Physician Extraordinary to Her Majesty; the great doctor who was called, in his day, 'The Nestor of English Physicians'. I have already mentioned this most brilliant luminary of Dr Watson's own profession; what I have not yet mentioned is that Sir Thomas belonged to the Devon branch of the family, and was thus much more closely related to Dr Watson than was even General Watson.

This obvious avoidance of all who might have helped him re-establish himself professionally, since he had retired from active military service, had puzzled and—I confess—disturbed me not a little, though I could never permit myself to enquire into what were private matters. But now, having listened to the arrogant German military attaché, and been the pained witness of Watson's distress, I understood that it was an irrational sense of guilt which had made him cast himself out from the society to which, both by birth and by professional achievement, he was entitled to belong.

Now, as we drew near to Baker-street, I found that I was not in despair of my friend's future. I thought that I perceived where the trouble lay, and I flattered myself that I had at least the prospect of a cure. I should make his work *with* me into work *for* me, and then again, turn it into work *with* me, so that he might become my indispensable partner. I had already evolved a practical scheme whereby he was now able to earn some money through my own activities: I had insisted, soon after we had begun to share the apartment in Baker-street, that he took a proportion of the several rewards to which I had become entitled. The finding of Mrs Farrington's (Watson calls her 'Farintosh') opal tiara had not yet been completed when we set up our joint establishment; and the modest reward that the lady had offered I shared with Dr Watson, reluctant though he was to take his moiety. With this as precedent, I was able greatly to augment his small regular income from the War Department, so that, at no great interval after our meeting—some five years or so—he was able to purchase an interest in a practice in Paddington, not far from the terminus of the Great Western Railway.

But money, as the popular phrase has it, is not everything; and my immediate task, as I now saw it, was to efface from my friend's mind the unreasonable belief that he had been guilty of some cowardice and that, as a corollary of this mischievous illusion, all the world thought so, too.

And let me confess that, observing in silence my friend's unhappiness, I felt a certain sense of guilt in the realization that, despite of Watson's dumps, I was conscious of a pulse-quickening elation. (I must say here that I now know my sense of guilt to have been as irrational as Watson's.)

One feels 'guilty' in being happy when those around are not so; it is in the very essence of our human nature to feel thus—but I look back and see that I was happy *despite of myself*; despite of what, in my immaturity, I thought of as 'my better self'.

For I knew that, as my racing friends of the *Adelphi* and *Pelican* and *Victoria* clubs used to say, my plans had 'paid off'; that, at last, I had been accepted for what I was: a professional man, albeit that I was the first member of a profession that I had created for myself—and by myself.*

Later in that same day—for it had gone three in the morning when we pulled outside the now familiar round-headed front-door—I found myself vindicated in a fashion at once practical and exciting. Two liveried messengers brought around two separate invitations to call 'at my convenience' on the writers; one was from Count Piper, the Swedish Minister; the other from the Secretary of the Dutch Legation, Jonkheer van der Does de Willebois.

---

* This remark is only partly true; another private detective of the day, Wendel Scherer, had made a bold bid for recognition as a 'professional man' in a police-court hearing before Mr Henry Jeffreys Bushby, one of the two magistrates at Worship-street. Scherer had refused to divulge the name of his client, claiming 'professional privilege', and though rebuked soundly by Mr Bushby, Scherer *had* put in the private detective's bid for professional recognition. Mr Holmes, nearly forty years later, had obviously forgotten Scherer's pioneering. But see page 12.—*Editor*

TWELVE ✣

Heirs and Graces

So far as the Chief Ruler of a nation is concerned, I am a firm believer in the hereditary principle. The system of either an elective monarchy or a republic (they differ in little but name) invariably and inevitably militates against that continuity of rule on which the stability of a nation mostly depends. Again and again, the United States has been forced to neglect pressing external and internal business because all its politicians of any importance are too busy campaigning for this or that presidential candidate to attend to affairs of state. The same is true, though in a lesser degree, in France; though there more attention may be secured to public matters because of France's larger and more experienced civil service. An elective monarchy in Poland had no other result than to extinguish Poland as a nation. In a republic, where the constitution calls for regular changes of ruler, it is inevitable that continuity of rule may be achieved only by converting the republic into an hereditary monarchy—as was done to the first French Republic by Napoleon I—or by the president's assuming dictatorial powers and by extending his term of office *sine die*. An hereditary monarchy always offers a people the better prospect of uninterrupted rule, and thus of social and financial stability.

But when I affirm that I am a supporter of the hereditary principle, this does not mean that I am equally a supporter of the principle of primogeniture. Indeed, I am strongly against the principle, finding that the eldest sons of kings (or queens) rarely possess the good qualities of the Sovereigns whose powers they will one day inherit. I think that the elective—or, if you prefer, selective—principle should be joined to the hereditary, so that *the most promising* child of the Sovereign should be chosen to succeed. One should never generalize, but eldest sons rarely make good heirs. Think, for

155

instance, what a tragedy it would have been for Kingdom and Empire had the late Prince Albert Victor, Duke of Clarence, been alive to succeed to the throne in May, 1910! Yet, by the strict application of the law of primogeniture, he it was, and not his wholly admirable brother, the Duke of York, who must have succeeded his father, King Edward VII. It was not altogether good fortune, as I have heard the innocent say, that this unhappily degenerate Prince was removed from the Line of Succession; but it was the greatest good fortune that sentiment was for once made subordinate to conventional morality, and, for the sake of the nation and of the world, Prince Albert Victor's accession to the throne was rendered impossible. This was one of the gravest decisions that the Crown's advisers have ever been forced to take; and that the Grandmother and Parents of this unhappy young man gave their consent, reluctant and heart-breaking as it was, to so terrible a solution calls for the greatest respect, no less than for the greatest sympathy. I shall probably have to return to this dismal tragedy later; I mention it here as it exposes, to my mind, the grave weakness of the hereditary principle: the far-too-frequent inheritance by the unsuitable, so that the patently suitable (in this case, the Prince's younger brother) is passed over. Even in Queen Victoria's immediate family, the Princess Royal would have made the ideal successor to the Queen; or, if a male heir had to be insisted upon, it should have been the Duke of Connaught and Strathearn, and not any of his older brothers.

These thoughts come to me because of the situation in Sweden which counselled King Oscar II to send for me to Stockholm, after I had spoken, at the Legation in Charles-street, Berkeley-square, with Count Piper.

The situation may briefly be described as follows.

The Heir Apparent to the joint crown of Sweden-Norway was, at the time of which I write, twenty-five or -six; no notably stable age for any man, but even less so for a headstrong, self-indulgent one, with too much money to subsidize his erratic and often unseemly impulses, and constantly subject, moreover, to the disturbing advice of acquaintances of no social standing and no moral worth.

The Heir was Oscar Gustavus Adolphus Bernadotte, Duke of Vermland, and Crown Prince of Sweden-Norway. Three years earlier—that is to say, in 1881—he had married Princess Victoria, daughter of the Grand-duke of Baden. This beautiful, intelligent and agreeable young lady was, however, to prove no counterweight to the pressures exerted upon her pleasure-bent husband by his unworthy companions, chief of whom was the low-born ex-assistant in the Royal Library at Stockholm, Johan August Strindberg, now, I admit, world-famous as a novelist and dramatist.

This man, of unbalanced but dominating character, was nine years older than Prince Oscar, who had been but sixteen when he met Strindberg in the Royal Library, and fell under his pernicious influence. Five years later, that is to say, in 1879, Strindberg published his first novel, *The Red Room*,* a satirical and violently abusive attack on contemporary Swedish society, especially as found in the capital city of Stockholm. That much of the inner knowledge displayed by the humbly-born author he owed to his friendship with the Crown Prince scandalized the better-bred, and the obloquy which rained down on Strindberg's head was shared, in a pretty equal degree, by his Royal friend.

The moral irregularities of which Strindberg boasted, and which, one may be sure, lost nothing in the dissemination by gossip, frightened King Oscar II and his ministers far less than did the openly proclaimed radical views of the half-mad but brilliant young writer. It has always been the fashion among certain young men born to high position to seek out and befriend persons from a far lower stratum of society; I know of no country and no age in which this phenomenon has not manifested itself—our own country being not at all deficient in examples of that irresponsible Royal predilection for what American colloquial usage felicitously calls 'slumming'.

What the young men of high position never seem to realize until it is pointed out to them is that they are being exploited by exceedingly clear-minded revolutionary ambitions; and that their 'tolerance', as they like to call it, is a mere weakening of their own authority and an opening of the door to decidedly intolerant Radicalism. It was certainly so in the case of those Radical elements, led by Strindberg, who were attempting—no less!—to destroy, by scandal, the stability and the very existence of the Dual Crown.

Aware that youthful excesses, even in a young man married to a charming princess, may be forgiven by the majority of people—especially in so tolerant a moral climate as that of Sweden—the revolutionary plotters sought to damage the reputation of the Crown Prince (and thus of Crown and Kingdom) in a manner which would effectively ruin him even in the regard of the most tolerant. They plotted to involve him in an affair of bribery, at the expense of the State; and here our own legislators may innocently have inspired the plotters, for the lively debates which centred about the passing of the Act for the better prevention of corrupt and illegal practices at Parliamentary elections, in 1883, had been widely reported in the foreign sheets. To explain the workings of the ingenious plot to dis-

---

* Published in Stockholm, 1879, as *Röda rummet*, and not issued in an English edition, as *The Red Room*, until 1913, the year after Strindberg's death.—*Editor*

credit the Swedish Crown Prince, I must briefly explain the development, in the early 'Eighties, of what now promises to become *the* major weapon of war: the submersible warship, commonly known as the submarine.

In 1878, in the foul waters of Liverpool Bay, the world's most improbable inventor was (after a near-fatal first trial) achieving remarkable success with the world's most improbable invention: a steam-driven submarine boat.

I call the inventor 'improbable', since Mr William George Garrett was a clerk in Holy Orders; an Anglican curate in Manchester. How he had conceived the idea of inventing a submersible boat, and whence he had acquired capital and engineering skill to build it, I never discovered. (He was young, though—and Irish; which may explain much.)

However, after some trials in Liverpool Bay, during which his extraordinary craft achieved a surface speed of no less than twelve knots, and during which it remained submerged for as long as six hours, Mr Garrett communicated with the Swedish engineer, Hr Thorsten Nordenfelt, the gun-designer, then working in his machine-shop at Erith, on the Thames, at the perfecting of the light quick-firing gun which bears his name. Hr Nordenfelt had already designed a twin-screw, steam-driven submersible boat, capable of sinking to depths of some fifty feet, and equipped with torpedo-tubes—the first submersible boat in the world, I understand, to have carried these weapons in a practical fashion.

Mr Garrett, the successful experimenter with undersea vessels, then joined up with Hr Nordenfelt, a no-less-successful experimenter in the same field, in active working partnership. The result of this 'pooling of resources' (as modern journalism expresses it) was the launching at Landskrona, in Sweden, of *Nordenfelt II*, the world's first really 'working' submarine—the father of to-day's underwater fleets, whose capacity for limitless evil we saw last May, when the defenceless *Lusitania* was sunk without warning and without pity, taking over a thousand men, women and children to their horrible deaths.

That even the earliest of the Nordenfelt submarines were designed to carry torpedo-tubes disposes, without further argument, of the claim sometimes advanced, that these underwater craft were originally conceived 'with a wholly innocent intention'. They were never conceived save to be weapons of war; but I think that we may justly concede that neither Mr Garrett nor the far more worldly Hr Nordenfelt ever imagined the use to which, in little more than thirty years' time, their joint invention would be put. But no human being of that not-so-far-off time—no, not even the German—could have foreseen that the comment of the *Kölnische Volkszeitung* on this appalling crime against humanity would be: "It is with joyful pride that we contemplate our Navy's latest achievement". But so it is—so it was that one of the Kaiser's most conservative organs of public opinion greeted the sinking of the *Lusitania!*

The launching of *Nordenfelt* II at Landskrona was what the illustrated journals called then—and still call—'a brilliant social gathering'. In this case, they were not guilty of journalistic exaggeration: it was a brilliant social gathering, with representatives of most of the world's more technically advanced nations, Great Britain being present in the persons of T.R.H. the Prince and Princess of Wales.

But it was something far more than a *social* occasion: here was the knowledge that, in the submarine, the nations, always justifying belligerency as 'preparedness', were being presented with a new weapon of war. The knowledge of this weapon, full of the most exciting potentialities for the destruction of others, had reached circles far beyond the purely technical ranks of admiralties or war departments. These uniformed or frock-coated men; these feathered and furbelowed ladies; though welcoming the opportunity of meeting, in social intercourse, their relatives in a hundred European royal families, had not come here to exchange drawing-room gossip, but to see whether or not the new weapon 'worked'. I look back on that day—at which, I should mention, I was not present—with a wonder growing as the years pass. I—we all, then—took it for granted that Royalty would necessarily be present at all such functions as the launching of a ship; and it struck us in no way strange that, at *this* function, there should have been present more Royal persons than usual. What it did not tell us—this plenitude of princes and princesses, noblemen and their ladies, and many presidential suites from republican states—was that, *somewhere*, a mistrust of the professional opinion was growing up. Would that that mistrust had developed to the point at which, I think, it must come—would that it had developed to that point thirty, even fifty, years ago!

Last Christmas—on Christmas Eve, to be precise—flying machines of the Royal Naval Air Service bombed Düsseldorff. Only four years earlier, in the bar of the *Lotti*, in Paris, Mr Orville Wright, the eminent inventor and aëronaut, had shewn me—more with contempt than with anger (though there was anger in plenty, too!)—a letter from the Private Secretary of the First Lord of the Admiralty, to whom Mr Wright and his brother, Wilbur, had offered their proven services in the design and construction of aëroplanes for the Royal Navy.

The letter, couched in those terms of a lofty and irrelevant imbecility which take one back to the spacious days when the Dutch warships took their uninterrupted way up the Thames, thanked the Messrs Wright for their kind offer, but explained to them that, after the most careful consideration by *expert advisers*, their Lordships were of opinion that aëroplanes would not be of any practical use to the Naval Service. And this insanity was written only four years ago!

So that, on reflection, it is possible that, had only 'expert advisers' made up the party at Landskrona, to see *Nordenfelt II* launched, the decision would have been against their Lordships' taking any further interest in underwater warships. One might well exclaim: "But what a happy outcome that would have been!"—Yes, indeed, save for the fact that Sweden was not the only country producing these craft. Herr Wilhelm Bauer, working for the Russian Government, had already achieved a success not incomparable with that of the Messrs Garrett and Nordenfelt. At any rate, not only 'expert advisers' were there—ordinary, common-sensible Royalty and Nobility came, sat, saw—and were conquered. Two Nordenfelt submarines were ordered by the Swedish Government; two by the Turkish; two by the Argentine; whilst other prospective buyers went away 'to think it over'. And now, two years later, with the two Swedish submarines in commission, came the next stage of a carefully worked-out plot to discredit the monarchy and, indeed, the whole social system of Sweden. The Crown Prince was accused, in one of the Radical newspapers, of having accepted a bribe of 50,000 crowns (a little over £27,500 sterling) to procure an order from the Swedish Government for the two submarines—with further craft to come. Eagerly, the other Radical newspapers—and not in Sweden alone—took up the scandalous tale; indignantly, newspapers of the Conservative opinion, took up the tale to shew what calumny political malice might heap on the innocent; between them, both sections of the press managed to obtain for the scandalous tale of the bribe what the Americans neatly call 'maximum coverage'. The second part of the plot now succeeded inevitably and easily to the already well-managed first.

This second part consisted in the supposed 'objective' answering, by the Radical elements, of the question: why did the Prince need the money?—a question which had the advantage of taking for granted that the Prince had accepted the bribe in the first place—something which was far from having been proved, though this type of dialectic prolepsis is part-and-parcel of the tactics of calumny.

In demonstrating the Prince's supposed need for money, the calumniators were all pretty sure that most people would accept as fact that he *had* taken the money. And why did he need money? To satisfy the rapacious demands of some irregular intimacies and of a crowd of irresponsible hangers-on. To rebut these charges, I reflected, as I listened to Count Piper's explaining all this to me, was to be no easy task. But, as I explained to *him*, there is a fundamental rule in warfare which is all too commonly forgotten: that decisive victories are achieved by the victor's having used a superior weapon or by his having used no better a weapon, but in a superior fashion. It is essential, I reminded the Count, to remember that battles are fought out by opposing factions using the same weapons: bows against bows, rifles against rifles—never bows against rifles.

"And the analogy, Mr Holmes—?"

"Simply this, sir: the most effective weapon that the enemy has yet used has been the *apparent* explanation of the bribe—it has been given an *apparent* reason, so as to persuade the unthinking that this must have been a true reason, and that, accordingly, the bribe *must* have been accepted."

"And—?"

"And, Count, if we win—and win we must—it will be, it *must* be, by exposing the falsity of the other side's specious arguments—by shewing that the so-called 'plausibility' of their arguments is not plausibility at all."

"And how do you propose to achieve this, Mr Holmes?"

"I think, Count, that I see the way, though I ask you to excuse my being more explicit at the moment."

"Time presses, Mr Holmes."

"Indeed, Count—but not to the point at which I may dispense with the essential precaution of assembling *all* my facts."

Count Piper's face reflected his worry. He rose from his chair and walked to the window, staring down for a few reflective moments at the meagre traffic coming out of Berkeley-square. He turned, and re-seated himself. In an almost absent tone of voice, he said:

"There is something that I ought, perhaps, to have mentioned before. There is a receipt—"

"A receipt, Count . . ."

"A receipt for the—shall we call it bribe? From the Crown Prince."

"Pooh! a forgery!"

"Even his father, the King, says not."

I rubbed my hands.

"Excellent!"

The Count looked horrified at what he obviously considered my misplaced levity.

"Excellent, Mr Holmes?"

"We know that the Prince is wild—even foolishly irresponsible. Yet, Count, is he what, in this country, is legally termed 'certifiably insane'?"

"Good heavens, no, Mr Holmes! What are you saying?"

"That only a person certifiably insane would give a receipt in such circumstances. You look astonished—doubtful. But consider: *why* should the

Prince have given a receipt? For something so secret that—oh, come, Count, need I explain the obvious? That only a *crétin* would not realize, in signing a receipt, that he was being paid, not primarily to influence the ordering of the Nordenfelt submarine boats, *but to acknowledge, in writing, that he had accepted money?*"

The Count shook his head doubtfully.

"The receipt—of which I have seen a photograph—is very persuasive. . . ."

"Then, in that case," I said, "the signer is a lunatic! Have I offended your sense of propriety, Count, in suggesting that your Crown Prince might be a lunatic? It's not such a grave charge surely? There are," I added, lightly, "always some lunatics about. It would be a dull world without them!"

"Then," Count Piper asked, mastering his irritation with a patent effort, "you are of the opinion that the receipt is a forgery?"

"I think so, yes. But it is not important."

"Not important, Mr Holmes! Why, heavens above!, if this be unimportant, what in the name of goodness *is* important in this case?"

"My demonstrating that the transaction could not have taken place. Then, even if the receipt *might* be genuine—that I doubt; but there is still a possibility that it *might*—my shewing that the transaction could not have taken place will equally expose the receipt as a forgery."

"Nevertheless," said the Count, shaking his head, "even if you succeed in doing that, the principal mischief will have been effected."

"And what, pray, is that? Oh, you mean the exposure of His Royal Highness's private irregularities? No, sir: once again our tacticians have done wrong. They have sought to fire a double charge where only one was needed. By attacking both his morals *and* his honour, the enemy have hardly done the Prince a disservice. They will have presented the two charges as one—so that, when we demolish one set of charges, we shall inevitably have demolished the other. Pray, Count, are you a subscriber to the telephone service?"

"Why, yes, Mr Holmes: the instrument is affixed to the wall behind that Spanish leather screen. Do you wish to make a call?"

"With Your Excellency's permission, I should wish to push on with my plans without the least delay. I have in mind a gentleman whose knowledge might well help me to solve this important problem. He is a subscriber to the telephone; may I please speak to him?"

"Of course! Let me summon a footman to obtain your correspondent."

"No, please, Count! Let me obtain the correspondent myself. The fewer who know even that I have seen you, the better; and the less that anyone knows, the better, too."

Though we had no telephone at Baker-street—I abominated the instrument; and do to this day—I was familiar with its operation. I cranked the handle, and soon the voice of the lady-operator was asking me to which subscriber I wished to be connected? I gave the number, and soon I was enquiring after Mr Holmes. I was connected with Mr Holmes, and made an appointment to meet him in the Savage Club, which, in those days, had not moved to its present handsome premises in Adelphi-terrace, but occupied one of the old houses in Savoy-place.

After I had replaced the receiver, the Count, who had risen from his chair, said:

"I could naturally not help hearing that you asked to speak to a Mr Holmes. Would I be incorrect in assuming that the Mr Holmes to whom you spoke was your brother Mr Mycroft Holmes, of the British Foreign Office?"

"You know my brother?"

"Well, indeed," said the Count, in a pleasantly warm manner; "Mr Mycroft Holmes is by no means unknown to this Legation. We have the greatest admiration for his diplomatic skill."

"The Mr Holmes to whom I spoke, and whom"—I consulted my Frodsham—"I hope to meet within the next half-hour, is not my brother Mycroft, but my cousin and good friend Mr George Holmes, the Secretary of the Institution of Naval Architects, whose expert knowledge of naval architecture—*and its cost*—I trust will be of great use to us, Count."

The Minister looked over the muslin blinds into Charles-street.

"Mr Holmes, I see that one of the Legation broughams is standing at the kerb. Permit me to offer you—"

"In a carriage with the Swedish bearings on its panel? No, I thank you—but I should like a hansom, if your Excellency would be so good—?"

The Count rang a hand-bell, which was instantly answered by a smart young Legation clerk, whom the Count instructed to send a footman for a hansom. Whilst we waited for the cab, the Minister said:

"Now, as to money, Mr Holmes—you know that you have *carte blanche* in the matter of expenses; and, of course, in respect of where you think fit to go, and whom you wish to accompany you. As to your fee, all that is necessary will be a note from you. We shall not argue."

"I thank your Excellency. I shall almost certainly wish to go to Stockholm, and to take Mr Holmes, the naval architect, with me. But we shall see. Ha! is that a hansom that I hear?"

"It is, Mr Holmes. My good wishes, and those of my Royal Master, go with you. Do not fail us, Mr Holmes!"

There are problems whose solution almost suggests itself in the manner in which we seek to solve them. As an exercise in detective science, pure and simple, my solution of the Swedish mystery will perhaps not rank with such *chefs d'oeuvre* as some others that Dr Watson has described, for my success in this affair was attributable, not so much to the observation and interpretation of clues as to what Serjeant Ballantine once recommended to me as "a jolly good look at human nature!" "Imagine yourself a thorough-paced scoundrel, my dear Holmes—and then imagine what *you* would have done!"

This, then, was what I did: I had "a jolly good look at human nature"—that is, human nature, not at its most attractive, in the persons of Hr Strindberg and even less reputable acquaintances of the Swedish Crown Prince. And, whether this confession be against me or for me, I had no difficulty, I assure the reader, in knowing what I would have done to effect the ruin of the Prince. What I also saw was that greed which would have prevented my stopping half-way—stopping before I had gone so far as to ruin the scheme that I had so carefully devised.

Over a sherry-and-bitters in the library of the Savage Club—a club whose friendly Bohemian tone I had already sampled in the company of Lord Crawford—I explained to my cousin what I needed.

"I cannot—that is to say, I dare not—make an approach to either Mr Garrett or Hr Nordenfelt, who could, naturally, give me the figures that I require. So, George, we shall have to try for the closest possible estimate of the cost, not merely of one of these submersibles, but of the machine-shop, tools, and so on, needed to produce the craft. Do you think that you could manage an estimate for me?"

"I see no difficulty. I know where the steel was produced; I know what the wages bill would be in a Swedish yard—yes, I could make more than a fair guess at the cost of laying down a keel and fitting the vessel out. There is no secret of the tonnage or of the horse-power. When would you like the figures?"

"As soon as possible. One of the craft is launched, five others are on the stocks. You can let me have an estimate of the money already spent, and the money needed to complete the craft not yet built? Capital! And now, George, I must make my last call. If the information that I seek is what I think that it ought to be, I must be prepared to go to Stockholm at once. Is it possible for you to join me?—my client will defray all expenses and settle your fee without quibble. How say you?"

I left George in the Savage, and walked the few yards to the Strand—the Savoy Hotel had not yet been built over the old houses. I hailed a four-wheeler, and soon we were trotting briskly eastwards, towards the City and Baron Rothschild's splendid place of business: New Court, in St Swithin's-lane.

Here, however, a disappointment awaited me. My growler had turned into the courtyard, and I had entered the large hall. An attendant, in the famous blue-and-red Rothschild livery, approached me, and enquired courteously how he might be of assistance. On my handing him my card and requesting the favour of a few minutes' conversation with the head of the Firm, the man shook his head. The Baron—or Sir Nathaniel, the footman called him—was not at New Court, but at his town-house, 148, Piccadilly.

However, on my insistence, telephonic communication was soon established between the City and Piccadilly; I spoke to Baron Rothschild, * and was invited to call at my convenience. I re-entered the cab that I had prudently kept waiting, and within twenty minutes I was again alighting—this time outside Sir Nathaniel's mansion facing the Green Park.

On my presenting my card, I was shewn immediately to a splendidly furnished study in the rear of the house, in which the world-renowned banker was awaiting me. As I was announced by the butler, Baron Rothschild rose to greet me with a courtesy bordering upon affability, offering me a warm grasp of the hand.

"Pray be seated, Mr Holmes. I am most happy and honoured to have this opportunity of meeting you. I have heard much of you from Mr Edward Baring; † I have long wished to make your personal acquaintance. And now tell me: in which way may I be of service to you?"

"To the Swedish Crown, Baron; to the stability of Europe, in fact."

The Baron shrugged his shoulders.

"It is the same thing—if you are acting for Sweden."

I bowed at the compliment.

* It was by this title—a barony of the Austrian Empire—that Nathaniel Mayer Rothschild (born 1840) was generally known, though 'officially' he used his English title as baronet, that he had inherited, in 1876, by special remainder, from his uncle, (Baron) Sir Anthony Rothschild, Bart. In the year following Holmes's call on him, (Baron) Sir Nathaniel was to be raised to the peerage of the United Kingdom, as *Baron Rothschild* of Tring, co. Hertford, a title which is still in existence.—*Editor*

† Of the famous banking family, associated with Baring's Bank. 'Eminences grises', as well as bankers, the Baring family gained no fewer than four titles under Queen Victoria: Baron Ashburton, Viscount Cromer, Earl of Northbrook and Baron Revelstoke (to the last of which the Doyle-Watson pseudonym, 'Lord Leverstoke', must be a reference).—*Editor*

I then explained the situation, as it was known to me; not failing to give the Baron my surmises as well as my facts.

"I see, Mr Holmes: you wish to know whether or not the Messrs Garrett and Nordenfelt are still working with their original capital—a sum easily determined—or whether or not they have raised additional capital? Yes, indeed. In the first place, I can tell you that they have not approached *us;* but, as there is nothing better than confirming one's suppositions, will you permit me to make a telephone-call to New Court?" This was soon done; the Baron spoke to one obviously in his confidence; nodded, and disconnected the exchange. "No—as I thought: they have had no money from us, either originally or lately."

"Thank you. Is it possible, Baron, for you to find out whether or not any additional capital has been raised—not only in London but on any of the markets of the world? And if so, how much has been raised?"

The Baron smiled.

"Within a few hours, Mr Holmes; and I shall be pleased to do it. We have been of service to the Swedish Crown; this gives me a further opportunity to serve. How shall I communicate with you, Mr Holmes?"

"By telegram will do. I leave the discretion of its wording to you. My friend Dr Watson enjoys my entire confidence—but, as for the others—"

"Exactly. So be it, Mr Holmes. A telegram, then, before the end of the day—"

The telegram arrived at about nine o'clock. I tore open the familiar grey envelope with, I confess, some trepidation.

With a sigh of relief, I read this:—

> Attic wit by the northern field
> Got what Hubbard's cupboards yield.
> Favonius

I handed the telegram to Dr Watson, who read its cryptic message with wrinkled brow.

"Holmes: this is without meaning to me. Will you translate?"

"Thank God that I have received it! The honour of, not merely a man, but his country, also, is now saved—at least, for the present. What is it that you do not understand, Doctor?"

" 'Attic wit by the northern field . . .' Holmes: I can make nothing of this, I assure you!"

" 'Attic wit'. 'Attic' is a synonym of 'garret'—in modern colloquial English, at any rate. 'Attic wit', then, must mean 'Garrett intelligence'—or 'the intelligence of Mr Garrett'. Yes, this must be the meaning. 'By the northern field'. Associated with the northern field. 'Northern field' is the literal translation of 'Nordenfelt'. Thus: 'Mr Garrett, in partnership with Hr Nordenfelt'. So far, so good. When Mrs Hubbard went to the cupboard, Doctor, what did she find there? Nothing? Precisely! And that was the answer that I was hoping to get. Messrs Garrett and Nordenfelt have raised no capital. . . . Excellent!"

"And who is this 'Favonius', Holmes? He sounds like a character from Shakespeare."

"My dear Doctor," I replied, laughing (and almost slipping, far too dangerously, into the familiar character, not of Polonius, but of Captain Dacre-Buttsworth), "you really must familiarize yourself more with the more notable events of the racing calendar. The 1871 Derby was won by Favonius—and Favonius was owned by Baron Rothschild. The telegram, in short, tells me what I wished to know—and is signed by Baron Rothschild."

Three or four days later, George Holmes also presented me with some highly important news: that the capital spent by the Messrs Garrett and Nordenfelt had been just sufficient ("almost to a mere thousand pounds, I should say," was my cousin's comment) to defray the expenses of construction, so far.

"Pack your bags!" I said to Dr Watson, as soon as I had read George Holmes's letter, with the copious notes enclosed. "Then take a hansom to Cockspur-street, and book two first-class passages—saloon, of course—to Stockholm. In the meanwhile, I shall call on the Swedish Legation, and inform Count Piper that King Oscar may expect us with the best of news!"

The rest is easily told. We travelled to Stockholm: by train from London to Hull; and thence by swift passenger vessel of the most modern type, with every convenience from steam-heating to electric-bells. But we did not travel alone: Count Piper; his secretary; and Mr Richter, the Consul-general, accompanied us. On one thing I insisted: that a secret session of the Riksdag, the Swedish Parliament, be held, and that I address it. To this proposal there was no objection, and, on the advice of King Oscar himself, I spoke in German, rather than English, as most Swedes of the educated classes are more familiar with German. At Stockholm, we were joined by George Holmes, who had come to Sweden by a different route.

My speech to the Riksdag was short—and, I think, completely to the point. I explained that I had asked for the honour of addressing the two Houses of Parliament *in camera*, since the scandalous rumour of the Prince's having been bribed by the Messrs Garrett and Nordenfelt had made it necessary to discuss this partnership's private affairs—and such a discussion, in public, would be grossly unfair to an honestly conducted firm. There were murmurs of approbation from all sides of the chamber as I made this observation.

"Very well, then, Your Majesty, my Lords, Gentlemen—this is the long-and-short of the matter. I have expert evidence, both here, in the person of Mr George Holmes, and in London, in the person of Baron Rothschild, to prove that, in the first place, almost all the capital originally possessed by the designers of *Nordenfelt II* has been expended in the production of this and her sister ships—Mr Holmes estimates that, between them, the Messrs Garrett and Nordenfelt have less than a thousand pounds sterling left. And, in the second place, that no banker, big or small, has been approached either by, or on behalf of, the partnership. For this statement, I have the word of Baron Rothschild.

"The question now remains, Sire and Gentlemen: if the Messrs Garrett and Nordenfelt have spent *all* their money on the construction of their submersible craft, and—as Baron Rothschild tells us—they have raised no more, *whence came the fifty thousand kroner that the Crown Prince is supposed to have taken in order to procure an order for the makers of* Nordenfelt II?

"The Messrs Garrett and Nordenfelt did not pay it—even supposing that they had wished to do so; *for they did not have it.* And if someone else, you may suggest, paid it over on their behalf, *why should that third party have done so?*

"In short, Sire and Gentlemen, there was no fifty thousand kroner. There was no bribe. Only a malicious tale—among a dozen equally malicious tales—to discredit the Crown Prince, to discredit the Monarchy, and—in the end—to discredit Sweden herself."

As is now well known, that was the end of that particular scandal, though there were others, but none with so grave a danger to Sweden's monarchy—with these I had nothing to do; the Swedish *police des moeurs* were competent to handle them.

Nothing could be done to prevent the publication of *The New Kingdom*, in which Strindberg poured out his venom on Swedish Court life—though he did find it convenient to absent himself and his family from Sweden for several years.

The gratitude of King Oscar and the Government was enheartening for me. On the day following that on which I had been permitted to address the Riksdag, a grand dinner was given by Their Majesties, at which I found myself the guest of honour.

At a brief ceremony held immediately before the dinner, in one of the smaller rooms of the Palace, His Majesty was graciously pleased to invest me with the insignia of the Polar Star. It was not to be the last of my

Orders bestowed by the Swedish Crown—but, as my first, I took, I confess, a deep pride in my having earned it.

Her Majesty made me many pleasant compliments during the course of the evening—nor did she forget to be gracious to both my cousin and to Dr Watson (both of whom received tie-pins with the blue-and-gold shield of Sweden, flanked by the Sovereign's intertwined initials). I have omitted to mention that Queen Sophia was the daughter of the late Duke William of Nassau, and I believe that it was at her suggestion that, on my return to London, I was approached by the Dutch Minister in London, Count Charles de Bylandt, to solve what turned out to be a far more complicated matter than the Swedish business.

Before I go on to relate what had happened in Holland that my peculiar skills should have been needed, I must comment briefly on a development which is not only clear to me now, but which, even in those early days of my career, was not at all unsuspected of me—and, in truth, of not a few other people: that my professional skill (it is becoming fashionable to call it *expertise*) was manifesting itself in two coupled, but still distinctly different, aspects.

Perhaps I may make myself better understood if I remark on the fact that the clues by which we may arrive at the solution of any mystery are readily classifiable under two heads: the static and the dynamic; the permanent and the impermanent; the—if you do not object to the expression—the dead and the quick. There are many ways of describing the essential difference between the two types of clue, but an example will probably effect more than paragraphs of added explanation will.

For instance, a burglar, on leaving the scene of his felony, may tread into a muddy patch, and leave a clear impression of his boot. By means of plaster-of-Paris, this impression may be rendered permanent—that is, a cast may be taken of the print, which may then be used to identify the boot which has made it, and thus—one hopes—the wearer of the boot. The modern classification of the finger-print has added yet one more important item to the list of permanent clues.

But there are other types of clue which do not depend upon the criminal's leaving behind him cigar-ash, boot-prints, finger-prints, blood-stains, and so on. These are the clues which reside in the behaviour, *before, during and after the crime*, of the criminal and (if he have them) of his associates.

The detection of crime and the criminal by the observation of the second type of clue may be able to dispense altogether with such deductions as may be drawn from the presence or absence of the material clue. Indeed, a curious result of this ability to dispense with the material clue, in favour of the psychological clue, is that, after a time, one finds oneself coming to be more and more concerned with human behaviour, and less and less with the personality, as such. As I remarked to Watson on more than one occasion, one may never foretell what any one man may do, but one may say with precision what an average number will be up to. Individuals vary, but percentages remain constant, so that the pattern of behaviour, generally, rather than the pattern of one man's behaviour, is what should be the object of a puzzle-solver's attention. Sooner or later, however individualistic we fancy ourselves—or, indeed, seem to be—be sure that we shall come more and more to conform to the general pattern. It was for this reason that I concentrated my logical processes less upon the individual and more upon the pattern of behaviour into which, I realized, he must fit. Crime is common; logic is rare. Therefore it was upon the logic, rather than upon the crime, that I chose to dwell.

The inevitable result of this intense preoccupation with the *patterns* of human nature was that I gained, of course, a profound understanding of it; in no long time I came to be able to tell, without recourse to the dropped ash, the mark of the bicycle-tyre, the bloodied door-knob, not only what a criminal had done—and who that criminal must be—but what criminal intent must assuredly lead to.

In my work, especially that which brought me into contact with what the Americans call 'The Four Hundred' and we, less generously, 'The Upper Ten', I frequently met the late Sir George Lewis, whose lucrative solicitor's practice and great personal influence were derived from his having persuaded our aristocracy that, when in trouble (and that was not rarely the case), the only possible rescuer was Mr Lewis, as he was then.

Now, I have nothing to say against Mr Lewis or his often quite dazzling achievements; there was nothing bogus about him. He knew his Law (and, at the beginning, despised me because I did not); but that which had brought him to such power as the Distressed Aristocrat's Friend prevented his going further. Mr Lewis was too narrow. He could—and almost always did—find a means of suppressing this scandal or that (he was brilliant in his 'behind the scenes' handling of that revolting Cleveland-street affair); but his solutions were always legal, or, rather, legalistic. Either from a natural bent or because of his training as articled clerk to one of the shrewdest (and many thought the most slippery) of London attorneys, Mr Lewis saw a human being only as an entity with an odds-on chance of falling foul of the Law; and the rescue of that troubled human being as nothing save a perfectly legal trick to outwit the Law's punishment. Mr Lewis did not like me, because he feared, quite rightly, that my far-more-elastic methods would be bound—once his type of client had got to hear of them—seriously to challenge his monopoly as the Arch-Rescuer. As for my own feelings, I did not particularly care for Mr Lewis, who was a fellow-member of several of my London clubs; but as I had nothing whatever to fear from him, I bore him nothing like the detestation that he bore towards me.

Naturally, like any two properly-brought-up men, we met on terms of apparent amity; indeed, Mr Lewis went so far in concealing his animosity as to recommend to me several of his clients whom he had been unable to help. The cases of "Vamberry, the Wine Merchant", "Riccoletti of the Club Foot and His Abominable Wife", "The Service for Lord Backwater" and "The Arnsworth Castle Business" were all mine to solve on the apparently warm recommendation of Mr George Lewis.

But to return to what I was saying earlier, I soon saw that puzzle-solving fell into distinct classes: the first, in which the interpretation of the *material* clue was a vital step in my arriving at the truth; the second, in which my understanding of human motives provided the key to the solution. It was in the second class of puzzle-solving that my greatest success was achieved; and it was this type of success which gave me the *entrée* to strata of society which not laggardly grew more and more exalted.

I did not neglect those cases in which the material clue was of the first significance, though to *all* cases that I chose to accept my one unvarying rule applied: I chose to be associated only with those crimes which presented some difficulty in their solution. I worked hard to accumulate criminal statistics—or, rather, those statistics which would be of help to me in dealing with criminals. My earliest published monograph, "Upon the Dating of Documents",* was written, it is true, long before my second class of puzzle-solving had brought my talents to the notice of the Great; the same may be said, too, of my next three monographs— *Upon Tattoo-Marks* (1878), *Upon the Tracing of Footsteps* (1878), and *Upon the Distinction Among the Ashes of the Various Tobaccos* (1879), all of which were privately printed at my own expense. But my fourth privately printed monograph, *A Study of the Influence of a Trade upon the Form of the Hand*, most handsomely illustrated with lithographs of the hands of slaters, sailors, cork-cutters, compositors, weavers and diamond-polishers, appeared in 1886, after I had served the governments of Russia, Sweden and Great Britain, and a little before I was to be summoned to help the Russian Government once more, and both the Royal Family and the Government of Holland.

The year—1888—which saw my successful handling of the case of Prince

* *The British Antiquary* (not *Antiquarian*, as is sometimes stated), Vol. XXIII, No. 9, 43–50, September, 1877.—*Editor*

Alexander of Battenberg (whom Watson calls 'Count Von Kramm') also saw the publication of my article "On the Variability of Human Ears" in *The Anthropological Journal;* the year 1890 saw the publication of *The Type-writer and Its Relation to Crime;* whilst after my return to London in March, 1894, I wrote and published two further handbooks of detective interest, which will be noticed in due course.

I mention these small but important literary productions here to prove my claim that I had not abandoned the cut-and-thrust of a professional life far removed from the calm and ordered elegance of Court and Cabinet; the scent of the quarry, the 'wild pursuit', the view—the kill; that headlong action in which the chase takes over from contemplation; all that feverish hunt which has so often begun with my excited remark to Watson that 'the game's afoot'. Excitement never removed me from those exalted strata of society in which, after Mr Vanderbilt's first recommendations, I found myself 'accepted'; but on the other hand, those more quietly pursued solutions to the problems of the Great never weaned me from work in the less refined levels of society, where crime was endemic, but its problems simpler; and where there was not a little honesty, too—albeit that was sometimes only the honesty of half-witted brutality.

The motto of my grammar-school in Yorkshire was that cut-down (and so, in my opinion, pretty meaningless) quotation from Juvenal, that I prefer in its full form: *Orandum est: ut sit mens sana in corpore sano.* I don't know how many schoolboys or college men are impressed and guided by the school or college motto—I doubt that one in ten thousand even knows what it is—but I was one of the exceptions: I not only knew the motto of my school; not only felt myself enormously impressed by what, to me, was its obvious truth; I did (as they say in the Services) something about it—I kept my body and my mind as healthy, through sane exercise, as I might manage.

I boxed as often as I could; sometimes at Alison's, sometimes at the Victoria Club; sometimes (though in disguise) at those amateur rings in the seedier parts of Bermondsey or Bankside, where the winner, paid five shillings or even a mere hard-won half-crown, has to fight for it again as he passes through the brutal larrikins waiting to 'skin' him outside.

My sight in those days was not so defective that its imperfections might not be overcome by low-powered lenses, since all that I suffered from was a mild astigmatism; but I was reluctant to wear even a single eye-glass, because of the danger of my being hit in the eye by some ruffian. I contented myself, therefore, with a magnifying-glass, that I always carried with me. But practising with a pistol at the Villers-street shooting-gallery or with a Government Martini-Henry B.L. for one of the medals of the National

Rifle Association (I never, alas, got beyond the first stage—the Silver Medal of the Queen's Prize), I always wore a double eyeglass, whether practising as Mr Sherlock Holmes or as Captain Dacre-Buttsworth. And here occurred one of the most mysterious phenomena ever to trouble me by my inability to find even the wildest explanation: no matter how hard Mr Sherlock Holmes tried, 'the Captain' always beat him.

There is no doubt of this: memory plays no deceptive part here. Shoved away in my attic here at Fulmer is an old box full of score-cards, all marked with either my name or that of my *altera persona* *—my favourite *altera persona*, let me confess: Captain Dacre-Buttsworth, whom, later, I was to 'regularize' by obtaining his commission in the Post Office Volunteer Rifles. But of all that . . . anon.

This fact—and it certainly was a fact—obsessed me as a word or a scent or a note of music obsessed some of Poe's less normal characters; and it obsessed me the more as I realized the impossibility of discussing it with even the most discreet of psychologists without betraying the secret of Captain Dacre-Buttsworth's identity. A troublesome thought came (inevitably, one would suppose) after I had been persuaded by Watson to read that extraordinary tale of Stevenson's about Dr Jekyll and *his* other image, the villainous Mr Hyde.

Had I, in so closely identifying myself with the gallant, bogus and *déclassé* Captain, lost some of my own personality? Had I created, as Dr Jekyll with his self-administered drugs had created, not so much a different aspect of myself *as an entirely different person?* It was a disturbing thought; though, as I dwelt upon it, a more reassuring thought came to lighten my apprehensions. I remembered that 'Kangaroo' Hill had not accepted the bogus Captain of my assuming as an entirely different person—entirely different, that is to say, from Sherlock Holmes; for had not the shrewd racing journalist asked me bluntly who I really was? Still, the thought that I might have effected a Hyde-like change in my essential personality troubled me for a long time, and in so much as I have never yet found the explanation of the Captain's superiority in the aiming of pistols and rifles (I have had no opportunity to test his prowess with shotguns, the Captain never having got himself an invitation to a shoot), I suppose that I may say that this disturbing thought is with me still.

On our arrival at Pau in the autumn of 1868, my Father, besides entering me at the local Lycée, had also arranged for my regular attendance at the

* There is no doubt that, living and thinking in a still Classically-educated world in which even a 'Salutaris' soda table-water advertisement used Greek quotations in its copy, Mr Holmes used this phrase in its strictly Classical sense, in which *persona* is properly and primarily an actor's mask, and only metonymically the actor—the 'personage'—himself.—*Editor*

fencing academy of Monsieur Bencin, still acknowledged to have been the greatest *maître d'escrime* of his time. Though I had passed a few terms (we called them, as did the Etonians, 'halves' in those days) at Mycroft Grammar School, I had never really recovered from my serious illness of the winter of 1865–6, when, for several days, my family despaired of my young life. Seeing that I was still in great need of some restorative treatment, my Father decided that the balmy airs of that part of France by the Spanish border would effect a hoped-for improvement in my health, and our happiness was unbounded when it became clear that such would be the case.

I remember the year well as one in which my poor Father's never very flourishing finances—he had only his pension of some £1,200 a-year and my Mother's small income from her jointure to support a family of five—received a quite unexpected increment. My Father was never what, in Captain Dacre-Buttsworth's parlance, was called a 'racing man'; but he was interested in horses, and every now and then would lay out a few sovereigns on some animal which had caught his fancy. His 'method'—if there may ever be a method in this chancy business—was certainly not what 'Kangaroo' Hill would have called 'scientific'. My Father selected his fancies by name only, ignoring 'form', for all that Ruff * had no more careful a student. Years later, when I described my Father's 'method' to Arthur Binstead, as we were drinking a hock-and-Seltzer in 'the Roman's', he shook his head in compassionate wonder; and though I cannot recall his exact words as we sat within traffic-roar of the Strand, I find that he has repeated himself (probably not for the only time) in his amusing volume of reminiscences, *Pitcher in Paradise*. Let us assume that this is what Binstead indignantly told Phil May and me on that sunny morning of a Spring now gone these thirty years and more:—

> The fatuous folly of this incessant war against the satchels! Are not the monstrous odds against the backer sufficiently illustrated by so clear an object-lesson as the easy affluence of the bulk of his opponents? What but brains and an early perception of the way the game lay lifted Davis, 'the leviathan', from the carpenter's bench, Reynolds from the cab rank, Steel from the fish-market, Head from the telegraph needle, and Alec Harris from the bakehouse.

Not with such literary elegance did Binstead denounce the backer on that Spring day in, I think, 1884 or 1885; but, as Phil May observed, he got his message over clearer than did the semaphorist six fathoms down on the deck of a ship which had sunk in a pea-souper.

"So that's how your Governor betted, did he?" Binstead remarked, with a fine contempt for such follies. "And the bookies took the lot, I suppose?"

---

* *Ruff's Guide to the Turf*, the 'Bible' of the racing man.—*Editor*

"Only two of them," I answered, mildly, to draw him. "The other four honoured the bets. It was—"

"Wait now!" Binstead said, slapping the table with his huge hand: "I've got you! You're Tom Holmes's son. Good lord! I was there when Charlie Head took the lot at Goodwood in '74: £2,380 10s.—I remember the exact figure: Good Lord, I've heard it from Charlie often enough!—and never paid one sprat out—talk about skinning the lamb. I remember your Father took a hundred to twenty-five on Napolitain; and so did Lord Rosebery, except that he lost a century. So Tom Holmes was—pardon me!: *is*, I trust?—your Father?"

"My cousin," I said; "my Father was Captain Siger Holmes of the John Company: it's of his method of backing that I'm speaking. You know, Binstead, the system of—how shall I put it?—onomancy? Is there such a word? Divination by name?"

"If there isn't," said Phil May, sketching me on the back on a menu-card, "there jolly well ought to be! So your Governor patronized the system popular with the ladies? How well—(never mind about Binstead's prejudices!)—did he do? It isn't always the worst system."

"On the occasion of which I am thinking—very well indeed. He was a Blue Coat boy, and if Binstead will recall the year, 1868—?"

"By Jove, yes! Sir John Hawley's Blue Gown! That must be the animal? Romped home at Ascot, and, a week or so later, nabbed it at the Derby—Wells up each time. Now *that* was a piece of mobile kagmag! And your Governor backed it—?"

"The double event."

"Phew! The double! You don't say so! Blue Gown was odds-on, or nothing to bet for, in the Derby, but he started at fifties, or more, perhaps, at Ascot. Remember what your Governor took?"

"Two hundred and fifty to one—that was from Charlie Head, I remember; the others—Dunn, Percival, Steve Somebody-or-Other—"

" 'The Old Durham Ox'? Yes—Steve. I don't think he had another name. And what did your Governor win?"

"From the ones who paid—Head, Dunn, Percival and the one you call Steve—about ten thousand. They wouldn't accept more than a tenner each from my Father; and the ones who would—and did—welshed."

"Still," said Phil May, philosophically, finishing off his 'lightning' sketch of me with his characteristic flowing signature, and handing me the card,* "ten thou'—twenty monkeys—is better—or is it 'are better'?—than a poke

---

* Phil May was the best and the most famous of the 'lighter' artists of late Victorian times who contributed to the humorous journals and newspaper 'features', being a regular and deservedly popular contributor to *Punch*. His sketch of Mr Holmes has not, so far, come to light. Should it ever do so, it will be an artistic discovery of the first importance.—*Editor*

in the optic with a wet stick. How say you, Brother Pitcher? * Do I not utter the words of verity?"

"Of a surety, Phil!" said Binstead. "And to prove that you don't palter— is there such a word as 'palter'?; yes, there must be!—palter with the truth, let me assure you that I wish it had happened to me!"

My Father's lucky 'investment'—it was never repeated—made all the difference to what we thereafter enjoyed and what might have been our modest portion had the ten thousand not come (as by a miracle) my Father's way.

It was not wealth; and young as I was, I was never encouraged to think it so. I believe, though I am not altogether sure of this, that my Father sought the advice of both old Tom Holmes and of that other Holmes cousin who later became Paymaster-general in Ireland. At any rate, the 'investment' was soundly invested, and yielded some five to six hundred a-year, which took much of the financial burden off my Father, and enabled me to go, at the proper time, to both Universities, though later, as I have explained, it was through the generosity of my brother, Mycroft, that I went to Bart's.

* Arthur M. Binstead was a leading member of that brilliant team of writers who kept the 'Pink 'Un' popular for so many years. He always wrote under the style of 'Pitcher'.—*Editor*

THIRTEEN ❦

The Man from Devil's Island

That Dr Watson took considerable pride in his association with me is no secret; indeed, he has made as much clear in his many descriptions of my cases. Often, I regret to say, this pride led him into some indiscretions, which, added to the mistakes directly attributable to his deafness, not infrequently caused me no little trouble.

To take first the errors caused by Dr Watson's deafness, I can find no more striking example than in this paragraph from the episode that he (or Dr Conan Doyle, to whom I shall come presently) called "The Six Napoleons"; in which I am quoted as saying:

> You will remember, Watson, how the dreadful business of the Abernetty family was first brought to my notice by the depth which the parsley had sunk into the butter on a hot day.

Pausing only to observe that, if I have quoted Watson correctly, he has not done the same by me—I am surely never *that* ungrammatical?—I must say that this is what we may well call a *chef d'oeuvre* of mishearing.

It was not until the middle of 1904, I think,[*] that I read Dr Watson's account of the sinking parsley; and we had parted by then through my retirement. Had we been still living at Baker-street, I should have asked Mrs Hudson for two or three ounces of butter, nicely patted into a roll, a *bain marie* and some parsley. I should have melted the butter over the *bain marie*; the butter, of course, having already been decorated with a sprig of parsley; and then invited Dr Watson to observe that parsley does not, will not, cannot, sink into even completely melted butter.

[*] *The Strand Magazine*, May, 1904; *Collier's Weekly*, 30th April, 1904.—*Editor*

What I did tell the Doctor was that it was the depth to which the *pass-key* had sunk into the butter which gave me, not merely the clue, but the certain evidence that I was seeking.

It was in my *persona* of the Captain that I heard about the trick that dishonest servants played in the gaming clubs of London (and, I dare say, of most other cities). When the gambling had become what used to be called 'fast and furious' at tables on which silver, gold and banknotes lay as thick—and as unregarded—as autumnal leaves in Vallombrosa, the trick was for a club-servant to walk in with a tray of unordered drinks and plant the tray firmly on that part of the table on which the money lay. Looking up from an (almost certainly winning) hand, the member would give a brief and angry glance at the menial, and mutter, "D—n your eyes! I didn't order anything! Take that confounded tray and yourself off!"

With commendable obsequiousness, the servant would do as he was bid; apologizing for the 'mistake'. To the pat of butter which had been put on the bottom of the tray, gold, silver and—if the servant's luck was in that night—paper would be adhering.

With such an old trick of the gambling hells and even more reputable clubs the pass-key in the Stewart affair had been taken from the table on which it was lying. When I examined the pat of butter in which the key had been embedded, I saw that it had remained within the butter for some time; I was able also to judge, by the depth into which it had been pushed, the approximate weight of the tray (that is to say, approximately what that tray was carrying)—and, therefore, *who* had been carrying it. The fact that the key had been for some time in the butter gave me both the approximate time at which the theft had been carried out, and the period which had elapsed between the theft and the thief's being able to take possession of the key. From these several pieces of evidence, I was able, first, to say who could not have stolen the pass-key; second, who might have had the opportunity; and, third, who—of all possible suspects—*must* be the person who had purloined the key, which opened the vault in which Mr Stewart lay in his coffin.

So much for the inconvenient results of Dr Watson's deafness. The results of his indiscretions were far more serious, as I discovered one evening in the May of 1885.

I must explain that my relations with Scotland Yard had undergone some change. The notorious Benson affair, in which Detective-inspectors Druscovitch and Meiklejohn, with Detective-sergeant Palmer (an unlucky name for criminals!) had been sentenced to hard labour for their having accepted bribes from Benson, had—though now several years in the past—

made for a loosening of those friendly bonds which linked the professional police officers with the public. I was hardly to be classed with the public; yet, for all that I was on what the Americans call 'a retainer basis' with Scotland Yard, I had never been on a friendly footing with any of its subordinate members, and—though Watson insisted (and, indeed, still insists) otherwise—this reserve on my part was the natural response to a reserve established by Lestrade, Gregson, Jones and the others. This reserve—this mutual reserve, if you prefer—sprang not, as Watson insisted, from the irritation that the Yarders' individual and common vulgarities caused me, but simply from the fact that public confidence in the integrity of the police had received a grievous blow. This had come through the revelation (in which, by the way, I had had no part) that, from his splendid country seat, 'Rose Bank', near Shanklin,* Harry Benson, *alias* 'Monsieur le Comte de Montagu'; a convicted felon;† was instructing and governing a Scotland Yard almost entirely in Benson's pay.

At the beginning of my association with Scotland Yard, my relations with its staff had been amicable enough; but it was clear that, as my relations became more friendly, so did Higher Authority instruct its myrmidons to adopt a greater reserve, not specifically towards me, as towards any 'outsider' who might be suspected of exercising an improper influence over the Yarders.

Thus, by the middle of 1885, I had almost ceased—I speak now in the most practical terms—to be on friendly terms with the members of the Detective Force; the most striking—and, I must add, the most irritating—aspect of this cooling-off of amicable relations being the withdrawal of what I may call 'preliminary discussions'. It was not that I, Sherlock Holmes, had forfeited the confidence and trust of Scotland Yard; I was still 'on a retainer'; the more abstruse problems were still submitted to my professional examination. No, it was that, through the criminal venality of a group of senior Yarders, Scotland Yard's administration had lost—one hoped, only temporarily—all confidence in itself. The consequence was that, to natural caution of the outsider succeeded a perhaps understandable *suspicion* of the outsider—of all outsiders, simply because they were outsiders. Nor did the inherited and acquired character of the Commissioner, Colonel Henderson,** serve to modify this attitude of suspicion towards the outsider; in-

---

* Isle of Wight.—*Editor*

† Sentenced at the Mansion House, by the Lord Mayor of London, for having embezzled money raised to help the people of Châteaudun, occupied and ravaged by the Germans in the Franco-Prussian War of 1870.—*Editor*

** Lieut-colonel Sir Edmund Yeamans Walcott Henderson, K.C.B., late Corps of Royal Engineers. The two Assistant-commissioners were Lt.-cols. D. W. P. Labalmondiere and Richard Lyons Otway Pearson.—*Editor*

deed, as an Engineer officer of already narrow views, the Colonel, on taking up his appointment as head of the Metropolitan Police, had resolved on his own way of effacing the dark blot on Scotland Yard's reputation, a way which needed no explaining to the two military men who were his deputies. The Higher Command of the Army has always had a disinclination to take outsiders into its confidence; now, at Scotland Yard, these three diehard soldiers had what they considered an excellent excuse for 'keeping themselves to themselves', and even the most trusted of their consultants were again and again denied that early intimation of irregularity by which crime might have been prevented. Too often, alas!, the consultants were grudgingly told only when matters had gone dangerously far indeed.

This digression was necessary to explain why it was that, on a May evening of 1885, I was startled—shocked—by the sight of the man who followed Gregson into our sitting-room, after I had called "Come in!" to a knock on the outer door. I have, I flatter myself—and I had in those days—an unusual control over the outward expression of my emotions; but now, at sight of the stranger, I stumbled awkwardly to my feet, the basket-chair in which I had been sitting creaking noisily as I pushed myself up by its arms.

I stared—I know that I stared; for Gregson, seeing and correctly interpreting my confusion, permitted himself a vulgar grin as he said,

"Startled you, eh, Mr Holmes? I see you know the gent?"

'Startled' was hardly the word to describe the sense of physical and mental confusion—almost of horror—with which I recognized the pale face and slim form of the youth (he was still hardly more) whom I had last seen, paler and quieter even than now, dressed in full uniform, with his orders and decorations, *lying dead in his coffin.* I remembered—yes, I remembered to bow, and to indicate that my visitor should take a chair. Gregson's face still wore its idiotic grin; and, since one recalls only the trivialities of such moments, I recall that I reflected that Lestrade's grin would probably have seemed even more vulgar. Gregson took out his note-book.

"Let me introduce—er"—he read the name with obvious difficulty—"Mongsewer Chappy de Bang: Mr Sherlock Holmes. Now you're properly introduced, let's get down to business."

A slow smile passed across the pale, aristocratic features of my quite-unexpected guest. Without asking me if I knew French, he said quietly, in that language,

"Je regrette, monsieur, le malentendu, mais Monsieur le Flic vient de faire une erreur regrettable. Ce n'est pas de ma faute, mais il vous a donné mon métier au lieu de mon propre nom. C'est amusant, n'est-ce pas?"

The easy manner in which my visitor spoke and comported himself generally did much to restore my shaken aplomb; nor was I mistaken in realizing that he was deliberately setting out to put me at my ease. I turned to Gregson.

"What did you say that this gentleman's name was?" I asked him, with an impatience not underived from my shaken nerve.

"I told you; I read it out to you," the Yarder said indignantly. "Here," proffering his well-thumbed note-book, "read it for yourself!"

I read it. 'Mongsewer Chappy de Bang' indeed! I hardly knew whether to laugh out loud or throw the fire-tongs at Gregson's stupid head. I asked:

"Do you really know what's written here, Gregson? Please be seated, both of you. *Do* you know, Gregson? No—? Then let me explain that these three words, 'échappé du bagne', are not a name but a description. They mean, in English, 'gaol bird' or 'old lag'. Is your companion a gaol-bird, Gregson?"

"Oh yes!—and from the toughest Steel * in the world. Tougher than anything that we have in this country, *I* can tell you! There's not many clinks tougher than Cayenne—no wonder they call that hot pepper 'Cayenne'!"

I turned to my strange guest.

"Do you speak English, monsieur?"

"Fairly well, sir."

"You sound to me as though you have learned to speak it very well, indeed. Well, now, since Mr Gregson does not speak French, shall we converse in English?—and shall we come to the point? I don't suppose that Mr Gregson has brought you here to discuss the time of day?"

"More important than that," said the detective.

"Then you had better tell me what brings you here?"

"I understand that you can remove tattoo-marks," Gregson said, matter-of-factly.

I sprang up with an oath.†

"You dolt!" I shouted. "What folly put *that* idea into your thick skull!"

"You told Lestrade yourself—or so I understood."

"Or so you understood—you d—d jackanapes! I told Lestrade no such thing! How could I—when it is not true?"

"Lestrade says different," the man said doggedly, glancing at the visitor from Devil's Island, who sat unmoving whilst I stormed at Gregson's meddling stupidity. "Or, Mr Holmes, I could be mistaken—"

"Oh, surely not, Mr Gregson!" I said, sarcastically.

---

* 'Steel' was a corruption of 'Bastille', the popular—especially with criminals—nickname of the House of Correction, Coldbath-fields. Like that of 'Clink', originally the private prison of the Bishops of Winchester, in Southwark, 'Steel' became a generalized name for any type of prison.—*Editor*

† Watson has deleted this human failing from the record!—*Editor*

"—and it could be," he added, not heeding the interruption, "as it was *Dr Watson* who told him. At any rate, Lestrade was full of it when he came back to the Yard."

"He'll be full of something else if he goes around making such absurd statements. I take it that you, monsieur, wish to have a tattoo-mark removed?"

He was dressed in the conventional frock-coat of European fashion, and his shirt-cuffs were wide enough that he might pull his coat sleeve up without unfastening a cuff-link. Silently, he exposed his forearm. Neatly tattooed, about half-way between wrist and elbow, was this:—

Pr 14116

"I take it," Gregson remarked, conversationally, "that 'Pr' could stand for 'Prisoner'. I believe it's more or less the same in French?"

Neither my visitor nor I answered the detective.

"The marks have not been there for very long," I observed.

"Not long, monsieur. They are not tattooed on so long as one's sentence is under appeal. Once the appeal is dismissed—and it almost always is—then one is marked as a felon for life. I should, naturally," he added, quietly, "prefer to be without this decoration. Are you sure, monsieur, that you are unable to erase it? No . . .?

"A pity. Ah well, they were so sure at—well, let us say that they were so sure that you had the secret. *Alors!* this is simply one more disappointment to add to so many others!"

I did not tell this mysterious stranger that, had I mastered the secret of removing tattoo-marks, I should certainly not have exercised my skill on his behalf. I found his manner singularly engaging—perhaps my good impression was due in some part to his being so strikingly contrasted with the boorish Gregson—but it was impossible not to be favourably influenced by the young Frenchman's person and manner, both of which displayed every indication of good breeding.

"Don't you wish to know who I am, monsieur?" my visitor asked, with a slight smile.

"No, sir, not particularly. I imagine," I added, with a lightness to match his own, "that you are—or will be—what political expediency will need you to be. Nor do I think that even the presence of those marks will contradict the story, should it be necessary to tell it. There are precedents for everything under the sun—the Man in the Iron Mask might serve as a precedent for the story that I believe that you are about to tell."

"Yet, when I came through that door, sir, you recognized me?"

"I did not 'recognize' you—for that word means that I recognized your identity, and I do not know who you are. I recognized the *likeness* of a face that I—indeed, the whole world—knew. I was, for a moment, shocked by the likeness; even now I find it hard to believe that I am not talking to the young man who died six years ago, far away from this country—alas, deserted by his English friends."

"Who returned later to find a mutilated body—"

"*His* mutilated body."

"The Hottentots had *thoroughly* mutilated the body, sir. The corpse was accepted as that of the Prince, but—but *was* it his? A body was buried with full Imperial honours—yes, but *whose* body? That of the Heir to the Imperial Crown of France—or, that of an English soldier? Might it not have been expedient that the Prince should temporarily have disappeared?"

"So that, sir, is who you say that you are?"

"It is what I say that I am. Do you not believe me?"

"It would trouble my credulity to do so."

"Then how do you explain a likeness to the Prince so exact that, on first seeing me, you were shocked, as you English say, out of your skin?"

"It is not my business to explain the likeness. That it is astonishing is true—but then, sir, you would hardly be here were it not. Still, had I to explain the likeness, I would cite the well-known laws of human generation."

"It is somewhat insulting to a gentleman to suggest that he was born *à la main gauche?*"

"You raised the subject, my dear sir, not I."

"I said that I was the Prince Imperial, who had escaped—as did his cowardly brother-officers—the massacre of Isandhlwana, and—"

I raised my hand.

"No sir: let *me* complete the tale. Your English brother-officers *were* cowardly—but not in the way which is usually meant by that word. They *did* desert you—but not through cowardice; it was intended that you should fall victim to the assegais and knobkerries of the savages. Indeed, the party of Zulus were not all that they seemed to be: they were released prisoners-of-war, who had gained their freedom by promising what, to them, was no distasteful task: the murder of a white officer. Do I make progress, Monsieur le Prince? Excellent! But, at the last minute, just as his brother-officers, pretending panic, galloped away, the Prince realized that he was the victim of a plot to murder him. So that now it was *he* who—I don't know how this was effected, but doubtless we shall come to it eventually—suborned the natives; got them to mutilate an already-dead body, and let you, sir, go, on the promise of gold to make their already-secure freedom even happier. And this was how it was done."

"And then—?"

"Oh—then? Well, you foolishly returned to France, where though the authorities hesitated at murder—unlike the shameless English—they had no hesitation in cooking up both a false identity and a false criminal record for you—no one may beat the French at that kind of thing. They tattooed your arm with a number, and sent you away for life—just, as I said, like the Man in the Iron Mask. And now you are here, in Baker-street, preparing for the next step. By the way, have you suffered any loss of memory through your hardships?"

"None, I am happy to say."

"Have you yet seen your Mother, the Empress?"

"Not yet. You understand that she must be prepared for the shock of knowing that I am still alive. Why even the sight of me gave you, a stranger to me, a powerful shock."

This piece of impudence was said with so innocent an air that I could not forbear laughing out loud.

"Upon my honour, Prince, that's rich! Well, you haven't forgotten your Mother, then? And you remember, of course, that you are an officer in the British Territorial * Army; I take it that you can discuss the esoterics of the parade-ground and officers' mess with a fellow-officer—say, Colonel Henderson, the Commissioner of Police?"

The 'Prince' glanced carelessly at Gregson, who, at the silent invitation, leaned forward eagerly in his chair.

"Oh, Mr Holmes, I forgot to tell you—but it was the Commissioner who sent me along with—er, with—"

"Mongsewer Chappy de Bang. Dear me! And is the Commissioner entirely satisfied with your identity, sir?"

"Perfectly, sir. It pains me to note that you are not."

"Doubtless. But perhaps I can see a little farther into the future than can Sir Edmund Henderson."

"And what can you see that Sir Edmund can not?"

"I look back a couple of years and recall that Prince Napoleon was imprisoned by the Fallières Government—a mere matter of three weeks; but imprisonment, none the less. If I remember correctly, that was in the month following the unveiling, by the Prince of Wales, of a statue of the *late* Prince Imperial, at Woolwich—the two events may be not unconnected. Then, when the Fallières Ministry fell, President Grévy signed a decree putting all Princes of former reigning houses who were serving in the army or navy on the retired list. I imagine, from the way in which the Orleanists and the Napoleonists are now behaving, and in the present mood

* This adjective has changed its meaning—at least in this specialized connection—over the past century. In 1885, 'Territorial Army' meant the *home-based* army, as distinct from military units stationed abroad.—*Editor*

of French politics, that it will not be long before an expulsion order is added to the forcible retirement. I deplore the move, but I see it as inevitable. The Orleans and Bonaparte families will be expelled from France—perhaps next year, perhaps the year after—who can say? But soon."

"And then—?"

"And then, full of indignation, and thirsting for revenge, the expelled Princes will arrive in this country—and, if I am any judge of human nature, they will welcome your ability to embarrass and perhaps overthrow the French politicians who have banished them from their own home-land.

"But, my dear sir, and you, too, Gregson: I want nothing of all this. I regret that you came; regret even more that it was the Commissioner who sent you. Who sent you to him, I do not know, nor even wish to know. And now, without wishing to seem discourteous, may I bid you both good-night?"

I did not follow this precious pair—the well-bred, infinitely cunning, and even more dangerous rogue, and the fairly honest but dull-witted dupe. I saw Gregson hail a hansom, and waited until it had passed out of sight before donning my hat and coat and hailing another for myself.

I told the cabby to drive me to the Diogenes Club; I hoped that I would catch my brother Mycroft there.

I was fortunate; Mycroft was in the smoking-room, reading *Bell's Life in London*, and helping himself from a bottle whose shape proclaimed it to be filled—or formerly filled—with claret. He did not rise from his comfortable position in the worn saddle-bag chair, but said to the club-servant who had conducted me from the hall,

"Jenkins: bring another bottle—and a *leetle* more *chambré* than the last. I do not care for my claret *frappé*—or very nearly so." The man went off, and my brother said, with hardly a change of tone: "That visitor *did* irritate you, Sherlock. Pray tell me what he wanted—or what he was? Oh . . . how do I know that he irritated you? Because you could barely wait to see him off before you came here, to discuss him with me. And—oh, I see! Well, you were so impatient to hail a hansom that you stood, not within your doorway, but by the very edge of the kerb, to get both your boots and your gaiters splashed. No matter—ah!" as the returning servant brought the new bottle, and, after having set out clean glasses, and offered the label and cork for Mycroft's inspection and approval, drew the cork, wiped the neck with a snowy napkin, and poured out a little for my brother's tasting: "Excellent!" The man filled our glasses * and withdrew. "And now for your story—"

---

* This remark is not to be taken literally, but in the context of polite behaviour both in Mr Holmes's day and in ours. The wine was poured to the correct two-thirds height; this was the Diogenes Club, and not a modern wine-bar.—*Editor*

I related the events of the evening, and added:

"One wonders, Mycroft, that people have not yet learnt that complexity too often fails where criminality, kept strictly simple, ordinarily succeeds. I admit that the shock-using gambit is not ineffective—I was, for a moment or two, quite thrown, I confess, by seeing the young Prince Imperial walk into my sitting-room."

"You have come to see me," said my brother, "to find out whether or not I—or, at least, my Service—had anything to do with this evening's affair? My dear fellow: let me put your mind at rest. Her Majesty's Government had nothing to do with it; nor, indeed, had Her Majesty's Foreign Service."

"Forgive me, Mycroft," I said, "if I seem to have too tender a concern that eyes be dotted and tees crossed; but the British Government does sometimes act as a friendly agent for a foreign power? It was certainly so when Peel authorized the Postmaster-general's *Cabinet Noir* to intercept the Italian revolutionists' mail and to tip off the Neapolitan Government to the presence of plotters at home. And whom was the British Government helping when they left both Fieschi and Orsini free to make their bombs?"

"I am not splitting hairs, my dear Sherlock. Here, permit me to give you a little more claret? Neither for ourselves nor on behalf of others did we arrange the little comedy tonight. You have my word on that, Sherlock."

"Then I am satisfied. But on whose behalf, then—?"

"What of your all-purpose principle: *Cui bono?*"

"True. And I have tried to apply it. But who would wish to use a false French Pretender?—a Continental Lambert Simnel or Perkin Warbeck?"

"Any of the French royalists, I should venture—?"

"Yes, the thought had struck me, too."

"Sherlock: have you wondered what had happened had you known how to remove the tattoo-marks? Why do you laugh?"

"But I *do* know. Pray, Mycroft, don't look so astonished! I certainly had the means of removing the marks from the false Prince's arm. A little soap and water would have effected the erasure. The figures were merely *painted* on; not tattooed. My sight is defective in some respects, but I was not deceived there. I don't think, either, that I was expected not to appreciate the significance of the rather crude prison-marking." I took out a pencil and drew this on my cuff:—

Pr 14. 1. 16

"What, Mycroft, should have been conveyed by that marking?"

"Well, if a real prisoner had been about thirty, he could hardly have been admitted to Cayenne on 14th January, 1816. Therefore we are not dealing

187 The Man from Devil's Island

here with a date. 'Pr' *may* stand for *'prisonnier'*— on the other hand, it may stand for something else; say, at a venture, 'Prince'. So that, if the digits do not stand for a date, they might stand for letters of the alphabet. Like this"—and, taking up my pencil, and catching hold of my arm, he wrote, on my cuff, above the letters already there, this:—

N   A   P
Pr 14.   1.   16.

"Yes—'Pr' is certainly 'Prince', as 'NAP' is the English colloquial contraction of 'Napoleon'.* You are correct, Sherlock: you were intended to 'discover' the 'proof' of your caller's assumed identity."

"To what end, Mycroft?"

"To the end that this was a test, and, play it how you would, you had to shew your hand: you had either to join or reject the conspiracy."

"If one admit the conspiracy?"

"What else—?"

"A practical joke—? Any of those loutish friends of the Prince of Wales or of the Duke of Edinburgh—Lord Charles Beresford, Lord Aylesford, Charlie Buller, Bob Bristowe—could have thought up such a joke."

"Indeed, yes. But don't make the mistake, Sherlock, of underestimating these men; and for Heaven's sake don't think that, because a plot of theirs has the *form* of a jest, it necessarily has the *content* of a jest.

"Their Royal master and boon companion may be more German than English—but he is the only one in that select band who is: the rest are far more French than English; the Duke of Edinburgh is so gallicized—or has so gallicized himself—that he prefers the argot of the Parisian *apache* (of which, by the way, he is a master) to the diction of the Faubourg St Germain, a district which bores His Royal Highness to extinction. All these men think of Paris as their first home: there they can meet those friends of the Prince of Wales who've made England too hot to hold them.

"They're all friends of, and devoted to, both the French pretenders—royal and imperial: even the respectable members of the Orleans and Bonaparte families they like. Yes, Sherlock, this was a test, to see on which side you'll come down when, in a couple of years' time, all the French princes will be expelled from their native land, and will have come here, to do their plotting from this side of the Channel.

"And—I see that you wonder how they are going to keep their Perkin Warbeck concealed from discovery until the time to produce him is ripe?—I think that the late Prince Imperial belonged to no unusual physical type:

* Cf. the card-game *nap* (French, *Napoléon*).—*Editor*

Italian pallor, somewhat effeminate build: there are hundreds like him to be seen any day in Soho or Saffron-hill. Did you notice any signs of what the stage people call 'make-up'?

"I thought so. Be sure that you did. But wipe away the 'make-up', and you have some young French or Italian fellow who bears only a type resemblance to the Prince Imperial."

"Do you think that they thought—?"

"That you might have fallen in with their plans? Hm! Well, my dear Sherlock, you have already performed some very useful services for one or two of our European royalties. I'm happy, though, to see that you rejected the invitation to engage in intrigue. Republican or not, France is a country with which we must stand well. You did rightly, Sherlock! I approve your judgement. I shall take care that your decision is made known to Olympus." *

"What disturbs me somewhat, Mycroft, is that Lestrade talked out of turn."

"Not necessarily. He may have passed on information that he considered should be known to his superiors. You say that Gregson informed you that he was acting, in bringing this pseudo-Prince to Baker-street, on the orders of Colonel Henderson?"

"Yes—and that disturbs me even more. Why should Colonel Henderson, whether or not as Commissioner of Metropolitan Police, concern himself with testing me—or even with seducing me from my principles?"

"Because, my dear Sherlock, Colonel Henderson is a former officer of Engineers. He is also a Knight Commander of the Bath. Now, Sherlock, you must never neglect, not so much what people *are*—in this case, an officer of Engineers, a Knight Commander of the Bath—as what being what they are links them to. Do you comprehend me? The Duke of Cambridge, besides being Commander-in-Chief, is also Colonel Commandant of the Corps of Royal Engineers—and thus Colonel Henderson's perpetual commanding officer. Now, where does this take us? The Duke of Cambridge is the Queen's cousin; the Duke of Edinburgh is her son. Both are Knights Grand Cross of the Bath—and our Colonel Henderson is a Knight Companion of that Order. All three are members of at least five London clubs in common. Do you see any difficulty in the Duke of Edinburgh's persuading the Duke of Cambridge to *ask* Sir Edmund Henderson to send Gregson,

* This expression, whose meaning is obvious, was peculiar to my brother, who, when the context required it, referred to the 'dwellers in Olympus' as 'Olympians', and their behaviour or decisions as 'Olympic'. As the famed Olympic Theatre, in Wych-street, was then, like a much advertized Scotch whisky, 'still going strong', Mycroft's references to 'Olympians' and 'Olympic' could conveniently be mistaken, by any casually listening ear, for references to the theatre or its players or patrons.—*S.H.*

with the *soi-disant* Prince in tow? Of course not. And now, Sherlock: one earnest word of advice. Not a word of this to anyone. Not to anyone at all, do you understand?"

"I feel inclined to rebuke Dr Watson for having been too free with his confidences to Lestrade."

"Forego the expression of your righteous indignation! There is no need to remind the good Doctor that his indiscretion came to anything. He will have forgotten by now—let him forget. You did well. The other day, She Who Must Be Obeyed * was graciously pleased to mention to Lord Granville † that her cousin of Sweden had spoken most favourably of you, and Her Majesty gave it as her own opinion that you must be an exceedingly accomplished young man."

"I am most gratified to hear it."

"Lord Granville told me so himself. You see now how unwise it would be were you to seem to criticize, even by implication, one of Her Majesty's sons—especially since he was the loser by the jape or test? Good! I see that you are of my opinion. A silent tongue, Sherlock, remember!"

* London Society's discreet mode of mentioning the Queen in open conversation. (Cf. 'Mr Smith' for Mussolini.)—*Editor*

† Earl Granville, K. G., Principal Secretary of State for Foreign Affairs.—*Editor*

FOURTEEN ❧

Dr Conan Doyle and
some others

Though it was between the two doctors of medicine—John Watson and Arthur Conan Doyle—that an intimate and enduring relationship developed after their meeting in the early part of 1886; the year in which the official Golden Jubilee celebrations began, and a year of which I may say without exaggeration that it was the busiest of my whole professional career; it was I, and not Dr Watson, to whom Dr Conan Doyle first procured an introduction.

I had long ceased to attend the lectures of Dr Klein—or, indeed, any other lectures—with anything like regularity; but I had not given up attendance at lectures and demonstrations altogether; and I had long formed the student's habit of glancing at the notice-board as I walked to or from the Pathological Laboratory, sometimes looking in at the Dissecting Room as I passed.

For those who do not know the customs of the world of the great teaching hospitals, let me point out here that a lively fraternal spirit irradiates what, to the stranger, might seem a world austere, cold and even, in some respects, unfeeling. In fact, this is not so: the intense loyalty that membership of any hospital generates in the average breast is felt, at the same time, as a loyalty to the much larger world of the Hospital generally. One may be a loyal son of Bart's, as I was—and am still—but even the tyro medical student felt, as he was made to feel, that he belonged within a world-wide dedication to Healing, whose beginnings go back to a time beyond which the memory of Man travelleth not.

Well, one day in—I think that it must have been—at the end of February or the beginning of March, 1886, it happened that, among all the lectures and various other entertainments offered by the notice-board of Bart's, there was one which literally caught my eye and immediately engaged my interest: a lecture by Mr (afterwards Sir) Anderson Critchett, without doubt the most eminent of British oculists—at least, at the time of which I write.

The lecture, *On the Effect of the Electric Light on the Human Retina*, was to be given in the Great Hall of the Royal College of Surgeons, in Lincoln's-inn-fields, under the chairmanship of Mr John Marshall, F.R.S., then the President of the Royal College.

To-day, when the electric light is a commonplace, and—in an aspect at once reassuring and sinister—sends its miles-long fingers of light probing the sky above darkened London, it is hard to realize that, less than forty years ago, it was a novelty to be the constant subject of comment in the newspapers and of everyday gossip. The great Electrical Exhibitions of Paris, London and Vienna, had, in the American phrase, 'put Electricity on the map'; and the merits of the various types of incandescent lamp—the Edison, the Swan, the Bernstein and so on—were widely discussed.

I had often dined at Mr Critchett's * fine house in Harley-street, where his brother, the 'light' playwright, 'R. C. Carton' † was never the least noticeable of the guests, who would, as often as not, include such medical notables as Sir Richard Quain, Sir Morell Mackenzie and that other, more successful laryngologist, Sir Felix Semon, one of the two surgeons (Sir Frederick Treves was the other) most trusted by the late King.

Mr—Sir Anderson—Critchett was a fine speaker, and I decided to attend his lecture. My own sight, as I have mentioned, was defective in a somewhat erratic fashion: I could see well; indeed, minutely: in certain lights; in certain types of illumination, I could hardly see at all. I wondered, naturally, if I might gain something of advantage to myself in listening to my esteemed oculist friend. (In any case, I reflected, I could pay him the compliment of swelling his audience.)

Now, Dr Conan Doyle, who had already had some literary success in writing for various journals—to one of which, *The Cornhill*, we had taken out a subscription—and little success in his medical profession, had written to me to ask if he might discuss with me my views on the Bertillon system of 'anthropometry', as Monsieur Bertillon himself had named it. Dr Doyle had suggested two or three days on which he would be in London, and I had replied by suggesting that we might meet at the R.C.S., and then return together to Baker-street, with, perhaps, the possibility of dinner at

---

* Students of Victorian literature might ponder on the fact that, whilst a scholar at Harrow, Critchett was believed to be following in the path of that famous Harrovian poet, Byron.—*Editor*

† Author of *Liberty Hall, Lord and Lady Algy* and other late-Nineteenth Century successes.—*Editor*

Simpson's, later. He accepted the arrangement; chose to meet me at the R.C.S., and spoke to me both before and after the lecture.

Since Dr Doyle came to occupy so important a place in the lives both of Dr Watson and myself, I shall have a few words to say about him here. But first I must recall the astonishment that I experienced when he told me why he had welcomed my suggestion that he hear Mr Critchett's lecture. He quite astounded me by remarking, in a most casual manner:

"I have begun a story about a man with three eyes; * but I realize that I ought to know much more about the mechanism of ternocular vision. In the first place, what purely *physical* differences should we expect to encounter in an organism provided with three eyes? If the normal binocular vision that we know—that, incidentally, we share only with the primates—has given us the wonderful range-finding device of parallactic displacement, what benefits in addition might we not expect from that third eye? I mean, Mr Holmes: if binocular vision gives us the three-dimensional image—the image in the round—what could ternocular vision not give? Four-dimensional images? Are there four dimensions? And if there is another dimension, of what nature is it?"

Caught up by his own enthusiasm, Dr Doyle rattled on. I may, after this lapse of years, now confess that I thought the man had a screw loose; though I did remind myself that in any gathering of professional men, one might expect that fervid dedication to a hobby which must seem, to the outsider, something little short this side insanity. I said:

"But—I don't know, Doctor: I am thinking of the title of the lecture—but I feel that Mr Critchett will hardly touch on the aspects of three-eyed ophthalmology?"

"Oh, good gracious me, of course not," Dr Doyle agreed, with great good humour. "I know: he's speaking on the known or assumed effects of the electric light on our normal human vision. Yes, indeed. But *I might pick up a hint or two*. Ah! here we are!—we must go into the lecture."

I followed Dr Doyle in with, I admit, considerable misgiving. I had invited him to speak to me on the subject, not so much of Monsieur Bertillon, as on my opinion of the Bertillon system; and I had more than half-committed myself to a dinner with him—and on that evening, too. I sat through Mr Critchett's lecture in a mood of deep depression.

As it happened—and as is so often the case—my fears were groundless. If Dr Doyle had suggested to me that he was 'not all there' on the subject of

* What has happened to this story, for whose actual commencement we have the written authority of Dr Conan Doyle's younger brother, Innes? There is no proof that it was ever finished, or, if finished, that it was ever published. Its discovery, even in MS. form, would be of first-class literary importance.—*Editor*

three-eyed men, he achieved, without effort, his convincing me that he was sane enough on all the other subjects that we discussed—the principal, of course, being the Bertillon system, of which I professed myself a most enthusiastic admirer.* Indeed, the more that Dr Doyle talked—and he was what is now called a 'compulsive' talker—the more he put me at my ease, though never to the extent of engaging my affection. After the lecture, we walked from the College to the cab-rank in Carey-street, and took a hansom to Baker-street, where I introduced my two Doctors.

Once or twice, my friends of a literary turn have compared this meeting with the encounter of Dr Johnson and James Boswell in Tom Davies's book-shop. But the analogy is defective: Dr Watson was no Johnson, and neither was Dr Doyle a Boswell. Watson lacked the arrogance, the self-sufficiency of the Great Cham of Literature; Dr Doyle had no need to seek a hero further than himself. What Dr Doyle saw in Dr Watson—and I say this in no critical sense—was a means whereby Dr Doyle might (and let me be quite blunt here) turn an honest penny in an activity other than medical.

Watson was at Baker-street when Dr Doyle arrived in time for tea and the crumpets that my friend liked to toast before a gently glowing fire. It was evident that the two men took an instant liking to each other; a liking not altogether explained by the fact that each had taken a first-class medical degree at a first-class medical school, and that, for different reasons, neither had made much practical use of his superior professional qualification.

But, as the day progressed, we drove over to Goldini's, in Gloucester-road, for oysters,† an omelet *à la turque*, a fine Dover sole, grilled, and roast ptarmigan (since, I recall, it was in the close-time for partridge or pheasant or grouse). With this quite epicurean little supper, we had a truly excellent Montrachet.

Dr Doyle proved first-rate company, and his reminiscences were none the worse for shewing the evident marks of polish. Like Dr Watson—and, indeed, like me—he had travelled far afield, but to places not even as familiar to the English as Afghanistan. He had, as a medical student, voyaged on a steam-whaler to the Arctic; as a Bachelor of Medicine and Master of

* Dr Watson mentions this "enthusiastic admiration of the French savant" (Bertillon) in "The Naval Treaty", and many have found this professed admiration inconsistent with the offence that Holmes took when Bertillon's 'anthropometrical' system was favourably mentioned by Dr Mortimer (in *The Hound of the Baskervilles*). There is no inconsistency: Mr Holmes was indignant, not that Dr Mortimer should have praised Bertillon, but that the tactless medico had the impudence to give, as his opinion, that the Frenchman enjoyed a fame greater than that of Mr Holmes.—*Editor*

† Though it is impossible to determine the exact date on which Mr Holmes and Dr Watson first met Dr Conan Doyle, the oysters indicate that it must have been before the end of April.—*Editor*

Surgery, he had gone, the ship's doctor, out to the then very primitive ports of West Africa.

As he talked—most engagingly, I admit—a curious fact positively forced itself upon my acceptance: Dr Doyle, M.D., B.S., M.B. (Edinburgh), not only had no wish to succeed in medical or surgical practice—*he had never wished to become a medical man*. And, as the meal progressed from one enjoyable course to the next, it was clear that it had been to please his mother's ambition, and not his own, that he had studied—and studied diligently and successfully—to 'professionalize' himself.

Of this lady, whom he called (in obvious respect and not a little fear) 'the Ma'am', he spoke frequently; and when I met her, some months later, I had no occasion to revise, save in the most trivial particulars, the picture that my mind had formed of her from her son's description. She was a small— even dwarfish—woman of that precise Irish gentility that Thackeray caricatures, not altogether unkindly, under the representative type of 'Mrs Meejor O'Dowd' of the Rathmines social set.

This little old lady—as yet unseen by me—interested me, for, as the supper progressed and Dr Doyle, in a manner typically Irish, became ever more expansive and confiding, it was clear that 'the Ma'am' was (and, I reflected, almost certainly would remain) the most powerful influence in his life—*but to make him behave in a manner exactly contradictory to her wishes*.

She had had, like most other female members of the Anglo-Irish *bourgeoisie*, the desire to see her son 'secure' as well as 'respectable'—a desire to be achieved only in his becoming a member of the professional classes. Well, in this respect, Dr Doyle, with a commendable filial obedience, had done what 'the Ma'am' had wished; but no sooner had he qualified than he applied himself assiduously to his becoming the last thing that a mother of 'the Ma'am's' type would have wished her son to be: a writer. Dr. Doyle explained to us that he had had, so far, no success as a medical man; and that writing, as a means of livelihood, had more or less been forced upon him. But that this was not so was apparent from the lack of interest that he displayed in talking of the great medical career which had been denied to him, and the fevered enthusiasm which possessed him when he began to describe his as yet paltry literary success.

There was nothing unusual about Dr Doyle in that he was prepared to risk much to escape from a constricting middle-class environment: almost all the great French writers of the last century, for instance, had 'escaped' from the Law to follow a literary career. I recall without effort the elder Dumas, Balzac, Jules Verne, and I know that there were many others. What had not yet become apparent to Dr Doyle—or, perhaps, he did not wish to admit it—was that his failure to establish a medical practice at

Southsea had been *intentional*. He may not have realized this, but it was intentional, all the same. He wished to fail as a doctor, so that he might plead the *force majeure* of failure to 'excuse' his attempting success in a different field. He had become a fully qualified medical man, to please his mother—and, of course, his sense of filial duty—and now, having pleased his mother by becoming a doctor, he was pleasing himself by trying to become a writer.

Perhaps the fundamental difference between Mrs Doyle's plan for her son and that son's interpretation of the plan was this: the mother wished to see her son an anglicized Irishman; that is, Irish, with all the advantages that adoption of acceptable English characteristics could give; the son wished to become completely English, but to retain such Irish characteristics as might be of advantage to him.

In the matter of religious belief and affiliation, Dr Doyle clearly demonstrated a wish to break with family tradition. The Doyles were not only Romanists, but doggedly, even aggressively, so. Dr Doyle's artist uncle, the Richard Doyle who designed the present cover of *Punch*, resigned from a lucrative position on that famous journal when its editor attacked Cardinal Wiseman (known to *Punch*'s and other contemporary caricaturists as 'Soapy Sam'). Dr Doyle himself had attended the well-known Jesuit academy, Stonyhurst; but long before we had reached the *Cérises à l'Eau de Vie*, which was the much-lamented Goldini's *spécialité de la maison*, he had shewn a breadth of mind which, if not altogether incompatible with Jesuitism, was quite incompatible with his mother's religious beliefs. The talk had come back to the subject of the three-eyed man, and I had mentioned that there was a reptile to be found on some South Sea islands whose ancestor, countless generations back, had possessed three eyes, since its present-day descendant still sported the third eye, though only in vestigial form.

From the consideration of the three-eyed Polynesian lizard, the talk then moved on to a look at the pineal gland, on which I mentioned, as a matter of possible interest, that one dissection, at Bart's, had revealed that the cadaver's pineal gland quite shocked the demonstrator and us students by its eye-like appearance, even to the existence of rudimentary cornea and lachrymal duct, the pupil being represented by a macula like the eye-spot on a frog embryo.*

This casually mentioned item of information greatly excited Dr Doyle, who pressed me closely to describe, not so much the abnormal pineal gland itself, as those qualities by which its resemblance to a human eye became

* This unusual case is fully described in "An Apparent Third Eye in a Human Subject", by W. H. Flower, F.R.C.S., F.R.S., Conservator of the Museum of the Royal College of Surgeons; *British Medical Journal*, 1881, I, p. 842.—*Editor*

the more marked. At last, when I had quite taxed my memory to recall what I had seen in the Dissecting Room at Bart's, he said, with what I may call only a 'rapt' expression:

"An eye!—an eye, but *inside* the head, looking out—where?—and at *what?* And what do *you* think, Mr Holmes?—Doctor?: that the strikingly optical form is an *anticipation* of what the pineal gland must inevitably develop into?—or that here we have no more than—though no less than—mere atavism, like those coccygeal processes that I have seen in our medical museums, which are truly the tails with which our primate ancestors swung from trees?"

Neither Watson nor I had anything to suggest as answer to these excited (and, I thought, rather wild) speculations, but I did throw in that the gift of a third eye was something to be acquired by the saintly disciplines of the Thibetan Buddhist monks; that, presumably, Thibetan Buddhism did consider the pineal gland an eye; and that, atrophied as it normally was, it might be restored to full functioning by these disciplines. It was then that I realized how greatly Dr Doyle had passed beyond the narrow theology of his mother's creed.

He was an exceptionally well-read man; indeed, I may confess that his reading had been far wider than had my own, and he certainly knew as much as, perhaps even more than, I, on the subject of Buddhism in general and on its transcendental philosophy in particular. It was easy to see how far he had come from the strict Roman Catholicism of the Doyle household and of Stonyhurst College.

He was a stout man, of above average height; addicted to all those group sports in which Dr Watson had once shone—football, hockey, lacrosse, cricket, cross-country running, and the rest—to which Dr Doyle had since added rowing, swimming and bicycling (the last on a tandem-tricycle in which the bulky doctor-writer took his invalid wife out for an airing). That he was a good-hearted man, one may not deny; but, as I listened to him over the supper-table, I was taken with an uneasy conviction that, in many instances of his doing good to others, he had been actuated more by principle than heart. This is by no means to condemn principle, which has become less and less apparent among us since I was a boy; but principle does not *usually* go hand-in-hand with that spontaneity which, so Dr Doyle claimed or implied, marked each generous impulse.

The talk turned to heredity in general, and from the general we turned to the particular. I recall that I remarked that Dr Doyle's physical characteristics were such as the ancient writers attributed to the Celts: the large frame, the blue-grey eyes, the fair hair. This seemed to please him; my next observation that he could belong to any one of three Nordic elements in the modern Irish people—the Menapian invaders of about 200 B.C., the Norse of about a thousand years later, or the Normans of the twelfth century—pleased him less. "Norman," he corrected me, briefly. "My Mother's chief interest, apart from the care of her family, has always lain with heraldry and genealogy. My Mother, before her marriage, was a Power, and the Powers—or De la Poers (the present Marquess of Waterford is head of the Family)—*as you know*, trace their descent from long before, not merely Henry II, but William the Conqueror.

"The Doyles," he added, somewhat stiffly, "are not less well-descended."

There were, it was clear to me, two strong and mutually antagonistic impulses which had gone to the formation of his ambiguous character: one, the Irish repugnance to conform to the orderly life; to see, in the disciplines of the professional life (his father was an established civil servant) * that 'slavery' which is the theme of all Irish songs (especially those written by comfortably-off exiles from the Emerald Isle) and of not a little of Irish prose; the other, that equally Irish tendency to identify itself with, and share in the benefits offered by, 'the Tyrant'.

His uncle, Henry Doyle, with a prudence that it takes the unimaginatively prudent to find wholly admirable, had contrived to unite the two conflicting impulses—or, rather, to reconcile them—and to follow both Apollo *and* Pluto. A professional artist, he had used that sighing for 'the freedom of Art' to establish himself comfortably as a civil servant: he was the Director of the Irish National Art Gallery in Dublin.

If, though, he had broken with his family in several important respects, it must be said of Dr Doyle that he had broken with the traditional ideas and sentiments of that family, and not with the members themselves. He could not—or firmly professed himself to be unable—to see the least fault in any of his relatives, near or distant; and this fatuous loyalty he carried to sometimes laughable excess. For instance, though his grandfather, John Doyle, was one of the leading political caricaturists of his time; and his son, Richard, was one of *Punch*'s leading artists; and though the above-mentioned Henry's artistic capacity was never in doubt, Dr Doyle insisted that his father, the Deputy-surveyor, was quite their artistic equal. He had been, said Dr Doyle, 'drawing exquisitely since childhood', and to prove his point he produced for our admiration some of the most contemptible scrawls that it has ever taxed my charity to praise.

I cannot say, looking back, that the mutually opposed impulses, reconciled though they may have been, dwelt in complete concord within him; he seemed, if I may so put it, to be, not so much 'repressed' (to use the

* Deputy-surveyor (*i.e.*, Head), Office of Works and Public Buildings for Scotland.—*Editor*

jargon of the modern psychologists) as 'compressed'—shut in, boxed-up, tied-down. I was reminded, in listening to his guarded speech and carefully modulated tones, and in observing as unmistakable evidences of an almost brutally arrogant nature an item of his composition, of a lashed-down steam-boiler, only waiting for that small extra pressure to blow up.

I considered his shyness, his diffidence, his reserve, all suspect; nevertheless, factitious though they might have been, they operated upon his impulses exactly as more genuine qualities might have done.

He told me that he had long wished to have my opinion on Bertillon's 'anthropometry', but "hadn't cared to approach me". I raised my eyebrows at this; and he added, with a self-deprecatory smile:

"I have seen you more than once; in fact, it was only a week or two ago that I saw you at Bart's—you were passing through that narrow part between the Fives Court and the Quoit Ground; I had just come out of the Abernethy * Ward. You passed me."

"I remember. I was on my way to the Steward's office. But, Great Scott!, why didn't you speak to me?"

He shrugged his broad shoulders.

"I can't really say, Mr Holmes, except that—well, I funked it."

I shook my head and drank some more of my brandy; I had no comment to make on this puzzling nonsense. (Nonsense; because I was but five years his senior.)

He had learnt of me, he said, through my cousin's having spoken of me to his uncle, Henry Doyle, of the Irish National Gallery.

"You mean my cousin the Treasury Remembrancer, at Dublin?"

"Yes." He leaned forward, his elbows on the table, his square chin resting on his big boxer's hands, and "fixed me", as Coleridge wrote, "with his glittering eye". "Have you ever thought, Mr Holmes, what wonderful stories your exploits would make—properly written up?"

'So here it is!' I thought. 'Here we come to the nub! Here is what this smooth Doctor has been wriggling his way towards all the evening!' I said, carelessly,

"I imagine that the exploits of very many people would make good stories—properly written up. But is it your suggestion that you write up mine?"

The rest the reader knows. Dr Doyle's proposition was simple: that I should authorize Dr Watson to describe certain of my cases to Dr Doyle (Dr Watson writing them up, if he had the necessary literary ability), and

* Note the name; see page 123.—*Editor*

that, after editing and any necessary re-writing by Dr Doyle, he should endeavour to sell them to some respectable journal. I excused myself from any financial participation in this curious venture; but was, obviously, the witness to the fact that, for collecting the material and writing up the notes, Dr Watson would receive two-thirds of the amount received. Appealed to by both parties, I gave it as my opinion that such terms could be justified only if Dr Watson actually wrote the cases up—but as Watson assured me that he could, and as Dr Doyle seemed content with his one-third, I said no more. I was not altogether sure that this arrangement would not do me more harm than good—indeed, I am still not sure on that point—but, seeing how eager my friend was to 'complete' (as the house-agents say), and reflecting that here might be his perhaps unique opportunity to acquire capital for the purchase of a practice, I ignored my misgivings and gave my conditional consent. I must say that the pleasure that Dr Watson shewed was, for that moment at least, adequate recompense for the repression, in the interests of friendship, of my more prudent instincts—just as I am compelled to admit that the passage of the years have rather justified Dr Doyle than condemned him. In his handling and managing of Dr Watson's romanticized versions of my cases, Dr Doyle has done handsomely by my friend—at no little profit to himself. Nor, perhaps—since I would be honest in these matters—have I lost by the venture sealed that night over the Vieille Fine Champagne Maison of 1865 which, Goldini's being what it was, was the oldest brandy there.

Publicity is something which has little appeal for me, for to court publicity is to be asked to pay the price of caring for the opinions of others—and the opinions of the mass have never been of interest to me. It is for that reason that, even now, I find myself wondering whether or not I acted rightly at Goldini's on that evening of nigh on forty years ago. Of course, it was over and done with before we left the restaurant, on every table of which (save our own) the chairs had been piled in silent reproach at our late-staying. But, I wonder. . . .

The 'fortune' that Dr Doyle promised was not speedy in arriving, though when it did come, it came in full measure and overflowing, I am thankful to say. The first case that Watson wrote-up for Dr Doyle's editing was that on which he accompanied me for the first time: the affair of the Mormon who was found dead in a house in Lauriston-gardens, Brixton.

Dr Doyle had great trouble in selling this story; and nearly eighteen months passed between our agreement at Goldini's and its appearance in *Beeton's Christmas Annual* for 1887. And for this well-written (even, as I thought, *over*-written) account of an important case, Dr Doyle managed to extract from the publishers of *Beeton's*—Ward & Lock, of Paternoster-row—only £25, and that for all the rights in the tale. ("A measly pony!" as Captain Dacre-Buttsworth would indignantly have expressed it.)

But, as Dr Doyle explained—and events have certainly proved him right—it had been necessary to 'make a start'; and the bad bargain was to be excused on the grounds that unprofitable publication was better than none.

Well, both my Doctors did well out of the venture: Dr Watson was enabled to return to practice; Dr Doyle did even better, accepting, from the new King, that knighthood that I myself refused.

Dr—now Sir Arthur—Conan Doyle more or less takes his leave of these memoirs now; but there is one aspect of his nature that I must mention, since it had some influence on, not so much Watson's style of writing, as on the form that the stories of my cases took when presented to the reading public. I mean that the selection of pseudonyms for some characters from real life was principally under the control of Dr Doyle. And, I must record, this selection was not infrequently dictated by personal prejudice of the most unrelenting kind. Dr Doyle, it is often forgotten, was an Irishman; and the Irish, as with all peoples who have had a long period of illiteracy in their history, have exceedingly long memories—not at all always for benefits received. They remember old wrongs, and they nurse old grudges; nor are they absolved, *super nivem dealbati*, of either their retentive memories or their emotional (rather than intellectual) resentments. In the sense of forgetting nothing and forgiving nothing, Dr Doyle could not have been a more typical Irishman—and his editing of Watson's 'cases' reflects at every point a truly Hibernian bias.

Watson once remarked to me that Dr Doyle had "a lot of imagination". I replied that it was his tragedy that he had far too little.

FIFTEEN ❦

A Mission
delicately accomplished

In those seemingly far-off days, the Fifth Avenue Bath, in East Forty-sixth street, advertised itself as having 'The Finest Turkish and Russian Heated Baths in N.Y. City', and, so far as my own experience is concerned, I never found a better Turkish bath, save, perhaps Nevill's, in Northumberland-avenue.

Watson has mentioned somewhere in his writings on me that I am partial to the Turkish bath; this is true—and the partiality developed early in my life. I am a man who seldom takes exercise for its own sake (as I believe Watson has also mentioned somewhere else); I look upon aimless bodily exertion as a waste of energy, and I seldom bestir myself save where there is some professional object to be served. It used, at the beginning of our acquaintance, to astonish Watson that I should have been able to keep myself in training in such circumstances; but, as he has had the honesty to point out, my diet was scanty and my habits almost austere. I had read, at college, that the body accumulates waste products which are not easily eliminated in the normal way, but which have to be, as it were, shifted if such poisons are not to remain within the body to the detriment of physical and mental health.* I learnt, at the same time, that the Turkish bath is the most effective eliminator, not only of all these accumulated wastes, but also of the grime and dirt that the skin absorbs from our London air. It was fortunate that I liked the Turkish bath; it was no hardship to me to endure even the hottest of its hot-rooms—and it was in such a hot-room that I found myself (quite blinded by steam) on a winter's day in 1879.

---

* That Mr Holmes had been overheard expressing these views almost certainly supplies the explanation for the impudent attribution to him of an endorsement for 'Eno's Fruit Salts', a laxative let loose on the British in one of the most sustained and costly campaigns in the history of Advertising.—*Editor*

The Fifth Avenue Bath, which adjoined the Windsor Hotel—named, I was told later, after some real or imagined connection with the Victorian Prince of Wales—was popular with the American businessmen of the neighbourhood, who patronized the bar of the Windsor both before and after their Turkish bath.

I had asked the attendant for something; I don't remember what; when a voice from the thick and impenetrable fog of steam, said,

"Say, sir, you sound like you come from the Old Country?"

I said that I did. The next question—for I had by now become accustomed to the first—was not so usual.

"Say, do you know the Prince of Wales?"

I said that I had had the honour of being presented to His Royal Highness, but that I could not fairly claim the honour of having his acquaintance.

The comment on this reply quite astonished me.

"He'll be," the voice from the fog said, both confidently and admiringly, "the tarnationest ring-tailed curly wolf you Britishers'll ever see on that throne of yours. Say! don't he spike his cocktails with red pepper and pick his teeth with cactus? I'll *say*. . . ."

It was an extraordinary experience, this talk in the boiling steam of the Fifth Avenue Bath: like two ships speaking each other in the densest of Channel fogs. I shall not repeat the conversation with my American friend; but what he had to say was not only then unknown to me—it was, as I learned later, true. In short, Prince Albert, as the Americans called him, had earned himself considerable admiration for having challenged Lord Randolph Churchill to a duel.

"Don't they tell you all this in your newspapers, sir?"

I admitted that 'they' did not.

I discovered the facts easily enough when I got back to England; and as they are still as unknown to the people of the Empire as they were to me in New York in 1879, I shall briefly rehearse them here.

Like so many of the 'romantic' episodes in which the Heir to the Throne played the part of principal character, this business of the duel was shabby enough. The Prince, always in pursuit of another man's wife, had been paying irregular court to Lady Aylesford; * but in the autumn of 1875, having to embark on a tour of our Indian Empire, he had perforce to say *au revoir* to her ladyship, upon which one of the Prince's 'best friends', the Marquess of Blandford, had eloped with Edith Aylesford to Paris, and there, in the fullness of time, had given her a son.

* Known to the 'racing fraternity' of Britain as 'Sporting Joe,' Lady Aylesford's husband, the Earl, sought to divorce her, citing the Marquess as co-respondent. He was told by the learned Judge that his own openly immoral conduct had deprived him of the right to bring suit in such an action.—*Editor*

'Sporting Joe' Aylesford, warned by a telegram what was happening in England, left India and hurried back—too late, alas!, to prevent his wife's having left for Paris with Lord Blandford.

So far, so bad; but worse was to come. The Prince now returned to England, very angry indeed with Lord Blandford, not only for having broken up the Indian party, by compelling Aylesford to come home, but—more—for having decamped with a lady on whom the Prince had been casting sheep's eyes.

In the seedier circles that Aylesford adorned and the Prince frequented, the Heir expressed, in his thick German accent and always childishly simple vocabulary, his low opinion of Lord Blandford.

In Paris, his lordship, living in open sin with Lady Aylesford, heard none of these disagreeable remarks; they were, however, heard—and resented—by Lord Blandford's brother, Lord Randolph Churchill, even then grossly unbalanced by the foul disease which was eventually, first to paralyze, and then to kill him. But before the doom fell, and on the imbecile in the wheel-chair was pronounced that final (and, as some thought, not undeserved) sentence, Lord Randolph sought to ruin the Prince—for having spoken lightly of his elder brother's name.

Here were all the elements of the most grotesque farce—no wonder that the remnants of self-respect in these enchanted circles managed to keep the folly hidden, even from such as I! Mouthing his drunken threats that, if the Heir to the Throne did not 'lay off' Lord Blandford, then 'Randy the Fox' would publish the letters that the Prince had himself written to Lady Aylesford, Lord Randolph staggered from bar to bar, from club to club, from loose woman to loose woman, from shady racing tout to even seedier members of the Jockey Club, such as Sir George Chetwynd—his making the rounds of London low society subsidized by the money that he had got by marrying the daughter of the teamster-turned-millionaire, Leonard Jerome.

For reasons which may perhaps become obvious, I was never in a position to cultivate an intimacy with the Prince of Wales; so that I do not know whether or not his friends were astonished when, infuriated by Churchill's threat to publish the 'love letters' to Lady Aylesford, the Prince not only challenged Lord Randolph to a duel, *but sent the challenge through the Prince's Private Secretary.**

Randolph Churchill, who was as insolent as he was truculent, now had the good sense to consult Mr George Lewis, to whom Lord Randolph gave some simple instructions: give Lord Randolph a cast-iron excuse for not ac-

---

* The *very* grey *Eminence Grise*, Francis (later Sir Francis, then Lord) Knollys, one of the most self-effacing and powerful Royal servants of the Victorian era. His sister, Charlotte, then one of Bedchamber Women of the Princess of Wales, made herself equally indispensable and powerful in the service of the Prince's wife, afterwards Queen Alexandra.—*Editor*

cepting the challenge, whilst, at the same time, preserving Lord Randolph's 'right' to exercise the traditional Churchillian insolence. Most of the details of this unhappy episode I got through the kindness of my cousin Richard Holmes, then Librarian at Windsor.* He also gave me a copy of the answer that, on Mr Lewis's advice, Lord Randolph sent to his angry challenger; the note (after a long and quite inexcusable delay) being sent through Lord Randolph's 'second', Lord Falmouth. The note was worded as follows:

> Lord Randolph Churchill requests me to present his loyal, humble and dutiful respects to His Royal Highness the Prince of Wales, and to state that though he is willing to meet any gentleman that [sic] His Royal Highness may care to nominate, he cannot lift his sword against his future Sovereign.

Thus, through the adroitness of an attorney, was avoided a scandal which might well have rocked the throne; the trivial price was the temporary social-banishment of Lord Randolph.

Here again, what this present war has taught us to call 'camouflage' served its purpose, though the credit for compounding the benefit of the 'camouflage' by removing—even though but temporarily—Lord Randolph from the social scene must go, not to Mr Lewis, but to the far more adroit, and far less self-advertising, Mr Francis Knollys. It was on his advice that Her Majesty approved of the appointment to the Lord-Lieutenancy of Ireland of the Duke of Marlborough,† father of both Lord Blandford and Lord Randolph Churchill.

This did not mean that Lord Randolph had to give up his mischievous parliamentary activities; it *did* mean that, with a 'reason' for being with his father in Dublin, Lord Randolph's absence from 'the Marlborough House Set' was accounted for—at least, to the satisfaction of the newspapers.

Lord Randolph's estrangement from the Prince lasted exactly ten years; the wonder is—considering the unintelligent obstinacy of the two men concerned—that it was ever ended.

When I first had the details of the challenge from my cousin, I was at first astonished that such belligerency could be manifested by so apparently easy-going a pleasure-seeker as the Prince. But, not so very long after my cousin had told me about the duel, I had further information which shewed

---

* Sir Richard Rivington Holmes, M.V.O., son of John Holmes, Assistant Keeper of Manuscripts at the British Museum, skillfully combined the careers of soldier and librarian. He was lieutenant-colonel of the 1st Volunteer Battalion, Berkshire Regiment (Dr Watson's regiment) before being appointed Librarian at Windsor Castle.—*Editor*

† John Winston Spencer-Churchill, K.G., D.C.L., 7th Duke of Marlborough. He was Lord-lieutenant (commonly called 'Viceroy') of Ireland, 1876–1880. He died in 1883.—*Editor*

that the Prince's amiable manner did, indeed, conceal a quick and violent temper. It seems that, at one of those gatherings with his intimates that the Prince of Wales enjoyed, Reuben Sassoon (the man who presented the Prince with those engraved mother-o'-pearl counters afterwards notorious in the Tranby Croft affair), following immediately behind the Prince as the party went down-stairs, playfully put his arm about His Royal Highness's shoulder. The Prince so hotly resented the impudence of Sassoon that the Prince repelled the odious familiarity with such force as to throw the Levantine * down the staircase and to break his arm.

So that, as I remarked to Dr Watson, the Prince *had* a temper—and, by all accounts, a dangerous one at that!

Now, ten years had passed since the Heir had issued his unaccepted challenge to Lord Randolph Churchill; and, as I have said, the breach between these two self-indulgent simpletons (for so I have always considered them) had been healed. I had known nothing of the breach; it would have been difficult to remain unaware of the healing: the newspapers saw to it that we were all well-informed.

What I did not realize as I saw that Lord and Lady Randolph's reappearance within 'the Marlborough House Set' was reported in *The Morning Post, The Times,* and those other newspapers which print *The Court Circular,* was that I was to be deeply involved in a matter, still secret, most closely connected with the origins of the duel that Churchill had refused.

I must say here that though my summons to Windsor had not yet come (for all that I knew of the Queen's approval of me), I had further ingratiated myself with Her Majesty through a small service that I was able to render her and her son in the suppression of some scurrilous libels on the Prince.

For some years past, beginning at Christmas, 1870, and continuing until the Christmas of 1876—the year in which the Prince challenged Lord Randolph to a duel—pamphlets, highly critical of, and most offensive to, the Prince of Wales, had been published; and though the name of an author was missing from each pamphlet, that of the publisher appeared boldly. It was Mr Samuel Orchard Beeton, a man of decidedly Radical views, whose wife wrote the most successful book of cookery and household management ever issued to the public. The first of these anti-Royal pamphlets was entitled *The Coming K——,* and was an immensely clever skit on the then-very-popular *Idylls of the King,* by the first Lord Tennyson. To quote the

* The word 'Levantine' is used here by Mr Holmes in the literal sense of the word, 'Eastern', though, in modern usage it means rather 'from the Middle East'. The Sassoons were Parsees, who had migrated from Persia to Bombay. With the realistic Victorian respect for money, British Society welcomed them with open arms—the welcome led by the Prince of Wales.—*Editor*

opinion of my friend, Sir Sidney Lee: * "The brochure purported boldly to draw the veil from the private life of the Prince and his comrades, and to suggest his unfitness for succession to the throne". To this opinion, I might add that the brochure did a little more than merely purport "to draw the veil"—most people in a position to know the facts considered that it *did* draw the veil . . . and drew it most efficiently.

Five of these scurrilous pamphlets were issued, at yearly intervals; then the bitterly Republican Mr Beeton † died, and, as we may presume that no other publisher was willing to accept the odium and worse of publishing the pamphlets, their issue ceased. But, it was widely asked, for how long? The Republican movement, for all that its most influential leaders, Mr Joseph Chamberlain and Sir Charles Dilke, had seemingly 'conformed' to our traditional social system, had not really abandoned their Republicanism; and a new generation of Radicals—products of and exploiters of the Education Act of 1870—were openly working for what they called 'socialistic reform', by which euphemism they really meant the disgrace, followed inevitably by the abolition, of the Monarchy, that (no matter my opinion of the Heir and most of his brothers) I was dedicated to uphold.

As the Jubilee Year approached, the voice of 'Reform' grew louder and more insolent; and those in authority wondered if the admittedly talented author of *The Coming K——* and its successors might not find a new publisher in time to produce a new and perhaps even more scurrilous pamphlet in time for Christmas, 1886. The first task was to identify the anonymous author; and then, having tracked him down, to silence him—or, at any rate, his libellous pen.

He had hidden his traces well; but not so well that I could not flush him out of his anonymity; and now, armed with his name, I used against him the reasons for his having wished to remain anonymous. Here again, I had usefully employed my family connections, not only to uncover Mr A. A. Dowty, but also to hamstring his literary talent.

For Mr Dowty, too careful of his salary and pension as an established civil servant to put his name to his Republican effusions, was a senior clerk in the Paymaster-general's Department, in Whitehall, and, it will be recalled, my cousin Robert was the Treasury Remembrancer and Deputy Paymaster for Ireland. At my request, Robert Holmes communicated with Lord Wolverton, the Paymaster-general, and his lordship had our poetic Radical up on the mat. Dowty must have had a thoroughly unpleasant half-

---

* The second editor of *The Dictionary of National Biography*, in succession to Sir Leslie Stephen.—*Editor*

† American readers will be familiar, in another context, with the initials with which Mr Beeton signed his prefaces: 'S.O.B.'—*Editor*

hour. He was not dismissed; there was no need for further scandal, and now that his secret had been revealed by me, there was no more Radical nonsense to be feared from a frightened and chastened Mr Dowty. No pamphlet came out at Christmas, 1886.

I had no official recognition of my having found and silenced the author of *The Coming K——*, but I expected none. However, Mycroft was asked by Lord Granville to convey to me the information that Her Majesty and His Royal Highness were *deeply* obliged to Mr Holmes in this matter. I was content.

In 1884, the Crown Prince of the Netherlands, Alexander, Prince of Orange, died; the Heir to the Dutch throne was now Princess Wilhelmina, the four-year-old daughter of the King's second marriage. The Heir to whom the sickly Prince Alexander had succeeded was Prince William, the intimate boon-companion (though never quite the friend) of the Prince of Wales, to whom Prince William was familiarly known as 'Citron'. In the haunting of the least desirable society of London and Paris, Homburg and Baden, the two Princes were inseparable—and out of this strange companionship (for 'Citron' was the perpetual butt of the Prince of Wales's schoolboy humour) was to come either a tragedy or the rumour of a tragedy which was to have the most serious effects on the countries of which the two acquaintances were the Heirs.

The principal object of 'Citron's' generosity was the notorious Emma Crouch, *alias* 'Cora Pearl', on whom the Prince of Wales lavished some ill-advised attention and more material tokens of his interest. On 11th June, 1879, at about the time that the Prince of Wales was defending his good name in the regrettable Rosenberg case, 'Citron' died of pneumonia. As his constitution had been weakened by an irregular course of conduct, persisted in over many years, it could not stand up to an attack of pneumonia, or, indeed, of even lesser afflictions.

Now, from what the world knew of 'Citron's' excesses, a death through pneumonia would have been accepted, one would have thought, as the most natural, even if a somewhat deplorable, thing. If, one would have said, the Prince had not died of pneumonia, he would have died of something else—perhaps something worse.

But, in the seven years since his death, an ugly rumour had been circulating; a rumour whose credibility had been as progressively growing by reason of the 'evidence' which had been gathered and presented to support it. What that rumour was I was to learn at the Netherlands Legation, to which Count Charles de Bylandt, the Minister in London, had invited me.

One may live in any society and, in some inexplicable fashion, miss hearing even its most widespread rumours. So it was in the case of the rumour which denied that the Prince of Orange had died of pneumonia, and stated bluntly that 'Citron' had died at the hands of the Prince of Wales—*in a duel!*

We sat privately in the Count's study in Grosvenor-gardens, and after I had heard him out, I asked:

"Do you believe that the Prince of Wales killed the Prince of Orange?— or even that there was a duel at all?"

"We know that the Prince of Wales fights duels—we have that fact to go upon."

"No, sir; we do *not* know that the Prince of Wales fights duels. I know of one case in which he issued a challenge—"

"In the case of Lord Randolph Churchill?"

"Precisely. And you know, of course, that the challenge was declined."

"Yes. But, in this case, perhaps a challenge was given which was not refused? I was somewhat surprised, Mr Holmes, to learn that the Prince of Wales may, at times, exhibit a furious temper which, now-and-then, seems to verge upon the insane. Do I understand correctly that he broke the Indian Sassoon's arm by hurling him downstairs in a rage?"

"I believe, Count, that Mr Sassoon's arm was broken—but I think that the word 'hurling' may be somewhat of an exaggeration. But—yes, the Prince did cause Mr Sassoon's arm to be broken. Of that, there seems to be no doubt."

"Then," said the Count, reflectively, "there is no doubt, also, that we have here a history of violence?"

"Perhaps."

"I should respectfully suggest, Mr Holmes: not 'perhaps', but 'without doubt'. You know, do you, that this rumour is now widely believed throughout the Netherlands—not only by the common people (who are always ready to believe the worst of their betters), but by the Court itself? I think that it is time that the rumour be examined; and, if proven false, be no longer permitted to strain relations between our two governments—nay, between our two peoples. May I, on behalf of His Majesty King William III, ask you to resolve this difficulty?"

So, in an upstairs study in Grosvenor-gardens, began that long and close association with the House of Orange-Nassau in which, to the present, I have been of service to that Royal House in no fewer than five important affairs, and in some others of less importance.

I remember that, on my return from Grosvenor-gardens in a thick November pea-souper, Watson asked me whom I had been seeing; and I distinctly recall my answer: "I am afraid that I cannot tell you—at least, at the moment. I have been asked to help the reigning Family of Holland; but the matter in which I am asked to serve them is of such delicacy that I cannot confide it even to you."

I have just checked this reference; and I find that Watson did mention it—in that account that he has named "A Case of Identity" (to which I shall be returning shortly). Well, I told Watson that the delicacy of the Dutch case was such that I could not confide in him; and, as I sit here, pen in hand, overlooking a Channel so untroubled in this autumn sunset that one may hardly realize that the Seventh Seal has been broken, and that the Four Horsemen ride again for a world's destruction—as I sit here, I say, 'revolving many memories', I realize that I cannot confide the details even to these memoirs.

When I shall have finished this volume, I shall deposit them with the British Museum, to be opened only in sixty years' time—but who can say that all my wishes will be regarded? Who can say what will have happened in sixty years' time?

Will there be the same social system—with its traditional safeguards of testamentary intentions? Will there be a British Museum? Will there even be a British Empire? Will there even be a Britain?—or will it survive as no more than a satrapy of the German Empire, as Hanover, once a sister-kingdom of Great Britain, survives only as a province of the Kaiser's realm?

And, as for the Netherlands—why, Napoleon extinguished her independence; and a newer Emperor may do the same.

I shall, then, exercise, in this matter of the Dutch Royal House, as much reticence as I have exercised with regard to Dr Watson. Let it suffice here to say that, as the duel (which was supposed to have involved pistols) had to be presumed to have happened, I found myself seeking two essential items of evidence: the wound in the Crown Prince's body made by the hypothetical bullet, and the hypothetical bullet itself. In the event, neither the wound nor the bullet was hypothetical: the Crown Prince *had* died as the result of a bullet wound; but, as our necessarily far from delicate medical examination of the dead Prince, and our hardly less delicate verbal examination of the living, shewed, that bullet had come from no pistol fired by the Prince of Wales—nor even by one of his agents. The seven-year-old breach between the Houses of Orange-Nassau and Saxe-Coburg-Gotha was healed in the knowledge that the British Heir had not killed—intentionally or accidentally—the Dutch Heir. Now all that remained was to detect and name the real culprit.

I found the culprit, of course; but it was not a man; and since the lady could never be punished, I declined, even under pressure by the Highest, to reveal her name.

King William was justifiably angered; but my obstinacy served me here in good stead. The King, after reflection, withdrew his disapproval of me, and, indeed, became one of my most friendly patrons. I look at my note-book, as well as into those larger records of memory, and find that it was that refusal of mine to name Prince William's murderer which made me the trusted adviser of the Dutch Court.

I had always been interested in Holland: a small (and, since the loss of Belgium, in 1831, a much smaller) country, with a great colonial empire. Almost the first words that I said to Dr Watson, when I was introduced to him by 'young Stamford' in 1881, referred to my knowledge of Holland,* and I think that he makes reference somewhere else to my continuing inter-est in that country.†

I shall come later to the three other principal cases (that is, apart from the recovery of Prince William's letters in 1888) in which I had the privilege of serving both the King and the Government of the Netherlands: the three most important affairs of the 'Netherlands Sumatra Company' (as Dr Wat-son calls it) and the colossal schemes of the Baron Maupertuis; the shocking affair of the Dutch steamship *Friesland;* and—involving another ship, but involving, also, a perversion of scientific experiment with results so frightful that the implications make a story for which the world is not yet prepared.

In the meanwhile, I was hurried off from the affairs of Holland to those of Russia. In point of time, the Russian affair preceded that of the Dutch King; but, after having been approached by Baron Mohrenheim, the am-bassador in London, to go at once to Odessa, I pleaded the earlier necessity of King William III, and, by mutual agreement, the Baron and I arranged that I should settle the Dutch problem first; and then tackle, as they say, the far more serious matter of what awaited me at Odessa.

---

* *See* "A Study in Scarlet", where Mr Holmes refers to "a case in Utrecht in 1834".—*Editor*
† *See* "A Case of Identity", in which Mr Holmes mentions "something of the sort at the Hague last year".—*Editor*

SIXTEEN

I go to Odessa

I was summoned to Odessa for a meeting there on 2nd November, 1886; a date that I noted in my diary, not only in French, but in a highly contracted French: *mar. d. morts*, which ought to have meant (and certainly did to me) '*mardi, [jour] des Morts*'—'Tuesday, Feast of All Souls'—but was misread by either Dr Watson or Dr Doyle as a note concerning the death or murder of someone. It is thus that, I think, my purely political journey to the Black Sea port of Odessa appeared in Watson's note of my activities as "The Summons to Odessa in the Case of the Trepoff Murder"— I shall explain in due course how 'Trepoff' comes into this farrago of misread or misinterpreted information.

By the latter part of 1886—I maintain that it was one of the busiest years of my life—I had grown accustomed to commissions from High Places; and I was, therefore, not astonished when the German Ambassador, Count Muenster, invited me to Carlton House-terrace to "talk over a little matter that it might interest you to investigate." I was, further, taking tea with the Count in his study overlooking the Mall, not altogether surprised to learn that, in inviting me to call at the Imperial German Embassy, the Count had been carrying out the orders of Prince von Bismarck, 'The Iron Chancellor'.

I was however, I confess, quite astonished to know the reason why I, of all people in the world, had been chosen by Bismarck to undertake a mission involving little or no detective skill, as such, but only what, I am sure, my brother, Mycroft, would have done a hundred times more skilfully. I said so; but the Count shook his head.

"Why should you—or, rather, your principal—think that I am the right man for this enterprise?"

For answer, Count Muenster quoted the well-known lines of Goethe:

" 'Der den Augenblick ergreift, Das ist der Rechte Mann.' " *

"It seems, Count," I said, with a smile, "that it is not I who have 'seized on the moment', but the moment which has seized on me?"

He shrugged his shoulders, and added yet another line from *Faust*:

" 'Der Ausgang giebt den Thaten ihre Titel'!" †

"So be it. But why did the Prince choose me? Why *me*? I would have thought that an experienced diplomat . . . And why a *foreigner*, to boot?"

I am not easily thrown out of my stride, but it was as much as I could do to control my features when the Count said airily:

"Oh, your being a foreigner, His Serene Highness does not mind. It is that you are a professional detective which causes him to select you for this commission." And, before I might collect my wits, he added: "Are you at all acquainted with the Messrs Emile Gaboriau and Fortuné du Boisgobey? (Though the Prince thinks that they may be one and the same; of this I have no knowledge.)"

"I—But, a moment, Count, the name, 'Emile Gaboriau'—surely it is that of a writer of fiction?—stories about an imaginary detective named Le Coq? And—yes, indeed!—Monsieur du Boisgobey writes in the same vein! But what, pray, have these to do with me?"

"His Serene Highness," said the Count ponderously, "requested the Imperial German Ambassador in Paris to make enquiries. His report made it clear that, though the works of the Messrs Gaboriau and Du Boisgobey are presented in the guise of fiction, they are, in reality, a true account—and the detective, Le Coq, is a real person—or, more precisely, based upon a real person in the service of the Police Judiciaire. And," the Count concluded, fixing me with his ambassadorial eye, "since, next to the works of Charles Dickens, he esteems most highly the works of the Messrs Gaboriau and Du Boisgobey, it follows that he esteems a professional consulting detective of the highest standing—yourself, my dear Herr Holmes!"

He bowed, to add point to the compliment; I bowed, to shew that I appreciated both the compliment and the point.

Then we both bowed together.

"Then you will accept the commission?"

"How could I refuse?"

By the end of the 'Eighties, the standards of travel by railway had risen to match anything available to the most discriminating up to the beginning of this present war.

Though there was much which was confidential about my mission (no-

* The man who can seize on the moment—that's the right man!—*Editor*
† The result vindicates the deed.—*Editor*

one had forgotten how the Foreign Office clerk Marvin had communicated the text of the secret Anglo-Russian treaty to the *Globe* newspaper in 1878), there was nothing which needed to be hidden, at any rate as regards my destination and the purpose of my journey. Lord Granville, though he had ceased to be Foreign Secretary, kindly obtained my passports, all properly *visés* to secure me admittance through the most difficult of doors. Armed with these, I set out on the boat-train for Dover, from the old wooden Victoria Station, on the evening of Monday, 15th November, 1886, arriving at the Stamboul Station of the Oriental Railway on the sunny morning of Thursday, 18th November, very much travel-weary, and desperately in need of the refreshing bath which awaited me at the Péra Palace Hotel, hard by the delightful public gardens called 'Les Petits Champs'. (Those who wonder at the French 'atmosphere' of Turkey; its use of French, not as a subsidiary, but rather as the main language; should remember that, for centuries, the Sultans have been born of French mothers.)

I had taken the precaution of booking my accommodation at the Péra Palace, telegraphing from Baker-street in the International Hotel Code:

ALBADUO BEST SAL BAT GRANMATIN PASS

—which, in the strange language of the International Association of Hotel-Keepers signified:

FIRST-CLASS ROOM WITH DOUBLE BED, PRIVATE
SITTING-ROOM AND BATHROOM. ARRIVING
CONSTANTINOPLE BETWEEN MIDNIGHT AND
7 A.M. FOR ONE DAY AND NIGHT'S STAY ONLY

The telegram was *not* signed 'Holmes'—in addition to the passports with which Lord Granville had provided me, I had two other sets, one provided by my brother, Mycroft; the other by the Imperial German Councellor of Embassy, Count Herbert von Bismarck, the son of that Iron Chansellor who had invited me to be an independent witness—referee; arbiter; call it what you will—of a most secret meeting of three Emperors, *on the recommendation of a French writer of sensational fiction!* Surely no upward step in this world had been engineered by a mechanism so grotesque! (Indeed, on my way from Sophia, I had the mischievous impulse to register at the Péra Palace under the name of 'Le Coq'—though let me say that I conquered the impulse. Goethe says somewhere that one should never joke with women; he ought to have added that it is equally dangerous to joke with all his fellow-Germans, men and women alike.)

It had been suggested in London, by Count Herbert, that I should call for instructions at the German Embassy in Constantinople; but his unwise—not to say ludicrous—suggestion had been instantly and firmly vetoed by me. I was, of course, aware of the excellent reasons for the suggestion; excellent, that is to say, from the point of view of the German Foreign Service. Had the staff of the Embassy in Constantinople known that I, with passports from the *Auswärtige Amt* in Berlin, had passed through the Turkish capital without paying the local *Amt* 'the customary courtesies' (which means, in fact, an invitation of the Embassy to put me under surveillance—and not only during my brief stay in Turkey!), there would have been one of those inter-departmental exchanges of huffy letters which are, too often, the civil servant's only substitute for honest day-labour. As it was, I had no difficulty in staying in, and walking about, the beautiful capital of the Ottoman Empire without incurring the unwelcome attention of either the German or the Turkish secret police.

My train had pulled into the Stamboul Station at an early hour; so that, after having registered at the Péra Palace and had a wash-and-brush-up, changing my travelling clothes for a light-weight tweed suit of short coat and trousers, I ate a hasty breakfast in the hotel's magnificent *salle-à-manger*, and strolled forth to see what I might of a city whose beauties I might not have the chance of seeing again.

I did not wish to be bored with the chatter of a dragoman, but asked the hall-porter to find me an araba whose driver could speak either French or German, and who might be trusted to point out those places of historical or other merit that Baedeker—I had bought a copy in the hotel—marks as worthy the attention of the tourist. I explained that I wished to be conducted around the city, not deafened by the chatter of a professional guide; that I should pay as well as for the services of a dragoman; but that I wished to see what I might of the city at my whim, not at that of a guide's.

We stopped first at the post-office in the Grande Rue de Péra, whence I sent a reassuring telegram to Dr Watson, under the name of 'Dr Gower',* and a merely informative one to Count Herbert von Bismarck, also under an assumed name, to say that I had arrived at Constantinople, and that I was now ready to take the second step of my journey.

We visited the Great Bazaar, the small but beautiful mosque called the *Yeni Valideh Jami*, the *Chinili Kiosk*, a most elegant building in brilliantly-coloured brick and tiles of fayence, the old and neglected Seraglio, built by Mohammed II on the site of Constantine's Acropolis, the *Aya Sophia*

---

* Most probably because Dr Watson was an M.D. of University College, London, whose famous Hospital is in Gower-street. There *may* be an allusion to 'the benignities and zealës good' of that worthy character whom Chaucer calls 'moral Gower'.—*Editor*

mosque, that I found more impressive even than St Sophia—that we also visited. We visited three other mosques—those of Ahmed I, of Nuri Osmanieh and of Bayazid (this last a truly splendid affair, in the forecourt of which the gargling of innumerable pigeons reminded me of the feathered inhabitants of Trafalgar-square). I was anxious to see these mosques—testimony to Turkish architectural taste as well as to Mohammedan piety— since all are open to Christians until sunset.

I did not return to the Péra for luncheon; but had an excellent repast at Nicoli's *Brasserie Suisse*, only a few doors from the Péra. My reason for avoiding the Péra was a wish to spend as little time in the hotel as possible; all big hotels, in all big cities, are the rendezvous of professional and amateur information-gatherers and examiners of the passer-by.

In the afternoon, we visited many other places, until, quite wearied by a touristic energy which would have done credit to a German or an American, I paused to refresh myself with coffee and sweet cakes at Tokatlian's Café in the Great Bazaar.

At the Economic Bookstore, in the Passage du Tunnel, I bought several newspapers, for I did not know how long I should be at sea between Constantinople and Odessa. The advertised duration of the voyage is a day-and-a-half, and though travel in the Levant (contrary to the generally received opinion at home) is both comfortable and punctual, there are violent storms in the Black Sea which can greatly delay the traveller—or so Mycroft informed me.

So, then, I bought *The Levant Herald*, *Le Stamboul*, *Le Moniteur Oriental*, and—in both French *and* German—*Osmanische Lloyd*, the three languages in which these newspapers were printed offering a good deal more than a mere three points of view. I also bought a couple of old *Graphics* that I had not read, and an ancient copy of *The Illustrated London News*. With these, and a nostrum for seasickness prepared by the German chemist Ehrlich, in the Grande Rue de Péra, I felt that I might face the voyage to Odessa with some confidence.

On the following morning, after I had packed my grips and settled my bill, an irritating disappointment awaited me at Thomas Cook's, in the Rue Kabristan, just opposite the Péra Palace. I had called in to collect my ticket for the steamer, that I imagined would sail that afternoon for Odessa. Instead, I was told that I should have to spend another day in Constantinople; that no steamer sailed before Saturday, and that I had missed the Thursday boat, and that the Friday boat did not sail this week, but only next week. I saw that the mistake could not be blamed on Cook's, but I decided that, as the next boat did not sail until the morrow, I would book in at some other hotel, and fill in the rest of my time in the city as best I might. Accordingly, I registered once more, but this time at the Hotel Berliner, near the gardens of the British Embassy. On the following morning, from the Galata Quay, I went aboard the S.S. *Shmerinka*, of the Russian Steam Navigation & Trading Company, Captain Lyubyanoff, a commander whose arrogant but polished bearing, I wagered to myself, was never acquired on the bridge of a Black Sea merchant-vessel.

The Captain received me courteously, and himself accompanied the steward who was detailed to conduct me to my cabin, my impression that Captain Lyubyanoff was a great deal more than he pretended to be receiving more and more confirmation from the excellent English that he spoke. Now, since the passports that I had presented bore no English name, I wondered why the Captain had seen fit to address me in English. I asked him why, and he bade the steward be off.

"Sit down, sir, will you not? I do not know your name; and I do not enquire. But I do know that you are an English gentleman of distinction, and I am ordered to see that you arrive safely at Odessa. I shall carry out those orders. The source of my orders lays on me, without argument, the duty of affording you every courtesy, Monsieur . . . Vernet."

"And your name, Captain: is it 'Lyubyanoff'?"

"Yes, indeed."

"But you are not, I think, permanently employed by the Russian Steam Navigation & Trading Company? You have been, let us say, *seconded* to command the *Shmerinka*?"

The Captain laughed.

" 'Seconded'. I like that expression very much—very much indeed, Monsieur Vernet. (By the way, there is a *real* Monsieur Vernet in London—Consul-general for the Swiss Confederation—?)"

"A relative. No, Captain, he has nothing to do with the business which brings me here. And your crew, Captain: are they also seconded from a warship of the Imperial Navy? I ask, because—"

"You ask with justification. Yes, sir, all my men are my own; to be trusted in every way. And now, sir: may I hope that you will enjoy your voyage to Odessa. You will dine with me, of course?—and permit me to present to you—in your capacity of 'Monsieur Vernet', of course—my officers?"

Nothing could have been more agreeable than that short but choppy sea-journey to Odessa, and for that quality I have to thank Captain Lyubyanoff and his officers. (I have learnt since—it was no great secret—who, and what, they were; but I see no reason to disclose the real names behind their *noms de guerre*. I do not doubt that, by now, Captain Lyubyanoff knows perfectly well who 'Monsieur Vernet' was.)

To the quietly but elegantly dressed gentleman of middle-age to whom the Captain 'handed me over' at Odessa, I presented the passports which had been given to Mr Sherlock Holmes.

My baggage was carried out to the boot and top of a closed carriage of elegant but distinctly old-fashioned design, but without hammercloth or armorial bearings of any kind. The coachman was in a plain livery of traditional Russian type; two footmen, also plainly dressed, hung by straps from the rear.

"You do not know Odessa, I think, Mr Holmes?" Prince Melikoff—for that was the name of my conductor—asked me.

"Not even from my classical reading at school and university. My *Baedeker* tells me that it is a modern town, founded, by the Empress Catherine II, only as recently as 1794."

"Then let me take you around at least the centre of the city—you may not have such another opportunity; and we are in no hurry. Your first meeting with—with those Exalted Personages who expect you—will not take place until after dinner tonight. Come, let me shew you what is on its way to becoming the most beautiful city in Russia."

So we drove from the Harbour to the Catherine-square, in the centre of which rises imperially the splendid statue of that loose-living but firm-minded Empress, with smaller figures of her lovers supporting the plinth on which she stands. From there we drove along the Yekaterinskaya and into the Deribassovskaya, the Bond-street or Rue de Rivoli of Odessa.

I was taken to the Sobornaya-square, and shewn the superb Cathedral of the Transfiguration, in which the famous Prince Vorontzoff lies buried; the New Russian University; New Bazaar-square, the handsome Town Theatre, the work of two talented Viennese architects; and so to the famed Nicolayevsky-boulevard, which runs along the top of a plateau parallel with, and giving a wonderful view over, the harbour and sea. In the spring, my *Baedeker* had told me, this boulevard was the rendezvous of the fashionable world, and seeing the splendid mansions lining one side, and the well-laid-out pleasure-gardens on the other, I had no inclination to suspect *Baedeker* of exaggeration. The line of houses ends towards the north with two palaces of exceptional magnificence: the Vorontzoff Palace and the Imperial Palace. It was at the *porte-cochère* of the latter that our carriage pulled up; and, since this palace is also the private residence of the general commanding the Odessa Military District, it was in the sumptuously furnished study of this important gentleman that I was received on behalf of His Imperial Majesty the Czar.

The object of the meeting was, as Mycroft had put it, 'simple reinsurance, my dear fellow; simple reinsurance. The old Emperor"—he was talking of the German Emperor, William I—"is now ninety. He can't live for ever;

and Heaven knows what his successor (by whom I mean, not the dying Crown Prince, but the deplorable Prince William) will do with the theory of the *Dreikaiserbund*. So, whilst the German Emperor is still alive, the three Emperors wish to renew the contract of 1872.

"My dear Sherlock, such a compact has about as much inherent stability as a friendship between you and Charlie Peace. Yes, yes: I know that you knew and liked Peace—but you could hardly have *worked* with him; now, *could* you?

"Just so. Traditional German ambition, which ate up as much of Poland as it could, will not be content until it has completely absorbed—the analogy of the boa-constrictor is not inappropriate here, I think?—the Austrian Empire; and then, perhaps, once more discontented, it will seek to conquer European Russia—at least the Baltic duchies, and that part of Poland in Russian hands. The *Dreikaiserbund* is doomed, my dear fellow, not because of the probable opinion of Prince William of Prussia, when he ascends the Imperial throne in a few years' time, but because it is a compact inherently unstable. That is why I wish you to attend this secret conference—of which, I may tell you, we have had the agenda in detail for many weeks."

"But, Mycroft," I protested, "since you know all, why do you wish me to attend? What do you wish me to say?"

"I wish you, as the completely independent arbiter that Prince Bismarck has appointed you to be, to say that Her Britannic Majesty's Government, *for the moment*, *at any rate*, sees nothing objectionable in the re-ratification of the Pact of the Three Emperors. You may add—and, Sherlock, I *should*, if I were you!—that any Royalist association for the suppression of Liberal and Radical tendencies commands a great deal of sympathy in Great Britain, where the Republicans have been making themselves more odious by their bad taste than even by their disloyalty."

"Mycroft: what did you mean when you said that H.B.M.'s Government offered no objection to the *Dreikaiserbund*, 'for the moment'?"

"Oh—*that?*" my brother said, airily. "Why, yes; yes, of course. Simply, Sherlock, that—yes, indeed, my dear boy: you might add casually that H.B.M.'s Government would offer no objection to the continuance of the *Dreikaiserbund*, so long as one of its members—Russia—abandon its disturbing interest in Afghanistan; you know that all that wretched Afghanistan business is once again *sur le tapis?* Just tell them that, Sherlock, there's a dear chap—and I'll be as happy as a grig to see you back again. By the way, did you know that that dreadful fellow Marvin—who used to be one of Us until he revealed the text of the Russian treaty to *The Globe*—has written another book? * I lunched with Mr Murray at the Diogenes last week, and

---

* In 1878, Charles Marvin, a Foreign Office clerk, disclosed the terms of a secret treaty with Russia to *The Globe* newspaper. He was arrested and charged with the offence, but released

he tells me that the book was written and published within a week—though not by him, more's the pity! You read the account that Marvin gave of his betrayal of our secret? *—well, yes, of course you must have done—but this new book of his is really *excellent*, Sherlock. You must read it."

"You praise him, Mycroft? Was this Marvin not a sort of traitor? Was he not expelled from the Foreign Service?"

"Indeed yes. With ignominy. Had he been a soldier, he would have been drummed out. But he was still a remarkably clever fellow—his only fault was that he had—"

"Too keen a moral sense—?"

"My *dear* sir!—you sound as naïf as he was! No, no, Sherlock, Marvin both took the text of the secret treaty to *The Globe*, and was booted out of the Service, not because he was disloyal to the system—bless my soul, even Clausewitz could find a use for traitors!—but because he was disloyal to ordinary common sense . . . at least, as we understand it in Downing-street. He actually believed, poor fool, that treaties are made for the public good— at least, he thought that that was the theory—and that the public ought to be the best judges of whether a treaty be good or not. Worse, he thought that treaties are signed to have their conditions observed. What childishness! No wonder that he got the sack! And what a happy chance that his unsuitableness was revealed so early—before he had an opportunity to do any serious harm!"

"So, Mycroft: you don't object to this proposed treaty—re-ratification of the treaty, rather—of the three Emperors?"

"Good gracious no! What harm can it do to sign it? It won't be honoured—no treaty ever was—but it can do no mischief. By all means, Sherlock, attend the planning and—if possible—the signing of this absurd document. At least you will have the opportunity of wearing your medals."

"You attach little importance to treaties, then, Mycroft?"

"My *dear* fellow—!"

"Then, may I ask, why are they signed in the first place?"

"Oh—*signed?* I thought that you were asking me what value *treaties* had. (And the answer there is: none at all.) But the *signing* of treaties—oh, that's most important."

"Would you be so good, Mycroft, as to explain why?"

"Well, Sherlock, you should, I think, reflect a little. The *terms* of any proposed treaty tell us what the Foreign Ministers of allies or enemies are thinking *at the moment*—this is always useful to know. Then, of course, the

---

when it was discovered that he had committed no offence under English law. He wrote an account of the affair in an amusing little volume, *Our Public Offices, embodying an Account of the Disclosure of the Anglo-Russian Agreement and the unrevealed Secret Treaty of 31st May, 1878.—Editor*

* *The Russians at the Gates of Herat;* it sold 65,000.—*Editor*

making and signing of treaties give much employment—not only to the Foreign Service draughtsmen and their clerks; to the Ministers and their aides; but to all the hundreds, perhaps even thousands, of skilled craftsmen whose skills are essential to the proper conduct of a diplomatic meeting at the highest level: the tailors, the lacemen, the jewellers, the coach-builders, the harness-makers, the saddlers, the bootmakers, the confectioners, the wine-merchants—and all this, not only for the gentlemen, but for the ladies also. Why, a Congress such as that of Vienna or Berlin gives more employment (to say nothing of more satisfaction to the persons involved) than twenty London or Paris Seasons.

"But there is another aspect of these treaty-making congresses—public or secret, makes no manner of difference—that you would do well to consider, Sherlock. Attendance at such meetings is what matters; one's importance is reckoned not by what emerges from the meeting—which is usually so trivial as to be not worth bothering about—but solely by the fact that one has been invited, and that one is present in the company of important and powerful men. Remember this, Sherlock; remember that you have now received the accolade of an invitation to an important affair. You are, you understand, not going to Odessa to help in the making of a useless treaty—you are going to Odessa to be present when it is being drafted."

"Are treaties *never* honoured, Mycroft?" I asked, to tease his airy cynicism.

"*Never*," he said, indifferent but decisive; "but they are *always* made use of."

I returned to London from Odessa by a route different from that by which I had gone out. Indeed, it was not for nearly twenty years that I once again visited Constantinople.

I left Odessa with some regret; for, despite Mycroft's dismissing the meeting as so much dressing-up in fancy uniforms and eating and drinking in circumstances of a princely opulence, it was not all play-acting, and I had the good fortune to meet several men for whom I might justly feel an unfeigned respect.

I was entertained to a sumptuous banquet by the General commanding the 8th army-corps, which has its headquarters in this, the fourth largest city of the Empire; and before being conducted to my special railway-coach by a detachment of the Savage Battalion of the Cossacks, of which Prince Melikoff, a Georgian of royal and ancient lineage, was hereditary colonel, I received a command to wait on the Czar at the Winter Palace.

His Imperial Majesty, a man of giant stature and truly commanding presence, received me with much warmth; he had heard of my work, he said, both from the Empress—a sister of the Princess of Wales—and from his brother-in-law, the Duke of Edinburgh. At dinner in the Winter Palace, I had the honour of being presented to the Empress and several other members of the Imperial Family, with whom, as a member of the Order of St Anne, I was already—at least in a formal sense—*persona grata*. After the ladies had retired—for the Emperor had adopted many of our English customs—I found myself in conversation with General Fyodor Trepoff, Commissioner of the Metropolitan Police of St Petersburg, who expressed great interest in both my theories and in those scanty writings based upon them! A man of open and enquiring mind, General Trepoff had been made a State Councillor, and I felt that the appointment was to be commended, since the Czar could not fail to profit by the advice of such a man.

I think that it was the presence of the General's name in my very brief notes, as well as my reference to the secret Odessa meeting as *'treppauf'*,* a cryptic reference to the fact that the meeting was at the Very Highest Level, which caused either Dr Watson or Dr Doyle to refer to "The Summons to Odessa in the Case of the Trepoff Murder". Perhaps, too, my hastily scrawled *'morgen'* † may have been misread as *'morden'*.

The trouble was that Dr Watson *thought* that he could interpret my only too illegible scrawls (intended for no other eye than mine), whilst Dr Doyle was *convinced* that he could; in both cases, the misapprehension has led to some curious errors, though none of any great consequence.

To return to St Petersburg: I left with the good wishes of Their Imperial Majesties, and—as Mycroft had laughingly predicted—with two more Orders: those of St Vladimir and the White Eagle. In the following January, my membership of the Order of St Anne was raised to that of the first class, His Imperial Majesty sending me, through the hands of Baron Mohrenheim, the splendid regalia which had been made, some sixty or seventy years earlier, by Keitel, the celebrated bijoutier to the Imperial Court.

I returned to England by way of Berlin—where I was received in a most friendly manner by Prince Bismarck, though it would be dishonest to assert that he did not receive me rather as a professional consulting detective than as an amateur diplomat. This was a reception for which I had been in no way prepared, and its effect upon me was at once both flattering and disconcerting: it was undoubtedly flattering to have one's detective abilities almost over-praised; disconcerting to have one's 'important' attendance at a *'treppauf'* conference dismissed out of hand as of no account.

The Prince, who read and spoke both English and French well, had, as I had been told, two favourite writers, Charles Dickens, for whose *Little Dor-*

* German *treppauf* = 'upstairs'.—*Editor*
† *Morgen* = 'tomorrow'. *Morden* = 'to kill, murder'.—*Editor*

rit he could not find sufficient praise, and the French writer of sensational fiction Emile Gaboriau—"Magnificent, Herr Holmes; magnificent!"

I was amused at the Prince's solemn efforts to ascertain the 'truth', as he called it, of stories that he himself read with pleasure *because* they were admittedly works of the imagination. He saw my amusement, but without taking offence; and explained himself thus:

"I do not ask you to tell me, Herr Holmes, that when I read that Le Coq did such-and-such a thing, this is historical fact. I do not ask you even to state that Le Coq is a real person. What I ask you is this: were there such a person as Le Coq, busy in the detective activities that Monsieur Gaboriau has invented for him—would he go about his tasks as Monsieur Gaboriau tells us that he does?"

Now, that question was what the horse-copers call 'tricky'. I had already given my opinion of Gaboriau—no very high one (though I rate him above Poe)—to Dr Watson and some others. I value honesty; and I like to pride myself on my being truthful at all times; but this, evidently, was one of those times where I might be counselled to produce the rule-proving exception. I said that I was sure that Le Coq would have behaved *exactly* as Monsieur Gaboriau makes him behave; only adding that, "Of course, the methods of the *Sûreté* are not precisely the same as those of Scotland Yard". With this opinion, into which he (like the majority of us in similar case) read what he wished to read, the Prince seemed well content.

I think that I may say that this was the most cynical man whom I have ever met, in that the charm of his manner in private conversation had nothing hypocritical about it: he was as genuinely attracted by art and letters as he was attracted by those ambitious plans to which he had, without hesitation or scruple, sacrificed every impulse of decency and honour. To me, he was courteous and even warmly friendly, for I offered (or so he thought) no obstacle to the least of his dark plans; had he considered me the least of all the obstacles in his path, he would have swept me aside—nay, more, crushed me as he might an irritating fly.

SEVENTEEN ⁊

At the Queen's Command

From this too-close contact with ruthless Autocracy, it was, I confess, a refreshing change to meet a Sovereign who, whatever her lapses from a strict perfection, displayed most of the more praiseworthy human virtues, and none of the more serious faults. It is true that Her Majesty could be tyrannical; though never enough to earn the name of Tyrant—all those unfortunate enough to be involved in the matter of the 'kidnapping' of the Queen's little dog, Cherry, from Sergeant Kendillon, of 'C' Division, to the Comptroller of the Household and the Lord Chamberlain, will not easily forget those uncomfortable hours during the dog's absence, when the Royal Lady 'held forth'. Like the majority of women—and none, in my experience, was more womanly than she—the Queen wished always to have her own way because she was convinced that hers was the right way. Yet no-one of such rigid principles—even of rigid prejudices—could have been more tolerant, in an age in which those who most loudly proclaimed their 'broad-mindedness' were the least tolerant of all.

Of unquestioning faith in that Church of which she was, by law, the Supreme Head, that generous tolerance that she extended to all other faiths should have shamed those who preached the Brotherhood of Man, yet objected to sitting down at dinner with a man who wore the wrong sort of waistcoat. Her Majesty extended both her patronage and her protection to all who seemed to her to be the unhappy victims of prejudice—Jews, Roman Catholics, Hindoos, 'unacceptable' by-blows of her own Royal Blood, paupers, orphans, artists, writers, foundlings, the indigent sick; and she saw to it that some at least of her Heir's time was spent in those good works to which she had given her patronage. With the Prince of Wales, I never did succeed in establishing friendly relations—though I must confess that the fault there lay with me rather than with him, who always offered the hand of friendship to me. But if, with His Royal Highness, toleration was sometimes practised to a fault, it was as a virtue that he had learned it of his Mother. Both the Queen and the Prince of Wales were innocent of, and always indignant at, that form of prejudice which derives from too acute an awareness of race. At a grand reception, where the principal guests included the King of the Sandwich Islands, the Prince of Wales was informed that Prince Frederick of Prussia had been offended at the precedence given to the King. The Prince of Wales's comment had a robust common-sense worthy of the great Dr Johnson himself. "Well," said the Heir, "either the man is a king or he's just a buck nigger. If he's a king, then he takes precedence of mere princes—and if he's only a buck nigger, then he has no business here."

This championing of the victims of prejudice, the Prince of Wales had learnt of both his parents; but principally of his Mother, the Queen. It was to see this formidable defender of the rights of minorities that I was now summoned.

I did not realize, when the telegram from Mycroft informed me that the Queen would be sending for me, that the problem to be discussed was the protection of a minority of one—and that that one-person minority was—the Queen herself.

Mycroft's telegram was typical, not only of my brother, but of all that secrecy-for-its-own-sake that the clerks of the Foreign Service are trained to respect above all other things; that obfuscation of the essential clarity with which all thought should be expressed, whether in writing or in speech; that dedication to a state in which "darkness was upon the face of the deep".

The telegram was worded as follows:

Herb Madge vulture presents. Seneschal yew seamy proter osmanwi farthing dip.

There was no signature.

I tossed the grey slip over to Dr Watson.

"There, Doctor: practise your hermeneutics on *that!*"

My friend wrinkled his brows over the message, and at last handed the slip back to me with an apologetic shrug.

"I confess, my dear Holmes, that this really does baffle me. On the other hand," he added, defiantly, "that's no wonder, since I haven't the code—"

"The *code?* Good gracious, Doctor: of which code are you speaking?

There is certainly no code here. Indeed, I am astonished that Mycroft permits himself to telegraph *en clair*. Now—now that I have told you that there is no code involved, do you mean to tell me that you can't see what my mystifying brother has written here? No—? You astonish me. Here—"

I scribbled on a sheet of paper, and passed the paper to my friend. I had written:

Her B. Maj. vult your presence. Essential you see me proteros man with candle.

Dr Watson picked up the paper; but laid it down again with a despairing shake of his head.

"Holmes, I confess that it's as much Greek to me as ever."

"At least there's one Greek word in it. Surely, Doctor, you know what *'proteros'* means?"

" 'First, foremost, forward . . .' Of course I do. But is it Greek? Oh, it is, eh? And is that *'vult'* the Latin word: 'he wishes'?"

"In this case, 'she wishes'. Yes. Can't you decypher the message now that I've given you these important hints?"

"Candidly, Holmes: not. It's so much double-Dutch to me. But if you can read it, what does it say?"

"This."

I took up my pencil, and wrote as follows:

Her Britannic Majesty requires your presence.
Essential you see me first Diogenes.

" 'Diogenes'? The club, of course. But how does 'man with candle' resolve itself as 'Diogenes'?"

"Didn't he go around Athens holding a lighted candle, in a vain but well-publicized hunt for an honest man?"

"Good gracious yes, Holmes. I remember now. Plutarch, if I'm not mistaken?"

"I imagine so. But I must catch a hansom; Mycroft hates to be kept waiting."

I changed my short coat for a more fitting garb; and gave my silk hat a rub on my left sleeve. As I was leaving the room, Dr Watson asked:

"I remember reading about him in Plutarch—"

"Who?"

"Diogenes. What I've forgotten is whether or not he ever found an honest man—?"

"My dear Watson: did you honestly expect that he did?"

Mycroft, like all those abstracted visionaries with whom life and fate have brought me into contact, always seemed to me to have his dream-clouded eyes fixed far too intently on the main chance. His first remark, when I found him in the library of the Diogenes Club was:

"Play your cards properly, my dear Sherlock, and this could be the making of you! May I trouble you to ring for the waiter? You will join me, of course, in a sherry-and-bitters?"

After the man had filled our glasses and left, I said, somewhat warmly:

" 'The making of' me! My dear Mycroft, I have only just returned from meeting two Emperors and the highest emisssaries of a third—"

"A meeting that I arranged."

"Just so. But, even allowing that every advance that I have made were attributable to your good offices, Mycroft—and that is far from being the case—that you should talk of any commission's 'being the making of me' is sheer, unmitigated balderdash, as well you know! I am not exactly 'unmade', Mycroft, don't you think?"

Not in the least put out by my warmth, my brother said, as though, for all the world, I had not said one syllable in protest against his patronizing attitude:

"The Emperor of Russia, the King of Sweden, the King of Holland— Well, their coats-of-arms adorn the windows of fifty tailors or haberdashers around Cork-street and Savile-row and New Burlington-street. But if you wanted a frock-coat, Sherlock, wouldn't you go to Poole or Davies, who have *our* Royal Arms on the window? Come, Sherlock!—be reasonable, be rational. Patronage by foreign royalty is like a foreign title borne by an Englishman—*it isn't quite right*. People can't help thinking that, if he's an Englishman, why can't he be an *English* baron and not some French or German or Papal nobleman? Well—to business! And, Sherlock, whether you like the phrase or not, this affair will be the making of you; you mark my words. So, my dear brother, pay careful attention to what I am about to say."

On the saddlebag chair at his side lay a flat leather folder, of the type that the French call a *serviette*, which closes by means of a flap capable of being locked to the body of the *serviette*.* As he opened the folder and drew out a large manila envelope, Mycroft continued:

"I am about to shew you something that I should not, in any official sense, shew you—or, rather, that you should not see. You will be shewn what I am about to shew you—but, as it is of a somewhat surprising (not to say alarming) nature, I thought that I would confer a decided tactical ad-

* And which is now called, by the British, a 'brief-case'.—*Editor*

vantage on my brother by letting him have a prior sight of the article in question. Here you are, then, Sherlock: tell me what you think of *this?*"

He drew a sheet of roughly quarto size from the manila envelope, and after a hasty glance around, to see that we were not observed, laid it on the table before me. It was a black-and-white lithograph of two persons—a man and a woman—in a bedroom, and the title, *The Bridal Night,* did nothing at all to inject even the least element of respectability into the drawing. The intention of the drawing was that it should be suggestive; and salacious it was.

Yet it would have been hard to say in what the smuttiness of the picture consisted; certainly, by any legal definition, it was not obscene, even though a little more of the lady's bosom was exposed than strict propriety requires. The tall husband, who is clasping his ecstatic bride to his chest, is decently clothed in an all-enveloping dressing-gown, and though the lady's night-dress is obviously thin, it is not at all diaphanous. Perhaps the sugges-tivenesss of the drawing lay in the skill with which the artist had captured the real or imaginary passion, ranging from a moderate hysteria to the full-blown *furor femineus,* whose detailed describing is the principal concern of certain French novelists, and had displayed it in every line and lineament of the young bride's body.

As I sat staring at the drawing, and still wondering in what its undeni-able impropriety consisted, Mycroft gently eased the drawing from my fingers, and returned it to its envelope; the envelope being replaced within the leather folder.

"I feel that it is safer if we do not leave it lying about. And now, let me briefly tell you the history of this drawing.

"It is unsigned, but the artist was Charles Leslie, the American R.A.—pupil and protégé of that other American R.A., Benjamin West. The draw-ing was given away gratis with *The Exquisite,* a journal published by Henry Smith, of whom—and of his publications—the less said the better. This drawing first appeared in *The Exquisite,* but was later re-published in two other of Smith's scandalous productions—both a great deal more salacious than *The Exquisite—: The Royal Wedding Jester* and *The Wedding Night, or The Battles of Venus.* You see that I have these titles off by heart: in fact, I exam-ined all three at Windsor, where they have all three copies. Our cousin Holmes, the Royal Librarian, kindly got them out for me. It was he who took an extra photograph of the drawing—which enabled me, my dear Sherlock, to shew it to you just now."

"It is certainly not the sort of thing that one would hang on one's draw-ing-room wall—though," I added, "I know several clubs whose smoking-rooms might even be improved by such art. But, Mycroft, what has this to do with me—and, even more to the point, what on earth has it to do with Her Majesty?"

My brother, whose face and manners had always more than half an impulse towards the histrionically affected, now pretended to surprise. He opened the folder once more, and took out the picture, again placing it before me.

"You appear to be curiously unobservant this evening, my dear Sherlock!—OR OUGHT YOU NOT TO BE USING YOUR EYEGLASS? Use it, my dear fellow, and take a closer look at the persons depicted. Ah! so you *do* see—you see at last, I perceive! And what do you see, Sherlock—?"

I said, staring at the drawing:

"But it can't be—"

"Oh, Sherlock, but it *is!* Of course," gently replacing the drawing in its envelope, and the envelope in the folder, "it was—let me see now—yes, nearly forty-seven years ago. We *all* change greatly in nearly fifty years, my dear brother—though, perhaps, some of us do not change so much as do some others. Yes, you recognize the originals now; but what took you so long?"

"The utter unexpectedness of it, I suppose. But—Her Majesty! And who is the gentleman supposed to be—?"

"Sherlock, Sherlock! I am disappointed in you. You look for scandal where none is intended! The tall young man who looks like one of the more dissipated and irresistible of Ouida's guardsmen is—well, who else should he be than—"

"Prince Albert—?"

"You were only six when he died, Sherlock; I may assure you that, even allowing for Winterhalter's flattery, he was a remarkably good-looking young man. Yes, Sherlock: the two young people, caught up in the raptures and roses of—perfectly legal—love are none other than Her Majesty and her husband, Albert the Good. And if you are now about to ask me what you are doing in this affair, let me tell you briefly that, in the first place, you are to be ordered—'commanded' is the right word, of course—to find and destroy the original of this picture, and then to see that the Republicans do not carry out their plan of distributing it broadcast as *their* rather tasteless contribution to the celebration of the Jubilee."

Her Majesty received me in private audience in one of the smaller drawing-rooms in Buckingham Palace.

I was introduced to the Royal Presence by Sir Francis Seymour, Master of the Ceremonies. No-one in attendance upon the Queen, not even a single footman; and the complete absence of ceremony with which I was presented, and the fact that General Seymour immediately after the presentation, begged leave to absent himself, so that Her Majesty and I were left entirely alone, indicated that I was come upon no matter of general report. It was unthinkable that General Seymour was ignorant of the reason for the Queen's commanding me to her presence; but it was evident that the matter about to be discussed had been confined to the knowledge of as few persons as possible.

With that Royal tact which was not the least part of her heritage, the Queen put me instantly at my ease, inviting me to take an armchair which half-faced her, and asking me to "speak up, Mr. Holmes; my hearing is not so acute as it was."

In recalling the grace and ease with which Her Majesty put aside my own diffidence—for I confess that I was unexpectedly nervous (I, who 'did not know what embarrassment was'!)—I would recall for the reader the almost sacred awe in which the Queen was held by *all* classes of her millions of subjects. In her small figure—she was barely five foot in height—dressed in the unfashionable and (so it seemed to me) shabby mourning; her hands grown ugly with the arthritis of age; her face blotched in that manner that the malicious Gladstone loved to describe in letters to his wife—there was yet a *presence* to which even those least susceptible of the claims of Majesty had to submit.

"There was power there, Watson," I said on my return to Baker-street; "and power which is fully and perfectly self-aware. Her Majesty is all three of Shakespeare's types of greatness, gathered up in one: she was born great; she has achieved greatness; and she has certainly had greatness thrust upon her."

"In respect of Disraeli's making her Empress of India, you mean?"

"Curiously enough, not altogether. I was thinking of the greatness that she has exercised by herself, not as the mere nominee of a political theory. The Queen, I know, was reluctant to assume the title—and I fear that, for all the politicians' politicking, her reluctance will prove to have been the inspired prevision of a day when India will no longer be ours. It is with the Anglo-Saxon peoples that we should be concerning ourselves, Watson, and—" Here I broke off, with a laugh. "Forgive me, Doctor: I am preaching again! And I was talking of the Queen and her greatness. Believe me, she is aware of it, she exercises it with the fullest consciousness of its value and power. Her assurance of her right to command is unquestioned by her—and she expects that it will be questioned by no one else. She expects no opposition, because she can see no reason why her commands should be questioned—least of all resented. She is the most extraordinary woman whom I have ever met—and I doubt that there have been a dozen such in the world's long history."

The dictionary defines the word 'legendary' as 'consisting of legends; fabulous, strange'; but of recent years the novelists have given this word a newer meaning—a meaning that I find ideal in the present context. For the modern novelist, 'legendary' means 'heroic' in the sense of a grandeur more than human; that almost divine superiority over all others which belongs to those heroes of Homeric, Scandinavian, Carlovingian and Arthurian legend. In this modern sense of the word, the Queen was indeed 'legendary'.

As with all such exalted personages, she was ever conscious of what she *symbolized*, as well as what, individually, she was. I had already spoken to the Czar; later I was to meet the Emperor of Austria-Hungary,* the Sultan of Turkey and—perhaps most typical of all these exalted 'symbols'—His Holiness the Pope. With all these Heads I was to encounter that constant awareness of their great responsibilities; the awareness of all those millions over whom they ruled as the guardians of their nations' or churches' † traditional social systems.

Of course, they could and did speak as individuals—the German Emperor laughed in no remote Imperial manner when I recalled for him the words of Mr Albert Chevalier's song "Knocked 'em in the Old Kent-road", for Kaiser William and I shared a great liking for the Cockney troubadour of the London music-halls. And others of the Illustrious whom I have had the honour to meet have proved themselves just as 'human'—once again to quote the novelists.

But that awareness that they lived and acted and spoke, not for themselves, but as the chosen (not a few thought of themselves as God-chosen) representatives, rather than the rulers, of those peoples of whom they were the constitutitional or autocratic heads, was something that they never forgot. Thus did the Queen so easily yet precisely move, in her speech, from the first person singular to the first person plural; carefully distinguishing between those sentiments that she uttered as a private person, and those that she uttered as a Monarch.

"Your name, Mr. Holmes, is, of course, well-known to Us." I rose from my chair, and bowed. "Please be seated, Mr Holmes. Your name has become quite familiar through the very many applications that you have made to Us through Lord Kenmare to accept the various foreign orders and decorations that you have thoroughly deserved. We were happy to give you the required permission, Mr. Holmes."

"I am deeply honoured and grateful, Ma'am."

---

* The strictly correct form is 'Emperor of Austria, King of Hungary', but Mr. Holmes uses, quite properly, the term in general use.—*Editor*

† Since the Sultan of Turkey was also 'the Pope of Islam', he was the Spiritual as well as the Regal leader of the millions of the Faithful.—*Editor*

"I also know, Mr Holmes, for what services these often quite high honours have been conferred upon you. My daughter, the Princess Royal, who, as you know, is the Crown Princess of the German Empire—by the way, sir, I understand that you speak German well?"

"I learnt it as a boy in Cologne, Ma'am, and my father never permitted me to forget it."

"Let us speak German, then," the Queen said, in that language. "It was the tongue of my dear Mother, of my much-loved Uncle Leopold, and—most important of all—of my sainted Husband, Albert. So let me have the pleasure of speaking and listening to the good old German tongue. But I interrupted myself: I was about to say that the Princess Royal keeps me well-informed of the sentiment abroad: your credit is very high; very high, indeed; with persons of consequence, Mr Holmes."

"Your Majesty flatters me in mentioning it."

Now it is true that those persons whose exalted position takes them apart from ordinary mankind, and, in so taking them makes them symbolic of the mass from which they have been removed, not only speak, as it were symbolically, but act symbolically, too. So that, even if they set a guard upon their tongues, they are too often betrayed, as to their intentions, by the symbolism of their acts.

If this seem a little obscure, let me strive to explain.

Her Majesty's drab mourning dress was relieved by the wide blue riband of the Garter and by the diamond-sapphire-and-ruby Star of that Order. She also wore a diamond-edged cameo-portrait of the Prince Consort: this emblem of her undying love for her dead husband, she always carried.

Now I was not unaware that the gentleman who had been chosen to conduct me to the Royal Presence would not customarily have been bidden to that duty, but I saw that the choice of Sir Francis Seymour had been deliberate on the part of the Queen: Sir Francis, before becoming Master of the Ceremonies to the Queen in 1876, had been Groom-in-Waiting to Prince Albert, until the latter's death in 1861.

The cameo, as a symbolic reminder of the Prince's constant presence, was always on the Queen's person; but the choice of one of the dead Prince's servants to conduct me into the room in which Her Majesty awaited me—well, this was surely underlining the significance of the symbolism; this could only indicate (but that I knew already) that I had been summoned to serve, not so much the Queen, as that undying love that, some thought, was paraded—and, perhaps, paraded a little too openly.

"You are aware, Mr Holmes, that Change—violent Change—is threatening all our old institutions; not constructive Change, sir—the wise expect, and accommodate themselves, to that; but destructive change, offering no alternative to that that it seeks to destroy. There is real danger in all this, Mr Holmes, do you not think?"

I answered with the well-known phrase of Schiller's:

" *'Was Hände bauten, können Hände stürzen.'* * One must see to it, Ma'am, that hands do not pull down what has been built up over so long a time."

The Queen nodded her agreement, but made no other answer. For some long moments she appeared to be considering what next to say, and when, at last, she did speak, it was in English once more. Pointing to a door different from that by which I had entered, and handing me a key warm from the hand in which she had been concealing it, Her Majesty said:

"In the empty room through that door, Mr Holmes, you will find a box on a table. Here is the key to that box. Open the box. There is a picture inside. Study well the picture—it is to discuss that picture that I have summoned you here. After you will have studied the picture, close and lock the box." I took the key in my left hand, rose, and walked to the closed door. A voice at my back said: "Shut the door behind you, Mr Holmes; I wish you to examine the picture in private."

In the box was, of course, as I had expected, the picture of *The Bridal Night* that Mycroft had shewn me. I studied this second example, though, with as much care as I had bestowed upon the drawing at my first sight of it, seeing if perhaps I had not overlooked something in my original examination. I had not, but I was reluctant to return too early to the Queen, lest she should think that I had not studied the picture with sufficient care; yet reluctant to dwell too long in the private room, lest she should think that I had stayed to gratify an unworthy impulse.

I recalled Mycroft's complacent "This could be the making of you!" For a reason that I could not quite grasp at that moment, Mycroft's remark— more, the attitude of mind which had inspired it—irritated me. I did not, I realized, wish to 'be made'; I wished to do my honest duty by my Sovereign and my country, let the cards fall where they might.

And all the time, as I was thinking of Mycroft's too-practical attitude with ever-increasing impatience, I was studying the drawing, wondering how I should describe it—how I should classify it—when the Queen began to question me.

It irritated me later at the Diogenes Club that Mycroft's praise should have been so sincere; it made my own spontaneous replies to the Queen seem a calculated business of the sort that Lord Holdhurst and his Foreign Service hold in such unaffected admiration. "Why, Sherlock, how *brilliant!*

* "What hands have built up, hands can pull down."—*Editor*

Why, my dear fellow, we'll make a diplomat of you yet! Why, God bless my soul, 'Pussy' Granville couldn't have done better!"

I found this praise for a non-existent cunning not only embarrassing; I found it positively repellent. I like praise as much as does any other man; but it must be praise that I have deserved; certainly not praise for something of which, had I been guilty of it, I would have been heartily ashamed. I had had no intention of being 'clever' or even 'diplomatic' as I came out of the private room, closed the door behind me, and silently handed the key of the box to Her Majesty.

"You locked the box, Mr Holmes?"

"Double-locked, Ma'am—and checked. The box is firmly closed—with the picture inside."

"Thank you. Please be seated, Mr Holmes." She touched a small silver striker-bell at her elbow, and glanced up at a fine French clock which ticked gently away on the marble mantel-shelf. The main door opened, and a footman held it ajar whilst another carried in a silver tray bearing decanters, glasses and a covered dish of what turned out to be sweet biscuits. The Queen never permitted footmen or other inferior domestics (for all that she was the most generous and thoughtful of mistresses) to look at her; at all times, until her death, they had, in her presence, to keep their gaze directed at the ground. The first footman, his eyes downcast, brought up a folding table, opened it, laid a cloth upon it (that he took from a drawer), brought up two small tables, one for Her Majesty, one for myself, and, having poured out the Queen's favourite mixture of vintage port and old malt whisky into a large cut-glass rummer, stood in an attitude of watchful attention by the tray.

"You will take some light refreshment with us, Mr Holmes?"

"I thank Your Majesty."

She gestured towards the tray.

"Port, sherry, Madeira, hock—brandy, whiskey—you have a wide choice, Mr Holmes."

"A little sherry, if you please, Ma'am."

"Then let me recommend the Solera. It is not very old—a mere quarter-century, I understand—but General Seymour recommends it, and it must therefore be excellent. Will you try it, Mr Holmes?"

"With pleasure, Ma'am."

The footman poured my Solera; handed the biscuits; and, with his companion, still with eyes downcast and not saying a word, left the room as quietly as he had entered it.

"We are now alone," said the Queen, "and may talk without interruption. Should I feel in need of another glass of Sir Morell Mackenzie's recommended mixture, no doubt you will not object to pouring it for me? Of course not. Well now, Mr Holmes, I shall not ask you if I may rely on your discretion, for had I had the least doubt of it, you would hardly be here now. But I do mention it, not to cast doubt on it, but to emphasize the need for a discretion far superior to any that you may have had to exercise in the past. Tell me, Mr. Holmes, what did you think of the picture that I have asked you to study? How, Mr Holmes, would you describe that picture— in, preferably, a short word or two?"

Now here, as Watson would say, was a 'facer'! To tell the truth, I did not know what to call the picture; how to describe it. I hadn't, to be frank, given a thought to the *necessity* of describing it, considering it to be, in practical terms, pretty indescribable (at least in the present circumstances). By what devious way of euphemism and periphrasis and circumlocution and—if need be—downright evasion, I had hoped to be able to deal with the matter of the picture without having to give it a classification, I couldn't have said; any more than I can say now. I imagine that, like any other man whom quite unimagined circumstance has made, at least temporarily, into a craven, I had hoped to 'wriggle out of it'. This, I now realized with all the horror of a sinking heart, was not to be permitted me. The Queen wished for no evasions; she had asked a plain question, and only an answer as plain would satisfy her. But I could not, for the life of me, find the right words.

"Come, come, Mr Holmes: you seem at a loss for a phrase? Well, sir: *how* would you describe the picture that I have permitted you to see? Did you study it, as I asked you?"

"Oh, yes, Ma'am—carefully."

"Well, then: what did you see?"

("I never bargained for this Mycroft; I swear I didn't!" I afterwards told my laughing brother.)

"Well, Ma'am, what was there to see?"

"I am asking *you*, Mr Holmes. What did *you* see?"

I sipped at my Solera, and the Queen regarded the snatched opportunity for delay with what seemed to me to be a tolerant but not respectful smile. At last, knowing that I had to go through with whatever lay ahead, I took a chance, and dived in, as they say, at the deep end.

"I saw . . . I saw two extremely personable young people, Ma'am: a very pretty young woman, and a most handsome young man. The legend beneath the picture informed me that these two had been married during the day, and that, therefore, their transports were perfectly regular—from the point of morality, Ma'am, as it says in the Marriage Service."

The Queen was now looking at me with a most peculiar expression, whose nature I was at a loss to understand. Her eyes were narrowed—those prominent, intensely blue, all-seeing Hanoverian eyes; and she had a small cambric handkerchief held to her lips. Silently she gestured towards her empty glass, and I rose to take the glass and fill it at the tray.

The Queen said rather huskily,

"The port first, Mr Holmes—about a third. Then the whisky from the *round* decanter. Thank you. Are you married, Mr Holmes?—they told me that you were not."

"No, Ma'am, I am not."

"But you are familiar with the Marriage Service?"

"Several of my friends have married, Ma'am, and I have been a guest at their weddings."

"I see." Then, suddenly changing back to German, she added: "And if you were married—?"

"Then, Ma'am, I should wish to inspire in my bride sentiments as warm as those displayed by the young lady in the picture."

"Are you serious, Mr Holmes? You would not dare to jest with me?"

"I was never more serious, Ma'am. And, as for jesting, it would not be that I did not dare, as that I did not wish. I have too much respect for Your Majesty."

She drank some of her strange—the Americans would call it a 'cocktail', I suppose—and appeared to be considering her next questions with more than her usual care.

"Would you describe the picture as indecent, Mr Holmes? Be truthful, now!"

"No, Ma'am, I should not."

"Indelicate, Mr Holmes?"

"In certain circumstances—yes."

"But not in all—?"

"No, Ma'am. Not at all in all circumstances."

"Can you explain this riddle?"

"Easily. The picture, *in itself,* is not indelicate; to issue it publicly—for it appears to have been included as an illustration in some journal—why, that would be intolerably indelicate. Not that the *picture* would be indelicate; its *publication* would be."

"Why, Mr Holmes?"

"Because, Ma'am, the intimate associations of marriage ought not to be made public."

"Yes, I see. Mr Holmes, do you know the two persons whom this picture—now nearly fifty years old—depicts?"

"Ma'am," I said, "I should be unpardonably obtuse were I not able to guess by now that the picture represents Your Majesty and His Royal Highness the Prince Consort."

"—As he became later," the Queen, with her perfect passion for accuracy in statement, could not help but add. "Yes, Mr Holmes. Mr Holmes, you cannot be under the illusion that I summoned you merely to shew you this drawing? You must have gathered that I had another reason?"

"Of course, Ma'am."

"Did you know that there is a plot to spoil my Jubilee celebrations by printing off and distributing hundreds of thousands of this picture—with, doubtless, some unseemly comments?"

"No, Ma'am," I said, untruthfully—but I had remembered my promise to Mycroft.

The Queen stared at me for a moment before she said,

"Hm! I would have thought that someone would have told you—. Very well, you did not know. But that is the problem: how to prevent these mischief-makers, these pullers-down of walls—I am glad that you like Schiller, Mr Holmes: he is a *great* poet—from ridiculing my sainted Husband and myself. I was distressed when I saw that picture fifty years ago—it would be intolerable were it to be reprinted in even greater numbers. May I rely upon you, Mr Holmes, to see that it remains where it is now—in that box?"

"Your Majesty may rely upon it that the picture will never again be published."

"Thank you, Mr Holmes. I trust you."

But as I said afterwards to Mycroft, was I mistaken in thinking that there was something of regret in the Queen's voice, as though, in some fashion, she had wished that the picture had *not* to be suppressed in the interests of delicacy and decorum?

Mycroft smiled.

"My poor Sherlock, what little you know about women!"

EIGHTEEN ❧

Dr and Mrs John Watson

Of course, it was inevitable that Dr Watson should have re-married—
sooner or later—and it was also inevitable, I suppose, that his second wife,
the former Miss Mary Morstan, daughter of the late Captain Arthur Morstan, 34th Bombay Artillery, should have failed to share the affection that
her husband, my friend of more than eight years, had come to feel for me.

It was in the December of 1887—the Golden Jubilee year had officially
finished in the previous May; but the country and the Empire preferred to
believe that Jubilee Year continued until 31st December, 1887, and were
celebrating accordingly—that Dr Watson's first wife died. Mary Ann Watson had been separated from her husband—*de facto* if not *de jure*—for close
on twenty years. The Watsons had parted, not so much from an unconquerable tendency to disagree, as from a hopeless failure to agree.

Dr Watson kept up a regular correspondence with his wife, and, after he
had learnt that she had been stricken of a malady fatal in those days, he visited her fairly frequently, for all that even her chronic illness could not
bring the parted husband and wife together. He was, I saw, genuinely distressed by her death, of which he had been the sorrowing witness—sorrowing, not only because of a normal human distress at another's suffering, but
also because he was witnessing the irrevocable departure of one whom he
had failed to make happy. Mrs Watson had lived for the last few years of
her life in Bournemouth, and was buried in the large and beautiful cemetery to the north of the town, at the junction of the Wimborne and Char-
minster Roads. The memorial service, that I attended, was held in the
chapel within the cemetery grounds.

Almost a full year had passed before, with the events most accurately described by the Watson-Doyle partnership in "The Case of the Four",* my friend and companion of nearly a decade met and was captivated by Miss Morstan, as, but in a very different way, was I. The trouble was that whilst Miss Morstan returned, though in no very passionate manner, my companion's affection, she had for me no liking at all; and, in the way of a woman, blamed me for such of Dr Watson's faults as she might hardly fail to notice.

At first it amused me that Dr Watson's imperfections should be attributed to my failure to (as Miss Morstan indignantly expressed it) "look after John"—a man who, though he had never told me his age exactly, must have been at least eight years my senior! Had I "done my duty by my professed friendship"—so Miss Morstan again—the good Doctor would not have been half-way to a death by alcoholic poisoning, or a death from bronchitis by smoking ship's shag, or a death from 'a loss of all moral sense'—thus Miss Morstan again—by frequenting the American Bar of *The Criterion* or 'Jimmy's' (as we called the 'snug' of the now-vanished St James's Restaurant). Had I done my duty, I should not have "dragged poor John out at all hours of the night, half-way across London and goodness knows where, to expose him to danger of I don't know what sorts, just for your own silly self-glorification". Considering that, though I *had* exposed the Doctor, as well as myself, to the poisoned darts of the Andaman Islander, as we sped down River in hot pursuit of Jonathan Small, it was also in pursuit of the Great Agra Treasure, *on behalf of Miss Morstan*, and I said so—thus breaking the cardinal rule laid down for the friends of lovers or husbands, *that they never defend themselves*—I ought not to have been astonished that Miss Morstan and I fell out.

I once said something to Watson in reference to the persecuted lady whom he calls 'Frances Carfax', and my observations on her, as a type, Dr Watson has carefully recorded. I could quote the words as being equally applicable to Miss Morstan:

> One of the most dangerous classes in the world is the drifting and friendless woman. She is the most harmless, and often the most useful of mortals, but she is also the inevitable inciter of crime in others.

If, in this passage about 'Lady Frances Carfax' and her type, we substitute, for the word 'crime', the word 'error' we have a passage which applies perfectly to Miss Morstan.

---

* Accurate enough, so far as the main events are concerned; but there are a number of inaccuracies as regards the less important details, all of which have been examined, and, to a large extent, explained by Sherlockian scholarship.—*Editor*

Ten years before she entered both our apartment and our joint life, her father, an Indian Army officer, had disappeared in mysterious circumstances. She herself had left India on the death of her mother, and had lived in no proper home, but only in an Edinburgh boarding-house, until she was seventeen, when she had suffered the loss of her father. Compelled then to earn her livelihood, she had adopted one of the few respectable occupations then available to young females without either income or family, and became a governess. If ever there was a young woman who deserved the title of 'drifting and friendless', that young woman was Miss Morstan.

Watson, of course, was smitten beyond the reach of argument or warning; he has left some record, poor chap, of his sentiments in the matter—nothing very original, and what millions of men have seen in their beloved in the first few hours of Love's awakening!

> My mind [*he wrote*] ran upon our late visitor—her smiles, the deep, rich tones of her voice, the strange mystery which overhung her life. If she were seventeen at the time of her father's disappearance she must be seven-and-twenty now—a sweet age, when youth has lost its self-consciousness and become a little sobered by experience.

Sweetness, like beauty, lies in the observation of the smitten; and had I chanced upon this maudlin guff at the time of writing, and not, as it happened, after Miss Morstan's death, I might have had some acid comments to make upon 'youth . . . a little sobered by experience'. It is as well that I did not; Watson had pain enough without my having added to it.

The fact is that Miss Morstan was neither self-conscious nor youthfully sweet. If it was inevitable that her orphan upbringing and unsupported battle to make her own way had toughened her in what (to me, at least) was a noticeable degree, it was also true that she had been hardened by her experience. If she had a tendency to faint, that, alas!, was the sign of the heart-disease from which she was soon to die; had her heart been stronger, she would not have exhibited even that sign of womanly weakness.

St Paul said to Timothy that the love of money was the root of all evil; I should say that regret for vanished money, as a fruitful source of trouble, runs the love of money a close second. And it was Miss Morstan's unconquerable regret for that half-million or so, lying at the bottom of the Thames, which made the rift between us. For, to Miss Morstan's world-sharpened wits, regret was one thing—idle regret, quite another. At first gently, almost casually, she would bring up the Treasure in her conversation:

"Is it *really* lost, Mr Holmes? Somehow, do you know, I can never bring myself to believe that. Is it *really* so irrecoverable?" she would ask, her round chin resting gracefully on her rounded knuckles; her big grey eyes fixed 'appealingly' on mine.

"I'm afraid that we must abandon all hope of our recovering it, Miss Morstan. The Thames, at that point—"

And yet once more, I would explain the conditions of the River at that point: the fact that tidal currents operate to scour the river-bed, and—

"But—I don't know: silly me, talking of such things!—but are there not such things as dredgers, Mr Holmes?"

"Yes," I would say, feeling the sort of weary uselessness with which his now-unmeaningly-spoken lines fill an actor at the end of a long, but not very successful, run, "there are such things as dredgers, but, in these particular circumstances—"

And the next line, coming as pat as the next line in a Shakespearean text, would be:

"I was wondering about a diver, Mr Holmes? Couldn't he—well, sort of hunt about, do you know? I'm sure he'd find the chest—or, at least, have a jolly good look—" (The implication was plain: *he'd* have a jolly good look— unlike that idle Mr Holmes!) "Can't one hire the services of a diver? Can one? Oh, that's interesting! Are they very expensive?"

Had Dr Watson not been always listening, with a maudlin grin, to this unchanging cross-talk, I might have been a good deal less patient than I always managed to be. On one occasion, I even persuaded my cousin George Holmes, then Secretary of the Institution of Naval Architects—he is now Sir George—to come along to Baker-street and give this over-persistent young lady a technical explanation of the impossibility of recovering, either by dredger or diver, anything which had fallen overboard at that particular part of the River which had swallowed up the Great Agra Treasure.

But I could see that, persuaded 'gainst her will, Miss Morstan was of the same opinion still; how much, I was to be quite startled in discovering.

Dr Watson records that I said of the young lady, at the very beginning of our never-warm acquaintance:

'I think she is one of the most charming young ladies I ever met, and might have been most useful in such work as we have been doing. She had a decided genius that way.'

Yes, I admit that I said this. 'Charm' is an indefinable quality, and too often exhibits the charming quality of hoar-frost on the morning meadows: here now, vanished with the day. But as to her talent for detective work, I have no words to withdraw. She would have made—no, she *was*, I say—a woman with a decided genius for tracking down the objective on which she had set her sights.

How this fact came to my amused notice makes a most curious story.

Not long after Miss Morstan had married Dr Watson on Wednesday, 1st May, 1889, at St Mark's, Camberwell (in which parish she was living), a letter arrived at the offices of The British & Imperial Heraldic & Genealogical College of Research, marked for the attention of Mr Augustus Walker, who, if the reader has forgotten, was one of my other selves. The letter is before me as I write:

> Ivydene,
> 45, Acre-lane,
> Brixton, S.W.
> 4th June, 1889

Dear Sirs,

Your name has been given to me at the British Museum as that of a Firm able to make enquiries relative to proving Family relationship.

Will you please inform me of the details of your charges? If they are not too high, I should like to make use of your services.

> Yours faithfully,
>
> [*signed*]   Mary Morstan

Now, this was a curious letter to receive from *Mrs John Watson*, of *38, Norfolk-street, Paddington* (just across the road from St Mary's Hospital), where Dr Watson, on his marriage, had set up in modest practice. Nor was 45, Acre-lane the address at which Miss Morstan had been living: Acre-lane is not in the parish of St Mark's, Camberwell; and had she been living there, she could not have been married in that church. The Acre-lane address was, therefore, an accommodation address.

'Mr Augustus Walker' replied as follows:

Madam,

I acknowledge, with thanks, your favour of the 4th instant, and note its contents.

The charges of this College are strictly related to the time spent on research, for which, in enquiries of an ordinary nature, the fee is 2s.6d. per hour, any requisite travelling expenses being charged for at cost.

You do not say whether the Search would necessitate enquiries out of London.

If you could give me more information, I could be more definite on the question of charges. The average enquiry, if needing no travel outside London, may usually be made for less than £1.

I await the favour of your further reply,

Assuring you, Madam, of our strict attention to your requirements at all times,

I remain,

pp. The British & Imperial Heraldic & Genealogical College of Research,

[*signed*]   Augustus Walker, Travelling Inspector

'Miss Mary Morstan' to 'Mr Augustus Walker':

. . . I wish to discover if there be any relationship between a Dr John Hamish Watson, born at Milverton, near Taunton, Devon, 19th March, 1847,* and either Mr J. G. Watson or Mr W. L. Watson, both of London. . . .

'Mr Augustus Walker' to 'Miss Mary Morstan':

. . . It would be helpful to both of us if you could furnish me with more particulars relative to Mr J. G. Watson and Mr W. L. Watson. I am sure that I need hardly point out that 'Watson' is one of our commoner British surnames. Is it not possible to give me their full Christian names, ages and place of birth? To search the Registers for a Mr J. G. Watson or a Mr W. L. Watson would not be merely a most expensive undertaking, but, I fear, almost a useless one as well. . . .

'Miss Mary Morstan' to 'Mr Augustus Walker':

. . . I can tell you only that the Messrs Watson are professional gentlemen whose place of business is in Nicholas-lane, Lombard-street, City, in which case, they must be over forty. I regret that I cannot be more definite. . . .

'Mr Augustus Walker' to 'Miss Mary Morstan':

. . . Would it be possible for you to call on us here, when I could see you by appointment? I find that persons making enquiries, especially Ladies, are some-

* Was this the real date of Watson's birth? Obviously he had had to give Miss Morstan a year of birth, for any coyness in this (to her) important particular would have stood little chance of holding out against her insistence on her 'rights.' He may well have 'settled' for the year 1847. As I said earlier, I never troubled to check the date at Somerset House. Sometimes the good Doctor seemed older, sometimes younger- but if his wife was satisfied with the date, 1847, well then . . . —S.H.

times—indeed, quite often—in possession of helpful information of whose possession they are unaware, but which often may be revealed in conversation. . . .

Did Mrs Watson smell a rat?—or had she a native or acquired caution which counselled her to keep her enquiries to the impersonal *milieu* of the letter? Whatever her reasons for not accepting 'Mr Walker's' invitation to talk matters over, she disappointed me, for I should have liked very much to test the sharpness of Mrs Watson's eyes by appearing before her in the guise of the Gray's-inn-road Genealogist.

However, a letter from another source enabled me to discover the identity of one of the Messrs Watson about whom Mrs Watson had written to me. Unbelievable as it may sound, it was Mr J. G. Watson who had written to me, and his communication certainly explained much:

1st August, 1889

Dear Sir,
    I trust that you will not have forgotten me, for all that it now some six years since we met on Messrs Chatwoods'* stand at the Amsterdam Exhibition of 1883, and afterwards dined together at the Hotel Polen?
    I wonder if might ask you to spare me a little of your *professional* time, to advise me in a matter which is troubling me greatly.
    I have had a call from a lady which, though seemingly rational enough (even if quite unprecedented in my long experience), *may* be the gambit of some novel game of fraud. The recent enterprises at the expense of the London Banks—the matter of Warden† must be as fresh in your mind as in mine—must make us all perhaps unduly sensitive to 'novel' approaches, but I should be happy to be assured by your own professional assessment of the matter.

This letter told me far more than I should ever have gathered from a search through the registers at Somerset House; indeed, since the writer had used his business letter-heading, the signature told me everything. The letter was signed 'W. L. Watson', and had been sent from the head-office of The Agra Bank, Limited, in Nicholas-lane, Lombard-street.

One should never reject an opportunity to acquire a reputation for omniscience. Immediately on the receipt of Mr Watson's letter, I sat down at my desk, took a sheet of writing-paper, and indited this letter to him:

---

* World-renowned British manufacturers of bankers' strong-rooms, whose exhibits 'created a sensation' at the Exhibition, and carried off all the prizes.—*Editor*

† Thomas Warden, secretary of the London and River Plate Bank, absconded on 1st October, 1883, after robbing the Bank of £110,000.—*Editor*

221B, Baker-street,
Portman-square,
London, W.
1st August, 1889

Dear Sir,

I am obliged by yours of to-day's date; of course I recall, and with much pleasure, our joint interest in Chatwoods' time-locked 'impregnable' strong-rooms, and our discussing their possible weaknesses afterwards over an excellent Dutch dinner. I hope that you will do me the honour to dine with me soon, at a time convenient to yourself. The Chef at the Union Club excels, I think, even the famed Soyer—but you shall, I trust, judge for yourself! A telegram will give me ample time to order a dinner for two.

In the meanwhile, to save time, let me reassure you in the matter of the call from a lady. There is no question of fraud here, unless over-obstinate optimism be a fraud. The lady, I suggest, wishes the Agra Bank to underwrite the cost of searching for the Great Agra Treasure, of which she is the legal heiress, and which is at present at the bottom of a river not a million miles from Lombard-street. The costs of recovering this sunken treasure—conservatively estimated at some £500,000—neither she nor her husband is in a position to defray.

Let me present you with the following *facts:*—

1. There is a treasure worth, say, £500,000.
2. The lady is the legal heiress to it.
3. The treasure is where she says it is.
4. There is absolutely *no hope* of raising it.

With regard to the last statement, the lady is of a different opinion—and so may you be. I merely give you *my* opinion—professionally, as you have requested; but without fee, as becomes dealings between friends. Were I a Director of the Bank of Agra, I should leave the Great Agra Treasure where it is.

Yours very truly,
[*Signed*]   Sherlock Holmes

I heard later, from Lord Carnwarth, a director of the Agra Bank (and whose uncle, the 11th Earl, as Colonel of the Bengal Horse Artillery, had known Captain Morstan, of the 34th Bombay Infantry), that Mrs Watson had approached the Messrs Siebe, Gorman, with a proposition that they should send one of their divers down to search for the Treasure on a speculative basis. The firm declined, and, I believe, Mrs Watson reconciled herself to 'accepting' her misfortune, by blaming her loss completely on me.

A permanent and irreparable division between Dr Watson and myself might well have been effected by his Wife's intransigent attitude towards me had it not been for a happy outcome of that long-past dinner at Goldini's. I refer, of course, to the dinner at which Dr Conan Doyle (as he now wished to be known) had proposed a literary partnership between Dr Watson and himself—a partnership to which, I make no bones about admitting, I gave my blessing.

The first of my cases that Dr Watson and Dr Doyle had written up had been that of the vengeance-inspired pursuit of the Mormons Stangerson and Drebber by the dying Jefferson Hope. To the somewhat romanticized account of this case, Dr Doyle had given the Whistleresque title of "A Study in Scarlet". On offer to almost every reputable publisher and editor in London, it had been turned down by all; it seemed, indeed, after one year of having been offered, quite unsaleable. At last, in despair, Dr Doyle— though with Dr Watson's consent—accepted the trivial, almost derisory, offer of £25 for the copyright, made by the Messrs Ward & Lock. A year after the unprofitable sale, the story appeared in *Beeton's Annual* for *Christmas*, 1887. The story attracted practically no attention; the critics ignoring it completely.

It was as well that Dr Watson had not relied upon Dr Doyle's plan to earn him the money needed for the purchase of a practice. That, fortunately, had come from the share of the profits of *our* practice that I had persuaded him to accept in the earliest days of our partnership.

It was with this money, that he had gained from his work on such cases as "The Service for Lord Backwater," "The Darlington Substitution Scandal", "The Adventure of the Noble Bachelor", "The Adventure of the Paradol Chamber", and so many others that Dr Watson has either described or merely mentioned in passing, that he was enabled to purchase the practice of old Dr Simpson, in Norfolk-street.

But, at the end of 1888, matters took a decided turn for the better, both for Dr Watson and Dr Doyle. The American editor of *Lippincott's Magazine*, who had come to England to meet and encourage authors of promise, invited some of these promising authors to dinner: amongst them, Oscar Wilde and Dr Doyle. The authors left the dinner-table having promised the editor a new book within a very short time. Mr Wilde obliged with the now well-known *Picture of Dorian Gray;* Dr Doyle, in collaboration with Dr Watson, produced *The Sign of the Four*, a highly romanticised account of the Great Agra Treasure affair.

Looking back, one may see that the two literary collaborators could hardly have chosen another plot: the Agra Treasure business was contemporary with the commission from Lippincott's; the memory of the events would never be more vivid in Dr Watson's mind; he was in what some lovers call 'the seventh heaven' of his amatory bliss—that only too brief period in which the loved one has only the most engaging virtues—and no faults at all. The book was written at the greatest possible speed, sent to America in the autumn of 1889, after Dr Watson and his bride had returned from a 'late' honeymoon in Lucerne, and published simultaneously in London and New York in February, 1890.

As all the world knows, the novel was not only a success, but also generated success. My exploits, exaggerated though their description always was—and was to be—evidently appealed greatly to many thousands of the public; and, in the quarter-century or so since *The Sign of the Four* first appeared, the tales about my adventures have earned both Dr Watson and Dr Doyle a considerable sum of money.

This money had still to be earned when Dr Doyle signed the contract with the Messrs Lippincott in 1888; but that a publishing-house of Lippincotts' eminence should *commission* a book about *me*, Sherlock Holmes, and *him*, Dr Watson, and *her*, Miss Mary Morstan, revived all the lady's wilting practicality, and made her see me, as she said in a burst of quite undiplomatic confiding, 'in a new light'. What she meant by this 'new light' was the power to see that, despite her deep-rooted objection to me (though more as a rival to her marital happiness than to me as a person), she must permit the friendship between Dr Watson and myself to continue—else otherwise how might her husband gather the raw material of his obviously-about-to-be-highly-successful writing?

Reluctantly, but none the less fully, she permitted Dr Watson to continue to see me and to accompany me on several of my expeditions; her permission being the more readily given, as her shrewd poverty-sharpened eye saw that his medical and surgical practice could readily spare Dr Watson on most days of the week. But his absence from our rooms in Baker-street troubled me more than I had imagined it could ever have done. For the first time since those unhappy days in Montague-street that a rigid and unrelenting control of memory had enabled me almost to forget, I was aware of, and saddened by, loneliness in its most oppressive form.

When young 'Stamford' had introduced us in Bart's, now eight years since, I had seen, in the rather battered former Surgeon-lieutenant no more than a convenient means of acquiring some desired Baker-street diggings whose rent I could not manage on my own. Not many months were to pass before I realized that, of all the men in the world, I could not have found a companion more suited to my own none-too-easily-satisfied requirements. We were not alike; our characters could shew even some striking differences; yet, for all those differences, our similarities of taste and outlook were more—and more important—than those qualities and idiosyncrasies which differentiated us. Even in the least important matters, we seemed to share many a common taste. We liked to smoke a pipe; and what we liked to smoke in that pipe was the strongest of tobacco—shag for me, Ship's for him; and even in so ordinary an indulgence as smoking, we exhibited some individual oddities—I kept my shag in the toe of an old Persian slipper; the mantelshelf was never without one or two pricks * of the strongest plug for Watson's briar.

We were men who liked a 'home', and we were as far from being domestic—or, rather, domesticated—as a bachelor and an honorary bachelor could be. We were restless men; always eager to be out-and-about, and we would have been miserable had we not had our flat and our personal possessions to come back to. We liked food, and we liked good wine and good whisky and good brandy—I, in moderation; Watson, perhaps less moderately. We were both intensely inquisitive: we liked to know 'what was going on around us'.

We liked London, and we liked—though not so much—the country, since we were essentially urban rather than rustic in our tastes. We greatly liked the theatre and recitals of good music; and I suppose that I am not guilty of the least exaggeration when I say that, in the quarter-century that I shared with Dr Watson, he or I—and usually both of us together—have seen every actor and actress of note; every great singer, from Sims Reeves to the De Reske Brothers; from Adelina Patti to Nellie Melba; every great music-hall comedian, from Nellie Farren to Dan Leno; from the Chickaleary Kid to Albert Chevalier. We visited all the theatres, from the highest to the least fashionable; from The Britannia at Hoxton, to The Lyceum, to see the never-to-be-matched Shakespeare of Henry Irving and Ellen Terry, with Telbin's incomparable stage-sets; from the high-class pantomime of Drury Lane, with Dan Leno and Herbert Campbell, under the superb management of Augustus Harris, to the earthy 'panto' of The Elephant & Castle, in the New Kent-road, where embryo talent was trying out its too-fanciful *noms-de-guerre* and still uncertain acting, but to audiences as critical as any which hissed off-key bel canto in the *Scala* in Milan.

We had, through visits which sometimes were as many as three or four in a single week, experienced the gradual physical glorification of the Theatre, growing, with each rebuilding, more and more magnificent.

And—I trust that my memory do not deceive me—I seem to remember that the actors and actresses grew in talent and stature with the progressive

* A cigar-shaped piece of ship's tobacco, whipped tightly in tarred rope.—*Editor*

glorifying of the Theatre. The theatre-studded Britain of to-day had its physical as well as its spiritual origin in the Theatre that Watson and I saw grow in the 'Eighties: a growth which reached its full and splendid flowering in the decade between the Jubilees.*

But I write now as though I had parted with Dr Watson for ever; yet that we had parted for only the briefest while was something that I could not know.

His absence from our rooms made them intolerable to me; and I sought a refuge from my loneliness, not only in those clubs—the Diogenes, the Carlton, the Union, the Travellers', the Medico-Legal—to which Mr Sherlock Holmes belonged—but also those others, of an inferior social standing, of which Henry Beatson, the clerk; Bert de Fratteville, the out-of-livery groom; Fritz Kassel, the German free-lance waiter, and Captain Dacre-Buttsworth, the shabby-genteel man-about-town, were members.

But—I missed Watson. In my restless perambulations around London, I found no-one like him; and, as I wandered from the Carlton to (though with a change of identity) *The Pelican*; from the Union to (again with a change of identity) *The Adelphi*; I came to the realization that I should never find anyone who *suited* me so well as Watson, with all his faults—sometimes irritating faults—had done.

Perhaps, I used to think at the moments of regretful sadness, I would never find anyone again with whom the possibility of a really serious quarrel was less likely to occur. Disagreements and quarrels between persons of the opposite sex are generated, I think, less by a difference of opinion than by the physical and psychical differences between the two protagonists in the sexual battle.

It is different in companionships between persons of the same sex: here, quarrels (apart from those small irritabilities which may come from the mere using of the same bathroom) are generated only by differences of opinion. In my case, I was fortunate: Watson had so few opinions, and those derived rather from idle listening than from any positive cerebration on his part, that he never—or, rarely (and then to no purpose)—argued with me.

But I find, in this sentimental recalling of my feelings of—yes, of abandonment—on the departure of Dr Watson with his second wife, that I have run ahead of my narrative.

It was not until the end of 1888 that I first met, in connection with the Great Agra Treasure affair, Miss Mary Morstan; it was not until the end of the following year that Watson plucked up courage to ask her hand in mar-

* That is, between 1887 and 1897.—*Editor*

riage—or (as I have thought not infrequently since) Miss Morstan decided that she might do worse than in accepting my friend's proposals. The years 1886, 1887 and 1888 were, without doubt, the most important in my life. I shall have to go back a little in my narrative, and tell what happened in those years, from my suppressing that unpublishable picture of the Queen until, with Dr Watson's marriage, I found myself once again a very lonely bachelor.

I have run through the last few pages of these memoirs, and I find, as I said above, that I must go back a year or two, to pick up the continuity—more or less—of my narrative.

In writing one's memoirs, I find, it is an impossibility to include everything, even in a life in which (thanks be to that inscrutable Destiny which plots our paths) almost everything has been of interest, and most of it a source of pleasure. But how may I include everything which has happened to me?—everything which has interested me?—everything, even, that I would like to recall and preserve for all time in the secret places of the heart? It is impossible. I can do no more here than pick out for mention, first, those things that I remember clearly, and, second, those things which are worth the remembering. Perhaps, if I were asked to say what are the things worth remembering, I ought to answer: the things which have demonstrated my progress as a developing human being.

I take up a note-book, and open it at random. Here is a date in 1888. I have called upon Her Majesty at Windsor, and on the way back to London, in the train, I jotted down something that the Queen had said that I thought was worth preserving. This is the fragment of conversation that I have preserved:

"You have a brother, I believe, Mr Holmes?"

"Two, Ma'am."

"A brother in our Foreign Service, Mr Holmes?"

"Ah, yes, Ma'am: my brother Mycroft."

"Yes. Mycroft Holmes. We have heard something of him. A clever young man, Lord Granville tells me."

"Your Majesty honours us all by your praise of my brother. I am happy that Lord Granville speaks so well of him."

"In my long life, Mr Holmes—I have been your Queen since I was nineteen; long before you were born; I have seen many clever young men. We have a number in evidence now—Lord Randolph Churchill, Mr Joseph Chamberlain, Mr Herbert Asquith, Mr Augustine Birrell and—until a couple of years ago—Sir Charles Dilke. Mr Holmes: do you know what happens to clever young men?"

"I haven't given the matter any special thought, Ma'am."

"No? Then permit me to tell you that *they get nowhere;* nowhere at all. As for your brother, Mr Holmes, he will, of course, do quite well in our Service—but that is *all*, Mr Holmes; that is *all;* he will never *get anywhere.* And do you know why?"

"No, Ma'am: frankly, I don't. I had always thought my brother Mycroft the cleverest of us three younger Holmeses."

"That's just it, Mr Holmes: your brother is *too clever—too clever by half!*"

So that was it! not that vaulting ambition which o'erleaps itself (in fact, Mycroft's ambition was rather to be the powerful *éminence grise* than a 'Pussy' Granville or Lord Edmond Fitzmaurice), but that too-sure-of-itself power to manipulate people and events, which, so disastrously for its possessor, succeeds only in looking like cockiness, and which ends by irritating rather than by impressing. But (I reflected) it took the Queen's honest and sturdy common-sense to point out this disagreeable truth to me!

Another remembrance from that time of my second great loneliness: Dr Doyle dined with me one night at the Grand Hotel; an excellent meal, I recall, in the so-called 'Louis XVI' Restaurant.

Since the occasion was related to the 'novelization' (as the Americans are now calling it) of the Great Agra Treasure affair, the talk turned inevitably to the means by which the romanticized account of the facts—later published under the title, as I have mentioned, of *The Sign of the Four*—was to be accomplished. A casual but relevant remark of mine, I remember clearly, brought a quite unexpectedly warm response from my guest, who stared at me for a long moment without speaking, before he burst out with this:

"Great Heavens, Holmes!—you surely are not under the impression that *I* wrote 'A Study in Scarlet', or that I am writing this new book on the Agra Treasure? My word! I do believe that you *do* think so!"

"I thought, naturally, that you were the writer in this collaboration with Dr Watson—that he supplied the material, and that you licked it into shape."

"Good gracious no! It is true that I do run over the manuscript, and make a few corrections—mostly from the point-of-view of what I know the Editor likes. But—*write* those marvellous adventures of Mr Sherlock Holmes! Not on your life, sir! Your very talented Dr Watson does that—but, stay, did you not know that?"

"I obviously owe Watson a profound apology. No, Doctor, I did not know that."

"Then I am happy to be the one to tell you that, in your friend, you have a fine writer—a really fine writer, sir! Perhaps, if this new book goes as well as we hope—you know that I have found a publisher who will do his utmost to promote sales?—your friend may be a wealthy, as well as a fine, writer."

(That, at any rate, was one of those hopeful half-prognostications which—to my great satisfaction—came true.)

In almost equal—and opposed—proportions, 1886 and 1887 (comprising, between them, the year of the Golden Jubilee) were both 'good' and 'bad' years. They were 'good' in the sense that I continued to be successful—more and more so; they were 'bad' in the sense that the calls upon my time became so heavy that, to combat the fatigue induced by an excess of employment, and to summon up reserves of energy to cope with the increased demands on my abilities and my time, I came very near to poisoning myself with cocaine.

The trouble was that, so near in time, but so far away, it seems, in certain types of knowledge, we knew so little of narcosis in particular and of the effects of the narcotics in general. It is quite astonishing to realize how ignorant we were; not merely thirty to forty years ago, but a mere decade ago, when the deadly heroin was introduced into medical practice as a *non-addictive* alternative to the habit-forming morphine and cocaine.

Much has been written in the newspapers lately, not only (and mostly correctly) on the dangerous effects of the narcotic drugs, but also (and mostly incorrectly) on the taken-now-for-granted 'wickedness' of those who use these drugs. A particularly mischievous—and altogether typical—example of the newspaper opinion on drugs is provided, I think, by a cutting from the *Daily Mail* of a year or two back. I have it by me as I write; its lurid and inaccurate journalistic denunciations are headed:

'DRUG DAMNATION'
'Society' Sensation-Seekers
Father Vaughan's Solemn Warning

(For a generation of the future, who may read these memoirs and who may not have heard of Father Vaughan, this self-advertising cleric was a professional warner, whose *Sins of Society* is, I am told by Mr Walter Heinemann, 'still going well', and who consorted, on easy terms, during the week, with that 'Society' whom he denounced from the pulpit of his fashionable church on Sundays and Holy Days. Every generation, since the Devil invented the milder forms of fraud, has had its Father Vaughan.)

Cocaine—as all these 'pick-me-ups'—is a snare and a delusion indeed: a snare, in that it offers a quick, 'painless' way to restored vigour; a delusion, in that it demands a price that the buyer had not bargained for.

The so-called 'sensation' that one gets from taking any of these 'uplifting' drugs is a benefit—if one may call it that—confined to the first, or, at most, the first few, times of taking. After that, one takes—one is forced to take— the drug, not to recapture that initial exhilaration (that, alas!, is gone beyond recall), but to bring oneself to a near-normality of being in which one may carry out one's ordinary daily duties.

And all this whilst one has to conceal the fact that anything is unusual!— to hide both one's craving and its uncertain and progressively ineffective relief!

That I was cured of this dreadful craving I owe, not only to the excellent advice of several of my senior colleagues at Bart's, but also to the sound, practical common-sense of Dr Conan Doyle, who, with no great love of Medicine, yet had a warm affection for Healing, of which he was a na-tural—and generally successful—practitioner.

But this preoccupation, not only with my to-be-concealed-at-all-costs malady (it was nothing else; and a fatal malady, at that), but with *conceal-ment in itself*, took almost all the satisfaction out of what ought to have been—indeed, *was*—if not my *annus mirabilis*, then at least one of the most memorable and productive of my several *anni mirabiles*.

On all sides I was successful and honoured: in the Birthday Honours list of 1887, I was nominated a Commander of the Order of the Bath (Civil), for 'personal services to Her Majesty'; in the following year, but still within 'Jubilee Time', my gracious and, to me, always kindly Queen appointed me Private Consulting Detective-in-Ordinary to Her Majesty; an honour spe-cially created for me, and one which has since been renewed by Her Maj-esty's son, the late King Edward VII, and by her grandson, His Present Majesty.

Honours of another sort, but not less flattering to my self-esteem, came in profusion. I was invited to accept the Presidency of the Criminological Section, and sit, as British representative on the Supreme Jury of the Brus-sels Exhibition of 1888, the year in which, following the publication of my monograph *Malingering* (a small study whose inspiration was the case that Watson calls "The Adventure of the Dying Detective") and my long article in *The Anthropological Journal* "On the Variability of Human Ears", I re-ceived the Honorary Fellowship of University College, London (Watson's *alma mater*), and became a Membre Associé de l'Académie des Sciences of Paris, an Honorary Member of the Imperial Academy of Vienna, of the Imperial Academy of Science of St Petersburg and of the Royal Academy of Science in Brussels.

Perhaps another, and more generous (and also, perhaps, less percipient) biographer of myself would state airily that I 'carried all these honours lightly and with becoming modesty'—as I have just seen stated in a life of that by no means gentle or patient character the late Lord Roberts. It may be that I have carried—and still do carry—my many honours with 'becoming modesty', but to affirm that I have carried them 'lightly'—which means, I suppose, that I was almost unaware of them; as a man must be aware of his boots only if he happen to go from the house without them—would be untrue. They not only weighed on me; they weighed heavily on me; and, more, their weight on my spirit was, at that time, an almost intolerable burden. For every honour meant more or less of involvement, on my part, with those persons or that institution which had honoured me; a fresh drain upon my diminishing quantum of energy; a fresh—and, at times, terrifying—need to conceal from the world the true condition of my spirit, mind and body. Looking back on those desperate days, I wonder (as must all who have survived shipwreck) how I came through with undiminished credit and not greatly diminished health. ("Your French blood, Holmes," Dr Doyle suggested; laughing but still more than half-serious; since he prided himself on his supposed Norman ancestry. "It's the blood of *stayers*."—And in this, I think that he was substantially correct: it was a remarkably shrewd observer who commented that, though often insignificant in victory, the French are splendid in defeat. I halted, by Whose grace I still do not know, a step this side defeat; but, as a great and generous conqueror of the French said, just a century ago, "it was a close-run thing".*)

Activity—that is to say, actual physical activity—seemed to have no relation to the demands that a case made upon me; I was as cast down by merely *learning* a dreadful secret (Watson calls it "The Case of Bert Stevens, the Terrible Murderer"), in the latter part of 1887, as I was by my strenuous physical involvement, between Tuesday, 25th September, and Saturday, 20th October, 1888, in the case of *The Hound of the Baskervilles*—the correct name, by the way (for once!).

I am particular in giving the dates precisely, because, exactly one week earlier—that is, on Tuesday, 18th September—Miss Mary Morstan, by calling on us at Baker-street, had set in train that dramatic series of events chronicled by Watson as *The Sign of the Four*. Indeed, now that I can 'recollect in tranquillity' a more reckless Sherlock Holmes of nearly thirty years ago, I see that even a person at the peak of his bodily fitness might have felt exhausted by a fortnight of such breathless and unremitting activity: from

---

* Said by the 1st Duke of Wellington ('The Iron Duke') after, and of, the battle of Waterloo, fought 18th June, 1815, and so, as Mr Holmes remarked, exactly a century before he was writing in 1915.—*Editor*

chasing a king's ransom down River, under a hail of poisoned darts from an Andaman Islander's blow-gun, to, only a week later, hunting a murderer and being hunted by his murderous hound, over the immemorial and treacherous wastes of Dartmoor. I see now that I attached too great importance—as well as assigned an incorrect reason—to my almost total physical and mental exhaustion. All which was needed—and let me recall here that both Dr Watson and Dr Doyle strongly urged me to take a holiday from my work ("What you need, my dear sir," said the latter, "is a jolly good rest!")—I found myself unable to take. I was not the first in the world to fall a hopeless victim to the duties that he had imposed upon himself; but here I was, chained to my self-imposed obligations as firmly and as inescapably as was ever Prometheus to his rock, whilst the eagles of voluntarily-undertaken work were tearing at my vitals.

And it was Dr Doyle who pointed out to me that my freeing myself from my addiction to cocaine could never be effected so long as the regular doses of cocaine had—or might appear to have—a valid therapeutic worth. A toper, he added, who thinks that he *needs* his morning pick-me-up will hardly be in the ideal circumstances to become a teetotaller.

One thing, I believe, saved me from total physical and mental collapse: the variety of my work; a variety which involved many different locations (as the Americans say) as well as many different types of problem.

I visited Holland again in 1887, in connection with what Watson has called "The Colossal Schemes of Baron Maupertuis"—real name: Maurits Klein *—and his Netherlands-Sumatra Company; an affair on which I shall have something to say later. In the August of that terribly hot year, I paid another short visit to America: this time in connection with the mysterious vanishing of the British barque *Sophie Anderson*, somewhere—apparently—in that notorious grave-yard of ships between Bermuda and Florida. I went from Liverpool to New Orleans by the Dominion Line's S.S. *Vancouver*, a large and very-well-found ship, which put in at Corunna and Havannah, though I did not disembark at the Cuban port.

I decided that in New Orleans, my excellent French would serve better, in any case, than my indifferent Spanish would have served me in Cuba; and from the greatest city of New France, I proceeded in a small but seaworthy vessel, to the supposed place of the *Sophie Anderson*'s disappearance.

I went thrice to Scotland in 1887: in the cases of 'Mrs Stewart's' death—

---

* A typical Watson/Doyle anagram. If for German *klein* ('small') be substituted the French equivalent, *peu*, we have 'Maurits peu', which may be rearranged as 'Maupertuis'. But there seems also to be an English pun here: 'Maupertuis' may be analysed as *mau(x) pertuis*, literally 'evil straits'—a condition in which 'the Baron' certainly found himself.—*Editor*

this took me to Lauder, in Berwick, a few miles north of Galashiels—and the missing 'Mr Etherage' (those acquainted with the Restoration dramatists will understand how easily Watson changes his name from Congreve), I had to spend only a few days in North Britain. The "Dundas Separation Case" occupied nearly a fortnight of somewhat begrudged time.

Mid-October of 1887 saw me in France, in the matter of some business in Marseilles; intricate, as Watson has noted, but of small importance: and almost a year later, I was back again in France—though in Paris this time—in connection with what Watson calls "The French Will Case."

In fact, this and the case called "The Unfortunate Madame Montpensier" are merely two stages of the case in which I was engaged to recover some possessions of the Royal House of France which had been seized under the Expulsion Order of July, 1886: Her Royal Highness the Duchess of Montpensier was the daughter-in-law of King Louis Philippe, and sister of Queen Isabella II of Spain.

Such things being too easily forgotten—the nine days' wonders of more than a generation ago—I should perhaps mention that feeling between Republican France and Royal Spain was, at that time, none of the best. Queen Isabella naturally resented that her sister should have been expelled from France, and that her personal property should have been confiscated 'for the French People'; but even three years before the expulsion of the French Princes, bad feeling had developed between France and Spain. On 20th September, 1883, the Kings of Spain and Servia had come to Frankfort, to be present at the German military manoeuvres, and three days later the Emperor of Germany appointed the King of Spain to command the Schleswig-Holstein Uhlan Regiment. This gave great offence to the French, and when King Alfonso reached Paris, on his journey back to Madrid, he was greeted by the French populace with hooting and hissing. It called for all the diplomatic skill of President Grévy to persuade the King to attend the banquet given in his honour at the Elysée Palace.

It was in this atmosphere of completely intransigent antagonism between a set of Republican politicians with whom our own home-grown politicians sought to remain on friendly terms, and two indignant Royal families who were treated as blood-relatives by our own Royal family, that I was asked to exercise my diplomatic skill. The award to me of a Companionage of the Order of St Michael and St George in the Birthday Honours of 1888 seemed, at the time, inadequate reward for all that I had endured at the hands of a most emotional French princess.

There was enough in London, too, to occupy my time and 'ratiocinating' (as Poe calls them!) energies. I saved the honour of 'Colonel Prendergast of the Tankerville Club'—really Colonel Takeley, of the Walsingham Club—

and I saved a London bank from considerable loss in that strange business of "The Red-Headed League" and its criminally ingenious inventor, John Clay.

Watson has noted most of the cases which, I suppose, saved me from a complete mental breakdown in 1887. I know now that my 'poisoning from cocaine', as Watson puts it, was the result of my having been poisoned by something far worse—and something, in this case, rather mental; spiritual; than physical. This was an experience *whose inevitable consequences I could plainly perceive:* consequences so frightful that I, seeing them so clearly, literally reeled from the shock. It was this horrible series of events, originating in what Watson calls "The Case of Bert Stevens, the Terrible Murderer", which made me so ill in the years from 1887 to 1892, when what I have called the inevitable consequences reached their terrible finale in an episode so tragic, yet so just; so heart-breaking, yet so inescapable; that even now, over twenty years later, I am unable to recall what my friend Kipling would call the Judgment of the Law without a chill of horror.

NINETEEN ❧

Wiggins and the Imperial Succession

Wiggins, in case the reader has forgotten, was (if I may so put it) the of-ficer-in-charge of that squad of barefoot, out-at-elbows street-arabs whom I had organized as my unofficial detective force: 'the Baker-street Irregulars'.

They had had considerable employment by me, and I had paid them well; some of the more ingeniously active among this more-or-less honest gang of ragamuffins often took back to their parents as much as three shillings for a day's work; * none went home with less than a shilling.

This juvenile detective force had been organized by me before I had met Dr Watson, and, Nature being what it is, all had grown out of the seatless breeches and elbowless jackets that they had been wearing when I first set Wiggins to recruit for me an Irregular platoon. Of course, as members of the squad had grown out of employment (since it was in their status and ap-pearance of street-arabs that their usefulness lay), the 'pensioners' had been replaced by new recruits. I had, in 'discharging' the 'too-old-for-service' lads, secured them respectable employment, in which, so I understood, all were doing well. Wiggins I had fixed up in the Central Telegraph Office at St Martin's-le-Grand, and I was affectionately amused by his turning up at Baker-street to shew us how smart he looked—and how proud he felt—in his neat blue serge uniform with the red piping and well-polished brass Post Office crown and numerals; the whole suitably topped with his telegraph-boy's peaked shako.

I had not seen Wiggins for some time, and his appearance, when I—lit-erally—banged into him at the corner of Nassau-street and Mortimer-street, quite startled me. It was Wiggins, right enough; but a Wiggins whom I had

* Then worth seventy-two cents.—*Editor*

never seen before, and a Wiggins whom, had the choice ever been presented to me, I had hoped never to see.

He would have dodged me, had he been able; but the circumstances of our meeting—colliding, rather—rendered evasion impossible for him. He muttered some sort of apology for having banged into me: "I never see you, Mr 'Olmes—and that's the Gawd's troof, sir!"—and looked about as furtive as any culprit caught in the act could ever have looked.

His eyes—how honest they once had been!—darted here and there; but my disapproving regard was steady enough; and beneath it, his own wilted and shrank away. He stared at the ground, whilst I stared at the absurd—but, in all their dreadful implications, too sinister for words—garments in which the wretched youth had dressed himself.

He wore a blue suit of short coat, waistcoat and trousers, in the brightest of navy serges, with a starched collar fully three-and-a-half inches high, and a plum-coloured satin cravat decorated with a tie-pin in which a none-too-small brilliant caught and threw back the blue and yellow of the gas-lamps.

On his pomaded hair—now dressed in a fetching quiff—he wore a billy-cock with a richly curled brim. His patent-leather boots had grey cloth tops with pearl buttons. Do I need to add that he wore lavender gloves and carried a silver-topped malacca?

Not even Captain Dacre-Buttsworth would have risked entering any of the half-dozen public-houses a pavement's width away in such company; and certainly Mr Sherlock Holmes could not have had a talk with the errant youth save in the half-anonymity of the darkened street. We walked along Goodge-street to the Tottenham-court-road, and up that dismal thoroughfare until we reached Grafton-street, on which we turned westwards again, and so came, through Fitzroy-square and all those innumerable small and squalid streets which lie between Great Portland-street and Baker-street, to 221B.

I did not ask Wiggins to come in; I had already learnt of his sudden rise to 'elegance' and 'wealth' all that I needed (but had dreaded) to know. I had, as I put my latch-key in the door, one last admonition for the sadly misled youth.

"Wiggins," I said, "you know that I shall not leave this matter as it is—I shall see to it that something is done? You understand that, don't you? Very well, then: my advice to you is to have nothing more to do with these people; when the police start their enquiries, you might do far worse than be absent from anywhere that they are likely to search. And what about your Mother?" I added, with all the friendly earnestness at my command. "Does she not wonder how you can buy such expensive clothes out of the modest wages that you earn as a telegraph-boy?"

Even at that relatively early age (I was thirty-four), I was not unacquainted with the action and reaction of the average human spirit; but I confess that Wiggins's 'reaction'—as the modern phrase has it—surprised me. If I had not expected shame—but, then, I saw now that I did not know, had never thoroughly known, Wiggins—

There was no contrition; there was not even a not-unacceptable defiance. No, indeed. Instead, the wretched boy grinned; God save us all!, but he grinned in a fatuous self-complacency which had my hand itching to wipe the grin from his vulgar features.

"Me Mum—?" he said, as the night wind brought the scent of *Jockey Club* from his scarlet breast-pocket handkerchief. He smothered a giggle in his gloved hand. "Why, Mr 'Olmes, sir: *she* don't mind. She's glad enough of the extry rhino—and what the 'eart don't know, the 'eart don't grieve about! Me *Mum*—? She's 'appy enough to know I got a rise!"

In all great cities, since that far-off time when great cities began to grow, the organized vice that my chance meeting with Wiggins had uncovered has existed. Its origin is always to be found in the meeting of the two social elements essential to its budding and flowering: a class of idle, self-indulgent Rich (these are the Buyers) and a class of work-shy, greedy, immoral Poor (these are the Sellers). I have heard it said that 'one may do nothing to stamp out this vice, unless one contemplate stamping out cities themselves'—and with this hopeless judgement one might well find oneself agreeing. But if, *in the long run*, this moral corruption is seen to be ineradicable, this does not mean that 'containing' it is a mere waste of time; if corruption may not be destroyed, it may at least be prevented from spreading. That, at any rate, was the view of those who went into action as a sort of *cordon sanitaire* in the matter of that house of unnatural ill-fame in Cleveland-street.

From the beginning of this appalling case, every legal authority—the Post Office police, the Treasury investigators and the Metropolitan and City Police—was hampered, not merely by the fact that each was pursuing its enquiries independently of all the others, but also by the fact that each had its own firm opinion on the way that the enquiries should be conducted—which meant, in practical terms, how much of what they were shocked to discover should be made public. (In this, perhaps, they were united: for each was of the firm opinion that the public should know nothing of the widespread corruption revealed by the interrogation of the telegraph boys and other regular frequenters of the house in Cleveland-street owned and run by the infamous Hammond.) *

* 'The Cleveland-street Scandal' centred about a male brothel conducted at No. 19 (now pulled down), run by Hammond, and patronized by perverts so Important that a 'cover-up' operation was called for to avoid a public scandal of literally Throne-rocking force.—*Editor*

Documentary evidence—not mere hearsay—that the *clientèle* of this deplorable establishment included persons of the highest social rank—among them, Lord Arthur Somerset, son of the Duke of Beaufort, and Superintendent of the Stables to H.R.H. the Prince of Wales—need not have given, in the broad-minded London of thirty years ago, the gravest cause for alarm. But the fact that the list of the Cleveland-street patrons also included that of an Heir Apparent to the Throne—Prince 'Eddy' of Wales, heir, after his father, to the Royal and Imperial Crown—put an entirely different complexion upon matters.

It being impossible to hush things up—too many people were in the know; too many people had talked—it was decided to try the next best thing: confusion. It may well be doubted that any official attempt to pull the wool over the Public's eyes was ever conceived and put into operation with less of intelligence and more of kack-handed stupidity. (It seemed, in hindsight, the merest triviality that this ill-imagined operation was delayed for several months because, confident that their Royal associate's presence in the affair would protect them, Lord Arthur and Hammond both declined to 'take the hint' to leave the country. Hammond went first; and Lord Arthur followed him—but not until his lordship, to the consternation of the police, continued to frequent the Park and to attend the more fashionable race-meetings.)

The case is well known. The compliant Editor of an obscure North London newspaper was urged to denounce the house in Cleveland-street, and to assert that the one nobleman who could *not* have been a patron—Lord Euston, son and heir of the Duke of Grafton—had been mixed up in the sorry business. The story ran through several issues of the *North London Gazette;* Lord Euston (on cue) sued Mr Ernest Parke, the Editor, for criminal libel; and Mr Parke meekly accepted (*pro bono publico,* I have no doubt that it was explained to him) a year's imprisonment. It was observed that the learned Judge (who was afterwards raised to the peerage; as was the—on this occasion only—inept Counsel for the Prosecution; Counsel for the Defence being rewarded with a mere baronetcy) was noticeably gentle with Mr Parke. The names of the Guilty—save for that of Lord Arthur, now safely in Paris—were never mentioned.

But something else, of which even those 'in the know' were ignorant, had come out of the trial and its shabby preliminaries: that this widespread perversion was linked intimately with what the Law regards as an even more serious crime: that of murder—and here, murder of the most vicious, most terrible kind. We are back now to the Terrible Murderer, 'Bert Stevens'— in reality, James Stephen, son of Mr Justice James Fitzjames Stephen, one of our greatest authorities on both English and Indian Law. His brilliant son, James, had been selected, by the Prince and Princess of Wales, to be the tutor of Prince 'Eddy', during the latter's terms at Trinity College, Cambridge.

James Stephen shared, with his Royal pupil, that unnatural appetite to serve which such places as the houses at 19, Cleveland-street and 11, Little College-street existed.

But, whereas Stephen had a natural disinclination to associate with any women save the ladies of his own and his friends' families—and then never save on the most platonic terms—it was otherwise with Prince 'Eddy', who could be, and was, attracted by several handsome females, some of his own class, others far beneath it. This 'abandonment' of his tutor for other friends, of both sexes, inspired such a jealousy in Stephen's breast that it literally drove him mad. A tendency towards insanity already existed in his family (his father was to retire, his sanity gone, in 1891); and, in James Stephen's case, this tendency developed into a homicidal mania.

A murder in Whitechapel in 1887 had been shewn by me to have been *most probably* committed by young Stephen, though there were two good reasons why a charge of Wilful Murder could not be brought against him: that the *motive* was not easy to demonstrate, and that the culprit, undeniably insane, could not have been brought to trial. There was, of course, a third and much more important reason for the case's never having been brought to Court: the culprit's intimate connection with Prince Albert Victor ('Eddy') of Wales, his pupil. James Stephen was judged, by a private panel of alienists, *non compos mentis*, and unable to stand trial, though it ought to have been borne in mind—and here was not so borne—that, under English Law, insanity *of itself* is not a defence to a criminal charge;* a reduction of responsibility is the supposed fact on which any defence involving insanity must rest. He was then committed, again by private order, to a 'home' (as such establishments are euphemistically called) at Hanwell. A man of high intelligence and considerable personal charm, and (being a criminal lunatic) possessed of superhuman cunning in the achievement of his desires, he soon persuaded the authorities that he had been 'cured' by their treatment. He was released in the spring of 1888, and by the time that he was once again under lock-and-key, he had committed those ten repulsive murders notorious for ever as those of 'Jack the Ripper'. The ten wretched victims of Stephen's maniac *Mordlust* cry out less loudly against his insanity than against my—yes, my *criminal*— failure to prevent the

* This theory is still supported in English jurisprudence. For a recent authoritative comment, *see* Shaw's *Evidence in Criminal Cases;* London: 1954.—*Editor*

262 I, SHERLOCK HOLMES

murders. I might plead ill-health; I might plead an excess of calls upon my time: fifteen cases—two of them involving journeys to France; one to Rome; one to Devon—between the first of the ten 'Ripper' murders, on 3rd April, 1888, and the last, on 13th February, 1890, after which my earnest representations *were* heeded, and Stephen—though not until after he had been permitted to return to his Fellowship at Trinity!—was committed to the lunatic asylum at Northampton, from which he was never to emerge alive.

In all my experience, I have never known a man so protected, by the wrong persons, for the wrong reasons, as was James Stephen—indeed, the whole family, of obscure origins and all apparently tainted with the hereditary insanity, were treated with a cringing admiration which positively prevented Authority's recognizing, not so much the fact that Stephen *must* have been 'The Ripper', as even the possibility that a Stephen could be capable of wrongdoing.

In the trial of Mrs Maybrick for the murder of her husband by arsenic, it was evident that the trial judge, Mr Justice Stephen (father of James Stephen) was mentally incapable of assessing the guilt of a child who had put a French penny in a chocolate-machine, let alone a handsome but 'difficult' woman of foreign birth, whose alien origins, and alien ways, had made her the object of the Maybrick family's xenophobia. In the laudable task of hunting Mrs Maybrick down, the Family 'democratically' (as the halfpenny newspapers like to put it) enlisted the aid of the servants—few defendants can have sailed so perilously near to death on a tide of such malicious below-stairs gossip.

Mrs Maybrick was defended—and ably, brilliantly defended—by Sir Charles Russell, who, after he had become Lord Chief Justice and Lord Russell of Killowen, continued his vigorous campaign to secure a Free Pardon for his client, in a well-argued document listing no fewer than *one hundred and thirty* points on which Mr Justice Stephen had misdirected the jury. Sir Charles pestered—there is no other word for it—each new Home Secretary as Governments changed; but, apart from the fact that he did secure the reprieve of Mrs Maybrick (no small triumph), he died without having set her free. In an article in *The Liverpool Post* that I recall from the time of Russell's death, the Editor, mentioning the Maybrick case, calls Stephen 'the mad judge'—the description is perfectly justified by the deplorable facts. Mrs Maybrick served the full term of her sentence: fifteen years. Not even the eloquence and authority of a Lord Chief Justice could spare her that—no Home Secretary, of whichever political flavour, was prepared to criticize a Stephen to the extent of letting the unfortunate victim of his insanity go free.

Mad Stephens, murders, widespread perversion, a well-organized and by no means secret conspiracy of Vice—it was against this background that the future of Prince 'Eddy' had now to be considered. Had he been merely as well-born and 'prominent' as the levanting Lord Arthur Somerset, the problem of the Prince's behaviour could have been dealt with. Lord Arthur—a major in the Royal Horse Guards, and medalled for service in both the Egyptian Campaign of '82 and in the attempt to relieve General Gordon of '84—had made an excellent soldier; and it was evident that Prince 'Eddy' was taking his military duties seriously. Alas! had he taken all his other duties as seriously!

But he was not a mere Duke's son, to catch the boat-train from Victoria for a Paris where the Law could not touch him; Prince Albert Victor was the Heir Apparent, at one remove, to the Imperial Crown—the constitutional ruler-to-be of the greatest empire of which the world's history holds record; the *symbol* of Monarchy, rather than Monarchy itself—and so governing, rather than ruling; and exercising the Royal and Imperial influence rather by the *mystique* of Kingship than by the imposition of Kingship itself. In such a position, exalted and unique, the Head of the British Empire governs through nothing but the respect that he or she exacts from the governed. The Sovereign may impose his or her will by no force, legitimate or otherwise; if he or she cannot be obeyed through the mere fact of asking, then the Sovereign—a *constitutional* Sovereign—cannot be obeyed at all. Bagehot, I think, summed up the matter well when he stated the three rights left to a constitutional monarch: the right to be consulted, the right to encourage, the right to warn.

Judged by these standards, Prince 'Eddy' was quite unfit to rule—and, whatever else it needed, the British Empire; a fifth of the world's land surface, a quarter of the world's people; needed a ruler fit to be consulted, fit to encourage and fit to warn.

It might be argued that the Prince's father, the Prince of Wales, led a scandalous life. This was true then—and it is true now; but there is a great difference between a 'scandalous' life and a life which gives scandal. The Prince of Wales's faults were numerous; but they were of a kind which did not alienate him from his people, either as Prince of Wales or as King. Had the faults of his son and heir become matters of common knowledge, those faults would have split Crown from People by an unbridgeable rift—*est enim magnum chaos*, as Lazarus said to Dives over a gulf which separated them no more irreconcilably.

So it was that the harsh practicality of statecraft insisted on the Prince's departure from a world that he could not help, and in which his presence could be only a hindrance. Had he been of lower rank, he could have been asked to resign his commission, or he could have been given a week's notice, or he could have been summarily paid off. But, as the Heir to the Throne, he had to go in a different and not quite so simple way.

I had no hand in his departure; the matter was never discussed with me. Only in looking back do I see the significance of the 'facts' which were hurriedly accumulated to present historians with the 'evidence' of a hard-working, completely normal young man: the opening of docks, the promotion to a dukedom, the 'falling in love' with Princess Hélène of Orleans (and the desired marriage forbidden by the Pope), the elevation to a Masonic Grand Mastership, the betrothal to Princess Mary of Teck. I was not in England—at least, not as Sherlock Holmes—when the Prince, seen off by his genuinely sorrowing parents, died 'of pneumonia following influenza', in January, 1892.

TWENTY ✧

I meet the Master-criminal

I have often mentioned the experience that I gained by my frequenting the 'crowd' which travelled the race-meetings of England, with *The Pelican* as its 'base headquarters'. Of all that I gained in this close association with 'the Boys', nothing else matched in importance the hint that I got of the existence of what I may call only a 'Master-criminal'. It is true that the 'master-criminal' is one of the favourite characters of the romantic novelist; but, as the news came to me, bit by bit, through a thousand significant fragments of gossip, I realized that I was being made aware of a person only too real—and correspondingly dangerous.

The name 'Moriarty' had been familiar to me since my boyhood; since, to be precise, the day when, at the Gymnasium Agrippina at Cologne, I was presented by the English master with a German translation of *Martin Chuzzlewit*,* as a school-prize. This work came in two handsome volumes, and I can see now, with the mind's eye, as clearly as I saw fifty-odd years ago, in the bare, whitewashed schoolroom, the title-page:

MARTIN CHUZZLEWIT
von
C. Dickens
Aus den Englischen
von
E. A. Moriarty

—my first introduction to our greatest English novelist, though in the language of Schiller and Goethe. The name 'Moriarty' was thus early and

* Leipsic, 1852, 8°; part of the *Gesammte Werke*, vols 14 and 15.—*Editor*

265

indelibly printed on my mind, and when, in mid-1872, a young man named James Moriarty answered my father's advertisement for a crammer for his scholastically-backward son, that son, attracted by the familiar name of the applicant, urged the father to appoint the young man to the vacant post.

Moriarty and I did not get on at all well; I found him impatient of my ignorance, and bullying in his (I am sure perfectly well-intentioned) efforts to discharge his duties to the satisfaction both of my father and of himself. He was a young man as conscientious—at least, in respect of his trying to instruct me—as he was humourless and, I thought, tyrannical.

The fact is that I was of a decidedly obstinate turn of character; and obstinacy, especially in the adolescent, cannot profitably be met with obstinacy; it must be met with pliancy, even at the risk of that pliancy's earning for itself the name of hypocrisy. The obstinate Napoleon was always skilfully handled by the pliant Cambacérès, Fouché and Talleyrand—heartless cynics to a man!—but the honest obstinacy of Generals Hoche, Dumas and Bernadotte brought them nothing but trouble. Yet, for all the dyspathy which existed as naturally between Moriarty and myself as between the average cat and dog, he remained conscientious, thoroughly honest in his intention to teach me, willy-nilly, and remarkably successful in that he managed to teach me so much. But I wish that I had liked him more, or that he had disapproved of me less; I might have learned even more than I did.

In the succeeding years, I heard of him once or twice; and in certain somewhat rarefied levels of scientific knowledge, James Moriarty had, it was clear, earned himself an enviable reputation. But it was not until 10th July, 1886—as I realized afterwards—that I first encountered, not exactly Mr Moriarty the Criminal, but let us say a presentiment that he had somehow involved himself in affairs which were then engaging my attention.

The occasion was the sparsely attended funeral of Miss Emma Crouch, the self-styled 'Cora Pearl', intimate 'friend' and remorseless plunderer of so many men. This woman, probably the most notorious adventuress of the last century, had died (not in the 'well-deserved' poverty to which British newspaper morality had condemned her; but in great pain from a fatal illness, poor creature!) in her comfortable apartment on the third floor of 8, rue Bassano, Paris, in the dawn of 8th July, 1886.

I had already rendered two or three trifling services for the Reigning Family of Holland: 'Cora Pearl's' death was the signal for the Netherlands minister in London, Count Charles de Bylandt, to send me an urgent telegram, asking me to call on him without delay. I called a hansom, and was with the Count at once. He explained that the woman, 'Pearl', had been—as I well knew—'supported' by the Crown Prince, who had died in

1879; and that it was believed that she had died still in possession of letters written to her by the Prince.

"Indiscreet letters—?" I asked.

The Count smiled.

"Could a letter written by the late Prince 'Citron' * to Miss Cora Pearl be other than indiscreet—?"

"Indeed not. I shall catch this afternoon's boat-train from Victoria." The time was about a quarter-to-twelve on the morning of Thursday, 8th July.

The Count appeared to hesitate.

"There is a much quicker way, if you should be pleased to consider it, Mr Holmes. The Royal yacht, *Maurits van Nassau*, has just left Thorneycroft's yard after a refit; she is lying at Symonds' Wharf, in the Pool, with steam up. I made so bold as to anticipate your acceptance, and the Captain is standing by to take you directly to France. Could you manage to return to Baker-street, pack a bag, and be at Symonds' Wharf by, say, two o'clock?"

"There is no need, Count, to return to Baker-street. I always keep a gladstone ready-packed for such emergencies. If I telegraph immediately to Billy, our page, he can take my traps down to Symonds' Wharf, and I can be away down-River by"—I glanced at my hunter—"one o'clock. You say that the Captain has steam up?" I took a telegraph-form from my pocket, and scribbled a hasty message for Billy. "There, Count: pray see that that is sent off at once, and my baggage will be at Symonds' Wharf no later than I."

I went down to the City through the dense mid-day traffic, which did not delay the Legation's skilful coachman; by one o'clock, I was in my cabin, and Captain van Oorschot had cast off. By three o'clock, with the *Maurits van Nassau* making a steady ten knots, even in the crowded River, we were off Greenhithe; by six o'clock—for we had increased speed on reaching the Estuary—the masts of the warships at Sheerness lay on our starboard quarter; and by ten o'clock, with our speed now a steady thirteen knots, the lights of Deal were twinkling through the sea-mist on our starboard beam.

By one o'clock on the following morning, I was seated, with a well-packed breakfast-basket, in the special that the Dutch Government had ordered to be waiting for me at Calais. Long before the shopkeepers of Paris had finished washing down the pavement before their premises, I had presented myself at the Sûreté, had shewn my diplomatic authority from King William, and, with an inspector of the *Deuxième Bureau*, was ascending the

* See page 207.—*Editor*

three pair of stairs which led to the sealed apartment of the late 'Cora Pearl'.

It took us—me, rather; though the French police (as Poe reminded us many years ago) are not backward in finding hidden things—more than two hours to discover the ingeniously-secreted letters. By late morning, the letters were in the possession of the Netherlands minister to France; and, declining an invitation from the Minister, by mid-day I was enjoying my *apéritif* at a table outside the *Café de la Paix*.

The funeral of Miss Crouch, at Batignolles, on the following day, was 'attended' by me, but in no official or respectful capacity. In truth—considering the number and rank of those with whom the deceased had been acquainted—it was a sad affair; a bare half-dozen mourners, among whom I recognized Jacques Offenbach, Henri Meilhac and Ludovic Halévy,* followed the coffin as I watched from the cover of some adjacent tomb-stones. I discovered afterwards that there were three others: "an Englishman, Mori; a Spaniard, Perez; and an unknown man who came to pass the time away"—thus a newspaper report of the funeral.

The unusual name 'Mori' struck me forcibly—unusual, that is to say, for a supposed Englishman. The Englishman, I reflected, must have given his name as 'Mori' to an enquiring reporter; and the more I reflected on this strange name, the more convinced I became that it was a pseudonym. What it most certainly must have been—that is, not only a contraction of 'Moriarty', but a pun on the Latin phrase *Memento mori!* (as who should say, 'Remember Mori[arty]!')—did not strike me, I admit, until I had come up against Moriarty, in his criminal aspect, some year-and-a-half later. Dr Watson has described the events in the case that he calls *The Valley of Fear*.

In such places as *The Star* (afterwards, from January, 1887, *The Pelican*) and much less salubrious establishments further to the East and South, I came to hear much of Dr Moriarty, and, in the hearing, to form the conclusion that, not only had a Master-criminal set himself up to administer the crime and criminals of the world's greatest metropolis, but that that Master-criminal was none other than my old crammer, James Moriarty. And with that conviction came the resolution that I would be the one to destroy both the Master-criminal and his Criminal Empire.

I look back on the three years which covered the period from January, 1888, in which month I first came face-to-face with Dr Moriarty, the greatest schemer of all time, the controlling brain of the underworld, to April, 1891, in which I set out to solve what Dr Watson has called "The Final Problem," as a time in which, however much my services were sought and

* Respectively: son of the famous composer (notably of *La Belle Hélène* and *The Grand-duchess of Gerolstein*), dramatist (co-author of *La Belle Hélène*) and novelist (Meilhac's collaborator on *La Belle Hélène* and other light operas).—*Editor*

given throughout Great Britain and the Continent, my whole energies were dedicated to the trapping and destruction of the Napoleon of Crime.

I look back through my careless jottings, as well as through my more formal notes, and I see with pleasure that Dr Watson has recorded, with more or less of accuracy, the more important of the cases which called for my attention during those three years. Compared with my self-set task of eliminating, if not Moriarty himself, at least the threat that his criminal dictatorship offered to our society, the cases, as recorded (or merely mentioned, *en passant*) by Dr Watson seem trivial enough.

Some, of course, he does not mention; or mentions so obliquely that one must have the key to the reference, before one may understand the reference itself. I instance here his mention of 'Bert Stevens, the Terrible Murderer'—a reference that I have already explained. Sometimes, the reference is even more obscure; though not so much by Dr Watson's intention to mystify or conceal, as by his having misread or misunderstood my notes: such is his strange reference to "The Giant Rat of Sumatra"—a reference that I shall *attempt* to account for later.

I note that, often, Dr Watson makes a single case serve two entries, under different names; such, I observe, is the double reference to "The Locking-up of Colonel Carruthers" and "Colonel Warburton's Madness", both referring to one case and one unhappy subject: a member of a well-known English family who need not be further identified. Again, that case (occurring in mid-October, 1886) that Dr Watson calls "The Second Stain", and describes, rightly, as the most important international case that I had ever been called upon to handle—words which were true enough at the time, but which must be modified in the light of subsequent happenings— had two successors, to both of which the title "Adventure of the Second Stain" must be given. The second adventure dates from July, 1889; the third, from later in that same year. Here is an instance of three cases classified by Dr Watson under one title.

International complications which did not take me abroad were encountered by me in the matter of "The Naval Treaty"—a case which occupied me for the last day of July and the first day of August, 1889; one of the busiest years of my very busy life. The case, as I remarked to Dr Watson at the time, was a very abstruse and complicated one; but it was also a case in which an odd element of the 'weird' entered,* and which had even

---

* That useful explanatory device, 'coincidence', may be invoked here, or we may 'explain' the 'odd element' by prevision—but the fact remains that the case titled "The Naval Treaty", in which two characters, given the pseudonyms Joseph and Annie (not 'Ann' or 'Anna'—*Annie*) Harrison, appear, was published in *The Strand Magazine*, October and November, 1893; and the American *Harper's Weekly*, 14th and 21st October, 1893. The pseudonyms were almost certainly the choice of Dr Conan Doyle. Now, *in the following year*, a London coroner sat on the

Dr Conan Doyle stumped for a 'psychic' explanation—given, as he had already come to do, to supplying such an 'explanation'.

However, there were cases at that time which did take me abroad; in the first case, it was a source of great satisfaction to me to see that my handling of 'Baron Maupertuis' in early 1887 was completely vindicated in the Netherlands Government's granting a charter to 'The Royal Company for the Exploitation of Oil Wells in the Netherlands East Indies', from which, under proper Government supervision, to-day's important Dutch oil-industry grew.* In those early days—now a quarter-of-a-century gone—the Dutch had only one well, in Pangkalan Brandan, on the island of Sumatra, a name with which Dr Watson had managed to present me with the least soluble of all Watsonian puzzles to date. He refers, in that case he calls "The Reigate Squires", to 'The Netherland-Sumatra Company'—a reasonable paraphrase of the real title of the company; but what was I to make of his reference to 'the Giant Rat of Sumatra'? When I turn the cap on the night-lamp, and the clock-face projected on to the ceiling tells me that it is ten minutes past three in what promises to be the most sleepless of dawns, then is the time for such problems as that of 'the Giant Rat of Sumatra'.

This vast and sinister rodent of Watson's (or Doyle's) mishearing-misreading-misunderstanding *must* have had its origin in something that I had said or written—and what might it be which had transmuted itself into 'Giant Rat'?

For all those 'colossal schemes' to which Watson refers, the 'Baron de Maupertuis' was by no means the principal in the proposed exploitation of Sumatran rock-oil, and I may well have referred to him, half-humorously, half-contemptuously, as 'ce rat de Sumatra' or 'ce grand rat de Sumatra' or even as 'ce rat géant de Sumatra'—using the word 'rat' here as in such well-known colloquial phrases as 'rat d'hôtel', 'rat d'église', and so forth. A *literal* translation of such a phrase as that with which I had dismissed the dangerous pretensions of the Baron might well have produced the Giant Rat of Dr Watson's fancy—a fancy not undarkened, be it noted, by the wild superstitions and brooding sense of Otherness of that Devon in which he had grown up. But, for the life of me, I could not remember having spoken or written such a phrase.

On the other hand, there was a certain difficulty to be expected in prospecting for Sumatran rock-oil: one major obstacle being the hostility of the

---

bodies of a man and a woman, and found that, after killing the woman, the man had committed suicide. Their names? *Joseph and Annie Harrison!* This is a fact that the parapsychologists seem to have missed, though no fact could be more unambiguously authenticated.—*Editor*

* Its direct successor to-day is the immensely powerful 'multi-national' Royal Dutch Shell.—*Editor*

Redjang people, who number not fewer than a million. Their name, usually spelled 'Redjang', is pronounced more like 'Rat-jyang', and might be mistaken, by an English-speaking person unacquainted with the Sumatran name, as 'Rat-giant'. Is this too catachrestic?—too far-fetched? But then, how far-fetched is the Giant Rat—?

But these, as I said above, are proper problems for sleepless dawns; the questions which refuse to be dismissed; the queries which *will* demand solution—provided that it be at the right hour for them; the wrong hour for the insomniac.

The other day, in a drawer of my writing-desk, I came across the gilt medal, about the size of a crown, which records that, in 1889, I made an ascent of the great iron tower erected by Monsieur Gustave Eiffel on the Champ-de-Mars. It reminded me how much, in the years from 1887 to 1891, my attention was taken up with the affairs of foreign dynasties and governments, but more particularly with those of France, for whom I served both her princely families and her Republican governments. (In this, of course, the aims and actions of the Prince of Wales and myself were in complete accord; I could never accept the proffered friendship of the Prince—between us lay what Lamb happily calls 'an imperfect sympathy'— but of the sincerity of his desire to unite Great Britain in an indissoluble bond with the two great nations of France and the United States I have not the least doubt.) Long after the unhappy self-indulgences of the Prince of Wales will have been forgotten, as the most trivial of snippets in the rag-bag of history, his lifelong (and, we trust, successful) efforts to promote a lasting friendship amongst the governments and peoples of Great Britain, France and the United States of America will be remembered with gratitude and held to him for his lasting honour.

It had been my good fortune to be able to facilitate the *rapprochement* between France and Russia which—despite the fact that Russia is an autocratic despotism and France a libertarian democracy (at least in principle!)— looks to proving itself the basis of a lasting treaty between them.*

For my assistance in this *rapprochement*, I was indebted to the esteem in which I was held by the Czar; by his son-in-law, H.R.H. the Duke of Edinburgh; and by the members of the Imperial Government generally.

On the question of improving France's defensive position, *vis-à-vis* her

---

* Despite what are now called the 'ideological' differences between Russia and France, the Franco-Russian alliance was signed in 1893, its principal terms including an undertaking, on the part of either, to assist the other in the event of an attack by Germany. The Treaty also provided for the development of the Russian railway system by French capital.—*Editor*

European neighbours—in particular, Germany—I found myself no less useful to France; my services no less frequently and importantly in demand. In an endeavour to dislodge the Russians from Sebastopol in 1855, the British troops had let the wind carry the fumes of sulphur dioxide towards the Russian lines; but the wind proving contrary, and the poisonous smoke returning to them who had sent it out, the experiment was discontinued; and the use of poisonous gas in warfare denounced by the British as 'barbarous', 'inhumane' and—God save the mark!—'unchristian'!

However, word had reached the French Bureau of Military Intelligence that the corresponding department of the German War Office had commissioned experiments to achieve a more practical form of poisonous gas than the sulphur dioxide of thirty years earlier. The French had obtained the names of the gases on which the German chemists had been working: they included chlorine, hydrocyanic, picric acid gas, phosphine and carbonyl chloride.*

Picric acid and phosphine, though poisonous enough to suit German requirements, were altogether too explosive to be safe for the aggressors themselves—the old story of the British sulphur dioxide during the Crimean War. But chlorine, prussic acid gas and carbonyl chloride seemed to have in themselves a promise of efficient toxicity combined with safety in 'launching'. On these three principal toxic gases, German chemical ingenuity based its hopes of an addition to the classic weapons of war.

I was asked by the French Government to undertake some experiments designed to find an effective counter to these—and some other, equally unpleasant—gases; and a laboratory, at Montpellier, equipped to my specifications, was placed at my disposal. The university has a faculty of Chemistry; there is also a national College of Chemistry; but my own laboratory was hidden away in one of the numerous factories whose activities contribute materially to the wealth of this prosperous southern city—familiar to me since my very earliest childhood. There were more factories than I remembered; and along the city's busy streets now ran electric tramcars, whilst the oil- and gas-lamps of my childhood had given way, in great part, to the electric light.

Since I had first visited Montpellier, I had read Stevenson's wonderful little book, and now, coming back to this golden land from which a memory, once imposed—by Phoenician, by Greek, by Roman, by Saracen, by Norman—never vanishes, I could look at it through Stevenson's eyes as well as through my own. If the factory-chimneys were smoking now, and something of my happy childhood was going up in the smoke, the sea,

* Better known, from the first World War onwards, as phosgene.—*Editor*

beyond Palavas-les-Flots, Maguelonne and Frontignan, was as blue as ever I remembered it, and on it were the 'white ships sailing . . . half veiled in sunny haze', of which Stevenson writes.

It is curious to reflect that the hint by which I was led to find the most efficient of these defences against gas I owed to one of Dr Watson's attempts to improve our domestic condition. I returned one evening, to find a large Doulton jar weighing down a stout table: it was a patent water-filter that he had bought that afternoon at Lipscombe's, in Queen Victoria-street, City, and that the delivery-van had just brought around.

At Montpellier, I had secured some good results with carbamide, synthesizing the urea by the classic Wöhler method; but, not quite satisfied that I had found a *general* defence against toxic gas, I remembered the filter that Dr Watson had bought for us, and speculating that the activated charcoal which could filter out the impurities from water might possibly serve a similar purpose with gas, I initiated some new experiments, and hit upon a solution of the problem which—if all accounts be true,* is proving effective in use.

By the dreadful paradox of our age, I was looking, in this land of almost unchanging youth, at a newer face of Death; nor was my research into a defence against poisonous gases the only 'Matter of Supreme Importance' (as Dr. Watson puts it) on which the French Government had requested my assistance. In underwater navigation, the French had made some quite remarkable advances, and their electrically-driven submarine vessels were unrivalled throughout the world. (Britain had nothing to compare with them.) They had, however, one serious—indeed, potentially fatal—drawback: the electric-batteries functioned perfectly only when the ship was on an even keel or, at most, on a very shallow incline, either when diving or rising. At too steep an angle of ascent or descent, or when rolling violently on the surface, the acid from the batteries would spill; deaths among the crew had been caused by the deadly fumes. I was able, after some experiment, to perfect an 'unspillable' battery, and since the very existence, let alone the design, of such a battery had to remain a State secret, the French Government generously allowed me a royalty on the invention equivalent

---

* Gas was first used in modern warfare by the German High Command, at Ypres, on the Western Front, Thursday, 22nd April, 1915, a date whose significance—*i.e.*, the Vigil of the Feast of St George, England's Patron Saint—seems to have escaped the notice of even the most dedicated of historians. This 'secret weapon' took the British and French entirely by surprise, the only counter possible to the victims being urine-soaked handkerchiefs or scarves. The gas used in this first attack was chlorine, to protect against which 'gas-masks' with charcoal filters were soon provided.—*Editor*

to what I would (it was estimated) have earned had the battery been placed upon the open market.*

But, far more important than the experiments in connection with the defence against poisonous gases and with the sealing of electric batteries for submarines—at least, the French Government thought it more important— were the experiments in aëronautics: the search for the means to make man-carrying aëroplanes out of the small models that Stringfellow had flown on Salisbury Plain forty years earlier. I was not—am not—an engineer, aëronautical or otherwise; and in the design of the various experimental craft, I had no hand; I was employed by the French Government, first to conceal the operations, and, second, to recruit, under conditions of secrecy, the men most fitted to become members of the experimental body.

France, as I well remember saying to Colonel Descharmes, then Military Attaché in London, when I met him at the Vienna Electrical Exhibition in 1883, had many claims to be considered—even in the 'Eighties—an 'air-minded' Power (to use an expression not then invented). If the present Royal Flying Corps and Royal Naval Air Service derive directly from the Balloon Company of the Corps of Royal Engineers, that takes the origin of our aërial forces back only to the 'Eighties of the last century, whereas the French Corps des Aérostiers was founded, by a Decree of the Committee of National Safety, in the Year II † of the Republic One and Indivisible. When Jourdan beat the Austrians at Fleurus in 1794, French 'spotters' directed the artillery, by semaphore, from what we now call 'observation balloons'. The Frenchman Giffard took his steam-powered dirigible balloon from Paris to Chelles, and back, at five knots, against a three-knot wind, in 1852.

It must be remembered that, when the French Government commissioned me, at the end of the 'Eighties, to recruit a company of aëronautical engineers, to develop a practical flying-machine for the nation's army and navy, it had already been demonstrated, by inventors of many countries, that man-carrying flight was a practical possibility. The French chemist Hérault, by the electrolytic production of aluminium, had almost solved the problem of the weight-power ratio which had limited the successful Stringfellow flying-machines to mere models—as it had the steam-driven (and equally successful) Phillips helicopter of 1847. The German Lilienthal, the Englishman Pilcher and the American Chanute had shewn that man-carrying gliders could be built. All that now remained was to develop a light-

---

* By the time that this was written, the 'unspillable' battery had become a commonplace; every motor-car being fitted with one. Mr Holmes, then, was not bound, in 1915, to treat the matter as any longer secret.—*Editor*

† 1794.—*Editor*

weight engine of sufficient power, to convert the hardly dirigible glider into the completely manoeuvrable aëroplane. Into my team I recruited a middle-aged * French engineer, Clément Ader, whose name caught my attention first because it resembled that of an English river that I knew well.†

Monsieur Ader it was who finally succeeded in obtaining for France the honour of being the first nation to produce a machine capable of man-carrying flight—but this was achieved long before the official announcement of the fact in 1897. French Military Intelligence skilfully concealed the fact that, from January, 1890 (at the same time as the miserable Cleveland-street charade was being acted out in the Central Criminal Court!), a practical flying-machine was at the disposal of the French Ministry of War. The singular use to which this machine was put, in the years immediately following its perfecting, belongs to a later part of these Memoirs—but I may mention here that by its use was effected the most remarkable escape of modern times.**

This talk of 'the most remarkable escape of modern times' brings me inevitably to what is perhaps a no less remarkable escape—though of a totally different type: namely, my own.

The last century saw the rise and flowering of what I may call the 'Joint Stock Idea' in international commerce and finance; in the course of that century, the private partnership was changed into the public company, which had the inherent tendency, so it seemed, to grow only as it fed on the absorption of smaller firms in the same line of business. I think that I may claim the credit—such as it is—for having seen that the development of 'Joint Stock' criminality had become, through the development of 'Joint Stock' commerce, an inevitability.

And, just as the joint-stock bank, say, of the Nineteenth Century may be traced back, as to its origins, not merely to Thirteenth Century Florence, but rather to First Century Rome, so the Empire of Crime that that criminal Napoleon, Moriarty, was planning and building-up had its precursors— the most recent (as well as the most successful) being the taking-over, by

* Clément Ader, French engineer, born at Muret, 1841; died, 1925. He was thus forty-eight ('middle-aged') when recruited into the aviation-team by Mr Holmes.—*Editor*

† This can be an allusion only to the West Sussex River *Adur*, which, nearing the sea between Washington and Henfield, enters the English Channel between Hove and New Shoreham.—*Editor*

** This must refer to Slatin Pasha (Major-general Sir Rudolf Carl Slatin), an Austrian soldier who was made, by General Gordon, his Inspector of Taxation in the Soudan, and, a year later, 1880, Governor and Commander of the Army in Darfur. Taken prisoner by the Mahdi in 1883, Slatin remained a prisoner in Mahdist-held Omdurman until he escaped— *how?*—in 1895. This foreign-born (though never naturalized) servant of the British Crown received the highest British honours.—*Editor*

Harry Benson, of Detective-inspectors Meiklejohn, Druscovitch, Palmer and the rest—the most influential officers then on duty at Scotland Yard. The barrister James Saward—'Jim the Penman'—had, somewhat earlier in the last century, come to the verge of organizing a criminal conspiracy, in that he provided a service of forgery and 'passing' for an ever-increasing criminal clientèle; but Saward stopped—or was stopped—before he could organize his criminal associates into a criminal 'Joint Stock' company.

But this, as I now realized, Moriarty, my old crammer, had done; and crime, like the air, being omnipresent, it was idle to suppose that there would be *any* criminal activity, from robbing the Inland Revenue with forged shilling-stamps to the armed assault on bank-messengers; from the defrauding of insurance-companies to the blackmailing of persons of wealth; which would not be considered and exploited by James Moriarty.

What I foresaw, once a mind as brilliant as Moriarty's had accepted, as fact, that crime might be organized and promoted on recognized business principles, was that there would arise, in Britain, one of those criminal empires which, under the name of Vehmgericht, Camorra, Carbonari—call it what you will—have plagued the governments and peoples of Europe for centuries, and, exported to the New World, are undermining society under a score of not less romantic (and deceptive) names: the Ku Klux Klan, The Scowrers, the Molly Maguires, the Mafia.

Moriarty, I realized, would have, in the organization of *his* Mafia, an advantage that none of the other organizers would have had: he would organize it with the lack of emotion of a book-keeper who had enjoyed an exceptional training in mathematics. Moriarty was not without emotion; but the only two emotions by which he was swayed were resentment and greed—the products of which cannot be other than acquisition and revenge.

That his unemotional attack—to use a term from piano-playing—on his chosen instruments would serve him better than any more heart-involving approach to the keyboard cannot be doubted. I knew his coldness, his frigid self-assurance. I remember how briefly—and how contemptuously—he explained to me, one afternoon in the summer of 1872, at Mycroft, the elementary facts of vector algebra. I have never forgotten the facts—as I have never forgotten the inhuman contempt.

I mention these matters, not so much because I wish to *condemn* Moriarty on moral grounds, as to explain why it seemed to me that his inability to share with the majority of mankind its emotional strength, no less than its emotional fallibility, could mean only that Moriarty could not exercise any selectivity in the choice of criminal action; that he must treat *all* crime only from the viewpoint of profit—and that he would as readily promote the moral corruption that we have seen in the Holborn Music Hall * and Cleveland-street affairs, not to mention the business of Oscar Wilde and his associates, as he would arrange the robbing of a bank or the kidnapping of a Duke's heir.

Dr Watson has recorded many of my opinions of this unique criminal; what Dr Watson has not thought fit to notice is that, in many important ways, the attitudes of Dr Moriarty and myself bore more than a merely superficial resemblance. I open Dr Watson's account of the case which gave him his second wife, and I find that I expressed myself in the following terms:—

> "Detection is, or ought to be, an exact science, and should be treated in the same cold and unemotional manner. You have" [I am addressing Dr Watson, of course] "attempted to tinge it with romanticism, which produces much the same effect as if you worked a love-story or an elopement into the fifth proposition of Euclid."

Like all other words, 'detection' has its general as well as its particular meanings; and what I had to say to Dr Watson about detection applies equally to my hunting a criminal or Moriarty's hunting a plunderable dupe. And both of us, there is no doubt, would agree that the 'cold and unemotional' approach to the hunt is the only proper one. In that opinion, Moriarty and I were united.

From the same *point d'appui*, I resolved to study the dispositions of the enemy's forces; to hunt him down; and then, without mercy, to destroy him.

The plans that I had made, through many a busy day and sleepless night, for Moriarty's destruction, though differing greatly in detail, had all one master-element in common: the recognition that any plan, if it were to have the least chance of success, must involve my disappearance—preferably, my seeming death.

Through my various *personae*, I could move through all strata of society; I could start, as it were, from the common loafer, too unenterprising even to mace the rattlers,† through the artful, the seedy-scholarly, the half-wittedly religious, the unemployable clerkly, to—in the character of Captain Dacre-

---

* 1870. Two youths, from greatly differing social backgrounds, were arrested as, dressed in female clothing, the better to pursue their infamous trade, they strolled in the promenade of the Holborn Music Hall. A son of the Duke of Newcastle committed suicide, following their arrest.—*Editor*

† Travel by railway without paying the fare.—*Editor*

Buttsworth, the self-supporting, self-respecting shabby-genteel. I realized, reviewing my gallery of alternative selves, that I needed at least two more, for I could not know how many of my disguises had been penetrated by Moriarty or some of his agents. Though 'Kangaroo' Hill had not recognized me in Captain Dacre-Buttsworth, he had given me several bad moments in suggesting that the Captain was not all that he would have wished the world to think him. And I had a strong feeling that there were not a few as sharp-eyed as Hill in the cohorts of Moriarty's criminal army.

I chose two clergymen of low rank—the gaiters of canon or archdeacon or bishop call attention to the wearer; the unpretentious garb of the lesser clergy does not. I 'created' a simple-minded minister of some not-easily-recognized form of Dissent, and to this 'creation' I added a minister of a different faith: a decrepit Italian priest, a type which, despite his wide-brimmed, low-crowned hat and rusty *soutane*, is as little remarked upon in London as in Milan. This latter was to be useful to me in making my way from Switzerland—where I had decided to stage my disappearance or 'death'—to Italy.

Of the details of that seeming 'death', Dr Watson made few—and those few not important—omissions in the account which (originally written to defend my memory against the attack of Colonel James Moriarty) has since been published under the title "The Final Problem".

When I write that there are few omissions in Dr Watson's account of my 'death' at the fall of Reichenbach, I must make it clear that much was omitted from his account—*but of facts concerning which he was ignorant.* He knew afterwards, of course, that I had rigged my own 'death'—and why; but he never knew (unless he discovered it from another source; but I think not) that the plan of my disappearance had been worked out with, and prepared—so far as its Swiss end was concerned—by, my cousin and most loyal friend Henry Vernet, who resigned his position as Consul-general in London so as to be ready at Meiringen to carry out his share of the operation.

Afterwards, I told Dr Watson that, as Moriarty, thrown by me in the *baritsu* equivalent of the 'flying-mare', went, 'with a horrible scream', over the brink of the fall, I began to climb up the sheer face of the cliff above the narrow pathway on which I had fought with Moriarty. This was true—as far as it went; what I never told Dr Watson was that, several days earlier, Vernet had paid a professional Swiss mountain-climbing guide to drive a set of the steel pins called *pitons* at intervals, to provide hand- and foot-holds; and that, before setting out to meet Moriarty, I had put on, beneath my waistcoat, a stout leather belt, with a steel eye-bolt, of the type used in mountaineering. Nor did I tell Dr Watson that, high above me, Vernet was waiting to pull up the rope, whose steel-hooked end was darkened (as was the rope itself) with lamp-black to render it almost invisible against the rock-face.

As Dr Watson has recorded, I drew him away from the scene of my 'death' by means of a false message, so that, finding the message a deception, and even hurrying back, he found no trace either of Moriarty or of me. What else could he think but that I had perished in the boiling waters of the Reichenbach Fall, locked fatally in Moriarty's arms—as he had been fatally locked in mine?

However swiftly Dr Watson had returned, he would not have seen me; no sooner had my opponent fallen screaming into the torrent beneath, than I turned away towards the rock-face, attached the hook of the rope to my belt, and, Vernet tugging from above, went swiftly up. As I told Dr Watson, there were two men awaiting me on that narrow path by the fall: Moriarty and a confederate; and that one man had fallen to death whilst the other had worked his way up and around the rock-face, so as to be waiting for me when I reached the top.

Since I had no wish to involve my cousin—a respected member of the Swiss Consular Service—in the public account of my affairs, the presence of Henry Vernet above the rock-face had, of course, to be scrupulously suppressed by me in recounting this adventure to Dr Watson. I therefore slightly varied the importance of the facts, rather than the facts themselves.

I told Dr Watson that I had escaped the malignant attentions of this second man; had fallen back upon the path, "torn and bleeding"; had taken to my heels and done "ten miles over the mountains in the darkness"; and had found myself, a week later, in Florence, "with the certainty that no-one in the world knew what had become of me."

Now all this was the truth—but by no means the whole truth. The second man—the watcher who knew that I had made my escape from the struggle at the fall's edge, and had *not* plunged into the raging torrent below; the watcher who now knew well that *I* was still alive—had certainly made his way, as I had told Dr Watson, around the rock-face, climbing up so that he might cast heavy stones down on me. But what I did not mention was what must surely have been this agile murderer's panicking astonishment to find, on his reaching the summit of the rock-face, that there had been another man in *my* party, as there had been another man in his!

At first—so, afterwards, Vernet and I put all the facts together—the Second Murderer, immediately on reaching the tall rock's top, had rushed to the edge, to take care of *me*—and so, for some moments, had been in ignorance, both of the rope by which I was climbing, and of Vernet, who was pulling on the rope. Seeing me below, this second man had grasped a large fragment of rock, and thrown it at me; following this first cast with an equally effective second. The first hit me a glancing blow—painful, though not fatal; the second missed me, but bounced off the *piton* that I was clutching with my right hand. I realized that, were the hail of heavy stones to continue, I must surely be killed, either as I hung there unprotected against the rock-face or, dislodged by a well-aimed missile, falling to my death on the narrow path above the Reichenbach ravine.

I could see the head—though not the features—of my assailant, as he leaned over the edge to better his aim; I could not see that Vernet, who had just caught sight of the assassin, had bent the rope a couple of turns around an upright *piton*, and drawn his revolver. My assailant first became aware that he did not have the small plateau to himself at the moment that Vernet, aiming his pistol in the half-dusk, fired point-blank at the figure crouched above the rock-face.

I heard the shot; I could not see how, with a screech of rage, the would-be-murderer leapt up, and with a curse on Vernet and me, took to his heels.

The sudden halting of the rope's upward motion startled me, too, and I fell heavily. By God's blessing, it was only a few feet, and I saved myself in clutching at one of the steel pins, on another of which I had cut myself rather badly.

Vernet, realizing that pursuit of the murderous stone-thrower would be useless, now began to haul on the rope, so that I managed to scramble to the top only seconds before Dr Watson returned from the false errand on which I had sent him. The noise of the falling water must have drowned the noise of the revolver-shot, and, seeing no-one on the narrow path, he assumed, as he has recorded, that Moriarty and I had fallen into the torrent, locked in a last and fatal embrace.

I was trembling with exertion and shock as I reached the top of the rock-face, and Vernet's willing arms drew me, almost fainting with exhaustion, over the cliff-edge. He dragged me a few feet within the low natural wall which fringed the small plateau; and stood guard over me, his pistol in hand, whilst I lay panting and supine on the mountain grass.

But a worse shock than the shock which accompanies an escape from sudden death awaited me. At last, when I could once again speak, I asked:

"Did you catch a sight of the man who was pelting me with rocks?"

"Oh yes," said my cousin; "I had a good look at him—I should recognize him anywhere!"—and he there and then gave me a description of the assassin-in-posse which, as I listened, made my blood run cold.

"Are you *sure?*" I asked. "Are you absolutely *positive?*"

"Of course I'm sure," said my cousin, somewhat huffily; and I could not but believe him. For all that he, like me, is a descendant of the Vernets, he is as much a Genevese as I am a Londoner, and nearly a quarter-of-a-century's residence in London had not diminished the Switzer's sharp eye and retentive memory. I knew, as I lay there on the grass, high above the Reichenbach fall, that what Vernet described to me, he had seen; and that what he had seen, he had accurately described.

Whom, then, had I sent hurtling down into the ravine?

The picture that Mr Sidney Paget, admirable artist though he was, has given us of Professor Moriarty conceals an essential truth: that Moriarty was not an *old* man. True, he was, as Mr Paget shews him, prematurely bald and lined of face; and his habit of carrying quite heavy books in the pockets of his rusty frock-coat had added to the traditional 'scholar's stoop'.

But, on that day by the Reichenbach fall, Moriarty was—being no more than seven years or so my senior—well under fifty; lean and wiry, and possessed of strength preserved through a regimen which excluded all vices but greed and revenge. That a man of forty-seven—provided that he were Moriarty—should have consented to meet and fight me on a ravine's edge had not astonished me; nor, indeed, had the physical strength that I had had to master to send my opponent to his certain death.

But now, shocked by Vernet's description of the man whom his revolver-shot had frightened off, I began to have an uneasy feeling that the identity of the watcher was no longer a secret from me. True, I had seen and spoken to Moriarty; had been locked in his arms for several struggling moments, until, with a *baritsu* throw, I had cast him from me—to his death.

They say—and they say rightly—that no man is too old to learn *something* new; and what I learned as I lay on the grass at Vernet's feet, was this: I had not learned enough about my arch-enemy. I may flatter myself that I am a master of disguise; but what did I know of Moriarty's talents in this respect? Could he disguise himself as I could? More to the point: *could he so disguise another that that other might be mistaken for Moriarty himself?* I had *seen* Moriarty; I had cast Moriarty to his death—

But had I—? And, if I had not, whom I had I sent screaming to perdition in the foaming waters of the rapids?

In my mission to destroy Moriarty, had I, perhaps, to begin all over again—?

[Here Mr Holmes's MS. ends.—*Editor*]

Bibliography

In the course of editing the MS. of Mr Holmes's memoirs, it was needful more than once to check a reference or to verify a statement; to pin-point a date or to expand, for the reader's better understanding, a remark too casual or mention too brief. The principal books which were consulted are listed in alphabetical order below.

To this list the Editor has added a selection of books which, though having no direct bearing on Mr Holmes's life and work, do provide a condensed yet comprehensive survey of the period against which he acted out his adventurous and significant life.

'A Foreign Resident'. *Society in London*. London: 1886.
———. *Society in the New Reign* [i.e., of King Edward VII]. London: 1904.
'An English Officer'. *Society Recollections in Paris and Vienna*. London: 1888.
———. *More Society Recollections*. London: 1908.
Anonymous. *Handbook to London As It Is*. London: 1879.
Anonymous. *Fifty Years of London Society*. London: 1923.
Arthur, General Sir G. *Queen Alexandra*. London: 1929.
———. *A Septuagenarian's Scrap Book*. London: 1933.
Ballantine, Mr Serjeant. *Some Experiences of a Barrister's Life*. London: 1882.
Battiscombe, Georgina. *Queen Alexandra*. London: 1969.
Binstead, Arthur M. *Pitcher in Paradise*. London: 1903.
Binstead, A., and Wells, E. ('Pitcher' and 'Swears'). *A Pink 'Un and a Pelican*. London: 1898. (*See also under:* 'Pitcher' and 'Swears')
Black, Mary. *Old New York in Early Photographs*. New York: 1973.
Booth, J. B. *London Town*. London: 1929.
———. *Pink Parade*. London: 1933.
Cardigan and Lancastre, Countess of. *My Recollections*. London: 1909.
Carson, Gerald. *The Polite Americans*. New York: 1966.
'Cosmopolitan, A'. *Random Recollections of Court and Society*. London: 1888.

282

Cowles, Virginia. *King Edward and His Friends*. London: 1958.

Crouch, E. E. (Cora Pearl). *The Memoirs of Cora Pearl*. London: 1886. (Spurious, but, written contemporarily, with fully authentic background—and with the facts *generally* correct.)

Davis, Lt.-colonel R. Newnham. *The Gourmet's Guide to London*. London: 1910.

———. *Diners and Dining-out*. London: 1913.

Eliot, Elizabeth, *They All Married Well*. London: 1960.

Ellis, S. M. *A Mid-Victorian Pepys*. London: 1923.

———. *The Hardman Papers*. London: 1930.

Friswell, L. H. *In the Sixties and Seventies*. London: 1905.

Gomme, Sir Laurence. *London in the Reign of Victoria, 1837–1897*. London: 1897.

Goncourt, J. and E. *Le Journal des Goncourts*. Paris: 1956.

———. *Pages from the Goncourt Journal: edited, translated and introduced by Robert Baldick*. London: 1962.

Greenwood, J. *The Seven Curses of London*. London: 1869.

Gribble, Leonard. *Famous Judges and Their Tales*. London: 1957.

Harper, Charles G. A. *A Londoner's Own London, 1870–1920*. London: 1924.

Harrison, Michael. *Painful Details: Twelve Victorian Scandals*. London: 1962.

———. *Rosa* [Mrs Rosa Lewis, of the Cavendish Hotel]. London: 1962.

———. *London by Gaslight: 1861–1911*. London: 1963. (Far less parochial than its title suggests.)

———. *Fanfare of Strumpets*. London: 1971.

———. *Clarence: The Life of H.R.H. the Duke of Clarence & Avondale, K.G.* London: 1972.

Hibbert, Christopher. *Social History of Victorian Britain*. London: 1975.

Holden, W. H. *They Startled Grandfather—Gay Ladies and Merry Mashers of Victorian Times*. London: 1947.

———. *The Pearl of Plymouth* (Cora Pearl). London: 1950.

Hughes-Hallett, Captain F. V. *Bran Mash*. London: n.d. (c. 1930).

Hyde, H. Montgomery. *Their Good Name: Twelve Cases of Libel and Slander, with some Introductory Reflections on the Law*. London: 1970.

Irving, H. B. *A Book of Remarkable Criminals*. London: 1918.

Jepson, Edgar. *Memories of an Edwardian*. London: 1937.

Kingston, Charles. *Rogues and Adventuresses*. London: 1928.

Laver, James. *Victorian Panorama*. London: 1948.

Lee, Sir Sidney. *King Edward VII: a Biography*. London: 1925–1927.

Legge, Colonel E. *King Edward in his True Colours*. London: 1911.

———. *More About King Edward*. London: 1912. (In both Colonel Legge's books about King Edward, whose Equerry the Colonel was, are to be found more or less scandalous stories which, sometimes with slight changes, are to be encountered, ten years or so later, in the 'anonymous' memoirs of Julian Osgood Field, q.v.)

'Lounger in Society, The'. *The Glass of Fashion: Social Etiquette and Home Culture*. London: 1881.

Magnus, Philip. *King Edward the Seventh.* London: 1964.

Marcus, Steven. *The Other Victorians.* London: 1969.

Maurois, André. *Edouard VII et son Temps.* Paris: 1931.

Maybrick, Florence. *My Fifteen Lost Years: Mrs Maybrick's Own Story.* New York and London: 1905. (Though 'ghosted' by an American professional journalist, this tale of a woman condemned by the insane Mr Justice Stephen is completely accurate as to facts, even when dealing with the intricacies of English Law in the 'Eighties and 'Nineties.)

Metternich, Princess Pauline. *The Days that are No More.* London: 1921.*

———. *My Years in Paris.* London: 1922.

Nevill, Lady Dorothy. *Under Five Reigns* (ed. R. Nevill). London: 1910.

Nevill, Ralph. *The Man of Pleasure.* London: 1912.

———. *Echoes Old and New.* London: 1919.

———. *Night Life, London and Paris.* London: 1926.

———. *Days and Nights in Montmartre.* London: 1927.

———. *The Romance of Paris.* London: 1928.

———. *Varieties and Vicissitudes.* London: n.d.

———. *Vanities and Vicissitudes.* London: n.d.

———. *The Life and Letters of Lady Dorothy Nevill* (ed. Ralph Nevill). London: 1930.

Nicholson, Renton ('Chief Baron Nicholson'). *Autobiography of a Fast Man.* London: 1863. (Though he was living in, and controlling the 'fast' life of London in, a generation preceding that in which Mr Holmes entered upon his career, the world of Nicholson was still healthily surviving twenty and more years after he wrote his autobiography.)

'One of Her Majesty's Servants'. *The Private Life of the Queen* [i.e., Victoria]. London: 1897.

'One of the Old Boys'. *London in the Sixties.* London: 1928.

Osgood Field, Julian (published as 'Anon'). *Things I Shouldn't Tell.* London: 1923.

———. *Uncensored Recollections.* London: 1924.

———. *More Uncensored Recollections.* London: 1925.

Pearl, Cyril. *The Girl with the Swansdown Seat.* London: 1952.

Pearsall, Ronald. *The Worm in the Bud: The World of Victorian Sexuality.* London: 1969.

Pearson, Hesketh. *Oscar Wilde.* London: 1945. (Far and away the best of the dozens of lives of Wilde which have been written, because of—not despite of—the fact that Pearson could sympathize with Wilde without being able to sympathize with Wilde's aberrations. It is also valuable for its vivid description of the Café Royal in the days when Wilde and Douglas—and Mr Holmes and Dr Watson [and, of course, Captain Dacre-Buttsworth]—frequented the red-plush banquettes.)

'Pitcher' and 'Swears' (Arthur Binstead and Ernest Wells). *A Pink 'Un and a Pelican.* London: 1898.

'Pot' and 'Swears'. *The Scarlet City.* London: 1899. (No other novel of this period has

---

* Colonel Edward Legge (*see* page 283) supplied a preface.—*Editor*

so brilliantly succeeded in painting the raffish world of the Empire Bar and the
English racecourses at the very end of the Queen's reign.)

Ribblesdale, Lord, *Impressions and Memories* (with a Preface by his daughter, Lady
Wilson). London: 1923.

Rochefort, Henri (Comte Victor-Henri de Rochefort-Luçay). *The Adventures of my
Life*. London: 1896.

St Helier, Lady. *Memories of Fifty Years*. London: 1909.

Sala, George A. *Gaslight and Daylight: with some London Scenes they Shine upon*. London: 1859.

Sichel, Pierre. *Jersey Lily*. London: 1958. (Rather more journalistic than literary,
this is still the best life of Lillie Langtry to date.)

Smalley, George W. *Anglo-American Memories*. London: 1907.

Soldene, Emily. *My Theatrical and Musical Recollections*. London: 1897.

Vizitelly, H. *Glances back through Seventy Years*. London: 1893. (The author was the
well-known publisher of Emile Gaboriau's and Fortuné du Boisgobey's detective stories—Bismarck's favourites—in their English translation.)

Yates, Edmund. *Recollections and Experiences;* London: 1885. (One of the best-known
journalists of his era—hardly inferior in fame to George Augustus Sala or
George R. Sims.)

The standard reference books of the period were also consulted by me. The principal were:

Army List
Baedeker
Bradshaw's Railway Guide
Burke's Landed Gentry
Collins's Illustrated Guide to London
Debrett's Peerage, Baronetage & Knightage
Dodd's Parliamentary Guide
Era Almanack
Foreign Office List
Handbook to London as It Is (1879)
Haydn's Dictionary of Dates
The Illustrated Omnibus Guide (London)
Law List
Lloyd's List
London Directory (Post Office)
Medical Register
Whitaker's Almanack
Who's Who

NOTE BY EDITOR:

In addition to the various newspapers mentioned by Dr. Watson as having been
regularly taken in at 221B, Baker-street, odd receipted bills from various London

newsagents confirm that the following journals were delivered to the Baker-street household:—

Annales d'hygiène et de médecine légale
Boston Medical and Surgical Journal
The British Medical Journal
Bulletin de la société médico-légale de France
Cornhill Magazine
Edinburgh Medical and Surgical Journal
The Graphic
The Illustrated London News
The Lancet
London Letter
Penny Illustrated Newspaper
The (National) Police Gazette

This, of course, even with the addition of the periodicals mentioned by Dr Watson in the Canon, can hardly be accepted as an exhaustive list of the reading matter delivered regularly at 221B, but in the absence of receipted bills and other evidence of ordering, the list is complete at the time of writing.

Two bills (one from Messrs Hatchard, of Piccadilly, the other from Messrs Bumpus of Oxford-street) cast important (but not unexpected) light on the seriousness with which Mr Holmes studied to perfect himself in his chosen art. The bills concern three works on cryptography that Mr Holmes had ordered.

THROUGH MESSRS HATCHARD:

Handbuch der Kryptographie, by E. B. Fleissner von Wostrowitz (Vienna; 1881).

THROUGH MESSRS BUMPUS:

La cryptographie militaire ou des chiffres usités en temps de guerre, by Auguste Kerckhoffs (Paris; 1883).
La cryptographie et ses applications à l'art militaire, by H. Josse (Paris; 1885).

Index

287